The Dragon's Disciple

Justin walked to the dresser and picked up her comb. He removed a strand of her hair, drew it slowly through his fingers. Standing there, thinking of her, thinking of her light and his darkness, he forgot himself. His gaze crossed the mirror.

Two glowing red glints appeared, strangely glimmering *beneath* the surface of the glass.

Caught! His stomach clenched and his eyes ached. He gritted his teeth.

A familiar voice filled his mind like steel searing into a mold, hissing and glowing with unbearable heat.

"My servant," it said.

"My master," he whispered.

DARK

❖

HEART

BOOK I
of Dragon's Disciple

MARGARET WEIS
AND
DAVID BALDWIN

HarperPrism
A Division of HarperCollinsPublishers

HarperPrism
A Division of HarperCollins*Publishers*
10 East 53rd Street, New York, NY 10022-5299

This is a work of fiction. The characters, incidents, and dialogues are products of the author's imagination and are not to be construed as real. Any resemblance to actual events or persons, living or dead, is entirely coincidental.

ISBN 0-06-105791-6

HarperCollins®, ®, and HarperPrism®
are trademarks of HarperCollins Publishers Inc.

Cover illustration © 1998 by John Howe.
Cover design by Carl Galian.

First paperback printing: June 1999

Printed in the United States of America

Visit HarperPrism on the World Wide Web at
http://www.harpercollins.com

❖ 10 9 8 7 6 5 4 3 2 1

Dedication

With sincerest thanks and gratitude to
Todd Fahnestock and William Quick,
for their inspiration, hard work, and
diligence. Without their help and
valuable contributions, this book
would never have been possible.

DARK
HEART

one

Justin lay hidden, watching as the girl entered her room, shut the door, and locked it. He sighed inwardly. She wasn't really a girl, but to him, she seemed so young. All of them did, all the girl-women who filled this modern world.

Her fairy face could transform from child to woman and back again in half a minute, allowing him to peer through her thin veneer of adulthood to the child beneath. The cosmetics she applied, the clothes she wore, the airs she affected, these were her defenses: the thorns of a rosebush that thought itself invulnerable, safely ignorant of the world's sharp shears. Shears to which youthful thorns were no threat at all.

She paused in front of the mirror and stared at her image. Standing behind her, he knew the silvered surface would show nothing but her own reflection against the walls of her bedroom, though he was close enough to touch her.

He wondered what she would do if he materialized

behind her. He could do it merely by wishing to. But he had no wish to terrify her, especially not now as she reached out to touch the glass before her, fingers brushing gently over the reflection of her face. He wondered what she was thinking.

With a small sigh, she unbuttoned her blouse and tossed it away. The silk fluttered down, a silent ripple of creamy femininity.

She crossed to her closet, hips swaying. She opened the door, looked inside, riffled through the clothing there. She tossed a few things onto the bed. The air smelled of her; he drank in her scent and sighed again.

She turned back to the closet, paused, reached for another pair of pants, stopped. She took her jeans off, kicked them away, and stood there in her white undergarments. He willed himself to ignore the display, to concentrate on her face.

She picked up a short, flowered cotton shirt and pressed it against her shoulders, the gesture impossibly vulnerable in her ignorance of his presence.

He still considered clothes a kind of architecture. In his youth, he'd worn rich fabrics, carefully cut and finely worked. The resulting attire had obscured virtually every portion of his body except his hands and face, creating an image that only a select few could aspire to. But that time was long gone, and those rules no longer applied to current fashions.

These days, in this place, the body itself was the major architectural structure, shaped and molded by pumping iron, rigorous dance, endless hours on treadmills, starvation, distance running . . . the machines and regimented tortures that were the real tailors of this time.

Smooth, tanned skin over well-muscled flesh was the most appealing garment now. The body as a self-creation, and clothing simply stretched over it, hiding little or nothing, only accentuating. Especially true for the young . . .

The girl moved closer to the mirror. He watched her fingers work at the back of her bra. Suddenly, inexplicably embarrassed, he turned away an instant before she bared herself.

He looked out the window into the beginning of the evening, listening to her movements instead of watching.

You were once this young, weren't you, Gwendolyne? And she resembles you so closely . . .

He caught the tiny, whispering hiss of her underwear sliding down her legs. A drawer opened and closed. He heard the rustle of silk moving across skin. He listened to her skirt rustle into place, to the soft sounds as she buttoned her blouse. He turned around.

Her long, dark tresses tumbled down around her shoulders. She took a comb off the dresser, her hair responding with tiny electric snaps and hisses as she pulled the teeth through.

Another half an hour and the child had become a woman. He watched her every move, from the way she twisted and styled her thick hair to the small movements her hands made as she brushed hints of rose onto her cheeks and lips.

No matter how many times he observed her, her

fascination never lessened. So like Gwendolyne. The memory of his dead wife burned in the light that danced around her.

A knock sounded: "Tina?"

The girl's mother.

"Zack is downstairs."

"I'm almost ready. Tell him I'm on my way."

Tina regarded herself in the mirror, pressed her lips together experimentally, nodded. With a final murmur of approval she turned her back on the mirror, snatched her purse from the nightstand, and clicked off the light.

He stood alone in the darkness, listening to her feet patter down the hall. He knew her name. He knew her destination. Tonight, as he often did, he would follow her.

Justin walked to the dresser and picked up her comb. He removed a strand of her hair, drew it slowly through his fingers. Standing there, thinking of her, thinking of her light and his darkness, he forgot himself. His gaze crossed the mirror.

Two glowing red glints appeared, strangely glimmering *beneath* the surface of the glass.

Caught! His stomach clenched and his eyes ached. He gritted his teeth. The two burning slits of red grew brighter. In the mirror, wisps of crimson smoke began to drift upward from the blazing eyes.

A familiar voice filled his mind like steel searing into a mold, hissing and glowing with unbearable heat.

"My servant," it said.

"Master," he whispered.

"My own gallant knight, Justinian, the honorable Earl of Sterling," the voice mused, as if enumerating the features of a particularly prized possession. The sound wrapped him in its coils. He could feel the pressure, suddenly found it hard to breathe.

"Yes, master."

"Are you well this evening?"

"Quite well, master."

"I rejoice in the news. Do inform me, my loyal servant, of your mission here. I'm curious."

"I am merely watching, master."

"As am I. Such a fragile flower, is she not?" The Dragon's fiery gaze bored into him. "And, of course, one so easily crushed. Like all such flowers."

Sudden heat flared in Justin's brain. He knew better than to try to evade the flames. He swallowed and said nothing.

The slit-eyes narrowed. Smoke continued to float up from their rims. "Ah, my Justinian. For the moment, at least, I choose not to crush. I am not small. I won't begrudge you your petty amusements."

"Thank you, master."

"Do you know what Kalzar Kaman has asked of me?"

Justin shrugged. "The dog? No, lord, I don't."

"The dog, as you call him, bids me to grind you into dust."

"For what, master?"

"For your inattention to your duty."

"And am I undutiful, master?" Justin paused. "I wonder why Kalzar doesn't say these things to me?" His voice was steady, his rage carefully cloaked in seeming unconcern.

The eyes in the mirror glinted red-orange. "He fears you, Lord Sterling. Did you know that?"

"Perhaps he has reason to fear me."

"You are both my disciples, Justinian. Mine. You know it. It was my hand that banished you from your ancient home. My hand that keeps you away. That is proof, if you need any. You wish to return, and I do not permit it."

"Yes, my lord. I know."

A moment of burning silence.

"What is it you seek in England, in any event? Your estate was broken up centuries ago. Nothing is left of what you remember."

"Home is more to me than the land I was born on."

"Perhaps. Kalzar tells me there is fine collection of modern eateries that stink of frying fat where your home once stood. The world you knew is gone. Perhaps I do you a favor by not permitting you to see the ruins."

"But that's not why, is it?"

"Of course not. You are headstrong, Justinian. It pleases me to make you feel my power. To know it in the hardest places and ways. So on the matter of your home-land I give you into the charge of Kalzar, whom you hate."

"And I do feel it, master. I feel your power."

Even though nearly seven hundred years had passed, some part of Justin still refused to believe that nothing of the England he once knew still remained. Surely some vestige of the impregnable castles and soar-ing cathedrals he'd known in his short time as the Earl of Sterling must yet endure, no matter how battered by the passage of the years.

"Perhaps someday I will lift my hand. But not yet."

The voice of the Dragon went silent for a moment, while Justin listened to the sound of his own heartbeat.

"Kalzar," the Dragon said suddenly, "has some justice for his complaints."

"Kalzar is rash and foolish. He puts us all in danger. I still think you should let me kill him."

"And free you for your homecoming. To England's green and pleasant shore?"

"Yes."

"I have a greater use for you in this new land."

"Then I ask that you—"

"Then you ask me *nothing*, Lord Sterling." The voice squeezed him more tightly. Justin shuddered, releasing one slow, anguished breath. "You will *obey*. As for Kalzar, if any disciple takes up claws against another, both will find themselves enduring a time beyond my mirror. Do you understand me, my lord?"

Justinian felt his ribs creak.

"Yes, master."

"Enough, then."

Suddenly the grinding coils that had crushed him relaxed. He gasped with relief.

"Now I bid you tell me," said the Dragon. "How have you dealt with the female detective charged with investigating the errand you performed for me recently? Detective Sandra McCormick appears to show more initiative than most of her kind. She steps too close to the truth."

Justin lifted his head, stared directly at the mirror.

"Nothing she has discovered endangers us in any way. I give you my word on it."

"And so you say. But I am not entirely convinced you have the right of it, though I will agree that matters have not yet reached a crisis point." The Dragon paused for a moment. "Well. You are one of my highest, Justinian. I have raised you because I trust you, and so I suppose I should continue to trust you. As you say, then. For now, she may live."

"Yes, master."

"Return to your tavern. Await my word. There may be another task for you."

Justinian nodded. "Yes, master."

The monstrous eyes flared once more, scorching his soul. And were as quickly gone.

The darkness returned and touched him, soothed him. The mirror was as it had been before Tina left, reflecting the room around it. But not him.

Justin moved to the French doors leading from Tina's bedroom to a small balcony. His hand slid over the latch and the door opened. He walked outside.

The rain had stopped. The stench of the city had been purged. The air smelled fresh and clean.

It was so like him, this city. Its surface could be smoothed and made fresh for a few moments, but the cracks beneath the cleansing seethed with a hundred years of rot, and could never be made pure again.

He looked down into the street. Time twisted in strange ways when he conversed with his master. Days might have passed. But this time, he'd been gone only seconds.

Tina ran down the steps toward a red Camaro that waited in the driveway. Justinian watched, feeling the weight of his own presence, of the many things both named and unnamable he'd done through the centuries. It was a heavy burden.

He braced one hand on the rail and leapt over it. A clap of thunder, muffled by distance, muttered from the fleeing storm. The dark, liquid grumble masked the splashing thud of his landing on the turf twenty feet below.

He watched the Camaro back into the rain-wet street, watched the flashy car drive a hole into the silver-washed dark, stood silent and unmoving until she had vanished beyond the spectral halos that marked the lonely street lamps.

How many other times? How many other roads? All different, but all still the same . . .

He waited a few more seconds, then moved off into the dregs of the night, on his way to do his master's bidding.

two

Detective Jack Madrone growled as he bumped into the car behind him, cranked the wheel, cranked hard the other way, and finally rammed his decrepit powder blue Mustang into the tiny parking space along the curb.

He yanked on the handle and opened the car door. It creaked, sagged an inch, and banged into the high curb. He had to pull up hard to slam it closed behind him with a rusty shriek of abused metal. He glared at the scrapes on the dull blue paint. *Too many people and not enough parking spaces in this goddamned town . . .*

The lights and sounds of Chicago gave the night a hazy, manic buzz. As he stepped out into the street a car swerved sharply to miss him, honking in irritation as it hissed past with a chirp of overstrained rubber.

"Ya, fuck you!"

He flipped the driver off, watched the taillights disappear, then crossed Ontario Street in mid-block and stepped up onto the sidewalk. Heavy clouds pressed down on the city. The early winter storms of the past few days had taken a breather, but that wasn't likely to last. At least, thank God, it wasn't snowing yet.

He smoothed a weathered hand across his lank black hair, scratched absently at the back of his neck. He needed to get a haircut. Needed a shower, too . . .

His twice-broken nose wrinkled as, lowering his arm, he got a whiff of himself. The day showed no signs of winding down any time soon. He shrugged his coat higher on his shoulders, pulled out a cigarette, and patted his chest and rounded belly in his perennial absentminded search for a light. He carried both matches and a lighter, and could never seem to find either.

"Where the fuck . . . ?" he mumbled around the cigarette, the bitter taste of unsmoked tobacco floating across his tongue. His glum expression brightened: "Ahh . . ."

He reached into an inside pocket of his rumpled jacket, pulled out a cheap green Bic lighter, brought it to his mouth and flicked. Orange and gold light reflected on his rain-slick face from the mercury-vapor streetlights overhead. His thin lips tightened around the cigarette as he took a long drag. In the harsh, chemical light he looked a hundred years old.

A moment later he spotted what he was looking for: a huge neon sign at the end of the block. Light flared from it, staining the concrete walls of the nearby buildings with color, lacing the puddles on the sidewalk with stripes of blue and green. *Gwendolyne's Flight,* written in some nearly unreadable script only a sign maker could love. Apparently the crowd stretching

along the sidewalk behind velvet ropes, all of them wait-
ing to get into the club, already knew where they were.
None of them even bothered to look at the neon words.
Or maybe they couldn't read . . .

Stupid fucking name for a nightclub, Madrone thought.

A gleaming black stretch limo pulled up in front of
the club and a picture-perfect plastic couple clambered
out, grinning toothily at the envious peons getting
soaked behind the rope. The man wore an open blue
Armani blazer over wide shoulders bulked up by
steroids and sculpted by years of pumping iron. His
movements were grandiose and sweeping as he waited
for the driver to open the door for his date. When the
woman emerged, long legs first, she wore a skirt so
short she shouldn't even have bothered. Or maybe that
was the bother. Madrone craned for a glimpse, but she
scissored the goody gate closed and pranced on into the
club. A taxi full of giggling, half-buzzed college girls
pulled up behind the stretch, and the hack leaned on
the horn for it to move out of his way.

He watched the frenetic scene, shaking his head.
He'd never understand the attraction of this hyped-up,
rich-blood club scene. Everybody was so impatient,
hell-bent to impress the rest of the assholes, spending
their nights sharing insults and drugs—coke for the
hopelessly old-fashioned, and designer dope for the
new-wave trendoids. *Maybe,* he thought, *you had to be
high to understand it.* But his own dope was Jack Daniels
or Budweiser, and he couldn't afford the price in joints
like these.

Still, he could remember standing in line right in

this neighborhood, thirty years ago, waiting to get into Coach Ditka's club, back when Da Bears ruled Chicago . . .

He walked down the street toward the club. *That little fucker better not have lied to me . . .*

As he pushed through the mob, he thought about Maxie. He'd turned him snitch about a year ago, busted him on some chickenshit possession rap, then arranged for the charges to go away. In exchange for a little verbal blow job every once in a while. But it didn't make any sense. Not really. Not unless the white-powder shit itself made sense, and it didn't either. Not for Maxie.

Maxie was born and raised rich. He'd had everything he'd ever wanted or needed, and he'd pissed it away going down on dope. In a way, he supposed he should feel sorry for the little punk, but you couldn't build a network of shitheads by feeling sorry for them.

Still, there were definite downsides to these pathetic, necessary arrangements. Like the fact that Maxie's brain was fried. It was well and good to have snitches, but how much could you trust the perceptions of a kid who only dropped by reality for the occasional visit, and never stayed long?

Better not be one of your brain burps, Maxie, you little fuck, Jack thought as he reached a doorman who looked like he'd been an extra in *Clan of the Cave Bear*. He inhaled sharply, then coughed at the throat-grating unfiltered smoke as he waited for the hired muscle to notice him.

"Twenty-dollar cover," the bouncer said, scowling at Jack's appearance. Jack decided the Army-surplus jacket and white T-shirt he was wearing was probably not their normal fare. Not unless you were wearing a gold Rolex, and he wasn't.

"Hey, pal, the shirt's almost clean," Jack said. "Like I give a damn."

The bouncer's face closed up like a bucket of concrete. "Outta here," he grunted, jerking his thumb at the far reaches of the sidewalk.

Jack grinned, dug out his badge case, and flashed the tin. "How about a free pass, asshole? Ya know, civic pride, help out the city. Like that?"

The bouncer looked at the badge, then grudgingly moved aside. Jack grinned at him again, tapped him lightly on one massive shoulder, and moved on into a kaleidoscope of whirling lights and raucous music. An immense round room opened up before him. The entrance led onto a pipe-railed balcony that overlooked the main floor. Daze-eyed celebrants leaned on the bright blue railing, sipping their drinks, mesmerized by the dancers below. Lights played over the dancers. Pinks and blues changed to reds and oranges as spotlights washed over the crowd of writhing people. The music was so loud it made the floor thump beneath his feet. The vibrations went straight to his balls. *Not bad,* he thought, *but not worth twenty bucks.*

He walked over to the railing, shoved some scrawny fag skinhead aside, and planted his elbows on the pipe.

"Hey!"

He turned and grinned at the fag. "Yeah?"

Or maybe he wasn't grinning after all, because the

fag stared at him, his pale face suddenly going even paler. "Uh . . . forget it."

"Yeah, you will," Madrone said, turning back to study the gyrating maelstrom below. It reminded him of funny old pictures he'd seen in the Chicago Art Institute, huge canvases by long-dead Italians, with ugly devils tormenting pits full of sinners as the flames licked up around them.

So he was looking for a camel jockey named Omar, according to Maxie the madman. On the face of it, the idea that a psycho killer would blurt out confessional gibberish about his crimes to a bartender sounded idiotic. But as Madrone peered through the flashing haze in the direction of the garishly back-lit bar on the main floor, he thought about the stupidity of evil. Of assholes who couldn't wait to melt their brains with booze or smoke or powder, the better to babble of their lunatic doings to anybody who would listen. He remembered one pussball, took after his old lady with a two-pound roofing sledge because she burned the TV dinners, then walked down to the local slophole to show his buddies the murder weapon. And had it sitting on the bar next to his Budweiser when they busted him. *If not for stupidity,* he thought, *I wouldn't close half my cases.*

Nick, he thought. *The bartender is named Nick. If Maxie isn't totally out of his gourd.* He paused to let his eyes adjust to the light before he muscled his way to the balcony bar.

"What'cha need?" the bartender shouted over the din, up to his elbows in dirty glasses as customers screamed at him for refills. Beads of sweat gleamed on his high forehead.

"I'm looking for Nick," Madrone shouted back.

"Not working tonight."

Madrone nodded. "So how do I find him? I've got the money I owe him." Madrone gave a tobacco-stained grin and flashed a wrinkled wad of cash. Doper-style money, in small, greasy denominations.

The bartender's eyes narrowed.

"Listen, pal. He's gotta keep his biz outta here. That means you, bud." The booze jockey paused, then shrugged. "He works Wednesdays, Thursdays, and Fridays. Down in the main bar. You can catch him then. But maybe better outside somewhere. Not in here."

"Okay, cool," Madrone said.

"Don't mention it," the bartender said. He sounded like he meant it. Really. Don't mention it.

Madrone shook his head and moved away from the bar. He took the stairs down to the main floor and fought his way through the jiggling crowd to the tables under the balcony, where expensively dressed couples ate overpriced food shaped like surreal little sculptures, shared tastes of party drugs Madrone figured were two steps ahead of the latest DEA lists, and watched the dancers. It took him a few seconds to find what he was looking for. The door said EMPLOYEES ONLY. He pushed on through and barged into the kitchen.

He nodded at the prep cooks and sous-chefs, who looked at him in confusion. The time clock was in the back, next to a scarred steel exit door. He flipped through the cards, looking at the names on them. Only one Nick. Nicholas Seder, in the section marked BAR. Bingo.

He plucked several time cards out of the slots. No sense in making it obvious who he was looking for. Nick's card didn't give an address, but that was all right. A full name and a social security number were good enough. Thank God for modern technology. It made a cop's life one hell of a lot easier.

"Hey! Who the fuck are you?"

Madrone turned. It was a short, plump, balding chef in kitchen whites, puffed up like a bantam rooster.

"No customers allowed back here," the little fat man said, his bushy eyebrows furrowed together. For some reason he reminded Madrone of a warped bunny rabbit. A bunny rabbit nervously clutching a meat cleaver.

"No sweat, okay, pal?" Madrone said. He pocketed the time cards and headed for the back door.

"Hey, you can't take those—"

With the heel of his hand, Madrone punched the square horizontal bar that was the locked door's emergency opening mechanism. His action sounded an alarm, but the thing popped open like a kid's jack-in-the-box. He walked out into the alley and let the door thump closed between him and Chef Rabbit. He heard the turn of a key in a lock. The screech of the alarm fell silent. He grinned. The Rabbit's courage clearly stopped short of chasing him into the night for a bunch of time cards.

He smiled, patted the cards in his pocket, and started walking.

It had started to rain again.

Fuck!

A stream of water pouring off the roof splashed down his collar and soaked his shirt. He yanked at his jacket. Great. Just great. Now his back was soaked, and he was freezing to death. Chicago. Fucking great.

Rain plastered his unkempt hair to his scalp and ran down into his eyes, making him blink. Thunder boomed and lightning scratched sudden bright claws across the sky. He turned up the soggy collar of his coat as far as it would go and headed down the alley toward the misty lights of Dearborn Street.

Despite his discomfort, Madrone felt pretty decent. Nick Seder, bartender, actually existed. He wasn't just a figment of Maxie's demented psyche. So maybe the mysteriously talkative Omar existed, too.

He'd just about written the Wheeler case off. Maybe, if this continued to pan out, he'd take Maxie out for a cup of coffee. Or give him a full freebie on his next bust . . .

A scraping sound, low and rain-muffled, rattled the wet concrete at his rear. He spun around, looking behind him.

Nothing. Sheets of rain, gray building walls, the restaurant's trash Dumpsters, and grimy, grease-stained cement. He stood for a moment, back stiffening, staring wide-eyed down the empty alley.

The scrape sounded again. What the fuck? That sound had been sharp, close—right in front of him. But he couldn't see a damned thing. Suddenly uneasy, he flipped open his coat, slipped his right hand inside to rest on the butt of the .38 Chief's Special riding his belt.

Across the alley from him, their straight lines blurred by the wind-whipped rain, two Dumpsters were backed up against the wall of a building. He stared at them. Was that a flicker of movement? Maybe . . .

He moved toward them.

"You in there, asshole?" He paused. "Let me see you!"

He took one last step, got his back against the Dumpster's side, and whipped his gun up. He spun and crouched low as he took a shooter's stance, aiming his weapon at the space behind the Dumpster.

Nothing.

All he could hear was the sound of the rain hitting the pavement . . . and the thump of his heart suddenly beating faster.

He grabbed the lid of the Dumpster, flung it up and over with a grunt, then stepped back. He wasn't sure what he expected—some wino seeking shelter from the storm, maybe—but there was nothing. Only the reek of rotting garbage.

He looked into the container. Nothing moved, not even one of those rats the size of German shepherds that infested the alleys near the river. He eased up slightly and stepped back, but the uneasiness twanging the knots of his spine wouldn't go away.

Maybe the rain was carrying strange sounds. He'd read about shit like that. Could the noises have come from the kitchen where he'd left Chef Rabbit?

He pulled a small flashlight from his coat pocket and looked around. He picked up a stick and rummaged carefully through the flattened liquor boxes, broken bottles, day-old food, and coffee grounds. He leaned further in and pushed some of it aside.

"What the hell . . . ?" Leaning down, bracing his waist against the sill of the Dumpster's edge, he dug further, got a solid hold on the thing, and pulled it up from where it was wedged between two heavy black plastic sacks. It seemed to be an animal skin. The weight of the thing was incredible. He hauled the skin out of the Dumpster.

In his time he'd smelled it all, everything from dead dogs to water-logged corpses boiling with plump, pale maggots. But he choked at the stench of this thing, whatever the hell it was. He turned his head away for a moment and took a couple of deep breaths. What in the hell was this?

Almost like rotting fish, but not exactly. He took a step back and swallowed a wad of puke trying to crawl up into his throat. He put the skin down, wiped his hands off on his coat, and then wished he hadn't.

Looking around, he spotted what he needed. He wrinkled his nose, holstered his weapon, picked the skin up, and carried it over to the faucet set into the building wall. He turned the valve and clear, clean water poured out. He knelt and washed his hands and the skin in the steady stream.

Standing again, he held the skin out and shook the water off it. It was heavy, maybe thirty, forty pounds. It looked like one of those suits dancers wore when they wanted to fool you into thinking they were naked. Except that this wasn't Lycra or any kind of cloth he'd ever heard of. This was real skin. Scaly skin. But like some giant reptile. Some kind of animal.

So who was skinning weird animals in the alley behind a fancy nightclub? One of the chefs? Must be a hell of a menu in there . . .

He bent over the soggy thing, nose twitching. The Dumpster stench was mostly gone, leaving it smelling like what it actually was. The odor was strong and memorable, very strange, but with overtones that were also familiar. Underneath the rot, there was a scent of something he knew, but he couldn't quite put his finger on what it was. Something like burnt oil . . . he arranged it on the sides and top of the closed Dumpster and leaned closer to get a good look at it.

Madrone heard the scraping sound again and whirled to face it, his back against the Dumpster. The bulky skin slid down and hit the blacktop with a wet smacking sound, like some monstrous kiss.

The noise had been right behind him this time. But there was nothing there! There wasn't anything to hide behind. Madrone looked around, feeling like some over-hyped idiot, even checking the sky above him and everything he could see up and down the alley. Rain blurred his vision, but he caught a glimpse of movement near the edge of the building at the far end of the alley, just off Dearborn.

"Hey!" He pointed his gun in that direction with one hand, holding the flashlight out to his side with his other hand. "Don't move!"

He felt even more like an idiot. Don't move *what?* There was nothing *there* . . .

He walked to the end of the alley, found nothing. He swallowed. He could feel sweat dripping from the pores of his scalp to join the rain streaming down his face.

Again, he heard a scraping sound right behind him. He spun around, weapon ready. His eyes flicked back and forth, but he couldn't see anything through the rain. That same strong scent that he almost recognized filled the air. It reminded him of the Chinese greasy spoon he always had to walk by to get to Mandy's Grill.

Scumbags were scumbags. Mostly they knew not to stalk cops. Unless they were nutzo. But a handful of times, it had happened to him. Not often, and he was still around to talk about it. Still . . .

He had fired his gun seven times in the line of duty.

This was different. He couldn't see anything, but he *knew* he wasn't alone. Something else was here with him. He could sense its animosity, the hot stink of its concentrated regard.

Something was stalking him. And all his years of experience and training weren't turning the tables. He stood frozen, basting in his own sweat, his nostrils filled with that bizarre stink.

And then he laughed. A short, ugly, mocking sound. "Yeah, right," he muttered. Bad dreams. What the fuck? Acting like some five year old, wetting his Jockey shorts over the monster in the closet.

He took a deep breath. He holstered his gun and walked back to the skin. Except for the patter of rain, the alley was silent.

He stared at the waterlogged pile. So what did he have here? Something for the morgue? Or for a veterinarian?

Suddenly he wanted a tall glass of Jack Daniels, and to hell with the ice. Whatever this thing had been, it hadn't been human. So it wasn't a homicide. But he'd never seen or heard of an animal with a skin like this. He stared at it some more.

All cops are curious. He knew he was, though he would never admit it. No point in making an asshole of himself by calling in backup for a weird skin. But there were people he could call quietly. Bigdomes at the University of Chicago, maybe.

He thought some more, then squatted down, grunting softly as his knees cracked. He balled up the heavy skin and tucked it beneath his left arm, leaving his right free to draw his weapon. Not that he thought he would need to.

He was still jittery. The mouth of the alley seemed to be a block away. The distant lights of Dearborn were part of the normal world, a world where you didn't hear noises that came from nowhere. That was where he needed to be. Not here, in an empty, rain-washed alley that stank like an open grave.

The back of his neck kept tingling as if somebody was watching him.

He looked over his shoulder again.

Still no one.

But the way the rain was pounding down, someone could be back there. Shit, they could be thirty feet away and he'd barely be able to see them in this mess.

His eyes flicked from one side of the alley to the other.

He was no hero. The heroes he knew were mostly dead ones. He preferred to be a live cop. And if a cop wasn't kicking ass, he'd better be bugging out, oh yeah. But he'd bugged out before and never been this scared.

Something dragged across the ground just behind him. Madrone stumbled as he tried to turn around.

"What the fuck . . . ?" He backed toward the lighted street only a few yards away now. Once again he drew his pistol. His hand was shaking, sweating on the grip of his weapon.

Two hands grabbed his shoulders from behind and Madrone spun, leading with his elbow. The blow whiffed empty air. The owner of the hands—a thin, well-dressed Chinese man wearing a dark suit and sporting gold Armani-framed glasses—ducked and came back up. Madrone grunted, off balance. His assailant jumped closer, grabbed the skin, and yanked, trying to jerk it away.

The skin was slick and heavy. Madrone almost lost control of it. But his fear boiled away, burned off by a rush of adrenaline. Here at last was something he could see, could strike at, could defeat. This was something he could understand.

He ducked away from the man's attack. He wasn't about to play tug-of-war with some Bruce Lee wannabe. He dropped his shoulder, spun to break the man's grip on the skin, and used the momentum of his weight to drive his elbow into the guy's solar plexus.

The man gasped, doubled over, and Madrone

brought the butt of his pistol down hard on the guy's neck. The man hit the pavement like a sack of wet cement. Madrone grabbed his collar, hauled him to his feet, and shoved him up against the wall.

"The position, asshole. You know the position. Assume the fucking position!"

He realized he was shouting. He forced himself to take a breath as he patted the guy down. No weapons. He stepped back, slipped his pistol back into its holster. Thank God he hadn't had to shoot the fucker. The paperwork would have been enormous.

"ID," Madrone growled. "Let's see some ID."

"Does it matter?" the thin Chinese man said. He met Madrone's gaze calmly. Now that the dancing was over, he looked like an out-of-place accountant. "I meant you no harm."

"Yeah, right," Madrone said. "You got a fucked-up way of showing it. Listen, you stupid asshole, I'm a fucking cop, and you're under fucking arrest! You gotta right to remain silent—"

"I want to help you, Officer Madrone," the Chinese man said, his voice as calm as if he were reading numbers off a spreadsheet. His mouth thinned to a tight line as he looked at Madrone.

Madrone blinked. "You know my name? I don't think I know you. Do I know you, asshole?"

"No, Mr. Madrone. You don't know me. But that doesn't matter."

He raised one hand as Madrone glared at him. "Leave the skin, Mr. Madrone," he said. Madrone stared at him in disbelief. Was that *pity* in his eyes? The hair on Madrone's neck stood up. He felt a chill, as if chips of ice were slowly condensing in his veins.

"I asked you how you know my name, asshole," Madrone said.

But the Asian ignored the question with that same frigid, infuriating accountant's calm.

"You have no idea how much disaster you are calling down upon your head," the Chinese man said. "That is why I am here. Leave the skin behind. Leave this place and forget Carlton Wheeler. You cannot change what happened to him. If you do as I say, you can save yourself."

Madrone stepped back, confusion rippling his sunken features. "Carlton Wheeler? What the fuck does this have to do with Carlton Wheeler? Who *are* you, asshole?"

The Chinese man let out a slow breath and fixed Madrone with an intense stare. "That skin will be the death of you."

Madrone made up his mind. "That's it, Charlie Chan. Hands behind your back, cross your wrists. Come on, *do it!*"

A loud scrape echoed suddenly behind him. He turned for just one second. But it was enough. The Chinese man jerked away from him. He was ten feet away and pounding for the mouth of the alley before Madrone could even blink. Madrone lunged for him, slipped, and landed hard on his ass.

"Jesus!"

But the man was gone. The sound of his rapid

footsteps lessened, then vanished entirely, leaving Madrone sitting flat on his butt, utterly confused.

Carlton fucking *Wheeler?*

Madrone shook his head to clear it, levered himself to his feet, then picked up the skin again. Limping slightly, he walked out of the alley onto the sidewalk of Dearborn, turned right, trudged to the corner of Ontario, and made his way past the club entrance. The trendy yuppies still standing in line peered out from under their Versace umbrellas at him, their expressions saying they wouldn't be inviting him in for a drink any time soon. Madrone felt them staring—though it was a different feeling than the *watchfulness* he'd felt in the alley—and supposed he couldn't blame them. Then the wind turned and he got a good whiff of what he smelled like. It was a miracle the yuppies weren't running scream-ing into the night.

He was already soaked, too wet to get any wetter without drowning, so that even though the incessant downpour pattered on his head and his clothes, it didn't add new dimensions to his misery. It just made him feel more like an idiot. It was a pisser to lose Kung Fu Charlie, but what bothered him the most was that noise he'd heard behind him. What the hell was that? It was just noise, except for the sense of *danger* he'd felt.

Madrone, still lugging the skin, ignored the yups and turned slowly, looking back toward the alley. All at once, he saw the dark opening as the maw of a huge ani-mal. He swallowed.

Watching every corner and shadowy niche, Madrone stuck to the streetlights all the way back to his car.

He wrestled the door open, tossed the scaly skin onto the floor of the backseat, jumped behind the wheel, and pulled out without even checking the traffic. Luck was with him. A few people sat on their horns, but nobody creamed him.

He blew past a stop sign on Ontario, turned right onto LaSalle, and headed north. He stomped the accelerator, ignoring the way the Mustang's overworked engine whined, and followed Sheffield up toward the lake, almost ramming a taxi as he passed the huge, dark bulk of Wrigley Field. He raced through the city and didn't let up on the gas until he turned onto Sheridan. He was getting close to home.

Madrone kept looking in the rearview mirror, knowing it had to be paranoia. There was no one following him. No one in the backseat. But he couldn't shake the feeling that someone—no, some*thing*—was after him. The fear did not leave him, and he began to wonder if he'd snapped. He'd seen other cops lose it. Maybe he was next. Christ, he was hauling around a fucking *animal* skin . . .

At a stoplight he turned, hooked his right arm over the seat, and stared at the mound of scales on the floorboard in the rear of the car. He considered opening the door and tossing it out. But he couldn't. The Fu Manchu accountant had mentioned Carlton Wheeler. And he'd tried to take the skin. What possible connection could there be between the two?

Madrone turned into the parking garage below his

building, waited impatiently while the card reader swallowed his keycard, burped it back, and broadcast a signal that sent the wide chain door clanking upwards.

He should have felt safe here. It was a secured building, one of the older high-rises along Sheridan that Lake Michigan had nearly swallowed a couple of decades before. He'd been living there then, when they had piled sandbags along the first floor to keep storm waves out of the empty apartments.

The place had a doorman, cameras, and continuously monitored hallways and elevators. But he didn't feel safe. He had to force himself not to run through the parking garage. He'd never noticed how dark it was in the garage before. Just a few old, flickering fluorescent tubes that cast everything into eerie blue shadows.

He kept telling himself his feelings were irrational, but that didn't stop him from shooting frequent glances over his shoulder and listening to the hollow sound of his heels echoing in the drafty concrete chamber. Like a tomb . . .

He thought about going back to his car and returning to the precinct house, even though his shift was long over, just so he wouldn't have to be alone. But that was crazy, too. Wasn't it?

He walked through the lobby, checked his mailbox, and exchanged a few words with the doorman, ignoring the way the man looked at the bundle of scaly skin under his arm. Looked at it and wrinkled his nose. Well, fuck him . . .

He pushed the button to call the elevator, and waited. The elevator took its own sweet-ass time, and another eternity passed before he finally got to his floor. The skin was cumbersome, bulky, and slippery, and he kept having to shift it to keep it from sliding out of his arms.

His keys clinked as he fumbled with them at the lock. Keys always got themselves tangled up whenever you least needed that kind of crap. He nearly slammed them to the floor in frustration before he got a grip on himself.

Blame it on fatigue, maybe, but he'd just be lying to himself. His hands were still twitching. Crashing off the adrenaline overload. He couldn't seem to shake the sludgy fear that oozed through his veins. Finally he was able to get the right key in the lock and turn it. He pushed into his apartment, shut and locked the door behind himself, and stood there breathing hard, clutching the skin.

Beside the door, the green light of the small alarm control box changed to red and began to blink. He flipped it open and reset it, then turned back toward the living room beyond the small entry foyer.

The only light was the weak city glow that leaked through the dingy picture window and created dim white squares on his faded green carpet, vaguely illuminating a week's worth of newspapers, crumpled Budweiser cans, and empty pizza boxes.

He wiped the sweat and rain from his forehead, walked into the kitchenette, and dropped the skin on the tile floor. That stink that Madrone couldn't place was strong now. It smelled as if someone had been cooking Chinese food. He reached for the light switch—

Something blotted out the light in front of the picture window.

Madrone's heart bulged straight up into his throat. Somebody here? *Here?*

But this was the fourteenth floor. Whatever it was, it had to come in through the window. The dead bolt had been locked in the door. The alarm had still been on and functioning. Nobody had come through that door.

So how could anything—anything at all—be here? It couldn't. It was plain and simple. Impossible.

"Huhnng . . ." he said. A low, choking sound of pure terror. He fumbled out his pistol, his fingers quivering so badly he nearly dropped it.

The shadows before the window shifted again, and a sudden blast of that now familiar stink filled his nose. But not cold and weak, like the skin on the kitchen floor. This was hot, fetid, boiling with life. And in that swirl of shadowed motion he saw the shape of it as it turned toward him.

It wasn't a second-story man, or some kind of genius lock-cracker.

It wasn't the Egg Foo Young guy, somehow miraculously returned for round two.

It was worse, far worse.

It wasn't even human.

Pointed wings rose above its low, squat head. Tightly packed muscles bulged on its massive frame. A thin, pointed tail whipped through the air behind it. As it stepped toward him, its great weight made even the concrete floor beneath the frayed carpet vibrate. Its red

eyes glowed at Madrone, burning him somehow, turning his fear into stark terror.

"Oh, sweet Jesus save us," Madrone moaned, raising his revolver.

The shadowy thing launched itself at Madrone too
fast for anything living to see.

Madrone pulled the trigger.

The monster barreled into him and slammed him
against the wall so hard the plaster cracked. His vision
blurred from the shock of the blow. He fell to his knees,
tried to suck in a breath, tried to bring his gun to bear
on it again.

He screamed as he distinctly heard his fingers snap
with a sound like crunching celery stalks. Suddenly his
arm was numb below the elbow, and he knew he wasn't
holding the gun any more.

He thought it should hurt as he fell backward to
the floor, but he couldn't seem to feel anything. Not his
hands, his legs, or his face. Nothing.

He tried to gasp for breath, and couldn't. In the
split second since he'd seen the creature, he had somehow lost everything, his gun, his footing, even the ability to breathe and feel. A rocking shudder ran through
his body. He finally managed to focus his eyes on the
thing that stood over him. As a gesture of resistance, his
glare was pitiful, but it was all that was left to him. And
he was Sicilian enough to feel some shred of defiant
pride in being able to do it. If only he could spit in its
face before it killed him . . .

What the hell was it? He couldn't see it clearly,
even though it was right in front of him, looming over

him. He could only see its silhouette, as if the room's shadows conspired to hide it.

He tried to reach out and touch it, but his arms wouldn't move. Something was horribly ... wrong. When the creature had overpowered him, it had somehow shorted out his voluntary nervous system. Now he lay there, sprawling and crumpled, completely at its mercy. The stench of his own urine assaulted his nostrils.

Wide-eyed and trembling, he looked up at the figure standing over him, as dark and hidden as some nightmare behind storm clouds. Only its red eyes burned.

Why couldn't he see what it was? His own hands, his bruised and bloody body, were visible in the dim light flowing through the window. Why not this ... *thing?*

Then, slowly the shadows seemed to fall away from it. It stood with its massive, scaled arms folded across its chest. Its clawed fingers dug into the swollen muscles of its own flesh, as though it was contemplating its next action. Green wings rose above its head. It was staring right at him. Madrone couldn't seem to move his head to look anywhere else but straight into its red eyes.

Then the thing spoke. Its voice was deep, rumbling from its chest like choked thunder, but its words were slow and quiet, softened with regret.

"I am afraid it is necessary that you die."

It was the last thing Madrone ever heard. The monster reached down and rammed one taloned fist deep into Madrone's chest, smashing aside ribs and cartilage to tear his heart from the bleeding cavity.

Detective Jack Madrone gave one violent, convulsive shudder. Then, before the pain even had time to register in his brain, everything faded to black.

The creature knelt beside the body. Madrone hadn't felt a thing, not at the end. That was good.

For himself, he could still feel the insane rush—the way that the rib cage bent beneath the force of his blow, the moist crunch as Madrone's ribs broke and separated to admit his clenched fist. The warmth of the blood and the fluttery, dying movement of the still-beating heart in his claws. And then the power, the incredible power of ending a life in a single motion—the memory sang through his arm as he stood there. Wet, warm blood streamed from his talons and dripped onto the carpet. He tossed the heart, now limp and still, to the floor.

He found the skin on the kitchen floor. He pulled the stolen time cards from the cop's pocket. Then he picked stray scales from the sleeve of the detective's coat and from his fingers. The creature searched for scales on the carpet and poured his finds into the skin. He wavered over the bullet casing from the cop's gun, gleaming on the carpet, and finally decided to leave it where it was.

The bullet had passed through him—unblessed weapons were useless against him—and was wedged in the far wall. He dug it out of the plaster, wondering where the mystery would lead investigators, sure it would confuse them, if nothing else.

Finally he wrapped the whole mess into a loose

bundle and tucked it under one inhumanly large arm. He cloaked himself in darkness again. Invisible to all eyes but those of others like him, he walked to the door. The tips of his claws closed on the doorknob and turned it.

Had anyone been watching, the door would have appeared to open and close as if by magic.

His mission completed, the creature who had once been—and would be again—Justin Sterling found the stairway to the roof. After a time he stood alone beneath the storm, breathing in death and rain. Then, in utter silence, he merged once again with the night.

three

It was well after midnight when Detective Sandra McCormick stepped out of the elevator onto the fourteenth floor and headed toward Jack Madrone's apartment.

"Whoever's doing this has a lotta balls. Gotta give 'em that." Her partner, a veteran cop named Lawdon McKenzie, kept his comments in a low undertone clearly meant for her alone. He'd pushed his way through the crowd of pajama- and robe-clad rubber-neckers clogging the hall between the elevator and Madrone's apartment to meet her. "Or maybe he's just stupid. You don't kill cops in this city."

Sandra nodded. "You don't kill cops in any city. Not unless you're nuts . . ." She paused. "You got a time of death yet?"

"The uniforms are telling me just after ten o'clock," McKenzie replied. "The lady next door called 911 at ten-fifteen. She says she heard a big thump and a gunshot. When she got her nerves back together enough to crawl out from under the table, she called." He thought about it. "It took her like maybe an hour to get her nerve back . . ."

The police had already cordoned off the door. Sandra and McKenzie worked their way through the throng toward the apartment doorway, which was guarded by one uniform, a young woman with a flat blue stare. At the door, McKenzie paused, irritation plain on his beefy features. He turned and faced the gawkers, who stared back at him with barely suppressed excitement.

Blood lust, McKenzie thought, disgusted.

"Show's over, folks!" he shouted. "Get back to your apartments. We have everything under control out here, so go on home. Please!" He lowered his voice and aimed a quick aside at the uniformed officer. "Get them outta here. Escort them to their doors if you have to. This is ridiculous."

"Yes, sir." The beat cop began pushing people away from Madrone's apartment door.

Sandra ducked under the yellow tape, crossed the threshold, and looked around. Something immediately struck her as familiar, but she couldn't pinpoint it.

She was still a little groggy. It was always a pain to wake up, get dressed, and leave a warm bed to come look at a dead body at this god-awful hour. But the captain had called her personally. It looked, he told her, like her man had struck again. One glance at the corpse confirmed why he thought so. Hole in the chest, heart on the floor. That pretty much said it all. Same as her prime-time case of the moment, the campus security guard, Baxter.

Crouching down, she examined the wound. She pulled a pen out of her purse and used it to peel back the bloody edges of the dead man's torn shirt. The edge of the wound was marked by several sharp incisions. Where the marks intersected there was a hole about five inches in diameter, straight through the rib cage. Fragments of Madrone's shattered ribs were visible below the skin and in the pool of congealing blood at the bottom of the hole, like bits of white teeth peeping from diseased gums.

Same thing as Baxter, she thought, *same exact thing.* She could only hope they could keep the circumstances of this murder as quiet as they'd kept Baxter's death. She could imagine the headlines if the story got out. Not one, but two now. A serial killer with a taste for blunt heart surgery. The media would go nuts.

But Jack Madrone had been a cop. That made it hot, hot and juicy, and somebody would drop a dime to a tame news hound. Somebody, somewhere. There wasn't a prayer of keeping it under wraps, even though the department would keep the actual details as confidential as it could. But stuff like this was so sensational, sooner or later somebody would leak even the most intimate trivia, let alone a hole the size of a baseball in a dead homicide cop's chest. And his heart like a lump of liver ten feet from the body . . .

She sighed and stood up. The crime scene forensics guys were still crawling all over the place like near-sighted, intense cockroaches. Most stuff was bagged and tagged, though the evidence was still in place. A flicker of light from the direction of the kitchen told her the shutterbugs were still hard at work, taking digital pictures of everything even remotely interesting.

Madrone's gun was lying some distance from the body, as though it had been thrown there by Madrone or the killer. Madrone's right hand was bruised, several of the fingers broken and swollen. It appeared there had been a struggle for control of the weapon.

And Madrone lost, she thought, an ugly quiver growing in her belly. She saw a lot of death, but a cop was different. Part of the clan. It could have been her.

A single bullet casing gleamed on the floor a few feet from Jack's body.

"It looks like Jack got a shot off. Anybody find the bullet?" Sandra raised her head, looking for blood spatter patterns or anything else to indicate the killer had been hit.

One of the forensics techs glanced up. "We think it was buried in the wall by the window. There's a hole there consistent with the angle of fire from where Madrone was standing. It looks like someone gouged something out of there." He shrugged. "We don't have any idea what kind of tool was used. Not yet."

McKenzie pointed at an ugly hole in the plaster wall, a very recent one, judging by the lack of dust and dirt in it.

"Somebody took the bullet? The killer? Damn, that's weird."

If the bullet was embedded in the wall, it had most likely missed its intended target. Why would a killer take it? What would he think the cops could learn from an expended bullet? Unless he knew about DNA, and he'd been hit . . . But the blood on the carpet, judging by its position, all appeared to be Jack's.

"Speaking of weirdness," McKenzie replied, "the heart's over here." He pointed at a plastic bag resting on the carpet. The inside of the bag was smeared with dark, congealed blood. "At least the nut case didn't eat it."

He grinned, his expression cynical. "Nice way to start the week, huh, Bruce? You just gotta love Mondays . . ."

Because Sandra had trained to black belt level in two different martial arts, McKenzie had taken to calling her Bruce, in mockery of Bruce Lee. "What'cha think?"

She shrugged. "Don't think much, yet. We got two now, and that's a real problem. One of them a cop, and that's a bigger problem."

"I can hear it now. Hole-in-the-chest cop killer stalks Chicago. Pictures at eleven."

McKenzie's many-lined brow wrinkled under his receding hairline as he paused, thoughtful. "I know it's a stupid question, but what the hell. It's the same killer, right?"

She nodded and stood up, though she never took her eyes from the gaping wound on Jack Madrone's body. "Yeah. It's the same."

"Chicago. That toddling town . . ."

"All over the place, Mac." She walked out into the living room. Old pizza boxes, wrinkled *Tribunes,* crumpled Bud cans, and a few dishes crusted with old food littered the coffee table and the floor. Some of the stuff was bagged. All of it had been dusted.

Sandra removed a cloth-covered elastic loop from her pocket, scooped her long hair into a controlled handful, and bound her mass of curls out of the way. She hadn't known Jack Madrone that well. She'd seen him around the Twenty-third District station on Halstead from time to time, talked to him once or twice. He always had a five o'clock shadow, always smelled of stale sweat, and always seemed to be mentally undressing her when she spoke with him. From what she gathered, he hadn't been very popular, but he had been a good detective. And nobody ever said you had to be a saint to be a good cop.

"You seen his jackets yet?" she asked McKenzie, who had followed her into the room.

"I called Twenty-three Homicide. He wasn't working nothing real big or nasty. But he did have one high profile. The Carlton Wheeler thing," McKenzie said.

"That lawyer. The rich crusader."

"That's the one." McKenzie squinched his eyes, trying to remember. "And another weird one, though not like—" He waved vaguely in the general direction of Madrone's corpse. "—Like ours," he finished. "Guy got scragged behind all the locked doors in the world, twenty-one floors up a ritzy Lincoln Park high-rise."

She nodded. "Yeah, now I remember. I heard Wheeler was actually a decent guy. Probably the only lawyer with a conscience in the entire city and somebody clips him."

"You gettin' philosophical, Bruce?"

Her lips curved in a small smile. "Not yet, Mac."

He grinned. "Just checking."

"Any similarities between Wheeler's case and this?"

"Yeah. They were both murdered."

She frowned at him. "Not funny."

He shrugged, ran a hand through the thin strands of what was left of his salt-and-pepper hair. "No similarities that I know of. Wheeler took a bullet in the brain. Nothing Hollywood—not like this."

"Was Madrone close to the killer?"

"Who, Wheeler's? What's the connection? Wheeler got his ass shot. Our guys get partly disemboweled."

She turned and stared thoughtfully at the doorway. "Maybe one similarity. There's an alarm on that door there. And we're fourteen stories up. You think Madrone was stupid enough to bring somebody home to rip his heart out?"

"Vampyra the hooker, maybe?" McKenzie asked. "Naw. He was an old hand."

"So how did the killer get past the doorman downstairs, past all these security cameras, through a deadbolted door with an alarm system? Wasn't it something like that with Wheeler?"

McKenzie looked as if he'd suddenly developed a bad case of gas. "Don't say that, Bruce. Isn't it bad enough already without crap like that?"

She wandered toward the picture window, paused, peered out and down.

"Was Madrone getting anywhere with the Wheeler thing?"

McKenzie pawed at his hair. "I don't know. I don't

think so. I think it was lookin' like one of those jackets that was going to stay open until the next Ice Age. I remember hearing something about it. Real smooth shoot. Ya never know, though. Maybe Madrone knew different. Maybe he *was* on to something."

"Maybe he uncovered something that made somebody nervous," Sandra said.

"I don't know, Bruce. Hell of a stretch. We'll have to go through his entire caseload. But we already got our gold-plated, Sherlock Holmes clue, right? That mini bomb crater in his chest. We seen that before already, and not with Carlton frigging Wheeler."

Sandra nodded. "So how *did* he get in?"

McKenzie got that pained look again. "There's no sign of forced entry on the door, but he went out that way. There's blood on the inside knob."

Sandra leaned over to examine the inside of the windowsill. The picture window was one of the old-fashioned kind that opened by sliding on a pivot. She saw water on the inside of the windowsill, reached into her bag, wrapped a hanky around her fingertips, and pushed the window. It slid open easily, and the space was more than enough to admit a man.

Baxter's murderer had also come in by an upper-story window.

"Mac?"

"Yeah?"

"Let's check on the Wheeler thing, see where the killer gained entrance. If they know."

"It's still a reach, Bruce."

"So, humor me. Woman's intuition, right?"

Mac grinned. "You believe in that like I believe in hitting the lottery, Bruce. Woman's intuition. Sure . . ."

"I think we got an acrobat, Mac," she said slowly. "Baxter was kinda like this, too. Hard to get at. What floor was that museum archive window on at U of C? Four, right? High enough, anyway."

"Not fourteen, though. Or twenty-one." McKenzie glanced around, his expression discomfited. He went to the window and looked out for himself. A gust of dank, cool air blew into the room. He pulled back in and shook his head.

"Had to come in the door, Bruce. There ain't no other way."

"There wasn't one with Wheeler, either," she replied. Wheeler, Baxter, now Madrone. And a killer or killers who specialized in impossible, invisible entry and exit.

"The S.W.A.T. guys said something about maybe a ninja. Spiderman right up the wall. Like in the movies." She rolled her eyes.

McKenzie snorted. "Those S.W.A.T. guys eat too many vitamins."

There was a piece missing from the archive room Baxter was guarding, but it had no great financial value, and the thief had left other nearly priceless pieces behind, including many that would be easier to fence.

She sighed. None of it made any sense. And neither did this. Madrone was a street guy, knew how to handle himself. He might have been an old timer, but his alarm system looked up-to-date. So did he know his killer? Did he open the door? Or was the killer waiting for him when he got home?

She didn't know which was harder to believe, Madrone letting down his guard so completely, or the killer wiggling through a window fourteen stories up.

"Madrone was a cop," Mac said slowly. "And Baxter was a security guard. Kind of a cop . . ."

Sandra rubbed her neck. "Yeah. That, too. So we got what, three similarities now? MO of the actual murders, problems with entry and exit, and maybe cops."

"Something like that," Mac agreed.

"Our Baxter guy snagged himself a souvenir," she said, moving out of the living room toward the kitchen.

"And maybe something like that happened here?"

"It's a thought."

"Let it pass, Bruce. Look at this place. You could probably move the fridge out and it would be hard to tell. Well, not the fridge, but—" Mac gestured toward the debris littering the living room. "I don't think Madrone was the kinda guy who kept an inventory of his empty beer cans and used newspapers. And that's about all there is in this dump."

Sandra wandered back to the window. Something about it was stuck in the back of her mind, like a tiny burr. She pushed her head out and looked down. Squinted.

Turned back into the room. "Hey! Anybody got a flashlight?"

A tech grunted, reached into his bag, and handed her one. A long-handled Maglite.

"Thanks." She adjusted the focus of the lens for wide-angle, then leaned out and aimed the beam at the brick skin of the building beneath the window frame.

There they were, just like the ones on the college building where Baxter had been killed. Those strange marks on the windowsill, the scratches in the brick.

"Hey, Mac," she said softly. "Take a look."

She moved aside as he pushed his bulk at the window, then poked his head out. He stared silently for a moment. "Jesus," he said. "Those look like—"

"Yeah. The same as the ones under Baxter's window."

They eyed each other.

"Look fresh, too. Like Baxter's," he said.

"Climbing equipment?" Sandra said. "Some kind of hooks or claws?"

"We checked that with Baxter and came up pretty much empty, Bruce."

"Yeah, yeah. So we check this, too. First thing we check is if they're the same kind of scratches." She turned back and faced the room.

"I got some stuff on the exterior wall I want checked," she announced.

The tech who'd given her the flashlight stood up and ambled over. "Yeah? Like what?"

Her voice went brisk. "There's scratches or marks out there, under the window. They look fresh. I want photos and casts. And then I want somebody to compare them with the same stuff we got from the Baxter scene."

The tech raised an eyebrow. "Baxter? Oh, yeah. I remember."

She nodded. "Check the whole building. Make

sure it isn't something from the window cleaners or whatever."

"Right." The tech leaned out and looked. "I did the Baxter scene," he remarked.

"Yeah, I remember you."

"These look like the same kind of thing. Not identical, you know? But the same kind . . ."

"Well, let's get it checked out."

The tech rubbed the side of his nose. "Maybe some kind of climbing equipment." He thought about it. "I dunno, though. Fourteen floors up? That'd be a hell of a production. Even after dark, somebody would have to notice."

Sandra shrugged. "Just get it all into the record. We'll figure it out later."

The tech nodded, then headed for the kitchen where the photographers were still flashing away.

Sandra turned, went back to Madrone's corpse, and stared down. His face looked old, older than she'd remembered him, and his features were twisted in an expression of terror. Terror frozen by death.

She squatted on her haunches and stared at the wound in his chest.

"Man, I wish I knew what the asshole used on him," she murmured.

Behind her, Mac grunted. "If ya know too much, Bruce, it takes all the fun out of it."

"Coroner said maybe like a steel pipe, with sharp, jagged edges. Something metal and hollow, rammed into him like a pile driver." She leaned forward. "But a clean incision, just like this one."

"Yeah, Bruce. But we figure that already, right? I mean, how many MOs are we gonna see where we get a hole in the chest and a heart on the floor? Maybe when somebody spills this one we see some kind of copycat thing, but nobody knows about it yet."

"I know, I know. *Man!*" She stood up, shaking her head, her features somber. "Hell of a way to go out, Mac."

"They all are, Bruce. They all are."

She glanced over and saw a couple of white-jackets from the coroner's office unrolling a body bag. They both looked incredibly young to her.

One of them came up. "Can we bag and tag him yet?"

"Yeah, I'm done. Listen, tell your boss I want full wound comparisons done between this one and the murder wound in the Baxter case."

The tech stared at her, a cynical grin playing across his youthful features. "I didn't do the pickup, but it's not exactly a secret around the office there's another one like this. I think you can count on a comparison."

She refused to take his bait. It was too late, and she was too tired, to play mind games with a baby-faced body hauler.

"Go ahead, cowboy. Get him out of here."

As she watched the two techs fit the body bag around Madrone's corpse, she felt that prickly little mind-buzz again. Something more, something that she'd missed. She tried to trace the thread through her mind.

"What—" McKenzie started to ask but she cut

him off with a motion of her hand. Her subconscious was trying to tell her something subtle, and she had to take a moment to listen.

What was it? The room? The window? The scrapes in the outside wall? All were similar to the Baxter murder, but that wasn't it. It was . . .

She sniffed.

The smell. It was the smell. She walked over to the window, sniffing the air all along the way. No doubt about it. It was there, ever so slight but highly distinctive, that oily burnt smell. She'd smelled that same scent, like hot sesame seed oil, in the room where Baxter had bought it. And that was odd. For one thing, the room in which Baxter was murdered had no food in it that night.

It was a museum archive, for Christ's sake. And now the same distinctive smell here. But this wasn't a museum archive. Food would be—

She headed for the kitchen. She opened the cupboards, then the fridge. No spices, no oils, nothing like that. Big Man TV dinners, boxes of generic mac and cheese, a couple of frozen pepperoni pizzas. Some salt and pepper, and that was in a drawer in the little paper packages takeout restaurants gave away. Sesame oil was a Chinese seasoning. But there weren't any Chinese takeout containers in the trash or in the fridge or anywhere else. In the living room, either.

McKenzie followed her. "What? What is it?"

"The smell. You smell that?"

He sniffed. "Yeah? So? Smells like Chinese food."

"Think about it, Mac."

"Think about what? So he liked Chinese food."

"Did he? Does it look like it?" She waved at the pizza boxes on the floor.

McKenzie shrugged. "Okay. Maybe not. Why?"

"The archive at the university smelled the same way."

His forehead wrinkled again. "Yeah, you're right. It did."

He thought some more. "So what's that mean?"

"Could mean nothing. Could mean something. But it's another similarity."

As the techs lifted the bag with Madrone inside, Sandra saw something. She moved closer and knelt by the stain on the floor that had been hidden by his body.

"Hey, Mac," she said, "what do you make of this?"

McKenzie made his way over and crouched next to her. Imprinted in the carpet, barely defined in the bloody fibers, was a strange depression about sixteen inches in length, roughly half that in width.

"What is that?" McKenzie cocked his head to the side. "Footprint?"

The print was an elongated star shape. Three prongs pointing toward the wall, one long prong opposing them, facing the other way.

Sandra leaned down and sniffed the print. "Yeah. Looks like it. Grab one of the forensics techs."

She waited until Mac found another photographer. The first was still busy getting pics of the scratches on the brick wall.

As he stepped back and light bloomed from his flash, she shook her head again.

"Great. Fucking great, Mac. What we got is Bigfoot, who's a Chinese food–eating, rock-climbing, frustrated heart surgeon. Our case reports are starting to read like some kind of *Star Wars* movie."

McKenzie chuckled.

But the thing *did* look like a footprint, though like no footprint she'd ever seen. For some reason she felt a sudden, chilly breeze along her spine.

"This case is developing a very big suck factor, Mac," she said.

"What kind of shoes do those really crazy climbers wear?" McKenzie asked.

"That's a good question. I haven't got a clue," she admitted.

"I'll look into it," he said.

One of the crime scene boys was dusting the door handle, lifting prints, and taking photos before he washed the blood off it into a sample vial. Sandra tapped him on the shoulder.

"I want a preliminary report, along with fiber and DNA data as soon as you get it."

The techie nodded. "Sure, Detective McCormick."

"You know me?" Sandra asked.

"Detective Sandra McCormick," the techie replied in a flat, noncommittal tone of voice.

"Good. So have somebody give me a call when the preliminary results come in. I'll come get the report."

"Sure." The tech had as little enthusiasm in his voice as before. He went back to dusting the doorknob.

Sandra moved away and let the tech do his job. She

looked at McKenzie. "What about Madrone's partner?"

"I don't know," McKenzie said. "Dunno if he even had one. I'll check it out."

"Okay." She sighed and stretched, looked around the room once again. "We'll keep the tapes up, keep this place off-limits. Mac, can you put out a bulletin to the hospitals? We'll want immediate notification of any gunshot wounds. Maybe Madrone managed to pop this guy after all. We can hope anyway."

"Sure, Bruce."

She rubbed hard at her face. Her skin felt like dough, flat and without elasticity. She yawned.

"I'm gonna go home and get some sleep. You should do the same."

"You watch yourself, Bruce. Whoever it is, they're taking down cops now."

She nodded. "You do the same, Mac."

He stared at her somber expression. "I want this guy," he said.

"So do I, Mac. So do I. So we'll get him. Right?"

He nodded grimly. "Yeah, right."

On the way home, rolling through the silent city, she thought about it. Most times, she'd walk into a crime scene and find some stupid hairball crying that he'd never meant to kill her, he just wanted to show her who was boss. Or that she was asking for it. Or there'd be some scumbag ranting that if he couldn't have her, nobody could. Or there'd be gangs or drugs or some other obvious indication of means, motive, opportunity.

But it always made her a little jittery when she had to run over the possibilities without a clear picture in her head of what had happened, some kind of familiar framework within which to set her ideas. Like a puzzle board. But when the puzzle clicked, when the identity of the killer became clear to her, it was an amazing feeling, one of the reasons she'd chosen this career in the first place.

Twenty minutes of driving through rain falling on empty city streets brought her to her condominium. The sky was still dark. Not even the first gray glimmerings of false dawn lit the horizon.

She turned left off Lakeshore Drive into the quaint gentrified area east of Michigan Avenue, between the Miracle Mile and the lake itself. After parking curbside, she checked the seat of her car to make sure she hadn't left anything to attract the smash-and-grab artists, got out, locked up, and walked to the front gate of her building, an old warehouse converted to condos for urban dwellers. A man was walking toward her. She marked him with her peripheral vision as she punched in her security code.

He passed her by, his footfalls loud on the sidewalk. Once his steps faded into the distance, she opened the gate, went in, and closed the gate behind her. She looked at the elevator, and then decided to take the stairs.

She took the steps at a quick pace, running to the beat of a rhythm in her mind. Her legs weren't burning even after eight flights, and her breathing had returned to normal by the time she reached her door. Martial arts training didn't buy you big muscles, especially if you were a woman, but you got endurance like crazy. *And that's something,* she thought, pleased. *I endure.*

She liked the thought.

No sooner had she entered than she heard the creak of a wheelchair. A man's silhouette blocked the light coming from down the hall. He paused a moment there, then wheeled himself toward her. Loose sweatpants hid his thin, wasted legs. A tank top covered his well-muscled torso. His shoulders and arms were ripped with muscle, carved like marble from the effort of moving his wheelchair all over the city.

In the half-light, the scars on her brother's face weren't too noticeable, but the part of his nose that was missing looked more grotesque than usual. He ran a hand through his blonde hair, scratched the side of his head, and adjusted his glasses, a fairly typical gesture for him. He smiled at her.

"Working late? Or did you have a date?" he asked.

She moved past him into the kitchen and opened the refrigerator, suddenly stricken with the urge to rustle up something to eat. "You know where I was, Benny. And if you don't quit teasing me, I'll never go out with anybody. Just to piss you off."

He deftly spun his chair about. He'd always been well-coordinated. She winced inwardly every time she thought about how much he'd lost in that motorcycle accident. It had been more than four years ago, and the tragedy still haunted her. She could only imagine how bad it was for him.

Four years ago, he'd received a full scholarship to

Cal Tech. He'd jumped on his motorcycle and raced off to his girlfriend's to celebrate. It was rainy and cold that day. Typical Chicago fall weather. He'd lost the bike on an icy curve, broken his back, and left a good chunk of his face on the pavement. His helmet had kept him from cracking his skull open and killing himself, and at the time he'd regretted wearing it. He'd felt, in the first few months after the accident, that death would have been preferable. He seemed to Sandra to have revised that opinion, but she never asked him if that was so. He'd tell her what he felt she wanted to hear.

The physical and emotional costs of that accident weren't the only ones Benny paid. His college plans had fallen apart and so had the relationship with the girlfriend. He spent six months in the hospital.

In Sandra's opinion, the whole situation wasn't fair. But she also knew that her opinion didn't change anything. The world was never fair, never had been. Sandra had known that for a long time now.

"But I don't know where you were. So tell me. A hot date with a hot prospect? Give me some details here, feed my fantasies. . . ." Benny said.

"The man in question had a hole in his chest and was rapidly cooling before we spent time together."

"You know, sis, you never go out with anybody living these days," Benny said.

Sandra looked up. "See, here we go again," she told the ceiling.

"Not all guys are assholes," Benny said. "Just because you married one asshole guy once upon a time doesn't mean that it's going to happen to you again."

Sandra shook her head. "You never give up, do you, Benny?" She took out a jug of milk and poured herself a glass. As she drank, she leaned back against the counter and relaxed. "I can pretty well guarantee that dead guys aren't assholes, at least not anymore."

"Okay, Ace. How's this, then? I think you should mope around your entire life, avoid any kind of intimacy with anyone except your invalid brother, hang out with the recently dead chasing fingerprints, hoping to find out that it was Colonel Mustard with a candlestick in the conservatory. It sounds like a fabulous life—at least for a David Lynch film. Not enough dwarves in it for Fellini." He reached up and adjusted his glasses.

"Fuck you, Benny," Sandra said, tipping her milk glass at him.

Benny sighed. "Even leaving out the incest angle, you'd be the first in a long time."

"Pity party now?" Sandra arched an eyebrow. She'd meant it in jest, of course, but as soon as she said the words, she regretted them. They steered too close to dangerous waters. Dammit, she was tired. She should go straight to bed. She wasn't alert enough to wrangle with Benny right now. He was smart, funny, and three steps ahead of her even when she was at the top of her form.

"You seemed to be in the mood for a bit of pity," Benny said. Sometimes Sandra thought he brought up these subjects just to watch her squirm as she tried not to hurt his feelings.

"All right, all right. I give up. I can't beat you with words, and I'm too tired to kick your ass properly. Can we save the yack-fest for another time when I've had more than, like, two hours sleep out of the last twenty-four? How's the computer game design coming?"

"Almost finished. The project's not due for another month. I'll be done in a week."

She nodded.

"How's the case?" he asked.

She sighed, shook her head, "I don't know. Not too good. I need to come up with something more for us to go on. I'm going to start checking specialty climbing shops or exotic blade-making shops or something tomorrow. The entire case sucks. And our guy did another one tonight. Just like Baxter."

Benny raised his eyebrows. "Yeah?"

"Yeah. It was family tonight, though. A cop named Jack Madrone. You'll probably read about it tomorrow in the papers under a suitably gruesome headline, no doubt, or maybe even catch it on the Net before then. We're trying to keep the details of the murder quiet, but the killings are so sensational somebody will leak it. Probably already has leaked it."

"Same way?"

"Yep. Same exact fuckin' way. Hole straight through the rib cage." She drank the rest of her milk and began rummaging again for solid food, a sandwich maybe, something to calm the rumblings in her gut. "Some kind of incisions on the chest surrounding the open wound.

"Yuck . . ." Ben wrinkled his nose.

"Yeah." She paused. "I don't mind telling you, Benny, this one creeps me out. Bad. Same feeling I got when I first saw Baxter's body. Never felt it before on any other case. You'd think that finding number two would give us something to go on, but the case just keeps getting more improbable. Murder is supposed to make *more* sense the more data you collect, not less."

He smiled. "You sound spooked."

She pursed her lips. "I don't know. Maybe. Yeah, spooked is right. And it takes a lot to spook me. But I'm intrigued, too. It's weird, the whole thing is, and I want to figure it out."

"Fine, then. Go for it. But do me a favor, huh?" Benny's voice turned serious. "If your killer is taking cops, just make sure you don't end up on his dance card, okay?"

"No," she said. "Don't worry. I won't."

"I always worry," he said.

four

A spattering of rain fell upon the dark rooftop. Deep music thrummed from below, a rhythmic base note under the twentieth-century snarl of the city.

Another sound intruded—the whoosh of air displaced by two mighty wings. A multitude of tiny puddles fled from the sound, blown from their resting places by the blast. Then came the thud and rustle of something heavy settling on the pebble-covered tar-strapped roof. Had there been anyone near enough to listen, they'd have heard the crunch of footprints among the rocks and the light scrape as a tail dragged along the surface. A series of small noises moved steadily closer to the skylight protruding from the roof's surface. Then came the scrape of metal against metal as the skylight edged open a crack, apparently under its own power. The faint glow from the room below created ghostly highlights on the falling raindrops nearby. Off-key mechanical music carried through the night, the electronic tones from the security panel as an unseen claw pressed the keys that disabled the alarm system. A whirring sound and then the skylight opened fully, a mechanical maw. With a rush of wind, a shadow dropped through. The glass skylight closed behind it.

The creature who called himself the Wyrm flapped his wings once as he settled to the floor. Shadows fled from him as his clawed feet pressed deeply into the thick blue carpet.

He moved across the room with a snake-like grace. Muscles rippled under his scaly skin as he crossed the plush rug, which muffled the sound of his passing.

A full-length mirror stood on a smooth, marble dais roughly seven feet in diameter. He ascended two steps to stand before it. The mirror was old, older than he was himself. It was framed in wood, intricately carved. Knights with spears and shields fought dragons whose curved necks formed symmetric patterns at the mirror's corners. The wood was layered in lustrous gold leaf, now cracked and flaking in places despite the loving care it had received through the centuries.

The Wyrm looked at his reflection. His flattened nose was ribbed with toughened skin, double ridged from the holes of its nostrils to the prominent bar of its brow. His mottled, scaled body was top-heavy, bowed by the heavy muscles required for flight. His was a physique built for strength, speed, and death—for chasing, trapping, catching, and killing prey.

He heard his muscles sing thrilling songs of carnage as he moved. They craved violence. They cried for him to open his huge wings and go hunting. To glide to the street and wreak bloody havoc. Dive into the petty humans standing below and scatter them like sheep before the wolves. To rend them with claws and slaughter them in great red waves of death.

The creature straightened and stretched, feeling his power. Shivers coursed through his body in waves. His wings filled the room from side to side. The curved claws at the tip of each of his wings scraped along the ceiling. The need to escape the confines of the tiny room was almost unbearable. His lips pulled back to reveal rows of sharp teeth, jagged and askew. The creature let out a soft, whispery sigh, and slowly returned to its crouch.

"Enough," he said. The creature's voice was guttural, harsh in the silence. He dropped the skin he'd taken from the detective's apartment onto the marble floor of the dais.

The creature brought his hands to his scaled chest, crossing them. A wet snapping sound filled the room. The creature grunted, clenched his teeth. Another snap sounded, quickly followed by a popping sound. The creature gasped as his wings crumpled down, bending and somehow folding into his back. The scaled skin around the wings warped and went flaccid, like a tent with the supports removed. The creature's low growl became louder as the process continued. Flesh tore away from underneath the scales. Bunched, powerful muscles receded to normal size. Bones twisted and morphed, growing smaller, more delicate. Claws pulled away from the edges of fingers no longer curled like talons.

Instead of a nightmare creature, a man stood before the mirror, his human body surrounded and obscured by a translucent, gleaming cocoon—the skin of the monster he'd been. He fell to the floor, writhing as the last of the old skin ripped away. The agony lasted only a moment, but the intense pain left him weak and unable to move. Finally, slowly, his strength returned. His hands pulled viciously at the scales covering his chest, tearing them away, revealing his human flesh underneath, red and angry as a newborn's. Justin emerged, wriggling naked from his prison, his raw skin shining wetly in the dim light.

Before he could take a breath the last miracle of transformation began. The redness of his skin faded before his eyes, leaving it smooth and pale. Healed. He was immortal. No illness could hold him captive, no injury or wound mar his body for more than a fleeting moment.

The face and form he saw reflected in the mirror were now quite human and very handsome, even obscured as they were by the strings of mucous that hung from his long black hair and naked body. The vile substance was a natural barrier between the human and the reptile parts of himself.

Justin gathered his hair into a ponytail and stripped the excess moisture from it. Droplets of fluid speckled the marble on the floor, already slimed and bloody from his transformation. He tried to think clinically, think about something other than what he was, what he'd done, and how he'd done it. Anything was better than thinking of that. .

He stared down at the dots of blood on the marble. They made him think of a too-close view of a pointillist painting, maybe a Georges Seurat masterpiece of a walk in the park. The dots of color that formed the picture would be nonsensical up close. Viewers could only make sense of them at a distance. Seen as it was meant to be seen, the painting gave the illusion of people walking through the park, an illusion comprised of tiny dots of white, pink, green, blue, dots of red . . . red like blood.

Justin clenched his fist, clenched his teeth. He closed his eyes and tried to think of something else. *No emotion,* he thought. *Keep it bottled up, stare at the wall, go another place mentally. Be anywhere but here.*

Tendons stood out starkly in Justin's neck and arms as he fought for control. His stomach muscles tensed. His eyes flashed open and he turned away from the mirror. The freshly discarded skin caught his eye. He grimaced in repulsion. Evidence of what he truly was, evidence he couldn't bear to see. Usually, he got rid of the skin as soon as possible. The Dumpster in the alley behind the club had always served, but no longer. He glanced at the other, older skin. He'd thought it safely disposed. But its discovery in the Dumpster had led to yet another bloody, screaming death.

No, he couldn't use the Dumpster any longer. Have to come up with something else . . . but he couldn't cope with that now. He could hardly cope with anything. Anything except . . .

He wrenched his gaze from the skin toward a more

pleasant view. Drawings of all sizes covered the wall. Some were rendered in charcoal, some were done in pencil. A few watercolors glowed like gems among the mostly black-and-white collection. There were scenes from all over the city, views of the Chicago skyline, sketches of nearby country landscapes as well as busy city crowd scenes, finished portraits, quick sketches, simple line drawings. Some of the art work had been pinned up in careful order, arranged in lines like well-laid bricks. Other pieces flowed in chaotic streams across the wall, corners overlapping, images turned at odd angles.

The wall was filled with Justin's own work. He rarely left it looking the same from day to day. He'd take drawings down and replace them with new ones often. His favorites stayed. His failed attempts rarely lasted more than a few hours. Sometimes his muse would send Justin out into the city for weeks at a time, and he would roam Chicago and its environs looking for suitable subject matter, sketching and painting everything that took his fancy.

Currently, Tina had center stage. Images of her dominated the collection of drawings. Tina laughing. Tina smiling coyly. Tina watching herself in the mirror, holding a blouse up against her chest. Tina diving for a volleyball, going for the save. Tina looking pensive. Tina the woman. Tina the girl-child.

Concentrate on the drawings, he told himself. His eyes fell on a landscape where the bare branches of winter trees were bending before a gale wind. *Think of that day when it blew so hard you could scarcely keep the pages from ripping off of your pad as you sketched. Think of that plastic bag that flew through the air and smacked you in the face because you were too busy drawing to notice it was coming . . .*

. . . just like Madrone smacked into the wall where you threw him before you killed him.

The death of the detective refused to stay safely buried in that part of Justin's subconscious that he never visited willingly. The joy he'd felt in killing the man thrummed through his bones. He looked down at his hand, now human and covered with slime. The warm moisture felt like the blood that had dripped from his fingers as Madrone's heart slid from them to the floor.

Justin choked and spun away, stumbled down the steps away from the mirror and the abandoned skin of his transformation.

And it goes to show you, doesn't it, Justin? If you try to resist the master, he lets you feast on the horror of your deeds after they're done.

He hadn't wanted to kill Madrone. No more than he'd wanted to kill the security guard Baxter a fortnight ago. But the Dragon would not be denied, and Justin now bore the weight of the Dragon's disapproval in addition to the weight of his own self-loathing.

Both men had been in the wrong place at the wrong time. That was all. But that didn't change or justify what had happened to them at his hands. Justin knew that as surely as he knew he'd had little or no choice but to kill them.

Baxter's death had been one of those unforeseen

things, totally unplanned. Justin had been at the university to retrieve an artifact at the Dragon's request, nothing more. He'd been in the main building at midnight, pulling an ancient chalice from its dusty display case. Baxter had startled Justin, startled him for several reasons.

Justin had been in the Wyrm shape that night, completely under the Dragon's compulsion, more passenger than free-willed entity. His mission nearly accomplished, he'd relaxed his watchfulness for a split second as the power of the artifact had pulsed through him. His senses were so acute in the Wyrm state that he was rarely surprised by his surroundings, but Baxter had run into the room at just the wrong instant. A second earlier or later, and Justin would have faded into the shadows before the guard saw him. In Justin's confusion, he'd reacted before conscious thought could kick in. The security guard hadn't even had time to draw a breath before his heart was on the floor.

And Carlton Wheeler, the lawyer. Justin's self-loathing turned to rage for a moment as he thought of that death. Omar had killed him. Omar, Kalzar's apprentice, sent to Justin to study the arts of the disciples. Sent to Justin to make his life a living hell, more likely.

Killing Wheeler was supposed to be a quiet task. A textbook assassination, a case the cops would open and close faster than a bad book. Justin had listened and taught Omar as he'd planned it, watched attentively as Omar set it up, practically held his hand as he pulled the trigger.

Wheeler's death was supposed to be airtight, a closed room murder mystery. No detective on earth could've tracked it to the killer . . .

. . . until that feckless idiot Omar had started babbling in bars about the murder to anybody who'd listen!

And then there was the cop . . .

Justin threw himself against the wall, pounding it with his fists. He knocked a hole in the plaster, ripping open the skin on his knuckles. Justin paused, staring down at the blood welling up from the uneven cuts on his fingers. The crimson flow slowed and stopped as he watched. The wounds mended and his pale skin gleamed pearl-like, smooth and perfect in the soft light.

"I didn't want to . . ." Justin whispered. The pain in his soul threatened to burst it. He whirled around, perhaps hoping he could escape the torment hounding him if he just moved quickly enough, but he knew from long experience it was no use. He'd made his choice centuries ago, when he accepted the Dragon's offer of eternal life in exchange for eternal servitude. If he'd known then what he knew now, would he have still made the same choices? Who knew? Certainly not Justin.

The fight went out of him and memories overwhelmed him. His back thumped up against the wall as he let the pain take him. Slowly, so slowly he could feel the texture of the plaster surface in all its detail against the skin of his back, he slid to the floor, trusting in the wall's support, until he felt his buttocks touch the carpet.

"I was wrong . . ." Each word he spoke was a sliver

of fear, a regret that stabbed him like a shard of glass in his heart. And each word could bring down upon him the wrath of the Dragon. The pain would be endless, unbearable, the damage physical as well as mental. And the injuries inflicted by the Dragon would not heal until the Dragon wished them to. The cuts would not close. The bruises would not heal. The pain would not cease, perhaps ever. Justin couldn't be killed, but if the Dragon wished it, Justin could spend his eternity in endless torment.

"I could have intimidated him," Justin murmured. "Taken the skin, rendered him unconscious. Who would have believed him when he described what he saw? He'd never tell a soul, because people would think he'd had too much to drink or had sampled the fruits of a drug bust or lost his mind. He'd probably wonder if that wasn't the truth himself."

But the dragon-like body that was the Wyrm was not fully under Justin's control. As an underling, a *dragonling*, in fact, the Wyrm was an extension of the Dragon, and it had its own drive, its own agenda, its own missions. When the Wyrm wanted blood, Justin was merely a passenger in his own flesh, a watcher from within. Even the transformation was most often a matter of the Dragon's bidding, out of his control. When he resisted the Dragon in the slightest way, he earned the kind of pain that would quickly kill a mere mortal, pain he endured until the Dragon felt he'd learned his lesson.

His options were always the same. Do as he was bid or feel the lash of his master's anger. He still resisted when he could, but he knew always that resistance was futile. The demons of guilt for the things he had done ate away at his soul, but he could no more change his actions than he could stop the world from spinning. Even as the accumulated pain of centuries of killing weighed upon him, he knew he could never inflict the amount of pain upon himself that the Dragon could.

And all his killings weren't futile. Sometimes he and the Dragon were in agreement. There were days when Justin understood that he must kill; there were people who deserved to die. Certainly he understood that! Had he not killed when he was still mortal? He'd certainly indulged in dealing death—in warfare and in what they would call justifiable homicide in today's vernacular. But this night's murder was neither of those things . . .

"To have your foresight, master . . ." Justin whispered. "To assuage my conscience by knowing how each of these steps ultimately serves mankind . . . it would be a balm to my soul."

He ran through the events of this evening, trying to find another way out, something he could have done to stop them.

He'd been in the alley, after returning from Tina's to the club to await instructions. He'd been standing in the shadows, wondering why his master had sent him here, when the alarm had gone off, indicating somebody was about to open the kitchen door into the alley.

Then he'd seen the cop find the skin, seen the fight with the Dropka disciple. From the moment the Dropka had appeared, he'd lost the option of dealing with the cop alone. And even then he'd known what the

Dragon would demand. From the moment the cop touched the scales of the dragonling cocoon, his fate was sealed, no matter how much Justin fought it. Not killing him then and there had simply been a precautionary tactic—a mysterious, monstrously murdered corpse was the last thing he needed in an alley behind his home.

Justin rose, shivered. He often hated what he'd become, but he saw no way to change it.

Perhaps a shower would pull him out of the depression that always followed a kill.

The shower didn't help. Afterward, he crossed to the closet. Throwing the door open wide, he pulled out a robe and put it on. The warm cotton settled over his wet skin.

You are my scalpel, Lord of Sterling.

The Dragon's words echoed in his mind from long ago, from the day when Justin had first voiced his doubts about his mission.

Scalpels must cut deep to save the whole.

That was undoubtedly the truth. But why did those words never give him comfort?

He understood intellectually that his immortal master had a plan for the world, one which resulted in actions that seemed on the surface to be deadly, brutal, and hideous, but which served the greater good of the whole of mankind; but as the tool who carried out those terrible acts, his soul lived in torment. He could neither take comfort in the larger goals his master pursued, for his master rarely shared his plans with underlings, nor could he shake the guilt for his dreadful deeds.

His mind understood. But his soul shrieked in unbearable pain.

Justin looked about the room and saw an accusing gallery of ghostly figures whose deaths he had arranged over the centuries. They weren't truly there, merely figments of his overwrought imagination, but they were still as real to him as they'd been on the day they died. They lived on in his memory as surely as they ever had in real life, forever trapped in that moment when they took their last breath while he watched. On the nights he killed, the images were most vivid, but the gallery of the dead never entirely vanished from his mind. Seeing them now, he knew there was no help for it. Sometimes he could hold them at bay, but not tonight.

Ghostly faces stared at him like death masks, each one contorted in fear and pain. Justin tried to ignore them. He wished desperately that he could sleep. He could escape them if only he could reach that oblivion. Justin's nightmares were always waking ones, for he slept the sleep of the dead.

Mortals dreamed, but not Justin. He tried to remember what dreaming was like, but since the day he'd made his choice, he'd never again felt the soaring joy of a good dream, the terror of a nightmare. No warm summer days. No grave-cold horrors. His ghosts found him when he was awake. Tired, defenseless against them, but awake nonetheless.

When he did sleep, it was as though he ceased to exist. Justin wondered sometimes if his lack of dreams meant his soul had left his body forever on the day he became immortal.

If so, there was little he could about it now.

Except regret the loss.

And he supposed the Dragon had provided a substitute for dreaming—of a sort.

The master's appearances in the mirror were strangely spaced. Those glowing red eyes would look out at Justin three times in the same day, every day for months at a time; then Justin would go decades without ever seeing the long, spike-toothed face of his Dragon lord in a reflection.

But the master often overwhelmed Justin's sleeping mind. The Dragon had settled there long ago and the weight of its demands were crushing. Although Justin never dreamed as mortals did, he did have Dragon-sent visions. He would see the death of his next victim, and he would see himself as the slayer. He would see where, he would know when it would happen, and he would feel their blood on his claws.

And then he would awaken and execute the Dragon's command.

Most of his victims had knowledge the Dragon could not permit to become public. The master didn't allow anyone who was a threat to his security to walk the world for long, and it was part of Justin's allegiance to ensure these people died.

When the Dragon or one of its disciples saw a problem, Justin was required to eliminate it, just as he had killed Jack Madrone. He had not waited for a dream to do it. The Wyrm had known what was required of him and had carried out the mission, no matter how Justin had felt about it.

It was only when Justin was unaware of the possible threat that the Dragon would cue him through the mirror or through a vision. If someone in a small town in Montana had somehow stumbled across evidence that might lead him to discover the master's secret, Justin had a vision. And when he awoke, he would travel through the mirror and deal with the problem.

Madrone's image now joined the throng of the dead surrounding Justin—his victims. The security guard, Baxter, stood beside him. Both stared at him, accusing, causing a pain in his heart that threatened to devour him.

The deaths were necessary. Justin knew that. He told himself that over and over again. But he never ceased to regret his part in them. From the Dragon's very first order to kill that first hapless priest, a part of him had rebelled at what he was asked to do.

But the Dragon required blood and death as the payment for the boon of endless life.

And the price of his service was rapidly rising.

The cost might soon be out of his reach.

Justin opened a small drawer in his black lacquer night stand. He pulled out a tiny crystal vial of white powder. He tapped a bit of the powder into a sterling silver cup above an ebony lamp inlaid with ivory. From a jade decanter, he poured a few drops of water into the cup with the powder. With a twist of his fingers, the lamp sparked to life.

Loathing himself even more than usual, Justin withdrew a syringe and rubber tubing from the drawer. Sitting in the soft chair beside the cabinet, he looped the rubber around his upper arm and pulled it tight with his teeth. He looked at the powder. Slowly, it began to melt and dissolve. When it was liquid, he sucked the heroin up with the syringe.

It was a vice that he knew better than to indulge. His immortality and healing abilities spared him from the degradation and death that awaited virtually all junkies among normal humans. He wouldn't even feel the terrible side effects of addiction—the wrenching pain, the chills, and the grinding need of withdrawal. But what was left of his self-respect died a little more every time he resorted to the needle to banish his ghosts.

Their images hovered before him. All of them, ancient ones and recent ones. Detective Madrone's incredulous gaze watched him, as did Baxter's. Then there was Becky Johnson, and the Italian priest who had fought so hard to live almost seven hundred years ago. A young bride, still in her wedding dress. Blackie Rogers, the cowboy. There were hundreds of them, thousands, and each one stared at him with burning questions in their eyes. Why? And why them?

Justin closed his eyes. His hand cradled the needle with its promise of a few moments of blessed peace, of relief from his haunted past. He was strong enough to resist the need, he knew it. He just had to find that strength where it was buried in him, somewhere deep down under the centuries of regrets.

The ghosts were stronger this time.

He plunged the needle into his arm.

Then something in the darkness moved. The

other ghosts parted for it. It was the form of a woman, young and beautiful, looking away from him at something only she could see.

"Gwendolyne . . ."

Her ghostly image turned as if she had heard him, the train of her heavy velvet dress trailing across the floor. Ghost for the better part of a millennium, she still looked impossibly young to him. She pushed a strand of her long hair out of her face. He saw her upturned nose, her brown eyes, the long graceful neck he had kissed so carefully on their wedding night as an assurance to his child bride that there was nothing to fear.

Her ghost stood before him now, searching for his face, but she could not see him cramped and slouched in the chair.

"No." That single word was a cry from his heart.

Again the sound of his voice called to her, and again she searched in vain for him in the crowd of victims haunting the room.

Justin? She mouthed the word. Her lovely, delicate hands reached out, as if blindly feeling her way through the impenetrable darkness of wrongful death.

Justinian?

"I didn't want to do it," he whispered. "God forgive me, I didn't mean for it to happen."

Where are you?

He closed his eyes again and put a fist to his forehead, pressing hard, as if he might push what was about to happen away with the strength of his immortal hand.

Justinian!

But he couldn't keep from looking at her. When

he opened his eyes again she stood before him, young and beautiful as she'd been in life. He huddled back into the chair. Her ghostly hand passed over his forearm and he shivered. So did she.

Justinian?

"Dear God, NO!" He fought the image, fought to control it, but the room around him had already begun to fade. His modern white stucco walls darkened into gray blocks of stone decorated with priceless tapestries, still glowing in their newness. Chicago's nighttime haze of light pollution streaming through his picture windows muted, became the golden glow of a single candle.

"NO! I will *not* go through this again . . ."

Justinian . . . what have you done . . . ?

five

Centuries twisted and intermingled. The cusp of the twenty-first century melted away like so much candle wax in a fire, just as the walls seemed to waver and fade when heroin coursed hard inside his veins. The emptiness of Justin's present vanished, filled like a chalice with voices from his past. The empty room in Chicago was gone from his senses, scattered like dust to the winds, replaced by a low-ceilinged bed chamber in the ancestral castle of the earls of Sterling, looking exactly as it had looked long ago and far away in the fourteenth-century English countryside.

But though his surroundings changed, Gwendolyne remained in front of him, as always an anchor to the man he'd once been and a reminder of what he'd become.

"My lord, what have you done?"

Justin stumbled forward into the room, into the arms of his wife. He clutched her soft curves to him, cherished the warmth of her flesh.

"Do not ask me," he said.

"The village is afire," she said. Her hands gently wiped the soot from his cheek. "They say you started it."

Still holding her, Justin collapsed onto the bed. He pulled her close to him, burying his face in her hair.

"The Black Death," he said. "It has arrived. Half a dozen of my tenants are already dead. I burned their houses with the bodies inside. I pray the fire will drive the disease away. I left only when it was clear that the fires would die down without spreading."

"You burned the village?"

"Yes, I burned it," he said. "It was all I could do. These are my people, their homes my property. Do you think I wanted to see their dwellings crumble to ash and scorched rock? But I had no choice. Do you want all the villagers to die? Their children, too, and our own children? Even after the fire, I can't be certain that I've destroyed the contagion. The Death may still be out there, walking among them."

His young wife pulled away from him, recoiling from the horror of his words. Justin sat up for a moment, then got up from the bed to pace the room like a caged wolf.

Gwendolyne watched him, her deep brown eyes glistening with concern.

"They simply do not understand," he said. "They see only their own concerns, their own little lives, going up in the smoke from the pyre. They don't know how terrible this can be, what is at stake here. Do they think I like ordering something like this? I would have sacrificed myself on their behalf if I could have stopped it.

But the plague is here. Perhaps it is the devil's will, perhaps God's own. It was certainly not my will that brought it into our midst, but mine is the task of stopping it, if such a thing is humanly possible. It may already be too late." He ran his hands over his face, as if by doing so he could wash the stain of this morning's actions from his memory.

Gwendolyne got up, put her arms around him.

"Tell me what happened, my lord. Why is there blood on your hands?"

Justin looked down, saw the scarlet stains mixed with the soot from the fires, saw the drying blood where he had smeared it upon her gown. He tried to speak, but the words were thick in his throat. He coughed, then began to speak.

"I killed a man. We came to burn his house and he went mad. He was in there weeping over the dead body of his wife. The plague had taken her. Neck swollen, the black spots. She was with child, near to term. We tried to take him out before we put the torch to the place, and he went mad. He struck Goodman Miller and picked up a scythe."

Justin looked away. He couldn't look his wife in the face. She wrapped her arms around the small of his back, held him tight.

"The miller managed to grab the scythe and I struck the man. He would not stop fighting, and I was forced to continue striking him until he went down." Justin let out a slow, anguished breath. "We dragged him to the village square. He kept saying that he'd built this house for her . . . they were going to live there . . .

he'd built it for her. He crouched there in the dirt crying like a babe. Blood ran down into his face from where I'd struck him. When the house caught fire, he broke free from our hold and ran inside. I couldn't stop him. He never came out."

Gwendolyne led her husband to the bed and sat him down. She dampened a cloth in the wash basin next to the bed and began to wash the blood and soot from his hands. If only the stain in his mind could be cleaned so . . .

"Milord, you did what you could. When this passes, those who survive, they will see that."

Justin sighed. "I stood there watching that man cry today, and all I could think of was you. What if you were the one in that house? What if it was me crying in the dirt over your body? I would have grabbed that scythe and threatened anyone who tried to keep us apart. I, too, would have chosen the fire." Justin looked into his wife's eyes. "But he was not me. I bear the responsibility for all of the people on this estate. I am not free to act merely on my own behalf. I am lord here. It is my duty to stop such madness. But how could I have saved him?"

"My lord, you did your best," she said.

"It wasn't enough. I told them today in the village that I would rebuild all their homes if I had to sell my own to do it, but nothing could bring back that man's wife, and he knew it. I told them that their homes and their dead had to go up in flames, or the Black Plague would take them as well. But they did not care."

Gwendolyne placed the cool cloth upon his face,

washing away the soot and tears. "Shhh, love, there was naught else that you could do."

"I . . . I don't even know if fire will save us. But I had to do something. I can't just let my people die, and I have seen that the plague moves from one stricken victim to the next. Perhaps by sacrificing the one village, I can save the rest. Perhaps . . . I had to do something! I am their lord!"

Gwendolyne pulled her husband down beside her on the bed.

Justin looked down into her face. She smiled up at him. Her serenity eased his troubled heart.

"From the first moment I saw you," Justin whispered, "I hoped that you would someday look at me with that gaze in your eyes." He smiled. "Your love gives me the strength to go on."

She took his hand in her own and pressed it against her heart. Soot from his clothes rubbed off on her white dress.

"My love," she said, "my heart pains me some days, so full it is with all that I feel for you."

"And you will stay here, won't you? You won't go into the village? You'll keep yourself safe for me?"

"I will be by your side, my lord, no matter what should befall us."

Justin looked into her deep brown eyes. He slipped one hand into her silky hair and smoothed it. "I am afraid for us all, you know. I don't want to die, my beloved Gwendolyne. I don't want any of the people I love, or any of the people who depend on me and whose work provides the wealth of this estate to die, either.

Surely there must be something more I can do . . ."

"Some things, my lord, are in the hands of God, not man. And you have done enough for today." Gwendolyne pushed him back against the pillows. Her lips pressed onto his. Her hair, the scent of her warm body, surrounded and caressed him. No matter what hell he had tromped through each day, no matter what unspeakable miasma clung to his skin after his travels and adventures, she always welcomed him into her arms. She smelled like flowers on a spring day. He clung to the familiar comfort of her embrace, let it take him far away from the smoke, the flames, the dead and dying he'd purged from his lands with fire.

But as he closed his eyes and pulled her even closer, finally at peace, the moment was snatched from his grasp, even as one nightmare was ripped away from him and a new, though ancient, horror seared into his thoughts.

He knew what was coming next; this vision from his past was far too familiar, and the hell that followed a frequent, if unwelcome, visitor to his mental gallery of guilt. He felt time sliding by, running through his ineffectual grip like a catapult's rope through ungloved hands, burning him unbearably.

He screamed, begged the fates to release him, but when he opened his eyes again it was too late. His wife was still before him, but horribly changed. Her face was drawn, her brown eyes cloudy. Even the soft scent of flowers that had surrounded her ever since he'd met her was gone, replaced by the acrid scent of disease and despair.

He was dying.

I am afraid it is necessary that you die . . .

"No!" Justin refused to believe it. He looked down at the fine linen sheet that covered him, hiding underneath its snowy expanse the strange and alien thing his body had become. He threw the bedclothes aside. As he'd suspected, the black spots were spreading. They dotted his shins, his thighs, his chest, and his arms like rot on a decayed fruit. Lumps the size of his fist, the swollen glands called buboes that gave bubonic plague its name, pushed up against the tight, bruised skin of his groin. His breath came in short, painful gasps—each lungful of air a burden dragged with great effort past the enlarged glands in his neck. His arms lay stiffly on the mattress, far away from his sides, pushed out from their accustomed positions by massive lumps in his armpits.

And he hurt, he hurt everywhere. The pain was unbearable, and it made him crazy. When the spots had first appeared, Justin had refused to believe he could be in the grip of the illness. The plague was for peasants. Surely his exalted position in society would protect him. He'd been blessed by God through the whole of his life, been given talent, beauty of form and face, the means to provide himself and his family with everything they could ever want. How could God desert him now?

But the Black Plague spared no one, king or commoner. It seemed to be God's own curse, and, as such, did not respect the order that He Himself had established.

When the black spots gave no sign of receding, but instead spread at an increasing pace, Justin hid his illness from his wife for the little time he could. Even then, with the evidence growing right before his horrified eyes, he refused to believe he would succumb. It was all too terrible to contemplate.

He had not known then the meaning of terror. He had not known what pain was. He had not known what it meant to be damned.

He knew now.

The pain intensified. He seemed to leave his body sometimes, though he could never escape the pain. It came with him, an unwelcome passenger on his mad voyages through delirium. He would strike out at his wife while he watched his own erratic actions in confusion from some impossible mental distance. He would say nonsensical things, and then not remember them a breath later.

Gwendolyne, his beloved Gwendolyne, had nursed him in his misery. She would come to him and put cool cloths upon his burning forehead. Even when he struck out at her in his madness, she'd wince, retrieve the dropped cloths, and resume bathing him to reduce his fevers. She ignored the bleeding scratches he made on her ivory cheek, the bruises on her body.

Then there were the times his sanity returned to him. Times like this. He lay on his bed, staring at his grotesque body. The pain was a low murmuring thing crouched at the foot of his bed. He knew that if he moved, it would leap upon him.

I am afraid it is necessary that you die . . .

The local leech stood over him, one of the parish priests. Justin screamed at the priest, tried to tell him that he wasn't wanted here. But his words weren't in any tongue known to man. They were the insensible cries of a wounded animal.

The priest stood there, holding a cloth-wrapped bundle of sweet herbs over his nose. The trailing ends of the perfumed rag hovered an inch from Justin's cheek. He tried to turn his head away from them, but the growths in his throat made it impossible. He moaned and lay still.

Gwendolyne stood behind the leech, waited in taut anticipation for his words. She was pale with worry, yet still so beautiful to Justin, even more so than usual now, despite her fatigue. He wondered if she ever rested at all. She had dressed up for him, in the elaborate gown and coiffure of a formal court appearance, going about her care for him as if nothing was seriously wrong, as if he weren't rotting away before her eyes. Her safflower gown was made of embroidered silk as bright as the sun, even through the faded palette of his pain-tinged vision. Her waves of soft hair were confined in some complicated way with ribbons and braids and the odd tumbling ringlet. He loved to run his hands through her silky hair. But that was impossible now. Even if he could muster the energy, he would not defile something so beautiful with his wasted hands.

Finally, the leech-priest turned his head toward Justin. He knew what the priest was going to say, and he cried out against it, but once again his voice sounded more like the howl of an injured wolf than anything a man would say. The priest spoke directly to him, though it was clear he was unsure if Justin was still capable of understanding him in his current state.

"I am afraid it is necessary that you die. It is God's will. You will be with him soon. One of my brethren will come to hear your confession and administer last rites."

Justinian heard Gwendolyne's stifled cry of anguish. He tried to find her, but he could not see her through the haze of pain surrounding him.

The door closed upon the priest.

After some time passed, Gwendolyne stood before him once again. He could see her now. Her gown was tossed in the corner, her corsets unlaced. Even as he watched, she removed them, loosened the ribbons on her chemise and let it fall off her white shoulders across her breasts, then past her waist to the floor. She was as naked as she'd been the day God made her. Slowly, carefully, she climbed into bed with him.

"No," he said. "No, please, my love." His words were barely comprehensible, beseeching pleas forced through his cracked, bleeding lips. "You must leave me."

She did not heed him. She pulled the cover over both of them and laid her soft, smooth body next to his diseased flesh.

"I cannot see my face," Justinian whispered frantically, "Gwendolyne . . . beloved Gwendolyne . . . how bad is my face?"

"Silence, love," she whispered, and in her voice he could hear the tears that she'd never yet let fall in front of him, "Every movement causes you pain. Sleep, my love. Silent be . . ."

"Please!" He wanted to push her away, but in his weakened condition, his movements were a mockery, less forceful than the flailing of an infant.

"Rest, my lord, please." She began to weep openly. Justinian could feel her tears trail across his fevered flesh.

It hurt him to see her pain, but there was one last boon he would ask of her before he sent her away. He wished to see for himself what the cursed hand of fate had wrought upon his flesh.

"A mirror, Gwendolyne. Bring me a mirror!"

"No, my lord, I beg you. Rest."

"The mirror!" he commanded.

Gwendolyne pulled a silver hand mirror from the chest at the end of the bed.

"It is here, my lord."

"Hold it up where I can see it."

"My lord, it will only pain you to see what you've—"

"By God, woman! Do it!"

She held it up to his face. The mirror wavered with the trembling of her hands and her silent sobs.

His reflection was distorted by the motion and his own dementia, but what he saw was plain enough.

It was the monster he'd become.

The vision at last ran its course as he looked in the mirror upon himself as he was today.

Blood in his long black hair, on his chest, and on his hands. Iridescent scales clinging to the ichor that coated his body. A needle full of a moment's forgetfulness hanging limply from his arm below the rubber tourniquet.

Finally freed from the past's lethal grasp, Justinian reached over and pushed the plunger. Heroin rushed into his veins and the castle around him melted away. The pain melted away. And with it, the vision of Gwendolyne . . .

Heroin was a recent addition to Justin's life, and not one he was proud of. Justin had known several Elder disciples of the Dragon over the centuries. For reasons he never understood, they did not suffer from the ghosts that plagued him. They carried out their missions for the master, many of them as bloody as his own, and never gave them a second's thought. Apparently the ghostly gallery that haunted him was unique among the disciples. The other Elders could not know the desire that burned within him to flee from those pale images.

In the beginning, he had turned to alcohol, but it wasn't strong enough. He metabolized the slow poison so fast that even in a swaying stupor, the ghosts could still follow him. He couldn't drink enough to banish them by passing out. And in some ways, his ordeal became worse during his drunken frenzies. He lost what little conscious control he had on what he saw, and all of his practiced mental defenses against the pain.

Still searching for surcease, he started dabbling in opium in the fashionably unfashionable salons of Paris just before the French Revolution. Like alcohol, the opium did not send the ghosts away completely, but rather softened his emotional response to them. The pain was still there, but it somehow didn't seem to matter as much.

Then Justin tried heroin. He'd been in San Francisco in the late 1960s, in the Haight-Ashbury. It was a time and place unique in his long experience. He soaked up the gentle atmosphere of the flower children, and along the way tried a few of the drugs from the pharmacopoeia the kids were experimenting with. Most had little or no effect on him; they were metabolized by his immortal body long before they affected his mind. Two of the drugs he tried were different. The first, LSD, was a mistake of epic proportions, one that cost several people their lives. But heroin, though a filthy habit, saved him from his personal demons, if only for a little while. The drug sang to him and the ghosts could not follow.

And the terrors and addictions that were the drug's deadly downside didn't affect him. His immortality and healing powers kept him safe. Even as he watched the children who'd introduced him to heroin's joys waste away and die before they reached adulthood, destroyed by the drug's embrace, he realized he'd found at last the release he was looking for.

Most men only had eighty years on this earth before they departed for whatever paradise they believed awaited them in the afterlife. He had been doing hard, brutal work for the Dragon—for all of humankind—for nearly seven hundred years, with no end in sight. Justin tried to believe he deserved his chosen form of oblivion. He knew better, of course, but there were days when his self-loathing was outweighed by his need for release.

He didn't know how long he floated in heroin's liquid arms before something brought his senses back.

At first, he wasn't quite sure what awakened him. Usually, while he was in a heroin haze, the roof could fall in upon him and he would barely notice it. But then, sometimes, a breath of air touched his skin and he would come back to full consciousness. As he did now.

The ornate mirror on the dais shimmered, as if the glass was dissolving. At first, he thought it was a fantasy induced by the drug. He forced his eyes to focus on the mirror. The glass shimmered again.

No. This was real. Someone was coming through.

When his master used the mirror, there were no preliminary signs, nothing to indicate that his presence was near. One moment, he was not there, and the next moment, he was the whole world. Though after all his years as the Dragon's servant, Justin was still unsure of what the Dragon looked like. He saw him only as the Dragon wanted to be seen. Sometimes the Dragon was smoldering eyes in the darkness. Sometimes he was a voice speaking from Justin's own reflection in the mirror. Once he'd even been a blonde beauty decked out in shimmering samite, complete with wings and a harp.

None of the disciples could control the mirror as the Dragon did. They could use the mirror, of course, at the Dragon's request—sometimes they used it, too, without the master's direct consent but never without his knowledge.

Again the mirror shimmered, and again. Justin watched with detached interest. He knew he should either stand to greet whoever was coming through or throw a black cloth over the glass to indicate that he did not wish to be disturbed. At the moment, all he wanted to do was to remain still, let time flow past him, enjoy the lingering afterglow of the drug. And so instead of doing what he knew he should do, he merely watched.

The shimmering intensified, then the surface rippled as though someone was skipping stones across it, as if the mirror was now a vertical plane of water. Features formed just on the other side of the mirror's surface, those of a dark-skinned man, his jet black hair cropped close to his head. Deep-set black eyes gleamed on either side of an eagle's beak of a nose. He had a face resembling that of a bird of prey. He seemed to stare at Justin from the moment he appeared in that shimmering other world.

The man wore a gray wool three-piece business suit and a hand-sewn silk shirt, both fresh from Saville Row, masterpieces of British single-needle tailoring. They fit him perfectly, like a second skin. The clothes were a disguise, giving the man the appearance of a top-flight corporate raider, a very successful businessman, a modern robber-baron at the peak of his form. But Justin could smell the dung heap behind the surface polish. The man concealed beneath the natty wool was an Arabian street thief from the fifteenth century. And all the suits in the world would never change it.

The mirror embraced the man as he stepped through its gleaming surface like a knife cutting through quicksilver. He looked about the room, his long, bony nose wrinkling in disgust.

"It smells like a charnel house in here," he said. He spoke with a perfect American accent, colored with shades of an Oklahoman's drawl.

"Does it remind you of the prison cells of your youth, Kalzar?" Justin asked. He straightened up in the chair. He tried to force his thoughts into order. *Steady and calm, keep it steady and calm,* he told himself. He cursed the remains of the narcotic in his veins, slowing his thought processes, making his reactions sluggish and fuzzy.

"Ah," Kalzar replied, "now that you mention it, it does have the stink of fear."

Kalzar stepped down from the dais, away from the mirror he'd just traveled through. He frowned as he stepped over the skins and fluids from Justin's recent transformation. Once on the carpet, he paused to wipe his shoes.

"You really should show more care, Justin. Doesn't this shock the cleaning lady? Cause her to ask embarrassing questions? Or do you simply murder them and then hire new ones?"

"That would be more your style," Justin said, still trying to see clearly through his heroin haze—and failing miserably. He sat back in his chair, waiting to see what Kalzar was up to, looking for a hint of the devious plan or uncontrollable urge to gloat that had led Kalzar here.

"There are too many people in the world, Justin. You wouldn't know that because you've spent your entire life in Europe and America. The East is different. If you'd spent time where I come from, you'd realize that the majority of people on this planet should be squashed like roaches."

"That doesn't sound like one of the five pillars of Islam. The Prophet would be disappointed in you."

"He's not my prophet anymore. I know who my god is. I know in whose *jihad* I fight."

Kalzar's vulture-like gaze flicked about the room, lingering on nothing except the drawings and the drug paraphernalia. He snorted.

"The weakness that surrounds you . . ." Kalzar said, venom dripping from each word, "after all of those years I put into you, after teaching you everything I know, this is where you end up." Kalzar waved a hand at the pictures on the wall, then gestured at the heroin vial, syringe, and rubber strip scattered on the small table by Justin's chair. "I suppose your raw talent must be quite impressive for the Dragon to turn a blind eye to all of these weaknesses. Once I thought you showed promise, but you're no disciple. As you are now, Omar could best you."

"Omar is a worm," Justin said, annoyed to hear a slight slur to his words; he resolved to keep his mouth shut until he was sure he could control his voice.

Kalzar's gaze flashed to Justin. All the old hatred, centuries in the making, was there. None of it had been mellowed by the decades they had been kept apart by the Dragon. Then he smiled suddenly, though the smile looked like a snarl.

Crocodiles look like that before they sink their teeth in, Justin thought.

"Remember how we used to fight together, Justin? Side by side, I mean, in the early days, before you took from me what was rightfully mine?"

The acid he's putting in those words must burn his lips, Justin thought, but said nothing.

"We would run down those pathetic druids in the forests of Scotland, back when Scotland still had forests fit to run in. You and I, we grinned at our own reflections on the swords of the Knights Templar before we slaughtered them like lambs. Together, we could have led a successful charge on all the armies of the world and won. And now look at you. See what you've become. I taught you everything, and look at how you waste it."

Justin levered himself to his feet, met his old enemy's gaze, saw the hate in Kalzar's face. Justin's jaw tightened but he forced himself to speak. This time, his voice came out low and deadly.

"Your arrogance stifles your tiny brain," Justin said. "Your memories are a delusion. We never fought side by side, Kalzar. I followed behind you to clean up the messes you made. To bury the whores you lost control with. To squelch the rumors you started with your endless bragging to the wrong ears. I did not steal your favor with the Dragon, Kalzar. The Dragon sent me to cover your tracks. I'm surprised the Dragon hasn't sent me to kill you. Perhaps our master is more forgiving than he seems. At least, so far he is ..." Justin let out a disgusted breath. "Yes, you taught me, Kalzar. Everything you know. I could never have compiled a finer manual on what not to do as a disciple!"

For a moment, Justin thought Kalzar would attack him. Kalzar's smile disappeared. The Arab's thin lips formed a straight, rigid line. Veins throbbed at his temples and against his white silk collar. His face was flushed, his eyes narrow. Justin waited, ready.

Kalzar mastered himself. His left eyelid twitched, and then he smiled again. "And you are such a fine disciple that the master has banished you from your homeland. Perhaps you are not so secure in the Dragon's favor as you think."

"Perhaps," Justin said. "Or perhaps you don't know the workings of the Dragon's mind. My stay here is for a reason, one which will become clear to me over time. Just as we could be ordered to kill a man today for what he will do in ten years, the Dragon's decision to keep me here is most likely to hold me ready for some coming task. I follow his orders. I have the intelligence and subtlety to understand what is at stake. That's the difference between you and me, Kalzar. You are the Dragon's bludgeon and I am his scalpel. That's the way it has always been." Justin walked forward, nearly nose to nose with Kalzar. "No matter how well you dress yourself, no matter how many accents you affect, you will always be a mere butcher. Not just because you're an idiot, but because you enjoy the slaughter, not the grand purpose behind it. You are a wretch, a festering sore on the face of the earth. I tolerate your continued existence because the Dragon can use you."

Kalzar narrowed his eyes. He was so angry he could barely speak. "You prancing peacock." Kalzar's voice was low but deadly, echoing throughout the room like a gypsy's curse. "You dance on thin ice, Justin. And one day you will fall through. It's only a matter of time." Justin could practically feel the heat of Kalzar's fury seeping through the fine wool of his impeccable suit. "And on that day," Kalzar spat, "I will be waiting to swallow you. Then I will tear *your* flesh!"

But the game grew old. Justin finally asked the question he should have asked the moment Kalzar stepped through the mirror. "What do you want here, Kalzar?"

No reply. The urge to fight was strong within both of them, and could explode into violence any second. Each lusted to shed the other's blood, to pour it out until the floor was lost beneath the crimson tide, until the *enemy* was too weak to stand, too weak to run, too weak to live. One day, each of them knew, the Dragon's edict forbidding them to fight wouldn't be enough to keep them apart. And each knew that day was getting closer, that the Dragon's long-standing edict wouldn't hold for much longer. *And,* Justin thought, *that brought up a very interesting point.* "The master ordered us to remain separated. How do you come here?"

The flames in Kalzar's eyes flickered. He flashed a smile. "I wish I knew for certain. I was standing in front of my mirror, and I wanted to look in on you. Of course, you know that has been impossible for decades now, divided as we are by the mandate. Imagine my surprise when it actually worked. I wondered what would happen if I stepped through. And here I am. What do you think that means, Justin?"

"It means the master will speak with you, Kalzar, and I will enjoy the aftermath. If you think you've found some way to travel the mirror without his knowing it, you're a fool."

"I really don't think so. I'm telling you the truth, you see."

"I don't believe you."

"You wouldn't." Kalzar smiled thinly. "But you're growing more sloppy every day, and the master knows it. Perhaps he hoped I would check up on you. Your recent actions endanger us all. Even I, isolated from you for a century, far away in Libya, know this. Imagine my surprise when I received a report from Omar saying that some female detective has been tracking you, and you have not yet killed her."

"I know about the detective," Justin said. "She knows nothing I don't want her to know."

"Oh, she doesn't, does she? How pleasant. Omar says she knows more than she should. So when *are* you planning to kill her?"

Justin shivered with rage. "Your oaf Omar has given the Dragon and his disciples a far bigger risk of exposure than I ever will. Like you, he talks about things to others who should not know. I have covered for him so far. His murder of Carlton Wheeler, which I planned for him, was flawless in every way, or at least it would have been if Omar had been capable of keeping his mouth shut. But he babbled about it, a piece of carelessness that would have led straight back to the Dragon had I not taken steps to prevent it. The woman detective knows nothing compared to the information Omar has dropped. I have followed Sandra McCormick's progress on the Baxter case closely. She's gotten nowhere with it, but tonight Jack Madrone, the policeman investigating Omar's murder of Wheeler, almost discovered everything, thanks to Omar's loose lips!"

"Omar is young, Justin. He is learning. It is your job to train him."

"If he does something stupid like that again, he's not worth training. I will kill him then. Lesser disciples must obey or the punishment is death."

Kalzar's eyes flashed and he gestured to the needle. "You have no room to talk. *You* are the one who lacks discipline. You have too many weaknesses. Serving the master, spreading his lesson should leave you no time, no room in your heart for your needles, your pitiful drawings, or your women."

"If the master had not decreed against it, I would have your heart in my hand, Kalzar, and I would squeeze it to dust before your eyes as you passed from this world. Perhaps the master has eased his mandate about this, too. Shall I test it?"

Justin walked toward Kalzar.

The Arab's eyes narrowed but he held his ground. He wanted the fight, but he wanted Justin to start it.

"I want you out of Chicago," Justin said. "And I want you to take Omar with you."

"Omar is here to learn, and he will remain here. Those are the Dragon's orders, not mine. I have, however, sent him on a small errand tonight, one needed to clean up the loose ends *you* left behind."

"What I do, I do for a reason," Justin said. "If Omar interferes with anything I have set in motion, I will destroy him. And then you. We shall see which one of us the master chooses to burn when he takes us both beyond the mirror."

Kalzar paused, waiting for something, perhaps a sign from the Dragon. No such sign came. Turning, he stepped on the dais. The mirror shimmered as he walked through it and was gone.

six

Sandra woke up for the third time that night, chased from sleep by nightmares. As she sat up, yawning and rubbing her eyes, sirens screamed beyond her windows. She looked at her clock—it was 4:45 in the morning. Her white gauze curtains glowed, lit by the flashing red lights of emergency vehicles. She kicked off the covers, winced as her bare feet hit the cold oak-planked floor, stood up, and stretched. Finally she walked to her window and pushed back the curtains.

Her bedroom faced the street—she'd chosen the room for its southern exposure and large expanse of glass. Fire trucks were parked at the greasy spoon across from her building. She could see flames and smoke billowing from inside the diner. Three firemen with axes were chopping a hole in the roof of the restaurant. More firefighters were on ladders, spraying the roof with water, while others worked on the ground to keep the hoses straight.

She ran her hands through her hair, massaging her

scalp. No relief from the headache caused by too little sleep and too much tension. She wondered why so many fires seemed to start at night. Maybe they were just more obvious in the dark . . .

She let the curtains fall closed, wandered back across the floor, and collapsed limply onto her bed. Between working late, the murder, and her nightmares, she knew she'd never get back to sleep. Maybe that was a good thing. She was afraid the nightmares would return.

They'd been the same for the last several days. Something was chasing her, hunting her. Closing in, even though she was running hard, faster than she'd ever run before. Just as it caught up with her, when she could feel its breath on her back, its sharp teeth on her neck, its claws brushing her skin, she'd wake up, heart hammering like a steam engine.

She shook her head, exasperated. *I don't jump at shadows. Not anymore.*

Not since she'd left her ex-husband. She'd left that waking, walking nightmare far behind. Chuck was out of her life. Permanently. And that was fine.

Anyway, the dreams she used to have about him were nothing like this. In those dreams, he would hold her underwater until she drowned. She could never break his grip, no matter how hard she struggled, and the more she screamed, the more water filled her lungs.

The highlight of tonight's nightmare had been that disturbing beast, sharp-toothed and armed with claws. When she woke up it slithered into the shadows of her mind, its precise shape forgotten. But though she couldn't remember a single clear detail, the dream still left a lingering chill in the air, a darkness around her heart.

Blinking her eyes, she crawled out of bed, opened her door, and, yawning, walked down the hall. There was a light on in the kitchen. Benny was up. The smell of brewing coffee filled the air. He swiveled his wheelchair around as she came into the room and raised one quizzical eyebrow.

"You're up early," he said.

Sandra focused her attention on his eyes, not on the scars where half his nose was scraped away. She knew the skin there wasn't wet, but it always looked that way, slick and shiny, so smooth it glistened in the light.

She forced her gaze to remain steady on his. She knew he hated it when people stared at his disfigurement. He'd been a cute kid before the accident, the sort of gawky, computer geek kind of cute that was all the more endearing because he never seemed to know he was cute.

The other scars on his face wouldn't be so noticeable, if not for his nose. The surgeons had told them they could do more restorative work, but Benny had refused. He insisted he'd already spent as much time under the knife as he planned to in his life.

And maybe he had a point. Who was she to judge? She wished she didn't think about it so much. She could only imagine how much *he* must think about it.

"*I'm* up early? What about you? Unless, of course, you haven't gone to bed yet." It wasn't unusual to find

Benny still tapping on his computer in the shank of the night, but she had never found him in the kitchen, making coffee at five A.M.

"Couldn't sleep," he said. The coffee machine bubbled and gasped into silence. He swiveled back to it. "Want a cup?"

"Yeah. Please."

He filled two mugs and put them on the kitchen table. She opened a cupboard, looking for the box of artificial creamer. After years of greasy spoon coffee, she liked the fake stuff better than real cream. Her spoon made small metallic chimes hitting the side of her cup as she stirred.

"Why couldn't you sleep?" she asked finally.

Benny shrugged, "Well, you know how it is. Those stewardesses, Bambi and Candi—"

"Yeah, yeah." She grinned. "It's tough being you."

Benny chuckled, then turned abruptly serious. "Bad dreams," he said.

"You, too, huh?"

"You had bad dreams?" he asked.

She nodded.

"Well, that's kinda strange, both of us getting the night frights," he said.

"Yeah. What were yours like?"

He shook his head, sipped his coffee. "Someone was chasing me. I can't really remember, but I think they caught me. That was when I woke up. Hey, did you see what's happening across the street?"

"Fire or something."

"Yeah."

"I had the same kind of dream, you know."

"You did? Someone chasing you?"

"Uh-huh."

"Shit, that's freaky." He sipped thoughtfully, then went on. "Maybe we jumped into one another's dreams. There's this guy on-line who talks about stuff like that all the time. I should ask him what it means." He paused again. "So . . . who was chasing you? I can't remember anything about the one after me."

"I can't remember much, either."

Benny shot an exaggerated glance left and right. "*Oooweeeooo.* Bugga bugga!" He wiggled his fingers and grinned. "You think someone's fuckin' with us?"

"Yes." She sighed. "You."

"No, seriously. Maybe it was some old Indian shaman you put behind bars years ago. He's come back for his revenge, sneaking into our dreams and messing with our heads."

"Yeah, right. I never busted a shaman, pal."

"Sure you did. And right before you busted him, he came to the realization that he was never going to get past level 13 of *Watcher's Chosen,* and in his insane but wise mind he decided to kill me for my insolence. I told you I designed that, didn't I?"

"Hmmmmm . . ." she said. "Your new game, right? Maybe you're on to something."

They grinned at each other like idiots.

She got up, wandered out of the kitchen and into the living room, and peered out a window. Rain had been falling all night, and it looked as if it wouldn't stop any time soon. Gray, dull, and misty out there. Fog off the lake. Not exactly the best start to a morning.

She stood silently, sipping and musing. It was always fun to chat with Benny. They hardly got to talk at all anymore.

Five years ago, she and Benny had almost never left each others' sides. Benny had been in the hospital recovering from his accident—and she'd been shaky herself, having finally broken free of Chuck.

What an odd pair they'd made then. The cripple and the emotional wreck. But each of them strong in the ways the other was weak—they were like two broken pillars that had fallen onto each other and formed an arch that would endure forever.

Sandra remembered Benny before his accident. She hated to admit it to herself, but she hadn't really come to enjoy him until after the motorcycle crash. Even as brother and sister, they'd been different, lived in different worlds.

But, even taking that into account, in the years right before the crack-up he'd been something of an intellectual bully. Quietly arrogant. She was sure he'd been picked on in high school for being an egghead, because he'd taken to stinging people in conversation as a sort of revenge on everyone who was more popular and less intelligent than he was. It had started as a defense mechanism, but later she'd seen him verbally vivisect half of their relatives during the course of an afternoon just to amuse himself.

Then, after the accident, he changed dramatically. How could he not? It was one of the things she admired most about him—he'd made something positive out of the most damaging experience of his life. It was amazing how someone who so desperately needed care and tenderness himself could turn and make it his mission in life to give that care to others.

She thought that in many ways, his new personality, too, was a defense mechanism, a reaction to the way people cringed at his appearance and his handicap. Perhaps he doubted that anyone would want to be around him after his accident. Or maybe he found out for himself how good it felt to help others. Or he'd just set out to prove to himself, and everyone else, that he could rise above what had happened to him. Whatever the reason, he'd changed his personality, and changed it for the better.

Now he was fast, fascinating, and fun to be around. If you could get past the grisly scars on his face, Benny was fabulous company. His light-hearted jests were never at the expense of others. He was a wonderful raconteur. He never poked at people's soft spots. He also seemed impervious to jibes aimed at him.

She wondered how much of this new facade was real interest in the people around him and how much of it was a new, rock-solid defense mechanism against his own pain. The way he joked about his condition sometimes worried her. She sighed, drained her mug, and returned to the kitchen.

"I'm going to take my coffee and go shut myself up in the dungeon again." Benny said. "I'm almost done with the latest thing in computer games, if I do say so myself."

Sandra smiled at him. "Okay. When you put the

final touches on it, tell me. We'll celebrate."

"Are you kidding? I'll be jumping up and down with glee—oops, cancel that, just a figure of speech. Rolling back and forth with glee!" He turned and trundled off down the hall.

Just before he went through his bedroom door, Sandra called after him. "Hey, Benny?"

"Yeah?" He performed a consummately graceful turn in the confined space of the hall. His feet on their rests came within half an inch of the wall as he whipped around.

"Can I get you to play webmaster for me? I may need some pretty esoteric information on this case."

"Sure. Why?"

"The murder scene had some pretty strange aspects. I'm thinking it might be some cult thing. So I wondered if there are modern cults responsible for similar killings. Like maybe if the Aztecs are taking hearts again, it should probably turn up on the Web somewhere, right? And there was something that looked like a footprint in the carpet, though not like anything I've ever seen. Anyway, I may need you to go digging."

"Easy. When?"

"I'll keep you posted."

"You give the word, Ace. I'm all over it."

Sandra nodded. "Thanks, Benny."

"Never mention it." He turned and went into his room.

Sandra watched until he'd vanished from her sight. She glanced at her empty coffee cup, then placed it carefully in the sink.

"Okay," she said to her rain-splattered reflection in the kitchen window, "another day, another dollar, girl." She headed for the shower. Benny's personality had helped. It really had.

But it was still probably going to be a lousy day.

By the time Sandra descended the stairs of her condo, the sun was rising, filling the world with a flat, gray light, and she was feeling pretty good despite the lack of sleep.

Half a bowl of sugar-coated cereal and a second cup of coffee did wonders for the body. She wished her mind were in the same state. Pausing at the gate of the small yard in front of the building, she looked at the gray clouds above her, at the way the whole world was shrunken into a cage of mist. Chicago in the fall . . . chilly.

Cab drivers were honking at the fire trucks still obstructing traffic in the street. In the building next door, a young mother was yelling at her wailing kid. The ordinary sounds of the city had her jumping today, had her adrenaline pumping.

The dreams she could not remember still clutched at her with heavy, invisible tendrils. Each time she thought she had the threads in her grasp, they snapped, broke away. Yet every time she concentrated on something else, they reached for her again, making her gut clench. Irrational, but there it was.

She shook her head in irritation and began walking to her car. The drive through the commuter-clogged

Chicago streets was uneventful, as she listened to traffic bulletins about huge jams on the Eisenhower and the Dan Ryan Expressway.

The tops of midtown skyscrapers that towered overhead were invisible now, enveloped by mist and rain, the Sears Tower off to the south completely vanished. Before she was ready for it, the Eighteenth District Station appeared, looming out of the gloom on West Chicago Avenue. She turned into the parking garage and grabbed the first available space.

She got out, picked up her briefcase, and closed the door. The soft *chunk* echoed in the garage. It was almost too quiet. Sandra narrowed her eyes and looked around. To all appearances she was alone. So why did she feel like something was *watching* . . . ?

She looked around again.

Nothing. She shook her head in irritation and marched purposefully toward the doors leading into the station. Inside, things were pretty much normal. Surly gangbangers, whores still in their evening drag, drug users, drug dealers, batterers, and all the people who'd had their ordinary lives interrupted by one or more of the above, surged and yammered at each other, the typical urban stew.

The uniforms in charge of dealing with the chaos looked stolid, braced against the tide of human misery. The desk sergeant gave her a wink as she passed by.

There wasn't a news hound in sight, so the lid was still on the Madrone story. Breathing a sigh of relief, she headed upstairs to her own turf, the detective squad room. McKenzie was talking on the phone to someone.

"Hey, Mac," she murmured as she sat down. There were several odd-looking metal gadgets on his desk. Some of the gadgets looked almost lethal. There were also some lengths of nylon rope in various strengths and thicknesses, some nylon straps, and a funny pair of leather slippers with rubber on the bottom.

The hair on McKenzie's balding head was in disarray. His wide, flat nose was wrinkled in the unconscious sneer he always wore when he talked to someone he didn't want to be talking to. Probably his wife. He and Linda had been together for twenty years, and from what Sandra could tell the last nineteen years had been one solid squabble. They seemed to enjoy it, though.

"No," McKenzie was saying, "I don't touch that stuff! Why would I move it!? No. Look, Sandra's here. I've got to go. Okay, I will. Good-*bye,* Linda. Okay, yes. Good-bye."

McKenzie hung up. "So, you made it in. Congratulations."

Sandra fingered the strange leather slippers on the desk. "What's with the funny shoes?"

"Climbers' shoes." McKenzie grunted. "You asked what kind of shoes climbers wear. That's them."

She lifted them, looked at the soles closely, then dropped them. "So I guess the scratches on Madrone's wall weren't from climbers' shoes."

"Madrone's partner was on vacation. Guy named Lyle Whitney. He's due back tomorrow."

"Okay, we'll do him as soon as he gets back. Anything on Madrone's case jackets?"

McKenzie shrugged. "We'll have to go up to Twenty-three for them."

She nodded, then picked up one of the metal gadgets, turned it over in her hand. It was a smooth, sturdy plastic rod with a mechanism of four hinged half-moons at the tip. A small bit of machinery on the stick connected tiny cables to the half-moons. When she pulled it, the moons swiveled back, narrowing the entire width of the mechanism at the end.

"What the hell's this, Mac?"

"It's called a camalot. Protection for climbers. Hey, you know how much this shit costs?"

"No idea," she said, looking it over.

"A lot."

"It's kind of like a work of art, though, isn't it?" The shaft of the implement was flat black; the cables were shiny silver. The half-moons were a rich, metallic lavender, perforated with irregular holes that reminded her of an industrial art exhibit she'd once seen.

"Yeah, sure, Bruce. Art."

"What does it do?"

"You pull that plastic thing down and stick it in a crack in the rock. Then let go and you can hang on the rock all day if you want to. That's what the lady at the rock-climbing gym told me." McKenzie shook his head again. "It looks like a high-end sex toy to me. I sure as hell wouldn't trust it with my life."

"It's metal. It could make scratches in brick or concrete, right?"

"I guess it could. But where are you gonna find

cracks on the side of a building big enough to stick that in?"

"Hmmm. Maybe they have smaller camalots? Maybe he used the smallest kind."

"Could be. I still think it's too thin."

"So what else have we got?"

"You're going to love what the lab came up with."

"Yeah?" She raised her eyebrows.

"Nothing."

"Huh?"

"Nothing."

"Nothing what?" Sandra asked.

"They didn't find anything. They had the preliminary report here about an hour ago. Just the essentials. Which weren't much, 'cause there wasn't anything for them to study. No hair other than Madrone's. All the fibers appear to match clothing or textiles found at the site. No prints except for his. No skin under his fingernails except his own. Even the blood on the doorknob was his. So we got zip. Zero. Nada."

"Great." She sighed and shook her head.

"Except . . ." McKenzie said slowly.

"Except what?"

He pushed his chair back and stood up, his hard mound of belly brushing the edge of his desk.

"We gotta go look," he said. "C'mon."

The lab at the morgue was crowded with equipment. In the middle of the room, a tech in a white coat was leaning over a microscope. Sandra recognized her but couldn't remember her name. The woman looked up and nodded.

"The Madrone thing," Mac said.

"Sure, Detective. Hang on, I'll be right back."

"You don't know what it is?" Sandra asked while they waited.

Mac shrugged. "Just what the report said, and it didn't make any sense to me."

The tech returned with a small vial, uncorked it, and tipped its contents out onto the stainless steel working surface. She aimed one of the light armatures directly on the specimen.

"What is it?" Sandra asked.

"That's a question, isn't it?" McKenzie said.

"It looks like a scale." She squinted at it. The teardrop-shaped thing, deceptively heavy for its moderate size, gleamed in multiple shades of translucent green. It started out dark green, almost black, on the curved part and gradually became lighter, almost clear, near the point of the teardrop.

"Where'd they find it?"

"They found it stuck to the lining inside the sleeve of his army coat, caked in blood. Hard to see," the tech replied.

Sandra pursed her lips. "Madrone have some kind of pet lizard or something? I didn't see anything like that."

Mac grinned. "Madrone? From what I hear, the closest thing he'd have to a pet would be a box of animal crackers."

Sandra turned to the expert. "Do you or your people know what sort of thing this scale is from?"

The tech shook her head. "We're working on it."

Sandra sighed. "You're covering your butt, but you don't have a clue, right?"

The tech grinned, but didn't reply.

"So now what?" McKenzie leaned back against the counter and patted his top pocket for his pack of cigarettes. He paused, looked at the attendant who was pointing at the ANYONE CAUGHT SMOKING WILL BECOME A *RESIDENT* OF THE MORGUE sign, then let his hands fall slowly to his sides.

Sandra shook her head. She turned to the tech. "I want to take this with me." She gestured at the vial, into which the tech had returned the scale.

"Sure. Do the paperwork, Detective." She gestured toward a rack of official forms fastened to the far wall. Mac went over and brought a sheaf of paper back. It took them ten minutes to fill out all the releases and declarations that preserved the chain of evidence. When they were done, Sandra slipped the vial into her bag.

"Later," Mac said to the tech.

"Not if I can help it," the tech replied, bored.

"Ouch. Touchy," Mac muttered as they left.

Sandra said, "I want to check out some S&M shops. You think?"

"Yeah? For what?"

"And maybe some specialty metal shops. See if they have any toys that might do the type of damage we saw on Baxter and Madrone."

"I can handle that," Mac said. "You comin' with me?"

"Nah. I'm going to visit the zoo."

•   •   •

They were so still. It was the first thing Sandra noticed about the reptiles in the zoo. After strolling around the circular room in the center of the reptile house, she came to a stop before the huge Komodo dragon. Its curled claws, its lethal snout didn't move at all. The only way she could tell the animal was alive was the slow in-and-out movement of its sides as it breathed and the way its pupils contracted as it watched her walk around the room. She wondered how quickly it would move if there wasn't an inch-thick glass pane between them. Would she be able to outrun it? Or would it run from her?

She looked at some of the other lizards in their glass cages, but the scale she carried could not possibly belong to the smaller ones. The Komodo dragon was the largest reptile she'd ever seen, and it still seemed as if it were too small to have a scale like the one in the vial.

She traced a half-circle on the glass with her finger. The flat, unblinking gaze of the dragon followed her smallest movement. So how did the scale get into Madrone's sleeve?

She turned away from the dragon and leaned against the rail that kept visitors from getting too close to the residents. She remembered coming to zoos as a child, and rooms like this one always gave her an eerie feeling. The stucco walls were painted a shimmering green, as were the round metal rails. Each transparent cage was like a doorway to some other world, with its own special habitat. The lush jungle of the vine snake abutted the desert domain of the rattlesnake, both so lovingly crafted that Sandra felt as if her world was the fake one. Beyond the glass were lands of sand and rock, leaf and tree and the wondrous, though often poisonous, creatures who made those lands their home.

She heard something move behind her.

"Detective McCormick?"

Sandra blinked and turned around. "I'm sorry. You startled me."

The white door marked EMPLOYEES ONLY stood ajar. A man in his mid-fifties with dark salt-and-pepper hair and glasses as thick as the walls of the Komodo dragon's pen smiled briefly at her. The first thing that struck Sandra about him was that he wasn't accustomed to smiling. The herpetologist was tall and gangly under his wrinkled white coat.

"Dr. Dawes?" she said, crossing the distance between them and extending her hand. He nodded and shook it rather timidly.

"I-I'm sorry to keep you waiting," he stammered. "It's just we had a kind of emergency here."

"Oh?" she asked.

"Yes. One of the coral snakes took ill."

"Oh, I'm sorry."

He shrugged. "There's always an emergency here. It's like dealing with a house full of children. Someone's always sick."

"I understand."

"So," he said, "how can I help you, Detective?" He pushed at his glasses nervously. "I must say that this is the first time I've had a police officer ask for my assistance. Usually when I'm called to deal with the public it's some distraught mother who has a child with a limp boa constrictor, or a hysterical society matron with a grass snake in the middle of her lawn party."

He's babbling, Sandra thought.

"Well, I do need your help, Doctor. We found something that I was hoping you might be able to identify for me."

"W-well, of course, whatever I can do to help . . ."

She pulled the vial from her blazer pocket and handed it to him. "I need to know what kind of snake or lizard this belongs to."

As soon as he took it, his eyebrows shot upward in surprise. He whistled and held it up to the light.

"I don't . . . believe I've ever seen anything like this." The light creases that marked his face deepened. Lowering the vial, he looked at her sadly. "I'm sorry, Ms. McCormick. I'd love to tell you what this is, but I'm afraid I don't know myself."

"It's not a lizard's scale?"

"Oh . . ." He stared at it again. "I don't think so. It's quite translucent, you see. Most lizard scales are designed to keep the light out, because most lizards live in such hot, bright climates. Built-in sunscreen. And, big as it is, the scale's not shaped like an anaconda's or a boa constrictor's." He turned the vial over and over again in his hands, watching the scale tumble around the small container. He seemed fascinated by it. "It's such a strange shape . . ." he murmured.

"What about—I don't know—an alligator or something? Could the scale have come from something like that?"

He shrugged. "It's very unlikely. If so, it would be a species I haven't seen before. Perhaps some deep jungle species. There are places in South America nobody's been yet, even in these modern times."

"Why couldn't it be a normal alligator?"

"Oh, no. The scale's much too thin and the shape is wrong."

"I see." Sandra leaned against the green railing. The chain of experts she had called had led her to this man. If he didn't know anything, she wasn't sure where she'd turn next. "Is there anyone else who might know what this is? Can you think of someone I might call?"

"I'll tell you what . . ." he said slowly, "if it's all right with you, I could keep the scale overnight and do some research. I might be able to discover its origin. At the very least, I may be able to come up with a contact that could help you."

She nodded. "Okay. I've got a form for you to sign."

She rummaged in her purse. "Let me call and clear this with my boss, and then we'll turn you loose on it. If this has anything to do with the killer we're after . . . well, he's bad. Really bad. Anything you could do to help . . ."

"If you don't mind my asking, how is the scale involved?" Dr. Dawes held it up to the light.

"I don't know. I wonder if the reason the killer went after the victim was because of this scale. But if I don't have any idea what it is . . ." She spread her hands and shrugged.

"R-right . . ." Dawes said, looking nervous. "I'll do what I can."

"Thank you." Sandra pulled a card from her blazer pocket and handed it to him. "Let's go make that call."

She shook his hand, then followed him deep into the bowels of the employee areas of the building to use his phone.

Later, she pulled out of the zoo's huge parking lot, grabbed her cell phone out of the glove compartment, and dialed McKenzie's number at the station.

She got his machine.

Pity. She'd wanted to explain in graphic detail how much a small snake eating an egg looked like Mac eating a burger. "Hey, Mac, it's Sandra," she said. "Check with the lab and see what they have to say about the scale's composition. Dr. Dawes didn't recognize it and now I'm wondering if it isn't something manufactured instead of shed. I'm gonna get some lunch, then go read up on lizards."

She followed the streets to Greektown, parked near one of her favorite restaurants, and walked inside. Rain trickled steadily down the awnings. A few people moved along the sidewalk, mostly dry under their umbrellas, and she muttered at herself for forgetting hers as she shook the water droplets out of her hair.

After ordering a *souvlaki* sandwich, *tzatziki,* and a raspberry lemonade, she went outside, sat at a small patio table under the awning, and watched the street, trying to sort out what little she already knew.

She looked at the busy Chicago sidewalk as she munched, her mind feeling as blank as the clean white tabletop in front of her. A woman took shelter under the awning next to her, avoiding Sandra's gaze as she straightened her hose and then moved on down the street. A redheaded kid in a scruffy green trench coat showed up right after the woman left. He stepped under the awning and paused, staring at her.

Sandra sat there, sipping her lemonade. When the kid didn't move on, she looked up. She stared back at him. He was of medium height, and thin. His trench coat covered his body from his ankles to his neck. Sandra guessed he was about eighteen, or maybe even younger, and he seemed familiar somehow. His face was pale and too thin, with a rash of pimples covering each cheek along with a thick sprinkling of freckles.

His hands were twitching. *Junkie,* she thought. She turned away from him and looked back at the wet streets. She watched the water drip off the awning.

"You a cop?" the kid asked.

Sandra looked over at him. "What's it to you?"

"You're the prettiest cop I've seen in a while." The kid smiled. It didn't do much for him. His teeth were scummy. His eyes had dark rings under them. "I think I'll enjoy making a trade with you," he said.

Sandra narrowed her eyes. "Trade?"

"You know, you scratch my back, I'll scratch your . . . whatever."

"Listen, fuckface, I don't just look like a cop, I *am* a cop. Move your scrawny junky ass on down the street, okay?"

His eyebrows furrowed, and he seemed, oddly enough, to be a little hurt. "Hey," he said, "I can help you. I know things you want to know. You better be nice to me or you're gonna get fucked up."

"That's it," she said flatly. Up and moving around the table, she reached for him. "You're outta here."

She grabbed his wrist, spun him around, pushed him up against the restaurant's brick wall. As she did so, one sleeve of his raincoat fell back, revealing needle tracks on his bony arm.

"Crazy bitch! I'm gonna kick you in the head," the kid snarled. "I'm doin' you a *favor!*"

"Yeah, yeah." He was squirming like a greased rat.

"Hold *still*, gomer," she hissed. In the struggle, something fell out of an inner pocket of his coat. He stiffened.

She looked down at a small bag of white powder, bent quickly and scooped it up.

"Okay, that's cool, you are now under arrest. She pulled out a set of cuffs. "Against the wall, asshole. Cross 'em behind your back. You know how."

"Fuck you!" the kid said and pushed away from the wall hard. The back of his head bashed into her cheek, catching her off guard. "Shit!" she yelled as they both went sprawling across one of the tables.

Plates, glasses, and food went smashing to the floor. The kid landed on her stomach, knocking the wind out of her. A woman sitting at the table shrieked, stood up, slipped on the wet pavement, and fell to the floor with them. The man with her yelled and stood up, yanked the kid off of his wife.

By the time Sandra got untangled, the kid was halfway down the block, really pounding along, his coattails flying. When she fought her way out to the street, he was lost in the lunchtime crowd on the sidewalk. She stood there for a moment, looking in all directions.

Nothing. No sign of him at all. Just sullen, half-soaked pedestrians and more rain.

She was wet again.

Damn.

Her next stop was the Chicago Public Library Main Branch, on South State Street. The scale and the funny-shaped footprint were the only concrete pieces of evidence she had from Madrone's murder. Though that was more than she had from the Baxter jacket. But she'd never been forced to work with things as strange as a green scale and a footprint that looked like something out of a bad creature-feature movie before.

Noon slid into afternoon, which turned into early evening. Sitting in the middle of a pile of encyclopedias, field research compilations, and reptile anatomy books, Sandra looked up and realized it was nearly seven o'clock. She'd learned a great deal about reptiles, but nothing that might lead her to some freakazoid killer with a supply of scales and a chest chopper.

Leaning back and massaging her eyelids, she decided she'd had enough for the day.

She selected three of the books she'd looked at to check out and take with her. Just as she reached the front desk, she saw a figure standing between the glass doors of the library entrance. Half in shadow and half outlined by the fading daylight outside was the junkie kid in the long, green trench coat.

She headed for the door. As soon as she did, the raincoat-clad kid bolted, flinging the outer glass doors wide and running for the steps.

She pounded out after him, but the steps were empty by time she got outside. "Damn!"

Just as she reached the street, she caught a flash of green disappearing into the alley. There were crowds of people on the sidewalk. Streetwise glances tracked her with automatic alarm, although none of them said anything. She pushed on through to reach the mouth of the alley.

Again she caught a glimpse of the edge of his coat turning the corner at the far end of the alley. Rain battered her face, hair and shoulders, soaking her as she ran along. When she reached the end of the alley, the kid was gone, lost in the crowd of commuters headed toward the stairs leading up into the State Street El station.

She stood there in the rain, feeling like an idiot, watching the people go by and hoping to catch a glimpse of russet hair above a green raincoat. Gradually, her breathing returned to normal, yet still she remained standing in the rain. Why would a kid who'd escaped arrest by the skin of his teeth follow the arresting officer? For hours?

What the hell . . . ?

The sense of menace she'd felt hovering about her since she'd seen Jack Madrone's body closed in on her.

Mac laughed at her woman's intuition, but she felt it suddenly kick into overtime.

Madrone had been chasing something. Only what he hadn't known was that something was chasing him, too.

Something deadly. Just like in her dreams.

The weird, disquieting sense of danger was still with her when she returned home. She entered the gate, punched the code, and opened the door. As she climbed the stairs, she kept one hand on the stair rail while her other hand rested on the butt of her pistol, hidden underneath her blazer.

Nothing leapt out of the shadows. She moved silently down the hall, the back of her neck itching, stopped before the door marked 807, and paused. Looked around. The empty hall felt ominous, shadowy. It never had before.

"Oh, stop it," she murmured aloud. She inserted her key in the lock and turned it.

The lights were on. But the same still, watchful silence seemed to shroud her. Inside the apartment now.

Sandra swallowed.

"Benny?" she called.

No answer.

"Benny!?" She yelled louder this time.

"Yeah, Sandra? What?"

His wheelchair came rolling down the hall. She went suddenly limp with relief.

"Sandra?" Benny wheeled himself into view and

cocked his head at her. "What's wrong with you? Why are you yelling?"

"Nerves." She shook her head. "I can't believe I'm such a dork."

"What's up?" Benny's ravaged face crinkled in concern for her.

"I got paranoid tonight. Someone was following me today. I lost him, but I still got paranoid."

"Who was following you?"

"I don't know. Some kid, a junkie. I don't know what he wanted from me, but he freaked me out. I tried to grab him, but he got away."

She closed the door to the hallway and stripped off her blazer, tossing it on the couch. She wandered into the kitchen, pleased that her knees seemed firm and her legs were steady, and opened the refrigerator.

She grabbed an unopened gallon of orange juice, closed the fridge with a shove of her hip, and hauled the container over to the counter. She still had vodka, if she could just find it. She thought a moment, then opened the left-hand cabinet.

There—she grabbed the bottle, dragged it down, and poured a hefty inch into the bottom of a tumbler. Topped it off with some orange juice. Then downed half the glass at a swallow.

"Easy, Sandra." He sounded concerned. She turned to face him.

"Don't worry," she said, "I just need to loosen up a bit." Stepping on the heel of one shoe with her toe, she worked her foot out, then did the same with her other foot.

She wiggled her toes. It felt wonderful—the first nice thing to happen to her all day. She waited with her eyes closed to better savor the sensation, as the liquor hit the bottom of her stomach and settled in for the night. Nice. Very nice.

"Loosen up," Benny said. "Sure. You're really freaked about this, aren't you?"

She turned and put the orange juice away.

"Nothing to worry about, little brother."

"Huh? I'm not supposed to worry when you walk in the door shaking and head straight for the liquor cabinet? You, who has about three drinks a year? Great. You worry about me all the time. But I'm not allowed to return the favor. Next time, let's trade troubles. Then maybe I can worry all I want." He turned his chair and scooted for the living room, obviously miffed.

"Really. Seriously. It's nothing, Benny," she said, walking out of the kitchen, carrying her glass and moving down the hall, following him into the living room. "I'm better now. Really. Look."

She spread her arms and did a mocking soft shoe. He grinned in spite of himself.

"Sandra—the last time I saw you like this was with—was when Chuck . . ."

She winced. "No, it's not like that. Not like it was with him. Never again like that."

She stared at him, knowing it was God's truth. It wasn't like Chuck. No man would ever knock her around again. It had taken two years worth of lessons in the martial art of kenpo, and four in aikido to convince herself of that, but she'd done it. Chuck, at least, was over with.

"You're really wound up, though, right?"

She could feel the knots of muscle between her shoulders, tight along the path of her spine. The knots were broadcasting small white flickers of pain. If she didn't do something about that, she'd be like a board come morning.

"Kinda," she admitted.

"You want to go dancing?"

She stared at him. "You know," she said slowly. "I think that's *exactly* what I want to do."

"I was kidding," he said. "Thought I was, at least."

"I'm not," she said.

If something was hunting her, even in a dream, let it dance to the music. She was sure as hell going to.

seven

Tina floated somewhere between bliss and terror. The backseat of the car was warm, and Zack's arms were around her. It felt wonderful. She really liked him, though they hadn't been dating that long; but while this wasn't the first time they'd made out, she liked to think of herself as careful. Tonight matters were going farther than she'd ever let them go before, and certainly much farther than she'd planned to let them go for a long time to come. She knew she was on unfamiliar ground. And she wasn't sure she wanted to be there.

Zack kissed her again. He opened her mouth with his and bit at her lips. It hurt a little, but it excited her, too, as did his hands on her body. The situation, though, was beginning to feel like it was spiraling out of her control.

Zack's hands twisted in her hair. The denim of his jeans, damp with sweat, felt rough on her bare thighs. She pulled away, just a little, because she wanted to see his face. His features were tensed, tight with need and passion. She felt his hands slide over her breasts, heard the rasp of his skin against the silk of her blouse.

Excitement and fear coursed through her like a hot drug. The feeling reminded her of the time her family had gone to Lake Powell, the time they'd all gone cliff jumping into the water. The sensation she'd felt that day while falling was a rush—it had thrilled her and scared her at the same time. She recognized the feeling coursing through her veins tonight. She was falling again . . . but this time she wasn't sure where she'd land.

Zack kissed her deeply. His hands were under her shirt now, a bit rough as they moved against her skin. The sound of their breathing was shockingly loud in the enclosed air of the Camaro. The windows had steamed over, blocking the view of the deserted city park outside the car, enclosing them in their own private fantasy world.

But that fantasy was starting to edge into something darker, the pleasure mixing with pain. Even though her body was clamoring for release, alarm bells had started clanging in some distant part of her mind.

If she didn't stop this now, it wasn't going to stop until it was over.

She pushed away, out of Zack's arms. Shaking, as breathless as if she'd just run a marathon, she huddled in the corner of the backseat.

"Tina?" Zack asked.

"Give me a minute here," she told him.

Even though Tina didn't always listen to her parents, there was one issue where she was in total agreement with them—a screaming baby, or a case of AIDS, or both, would cramp her style. She had every intention of enjoying a long and fun-filled run of parties and boys and beaches and college before she settled down into adult responsibility. To make certain she got the chance to enjoy the good life, she had to keep things from getting out of control in the backseats of cars.

"Zack, I'm sorry. I really like you, but I'm not quite ready for what's happening here."

"What do you mean?" Zack asked. He was staring at her, his eyes wide, hungry, frustrated.

She paused before answering, still breathing hard. She didn't want tonight to end. Zack was great—smart and good-looking—and he treated her like she mattered. But the last few minutes had been frightening as well as thrilling. And right now, Zack was looking really upset with her. But, dammit, she wasn't going to lose her virginity in the backseat of a Camaro. Someday she would decide it was time for her to cross that line, and maybe Zack would be the right person to cross it with her. But in the meantime, she had that shining future in front of her—and she wasn't going to throw it away because her hormones—or his—got the better of her.

She swallowed. "Zack, this is new territory for me. I'm not sure what I'm ready for here," she whispered. "But I know I'm not ready for what was going on."

She watched as the impact of that statement got through to him. His face tightened and she could almost *see* the rage hit him, grab him, shake him visibly. His breath rushed out in an audible gasp, like he'd taken a hit in the solar plexus. For a split second, he sat frozen into immobility, a terrible look on his face. Tina had a sudden urge to run, to grab the door handle, pull it open, and rush into the night before something bad happened in that car.

I've got to get out of here, she thought.

He grabbed her arm in a vice-like grip. "You're not gonna do this to me, bitch-tease," he groaned.

"Zack . . . you're hurting me." Tina could hear her voice shaking.

He pulled her implacably closer. "No, you're gonna give me what I want . . . what I need . . ." His voice, thick and choked, didn't even sound human.

"Please . . . please . . ." she begged, "I don't want this . . . let me go . . . let's go home!"

Then Zack moved, and it was much too late.

He was on top of her, pressing her into the seat cushions, ripping at her clothes, seemingly unconcerned about the bruises and scratches he inflicted on her as she struggled. She screamed, and he hit her in the head so hard she saw stars in the darkness around them. The pain blazed through her, burning her where it touched. She struggled, but Zack was bigger than she was and much stronger. And he was hurting her, hurting her terribly.

She screamed again. And again. And she fought him with every bit of strength she had.

"Please, God," she moaned. "Please, somebody, help me . . ."

•   •   •

God didn't find her, but Justin did. He hadn't seen Tina since he'd watched her leave with the boy the other night. The boy named Zack.

But he missed the sight of her, and longed for it again. He'd returned to her house, but she was gone. Wrapped in shadows, he'd discovered she was out with the boy again. He knew what the Camaro looked like, and where they usually went in it. He'd tracked the car through the Dragon-mirror, found it parked in darkness, the windows shrouded with a steamy film.

And a stink emanating from the car, easily scented by his hypersensitive nostrils, rich with blood and musk, overlaid with Tina's light perfume.

He found Tina naked, or nearly so, bruised and screaming in the arms of the young lout. Anger poured through him, a red haze of madness, a screaming rage that something he thought of as his had been taken by another, that something innocent had been attacked, was being brutalized right before his eyes. It had been centuries since Justin had felt such rage.

Without thought, he became the Wyrm, and the Wyrm gave himself up to his rage. He concentrated his anger into his fists and punched through the rear window of the car.

Zack, the violator, the boyfriend, was on top, thrashing and growling with lust, clubbing Tina as she struggled against him.

Thanks be, I am not too late, Justin thought as his claws wrapped about Zack's shoulders and ripped him out through the shattered window. The boy's face was terrified, but the Wyrm, seething with blood and rage, didn't care.

What he'd seen of Tina through the broken glass made him want the boy to feel all the terror he was capable of—and more.

Justin could hear her pitiful, terrified whimpering beneath the sounds of the boy's screams. He held the boy far above the ground, dangling him by the collar. He watched as Zack's skin purpled with oxygen deprivation. Finally, with a quiet snake's hiss of a whisper, he spoke.

"What do you think you've done here?"

He threw the boy back hard against the car.

"What the fuck are you doing, man?" Zack screamed, his voice high and cracking with terror. "What are you?"

"So you think you are a man. You think you have a man's rights. But a true man is never reduced to taking by force what should be given freely. You know nothing of what is due a woman," Justin said. "So I consider it my duty to make sure you will never live to become a man." The boy tried to back up, but, crushed against the side of the car as he was, he had nowhere to go.

The Wyrm slammed him on the side of his head, his heavy claws leaving a bruise on Zack's face that matched the one Justin had seen on Tina's.

Zack tumbled to the asphalt of the parking lot, screaming in pain, badly hurt. He cowered before his attacker. Justin reached down and picked the boy up by his arm. He could feel the skin tearing under his claws—scratched and bruised like the skin on Tina's arms.

The boy's agonized shrieks tore the night air. Justinian slammed Zack back onto the hood of his own car. The boy's head and shoulders dented the steel deeply. Zack gave a low moan as he crumbled, his body broken. Inside the car, Tina screamed and screamed.

"You're hurting me . . ." Justinian mocked him, as Zack came slowly to his senses, shaking his battered head, looking up through fear-filled eyes, looking for someone, something, anything, that would save him— and seeing nothing but a nightmare.

"Please . . . please . . ." the Wyrm said, in a high falsetto voice. "I don't want this."

The boy was so mangled he was hardly recognizable. Justin moved forward, seized Zack by his neck, and picked him up.

"No, please! Don't!" Tina's cries echoed in the night.

The Wyrm lifted Zack from the ground in one strong hand, shook him, choked him. The Wyrm smiled and narrowed his eyes. He drew back his other arm.

"I think," he said "that you've learned your lesson. What a pity you won't live to employ it."

A horrible cry tore from Zack's raw throat, from his shattered, distended jaws.

It ended abruptly, in the crunch of shattered bone and crushed flesh. And the soft patter of blood, dripping on the night-dark pavement . . .

eight

Tina sat in the wreck of the car, shivering in horror. She'd pulled herself into a small corner on the floor, wrapping herself up in Zack's letter jacket. She felt disconnected, as though she was watching herself from outside her body, from a great distance away. The pain from her bruises had receded to some distant point barely visible on the horizon, and she was beginning to wonder if she was in shock, so muffled were her sensations. As if she were wrapped in cotton.

Zack was sprawled across the hood of the car like some grisly hood ornament. She was certain he was dead. She'd seen what had happened to him, but not who had done it. Not really. A great dark shape had been all she could make out through the fogged-up car windows. But she could hear, even if she couldn't see, and the thing that had killed Zack was still out there.

Her only hope was that the killer, whoever he was, was through with his killing. When the creature had taken Zack, she'd locked the car doors. That was before she realized she'd played right into the killer's hands. Then the car doors had warped with the force of the killer's blows, trapping her inside. She was trying to work up the nerve to crawl into the front seat, see if the car would still start, try to get away.

But she felt the first move she made would attract the killer's attention, might even be her last move. And she knew that she owed more to herself than simply giving up and getting killed.

The tears began again and she swallowed. If she gave way to them, she was afraid she might never stop. The pain was coming back as she tried to plan, tried to save herself. She hurt all over. She hurt where Zack had beaten her, when the night had turned from love's young dream into some twisted slasher movie nightmare. She hurt where she'd slammed herself into the car doors, trying to get away while Zack was killed.

She could climb out through the broken back window, but there was glass everywhere, and her clothing was shredded, destroyed. It would be a slow, bloody, and dangerous process, and she'd be vulnerable to the killer every step of the way.

She was currently entombed in this car. She could only hope and pray that it was not what the killer intended. Wiping a hand across her eyes, she tried not to think of anything at all. *Please, just let it be over soon.*

"Precious Tina . . ." The voice was low and rumbling, and it came from behind her.

Tina squealed and spun around, looking through the shattered back windshield of the Camaro into the darkness of the night beyond. The city park outside the car's windows was dark, empty, deserted. She could see nothing, no one. But she knew he was there. She could hear him. And she could smell him—a strange odor like badly made Chinese food hung in the air. Rain spattered on the roof of the car, dripped off the chrome trim, and fell to the ground. A few trash cans stood at crooked attention against the wall encircling the lot, separating it from the children's playground. Beyond that was blackness. Fear and unexpected curiosity held her still, breathless.

Finally she could stand it no longer.

"Who's there?" she asked in a quavering voice.

"You would not know me, precious one, though I have watched over you for a very long time now." It was a man's voice, a rough, deep bass.

All the hairs on the back of her neck seemed to be standing on end, but Tina did not give in to terror. She was oddly reassured by the voice—at least the shadow she'd seen *seemed* human. Big, but human. She'd not been completely convinced of that when she'd seen it looming over Zack through the fogged-up windshield.

"Where are you?"

Slowly the darkness of the night . . . parted. The owner of the voice did not step out of the shadows, but rather the shadows seemed to melt away from him. Tina's eyes grew wide at what was revealed and she shrank back.

Jewel-like ruby eyes sparkled in a long, flat, reptilian face. Smooth, square scales glittered like emeralds in the darkness, covering his entire body. Thick muscles rippled under the gem-like skin. The creature's shoulders, biceps, chest, and stomach were so heavily muscled that the masses of those muscles met each other in starkly defined crevices. Its long, green wings pierced the night around it, then folded together behind it like some terrible parody of an angel's wings. Its wide mouth was solemnly held in a very human expression. Unless she had gone mad under the stresses of the last few minutes, she saw sadness, even concern there.

"Oh, my God . . ." she breathed out. Her hands gripped the Camaro's leather seat. "What . . . who are you?"

"Perhaps something of a guardian," the gravelly voice replied. "I wished to keep myself removed from your daily life. I did not think we would ever meet face-to-face. After tonight, I cannot in good conscience remain anonymous. Pain for you is pain for me."

Tina looked at Zack, winced, "Did you do this?"

The wide, flat head nodded.

She sobbed aloud. "I didn't want this to happen."

"I know." The hard, metallic edge to his voice caused Tina to look up again. The ruby eyes danced with inner fire. Tina rubbed her chilled arms and simply stared at the creature. It was frighteningly beautiful, so sleek, so shiny, so powerful looking. It reminded her somehow of the childhood fairy tales she'd read of dragons. How could something like it exist? It didn't move like a real thing, didn't speak like a real thing. Perhaps it was an angel of some sort, or a devil.

"Are you going to kill me?" she asked.

The big mouth smiled. "I would sooner kill myself. You have nothing to fear from me."

"Why should I believe you?" she asked, in spite of herself. She rubbed her arms again, warding off the chill of the night.

"You are cold," he said.

Suddenly she felt warmth on her arms. It was as though someone had brought the sun out in the night, though she could see no evidence of such a heat source, only feel the effect. The warmth coursed over her arms, her bare legs, and ended by warming her body.

She let out an astonished breath and looked at the creature. Her mind, though still hazy from shock and the events of the night, finally made the connection. This was a killer. Zack's body was still draped across the hood, and this . . . thing . . . had killed him.

She stared at his hands, which were not hands at all, but claws. They were wet with something. Blood. Zack's blood.

Tina screamed and fell back against the seat. The thing moved toward her, faster than she thought anything living could move. She scrambled around in her corner, trying to escape. Suddenly the scaled skin did not bring to mind sparkling gems, but bloody armor. Tina's terror struck her to the heart. She gasped, trying to get air. She couldn't breathe. Slowly the dark interior of the car faded away. Everything faded away. Even the dragon man faded away.

Tina regained consciousness slowly, in small increments, like drops of water falling into a pool. First she noticed the feel of the leather upholstery. She wasted a moment's thought to wonder why she was sleeping in such an uncomfortable place. That first fuzzy awareness was followed by a flood of sensation, sensation she nearly lapsed back into unconsciousness to escape. She hurt. Hurt all over.

It was when she asked herself why she hurt that everything came rushing back to her—the memories of what had happened that night. She was in the backseat of Zack's car. But Zack was dead and she was trapped here. The horror of it all smashed over her like a wave. She had no idea how long she'd been unconscious, or if the dragon man was still out there.

Then she heard a scraping sound. She sucked in a breath and pushed herself back against the seat, trying to merge with it, become invisible.

Again, the scraping sound. She searched the darkness surrounding her, trying to pinpoint the source of the noise.

Then she saw it—a figure approaching the car.

She cowered in terror. *Oh, God, what now?* she asked herself. The figure, silhouetted against the dim light from the moon, was right outside the smashed driver's side door, working away at it.

"Oh, no . . . oh, please God, no . . ." she whispered. Was that thing coming after her now? It had finished with Zack. Was it going to kill her now, despite its promise to let her live?

After a final, horrible screech, the door came free. She shrank away from it, as far from whoever was out there as she could get in the tight confines of the car. The figure wasn't the thing she most feared, that much she could tell for certain. He was human. In the scant light, she could see that his skin was dark, his hair and eyes black.

Tina had almost let down her guard enough to beg for help when she caught the look in the man's eyes. His expression didn't promise compassion or safety. His eyes were the eyes of a hunter. And at this very moment they were fixed on her as prey.

"So you're not dead yet?" the man said in a thick middle-eastern accent. "How careless of my friend. But much more amusing for me." He smiled, and his teeth shone white against his dark skin.

"Oh, my God . . ." Tina prayed as she never had in her life, trying to push herself back through the seat again. "Why me? What do you want?"

"Your pretty little head on a plate," the man replied. "I want to finish the job my *mentor* was too squeamish to take care of. Kalzar wants you dead. That's good enough for me."

"Please, somebody help me!" Tina screamed, even though she knew it was useless. After all the screaming she'd done on this night, surely help would have arrived if it was within earshot.

The man's smile faded. "No use screaming," he said. "It just makes me angrier. I will kill you regardless, but there are many ways to die. If you don't play nice, I'll make sure your death is long and painful." He reached for her. Before he could touch her, a sound from outside the car caught his attention—the sound of footsteps on the pavement.

"Mr. Omar." This voice was controlled, and held

the smallest trace of a foreign accent, but Asian rather than middle-eastern. The man with the hunter's eyes pulled himself out of the car so fast he almost bashed his head against the roof. Tina looked out past him and saw a teenaged kid standing calmly about ten feet from the car. There was nothing remarkable about him. He was just a kid, just like the kids she saw at school every day.

But by this time, Tina was convinced that nothing would save her, that this boy was just another in the endless stream of men come to destroy her on this night. She studied him—if he could keep the man he called Omar occupied for long enough, she could sneak out the door. There was enough wild country in the park that she would have a real chance to escape.

But from the looks of this confrontation, it would be over too quickly to allow her to fade into the distance. Omar was a perfect physical specimen: large, strong, fit, ruthless. The boy was small, lightly built, and—to all appearances—completely outmatched.

"How do you know my name?" Omar asked him.

"You're famous," the Asian kid said. His tone was scathing. "Didn't you know? There are posters of you all over the city with your face on them and *Killer* written underneath. Your *advertisements*. Haven't you seen them?"

As the boy drew closer, Tina realized that he wasn't as calm as he seemed. He was shaking. His hands twitched a bit as though he wanted to clench them into fists, but he kept them open and loose.

"You're a hero, huh?" Omar growled. "You like the girl, do you? Seems like everyone wants this girl. Well, if you want her so much, you can join her!" Omar lunged at the Asian kid, clawing for his throat.

What Tina saw next astounded her. Omar moved so fast she thought the kid would be on the ground before she could blink.

But the boy moved faster. Omar's hand whistled by the kid's head in a blur. She saw nothing but the wind left by its passing, ruffling the boy's hair. The kid spun away from the blow in a perfect circle, using the momentum of his motion to power a blow to Omar's neck as he stumbled, thrown off balance when his target failed to take the hit. Tina could hear the muted smack of flesh against flesh, the brittle crack of breaking bone. With a grunt, Omar crumpled to the pavement like a marionette with its strings suddenly cut.

Silence fell upon the night. The kid stood over the motionless Omar, clearly waiting for something. Then she heard the threats.

"I'm gonna kill you! I'm gonna fuckin' rip out your throat!" The downed man growled and cursed, tried to look up at the kid, but was clearly unable to use his arms or legs.

"Perhaps," the kid said. "Maybe one day soon. But not right this minute."

Tina had clambered over to the open door during the fight, hoping to escape. But it was over so quickly she never even had a chance to leave the car.

The Asian kid turned to her and held out a hand. The look of rage he'd given Omar softened to compassion as he met her terrified gaze.

"Please, allow me." He held his hand out to her.

She hesitated a moment, then took it. "You must hurry," he said. His voice was as calm as if he were helping her out of the car to attend an opera.

"Y-you broke his neck," she said, looking down at the growling, cursing Omar.

The kid nodded. "Yes. But it will not last. Even as we speak, he is healing. We have only minutes, perhaps only seconds. Please, hurry."

Tina didn't need any prompting. She stepped out of the car and around the fallen Omar.

A small smile crossed the kid's face as he looked over her shoulder.

"What is it?" Tina turned to see what he was looking at. She could see a faint glow of red and blue flickering above the treetops.

"Police," he said. "Someone must've heard the noise." The kid looked down at Omar, whose fingers were beginning to move. Omar looked up at them with such venom that Tina took a step back.

"You're both going to scream until your throats explode when I kill you!" Omar promised. He clawed at the ground, obviously trying to get up, but failing.

"Quickly," the Asian kid said. "Walk toward the street. The police will see you sooner there." He began leading her through the deserted park, across the playground, and up the hill toward the well-lighted roadway. She leaned on him heavily as she stumbled along in the dark, wincing as her bare skin was scratched by bushes and undergrowth. Thank God, Zack had left her shoes on.

"How much further?" she asked.

"Not much, and I think Mr. Omar will not readily follow you under the circumstances."

Tina noticed that she was hanging onto this boy like he was her last hope of heaven, and she tried to loosen her grip a little. Her hands wouldn't unclench. He looked down at her and smiled as if he understood everything she felt.

"Thank you," Tina said, and the tears burst from her eyes in a flood. She staggered. He held her up and she leaned against him as they made their way toward the sidewalk. Before they stepped out of the park and onto the sidewalk, she tugged the front of Zack's letter jacket together. It and her shoes were her only attire. She could hear the sirens now. They were drawing closer.

"Have courage, Tina. Your trials are not over yet," the boy said. They stopped by the edge of a building under a bright light. "Stay here. You will be safe here until the police arrive. Tell them everything you have seen tonight."

"W-what about you? Aren't you staying?"

He shook his head. "My place here would be difficult to explain, and I can serve you better from a distance." He let go of her and backed into the shadows even as the police cars rounded the corner, lights flashing.

"What about Omar?" Tina asked, frantic. She didn't want him to leave.

"He will not risk the possibility of being captured by the authorities. He is powerful, but he is not a Wyrm. He has almost assuredly recovered by now, so he

will not stay, nor will he try to get at you again tonight.
Stay within the light, Tina. Go to the police when they
come. I will be near."

With that, the Asian kid disappeared into the
night.

Tina turned and ran to the police car as it pulled up
to the curb beside her.

nine

Usually, the lights of the city made Justin feel at ease. The manic buzz of the electric arc lamps and the harsh definition of light and shadow in their unearthly glow were fitting companions to the low buzz and dark shadows that Justin always felt in his own mind. And in some rarely acknowledged corner of his thoughts, he felt they offered him hope. For while he could rarely escape that unintelligible static in the background of his own head, he could always fly above the lights, invisible and silent. When he did so, it made him feel better.

But tonight he was too disturbed for the usual soothing effects of night flight to kick in. That intrusive hum in the back of his mind was louder than usual, almost blaring. It harried him, tore at him until he wanted to scratch bloody gashes into his body. If he thought he had a chance to get rid of it, he'd give into the urge, tear his own skin until it was gone. But he knew it was hopeless. That buzz had been a part of him since the day he'd become what he now was, and it would continue to haunt him as long as he breathed. He flapped his powerful wings and let the wind take him, flying as swiftly as he could away from Tina, away from her now-dead ravager.

His acute night vision picked out the tiny sparkle of his skylight, far below. With a vicious twist, he tucked his wings closer to his body and dived steeply toward it. His muscles sang to him as he moved through the sky. As he neared the roof, rocketing through the sky like a comet, falling ever faster, he suddenly spread his wings to their fullest extent to slow his descent.

He felt his tendons creak and his blood rush through his veins. It took his mind off what he had just witnessed, what he had just done, and he reveled in the moment, at last forgetting himself in the joy of flight. The top of the building sped toward him and he felt an almost uncontrollable need to smash into it, to send cinder blocks and blood flying as he landed. He craved violence. *Let the building attempt to stop me,* he thought. *Let it try!*

It was a danger he faced every time he entered the Wyrm state. His anger was always pushing against his control, always threatening to turn him into some mindless, destructive beast. To control this violent form, his mind had to be focused on an even greater anger, an even more pressing purpose.

Again he spread his wings, unfurling them to their fullest extent to cup the heavy, wet air. Muscles burned along his back as the thin, leathery flaps strained with the demands he made of them. He slowed, then touched down lightly by the skylight.

His anger still pulled at him. *Rip the skylight off now,* it said, *and dive through and smash into the floor.*

Justin's feet scraped the roof. Tarred gravel crunched under his talons, the power pulling at him. Finally he could resist no longer. With a growl he lashed out.

The low brick wall that separated his building from the next blew apart at the blow. Bricks and clay-red dust flew onto the roof, landing with a clatter, until finally even the smallest fragments skittered to a stop.

Why had he killed the boy? The child had battered Tina, but he was young. He could have been saved. He could have learned. If Justin had just let him live, let him go, the boy would never have done anything like that again. Justin had seen that truth in the boy's eyes before he killed him. So what had possessed him? A bloody murderer, that's what he had become. The Dragon had not ordered Zack's death. The decision to kill had been Justin's alone.

Justin's dragonling body—like most of the gifts of the Dragon—did not respond well to thoughts of altruism. Just violence. That's all it understood. Justin knew that, and yet he'd gone to the car when he smelled the blood, almost certain of what he'd find, had used the shadows to hide himself, had come down on Zack like the hand of judgment for his sins.

And he had murdered the boy. He could have saved Tina without killing, without revealing himself. But he'd chosen the other path. The blood-soaked path. And he hated himself for it.

He growled into the night and ripped another chunk out of the knee-high wall.

You are a fool, Justin, he told himself.

He paced across the roof, trying to master the dragon form that wanted to slay, to rend, to destroy. His Wyrm self called to him to fly into the air, find another victim, or maybe many victims, and rip them to shreds.

He had played a deadly game and Zack had paid the price. His original intent had not been to kill the boy. It had been to insure Tina's safety.

And why did you think that was all that you'd get? Everything you touch runs with blood. Justin cursed himself. His howl of despair shattered the night.

He should have known he might lose control. He should have taken that into consideration, but he had failed to, and now he had alienated Tina forever.

What kind of protector are you? You should know by now. You cannot protect anything you love. You are no shield. You are only useful as a weapon, as a poisoned dagger that destroys whatever it touches. He dropped his head into his clawed hands. Justin had not been in charge of his body at all, despite his good intentions. It was as though his Wyrm state was nothing but an automaton assigned to slay. Once his anger sparked the machine's engine, there was no stopping it.

Justin roared into the night again and slapped his claws into the sides of his face. His talons bit into his scaled flesh and he ripped downward, tearing his cheeks.

Fiery pain ran through him. His muscles flexed in response. When his vision cleared, he realized he had leapt high into the air, and now was falling. The building was coming at him sideways. He hit the roof with a crash. Tar and gravel flew and one of his wings snapped. He roared again with pain as he slid across the gravel, crumpling a satellite dish as he rolled.

Tina had recoiled from him, had screamed at him to go away, had fainted before his eyes in stark terror.

Now all the good he might have done by saving her was erased. She was more afraid of him than she'd been of the boy he'd killed.

Slowly, Justin stood up.

His breathing calmed. His wing popped, shifted. The wet sound of cartilage rubbing against bone ground through his body. Slowly, ever so slowly, the wing rose behind his left shoulder and reformed to its natural shape. No wound ever lasted, whether Justin was in dragon or human form. He healed so quickly that the process was visible to the naked eye. It was part of the master's blessing. Part of the blessing of this cursed, vengeful gift of eternal life. He never had a lasting scrape or a scab. No virus could ever gain a foothold in his body. Bacteria in his blood stream died long before they could multiply. Even his veins were free of the heroin tracks that marked the arms of normal junkies.

Justin walked over to the combination latch and opened it. He dropped through the open skylight and into his apartment.

He let the pain soak through him during the entire

process of sloughing off his unnatural skin. He deserved it. Every moment of pain, every instant of agony. It should have been him back in the park lying there with a hole in his chest, not Zack.

When the transformation was complete, Justin staggered down from the dais, wet and numb. He tossed the skin into his new fireplace—much safer than a Dumpster, why hadn't he thought of it before?—and watched it burn. Then he showered and dressed.

Finally he slumped into his chair and pulled out his heroin and the tools he needed to use the drug. He'd had the fleeting thought that perhaps tonight, his good deed, the pain he'd rescued Tina from, would enable him to forgo his need to blank his mind, but even his good deeds turned rotten on him. He'd never forget the look on Tina's face just before she fainted. He'd seen the monster he was, reflected hideously in her eyes.

The preparation for the injection passed like a blur before him, and he let himself come to full attention only when he plunged the burning liquid into his arm. For a brief moment he enjoyed the rush of the drug as it raced through his veins—but his immortal body began to neutralize the drug's poisons almost before he could enjoy the glow, and then he slipped into the lassitude of the aftermath. His eyelids fell to half-mast and he sank deeply into the chair, hoping for the blank slate of sleep.

Send me no memories, he thought. *Please, no ghosts . . .*

The lights of his apartment were a pleasantly dim glow, and he closed his eyes.

No memories, leave me to sleep . . .
Justinian?
No . . .
Justinian?
I said no—
—Dreams, my lord . . . my dreams. They do visit me so strangely. They taunt me. In them I run, as I cannot now. My lord? Beloved Justin . . . do not leave me. Where are you?

Would the past never let him be? He cried out against it, but it was pointless. Now he sank fully into the vision, so clear in his memory that he might as well have been there, in the castle. He was curled in a corner of his bed in a cold stone room, cursing the servants who had left them, who had run in fear from the plague. Justin had refused to urinate in his own bed, and yet there was no one to bring him a chamber pot. He'd crawled through his room, defying pain and delirium and the easy path of succumbing to the illness. He'd finally found several of the glazed pots in a corner, empty and neglected. He'd dragged them back to his bed and mostly stayed there since then, unwilling to move a step further unless he had to.

The mongrel of a priest had declared Justin's castle off-limits, in the hands of the devil. Justin was not inclined to dispute the priest's contention. While he'd been delirious with fever, his children had died. His wife had struggled to nurse them all, had fallen further and further into despair and despond as they each passed, unshrived and abandoned by God's representative here on earth, to their maker.

And now only he and Gwendolyne lived inside
these walls, and Justin knew that they would not do so
for long. Though the plague's progress within Justin
had at last slackened, it had finally taken Gwendolyne
into its awful grasp. Fair Gwendolyne, his beloved wife,
now rotted under the same hand that had so nearly
destroyed Justinian and had laid waste to everything he
loved. When she died, Justinian planned to take his
own life if the plague did not take him, too.

The terrible force of disease worked upon Gwendolyne with a speed unlike anything he'd ever seen
before, consuming her with an unearthly vengeance.
He'd had two days from the onset of his first symptoms
until he'd reached the point where his legs buckled
when he walked upon them; where the pain was a constant, maddening thing; where boils had throbbed and
pulsed under skin; where the fever took his senses from
him and gave him visions and delusions of madness
instead. And he'd lived through it. The worst of his
fever had finally broken, leaving him weakened, ravaged
by the illness, barely able to move, but no longer delusional.

It seemed to Justinian that when the children died,
Gwendolyne had given up hope. After she'd buried the
last of them, she had succumbed herself. In the space of
hours, Justinian had seen Gwendolyne's illness surpass
his. Her slender throat was marred by a grotesque
swollen knot under her chin, and she whimpered from
the pain constantly, even in her sleep. When she was
able to speak coherently, she whispered to him of her
fevered visions, as she did now.

Justin steeled himself against the pain of movement and reached down for the chamber pot. Before he
could grab it, he realized it was too late. The warmth of
his own piss was turning cold against his skin, turning
his soaked nightclothes frigid.

He growled, a tortured animal's howl, and shoved
the pot from him. It fell to the ground and shattered,
littering the ground with shards of glazed pottery. He
let his head fall back, and it hit the bedstead. The blow
was not that hard, but his skin felt like brittle parch-
ment, and his bones felt as weak as grass stems. The
pain was such that he thought he had split open his own
skull. Sweat trickled into his eyes. For a terrible, fevered
moment he thought the moistness must be his own
brains, leaking away with the rest of his life. Harsh sobs
wracked his body. Beside him, he could hear Gwendolyne's pitiful whimpers.

"The dreams . . ." Gwendolyne's weak voice carried to him, "Justinian, 'tis fierce cold. It does coat my
body with ice. It touches my very bones. A coverlet . . .
canst thou reach one?"

Justin clamped his jaw and ground his teeth
together until he thought they must crack. He couldn't
bear to listen to this any longer. Fair, sweet Gwendolyne, reduced to this. He would die to preserve her,
but he could not endure hearing her any longer, not like
this. Her cries were as sharp as sewing needles thrust
into his ears. He had no more blankets. Their bed was
piled high, a foot thick with them, and still she shivered. Still he shivered. And now he had pissed himself.

I will not die like this, he thought. *I cannot die like*

this. I am a man of breeding. A man of honor. I will not die in a pool of my own urine.

"I will not go out like this," he vowed. "I will take matters in my own hands first."

Gwendolyne cried quietly at his side. "I am sorry, my lord . . . I am so sorry . . ."

She suffers past bearing, he thought. *I should end it.* The mad thought leapt upon him. He looked about for something he could use to end her pain. Standing near the doorway, near the corner where he had sought the chamber pot, was a tall mirror, ringed round with thick carvings.

The mirror's gilt frame was battered. But the glass face of the mirror was intact. If he could shatter it, he could use the fragments to end Gwendolyne's mortal suffering and his own.

Now he stared at the mirror, abandoned at the side of the entryway. He crawled out of his bed and across the floor. He reached out a shaking hand, took its frame, and pulled it toward him.

It was then that Justin's world changed forever.

"So you have found the strength for one last attempt at controlling your life, even as it slowly seeps from you?" the mirror said. The voice Justinian heard was low, gravelly.

Justin let go of the mirror as if it was a snake that had bitten him, and shrank away from it.

"What?" he said. He had been certain that the delusions had left him, that his thoughts were finally his own. But the mirror was speaking to him, so he had to be slipping into madness once more.

"I do not think that your ears have progressed quite so far into death as you would have me believe, Lord Sterling. Shrink not from me. It is my place to be here. And I think it would not offend any truth if I claimed that you have called upon me to appear here." The voice was clearly coming from the mirror, though he feared to gaze on it again. But he had to.

Justinian's hands trembled as he approached. He could not tell whether it was the sickness or his fear which caused him to shake so. Slowly, he raised his head and peered into the glass.

In the mirror gazing out at him was not what he expected to see—his own ravaged reflection. Instead, he saw a beautiful man's face surrounded by golden hair curling down to his shoulders. The man's eyes were the deepest shade of green Justin had ever seen, glistening like emeralds. They were fathomless. Justin looked at them, speechless. Eternity sped past him and he could do nothing. Time had no meaning and everything lived within that gaze, everything that mattered.

Finally, eternity came to an end and Justin blinked.

"Who—who are you?" he spoke sluggishly through his wasted lips.

"Your salvation, Lord Sterling," the mirror replied. "It is your nature to scream against death. When you were dying, your limbs fought the very air that you might grasp yet another breath and draw it into your lungs. It would be the falsest of lies, if I said that my reflection is other than thine own, in all ways that matter."

"Riddles," Justin said, "do not answer my question. Who are you?"

"That, too, is but a riddle, should you wish to solve it. But what I offer you now is more than a riddle. I will give you your salvation. I offer immortal life for you, for your beloved. All you must do is to take my hand . . ."

Delusion or not, Justin was willing to grasp at anything that might save him, might save his beloved Gwendolyne. With his hand, the hand that was not grasping the mirror, Justinian reached out, trembling with fear, to the golden-haired man. The hand of the mirror man seemed to have reached through the reflective glass as though it was nothing more than water. Justin took the hand, felt the shock as flesh met flesh . . .

He vanished beyond the glass.

He did not know how long he was in the world on the far side of the mirror, and he could never remember exactly what he heard or did. Only a few moments passed in the world he'd left behind before he stepped out of the mirror again. But he had changed in every way that mattered. His angel had burned away the lumps, had washed away the spots, had cleansed his entire being with fire. He felt the vigor of true health, and more. Beyond vitality, he felt invincible. His vision was crisp and clear. The smell of death in the room was strong, but he was above it now. Death could never touch him.

His beloved Gwendolyne still suffered here in this room, with death so near Justinian could almost touch its hovering presence. He had so little time. Justin lifted up the great mirror as if it was a child's toy, took it to the bed, and sat next to her.

Her eyes were closed. She slept fitfully, whimpering and twitching as the last stages of the plague ravaged her fevered body. Justinian touched her face gently. She didn't respond. Had she already slipped away? Was he too late? He put his hand under her dull, tousled hair, cupped her head and lifted it into his lap. He ran his thumb in a tender circle over her cheekbone, a lover's caress. She stirred under his touch. Her eyes opened and she moaned at the strain her new position placed upon her swollen neck.

"Justin . . . no . . ." she murmured. Her eyes focused on him, then. They widened.

"My lord," her shocked voice was weak, "you have recovered . . ."

"I am completely healed," he told her. "And now it is your turn to live again."

"Truly, my lord? A miracle!"

"It is, my lady. An angel has come here to deliver us. We are not damned, but are meant to be saved. Look here in this glass. Let him cleanse you of this malady, as he did me." Justin held her up to face the mirror.

As soon as she saw the figure in the mirror, her eyes went wide. "No!" she breathed with all the scant force she could muster. She pushed his arm and turned her face away. "What have you done?"

Justin's brow furrowed, and he gently turned her toward the mirror again, despite her struggles. Her strength was no match for his at the best of times, much less now. "Do not let your delusions get the better of your judgment, my wife. Look again. He can heal you. Do I not stand before you once again a whole man? Do you not see an improvement in me? This is our own angel, sent to us."

"He is no angel, my lord. He is a devil! You have made a pact with the devil, by my life! Can you not see his fangs?" Gwendolyne's eyes avoided the mirror in terror, and looked upon him with a mixture of pity and fear. She struggled to escape him, but he pulled her closer to him, holding her more tightly in his embrace.

"Look quickly, wife," he pleaded. "Your time draws near. I beseech you! Do not turn away."

"No. I would die a thousand deaths ere I make my bed with Satan. Recant, my lord. He has warped your mind. 'Tis no angel within the mirror."

"Open your eyes, woman, I beg you! Please, before the plague has its way with you."

Again she struggled to get away from him. Her weak movements were fruitless against his strength, and he forced her to face the mirror in desperation, angered that she would refuse her obvious salvation.

"Do it," he commanded. "Accept!"

"Never," she replied.

He reached out and dragged the mirror closer, but still she would not look. Again, he tried to force her to look . . . he tried to force her. He lifted her head ever upward. He . . .

And then the plague took her. She could no longer stand against it.

Her tears fell onto his arm as she died. Her tears . . . her blood.

Drops of blood on green scales.

"NO!" Justin lurched awake. His apartment was the same. The same mirror that had witnessed her death now stood on the dais across from him. His gaze fell upon his untidy gallery, the pictures he had sketched, some painstakingly, others hastily. Some of the works, mostly the architectural drawings, were precise. Not one line was out of place in them. Others canvasses were battlefields of slashing graphite—mostly the figures, the pictures of the women that had caught Justin's attention. All those women . . . they were all one woman. All of them were Gwendolyne. Each figure. Gwendolyne, whom the plague had taken from him.

His Gwendolyne.

. . . not blood. The plague had taken her, and her tears had fallen upon his arm.

He looked down at his arm, human now. Surely those had been tears . . .

"You're truly pitiful, Justin. A broken-backed, sniveling excuse for an Elder. If you were a horse, I'd shoot you."

Justin whirled around at the soft, deep voice. The American accent was too contrived to be real.

"Kalzar!" Justin snarled.

"Perhaps that's not a fair comparison," Kalzar said. "I'd shoot you anyway, given the chance."

His old enemy must have entered through Justin's mirror again, though he was not standing anywhere close to it. And this time, Justin had not been aware of the transition.

But Justin knew full well that there was no other way to get into the apartment short of breaking the sky-light or smashing the door down. And both were intact. That Kalzar could enter and leave Justin's sanctum at will lit a furious fire in Justin's stomach.

Kalzar walked across to the picture-covered wall, ripped down a picture of Tina. "I remember when you were more ruthless than this. Today, it's getting so that every time you kill, you have to run straight back here and stick that needle in your arm." Kalzar's burning eyes turned toward Justin.

"I told you not to come back here," Justin said, gripping the arms of his chair tightly with his hands to keep from trying to tear Kalzar's throat out with them. Kalzar healed as fast as Justin. It would be a waste of effort.

Kalzar's smile was a distillation of pure evil, his teeth glistening in the dim room. "I will have your heart this time, Sterling. Every time you stick that needle in your arm, you grow weaker mentally, even if not physi-cally. Do you think the master doesn't know that? He sees everything. One day, you're going to wake up and find my claws closing about your neck."

Justin stood up. He shoved the heavy overstuffed easy chair off to the side as though it was composed of air. It flew across the room and landed against the wall with a resounding crash.

"Why not try it now, Kalzar?" Justin challenged his adversary. "You parade around, growling and howling about your wounded pride. I think you spend so much time talking because you know I could tear you apart. Am I wrong? Come for me, and we'll find out!"

Kalzar seethed, searching for words. He bent over, and Justin could see him preparing to make the transformation to the Wyrm state. The Dragon had warned them both about fighting each other, had made it quite clear that their lives might be at stake if they ever did so. While Kalzar could not kill Justin, the Dragon could certainly kill one or both of them. But Justin wasn't worried about that anymore—death might come as a relief to him these days.

Still, those thoughts were insubstantial next to Justin's anger, next to the red haze of accumulated rage—nearly six hundred years' worth of rancor and ill will since he'd first met Kalzar—that engulfed him.

Kalzar stopped himself. Justin could feel how close the Arab had come to changing. The tightly stretched skin on Kalzar's clenched fists bubbled, trying to become scales, but he held back, held it in.

Justin baited him again, spoiling for a fight that would finally put this rivalry to rest one way or another. "You refuse my gauntlet, Kalzar. Why is that? Are you that afraid? Does the Dragon's last reprimand to you still sting? Or are you so sure of the loss you can't afford to try me?

"I remember when you were the Dragon's lieutenant, closer to him than I, but that's not the case any longer, is it? Who took that from you? Oh, that's right. I did, didn't I? I told you before. The Dragon is a surgeon and you are a club. He can only use you to make a bloody mess, not to do the real work." Justin walked up to Kalzar, and the Arab flinched with each step Justin took, tried desperately to keep hold of his rage. Saliva trickled out of the corner of Kalzar's mouth as he fought his urge to change, to kill.

Justin could feel the transformation trying to burst out in himself also. Just below the surface of his skin, he could feel his bones reforming, those great muscles swelling in his shoulders. The Wyrm in him wanted to be set free. Those burning eyes wanted to look upon Kalzar. That indestructible hide wanted to gleam in the bloody light of battle with a worthy opponent. Justin kept the Wyrm at bay, but only barely. The one thing that kept him from leaping upon Kalzar and ripping his throat out was the thought of facing the Dragon afterward.

"I never asked for your place of favor," Justin finally said. "I earned it. You disgust me, then and now. You curry favor like the lowest of flunkies, like a serf groveling before his lord. You run here and there, tearing off heads without ever asking why, hoping he'll notice. But he knows you for what you are. A beast incapable of planning, incapable of conscious thought. He needs generals. You'll never transform yourself into anything more than the gutter thief you once were."

Kalzar just stood there, fighting his instincts, fighting not to become a Wyrm.

Justin was momentarily impressed. A hundred years ago, the Arab would have launched himself at Justin in a foaming rage. Instead, he turned away, turned his back on Justin, struggled to halt the transformation, reverse it.

"Leave now, Kalzar," Justin spat, "and never enter my house again; otherwise, I will test the Dragon's warning. I will kill you, and risk the consequences. It would be worth it to rid this earth of the festering sore that is your existence."

Kalzar turned slowly to face him. Justin realized that the outcome here was still in question. The dragonling form was still just an instant away, waiting to be set free. Fire glowed behind Kalzar's pupils.

Kalzar opened his mouth to say something and hissed instead. A low growl rumbled from his throat.

The man rather than the monster struggled to find his voice, and finally spoke. "Oh, yesss," he hissed. "Yesss, Jussstinian. Tessst it!"

Justin was tempted. Oh, so tempted. But then sanity reared its head again. Why waste the energy on such a pile of steaming refuse? "Go, Kalzar," he said. "Go make more of your ham-handed mistakes. I'll see you in my dreams."

"Yesss," Kalzar replied. "Like you will dream of the girl you watch so carefully. Do you know that she nearly died tonight after you left her? Or perhaps as you will dream of the detective, who dares death to come for her with every breath she takes?"

"Get out of my city, Kalzar. I won't warn you again."

Kalzar's mottled face wrinkled in a grin. "You will have to kill them both soon. The master will feel your reluctance."

"Neither of them are a threat to the Dragon. They know only what I allow them to know."

"But we must be sure about such matters." Kalzar said, stepping toward the mirror. "They know something is going on. They have seen the signs. The girl has seen *you,* you fool! I have assigned their deaths to Omar. He needs more practice. Your 'delicate methods' don't make full use of his talents."

Justin snarled at Kalzar, horrified by his words. "No disciple kills in this city without my consent! That's final. Omar bungled the first mission I sent him on. Badly. If he kills again without my supervision, I'll rip his arms off and leave him in the mirror!"

Kalzar merely sneered at him. "Then do your job, Justin. The master wants your women dead. If you don't kill them, I will be forced to step in."

"I will handle them in my fashion!"

"The master doesn't approve of your fashion."

"You would like to think you know the master's mind, wouldn't you, Kalzar?" Justin said.

Kalzar's lips curled. "I just left Omar at a blues club on LaSalle Street," Kalzar said. "I guess this lady detective of yours likes the blues. Or perhaps I should say she *liked* the blues. Omar is fast, even if he's not always careful . . ."

Justin jumped at Kalzar, but Kalzar was ready for him. He sidestepped and rushed toward the mirror. Justin cut him off.

"You have the reflexes of an old man, Justinian!" Kalzar cackled. The Arab jumped sideways, snatching a hand mirror from Justin's drug paraphernalia. Justin glared in fury as Kalzar stuck the mirror in his face.

"See, my master!" Kalzar crooned, "Look upon this

trash, at the wreck of what was once one of your Elders!"

Justin half expected, as Kalzar did, that the Dragon would appear in the mirror, but nothing looked back at Justin but his own reflection.

Slowly, clearly confounded by the Dragon's refusal to respond, Kalzar rose from his crouch and turned the mirror to face himself. He gritted his teeth and his muscles twitched.

Not this night, eh, Kalzar? Justin thought. *The Dragon is not watching.*

With his eyes narrowed, Kalzar tossed the mirror on the floor. It shattered into sharp, glistening shards.

Justin stayed where he was.

"It appears," Kalzar said, "that the Dragon does not yet realize it is necessary that you die." He turned and walked to the dais and up to the huge mirror. "I will do everything in my power to change that." He stepped into the mirror. It rippled with his passage and was still.

ten

Sandra threw her blouse on the floor and shoved her closet door wide, then stood motionless a moment, wondering what to wear.

Tentatively, she fingered one of her flashier miniskirts, but finally pushed it back into the throng of hanging clothes. She wasn't in that sort of mood. After the kind of day she'd had, she wasn't interested in putting on a pair of spike heels and hamstringing herself for fashion's sake.

She tossed a black lace blouse on her bed and closed the closet. From her chest of drawers she took out a black satin chemise and a comfortable pair of jeans. And definitely, she decided, returning to the closet, a pair of patent leather flats . . .

Five minutes later, she scrutinized her reflection and nodded with satisfaction. Ten years ago, she wouldn't have dreamed of going out on the town alone dressed like this. Besides the fact that Chuck would have beat her silly for even thinking about it, there was the other factor. She was a cop. She knew too well what kind of predators were out there, just waiting for a woman to step into their midst dressed in something provocative. In their twisted little minds, a good-looking woman dressed in anything but a head-to-toe gunny sack was "asking for it." "It" being anything up to and including full-blown rape.

Slipping money, a lipstick, her driver's license, her shield and ID, her keys, and her off-duty weapon—a Smith & Wesson .38 snubbie revolver—into a small beaded handbag, she smiled. With the load of unfocused hostility she was struggling with, it just might be a real pleasure to run into some idiot who wanted to cross the line with her.

She narrowed her eyes at her reflection. A pretty woman holding a purse with a pistol inside. She thought about the redhead who had knocked her on her ass today. That embarrassment still burned. And the feeling of being stalked, the weird paranoia that had almost made her come unglued earlier. Maybe it was just cop jitters. But it felt real enough . . .

She grabbed her purse and left her room. Benny's door at the end of the hall was closed. She paused. Benny had let something slip earlier, and she'd almost missed it. She walked to his door and knocked.

"Yeah?"

She opened it a crack and popped her head inside. A gray-blue glow from his monitor lit the walls. He twisted around in his chair and raised his eyebrows.

"I'm a dork," she said, frowning. "A selfish dork."

Benny smiled and swiveled his chair around. He

beckoned for her to come in. "Yeah? How big a dork?"

"Big."

"How selfish a dork?"

"Very selfish."

"What color?"

She laughed and sat on his bed, leaned back on her hands. "C'mon, Benny. You said something when I came in and I blew past it."

Benny wrinkled his brow, "What's that?"

"You suggested we trade troubles. I was too thick to pick up on it. Your troubles. What's going on?"

Benny shook his head, but his mood darkened. He broke eye contact and looked back at the computer screen, then down at his chair. "Nothing. Same shit, different day. It's not important."

"It's important to me."

Benny was silent for a moment. It was tough to get him to talk about his own troubles. His attitude toward adversity was to act as if it didn't exist. He didn't like to dwell on the bad things. That worked well for him with most problems, but sometimes he let things fester inside. She knew she had to proceed with care. Too much sympathy and Benny would clam up. He hated it when people pitied him.

"Remember me mentioning a girl named Kylie?" Benny said slowly.

Sandra thought about it. Benny talked with so many people on the Internet. She could never keep their names straight. "Vaguely," she replied.

"Well, we've been flirting over the Net for months now."

"Okay."

Benny ran his hands through his hair. "A couple of months back, when I got that big advance for the game, I invited her out to dinner to celebrate. It was a gesture, nothing more. She lives in Maryland, so I figured there wasn't a chance in hell of it happening. No harm done. She could come with me in her imagination. Well, a week ago she writes and tells me her company is sending her to Chicago for some sales training seminar. She says she wants to collect on the dinner."

"How is this a bad thing?" Sandra asked.

"I told her to meet me at Ambria, over in Lincoln Park."

Sandra whistled. "Solid choice. But rich. So, what, you're Mr. Moneybags now?"

"She seemed worth it. She told me to wear a red carnation so she would recognize me. I suggested wearing my ON THE ENTERPRISE, YOU'D CALL ME SIR button instead. I got an LOL for that."

"LOL?"

"Internetese for Laugh Out Loud."

"So what happened?"

"What happened?" Benny snorted. "Nothing. That's what happened. I show up in my best suit and red carnation, wait there for two hours, and nothing." He looked at her pointedly.

"And?" Sandra said.

"And what? That's it."

"That's what? That's all you did? You didn't call her to find out why she was late?"

"Late? Don't you get it?"

"Yeah, she got lost or something came up. Give her the benefit of the doubt, Benny."

"No. She was there, Sandra. I'm sure she was at the restaurant at some point. You see, I didn't tell her about me. About this." He waved a hand at his wheelchair. "I didn't want to deal with the whole pity thing."

"I'm missing something here. You think she was there and she didn't even say hello?" Sandra asked.

"Obviously she walked in, saw me like this, and kept right on walking. Oh, sure." Benny threw his hands up in the air. "Old Benny's a good Net pal. He can make you laugh till you're blue in the face, gives you a shoulder to cry on. But he's just not good boyfriend material, is he? Doesn't quite have the face. Just doesn't have the right functioning equipment." Benny glared at Sandra, as though it were her fault.

Sandra kept her reaction from showing. She wanted to move over and throw her arms around Benny, hug him tight and tell him how much she loved him, and how that little bitch didn't deserve him. But she didn't dare get emotional. She didn't dare show pity. With Benny, it was the quickest way to get your butt tossed out of the room.

Benny fumed, oblivious to the long silence that filled the space between them. He seemed to be asking her with his eyes what he should've done different. He seemed to be waiting for her to admit that it was true, that he wasn't worth dating, that it was hopeless.

Sandra swallowed, and spoke. "So . . ." The only other sounds in the room were the soft hiss of Benny's breathing, the humming computer, and the muffled city noise beyond the window. "Are you done now?"

"Done what?" Benny's voice was sharp, slightly confused.

"Done feeling sorry for yourself." It was a risky thing to throw at him. She knew it, but she couldn't think of anything else. They were a pair of tough nuts, the two of them. They hadn't made it to this point in their lives by being weak.

Benny's face reddened. Sandra drew a breath. She leaned forward, ready to hug him and tell him it would be all right. But something kept her from that. She waited.

At first he didn't look at her. "No," he said, "I'm not done."

"Well, how long is it going to take?" Sandra was surprised at the steadiness in her voice.

Benny let out a long breath. He cracked a reluctant smile. "One night of playing *Cheerleader Carnage* on the computer should just about do it." He looked up at her, and his eyes sparkled.

Sandra smiled. "I love you, Benny."

"You always say that *after* you punch me in the stomach."

"I have to get your attention first."

He nodded, looked at her clothes. "You going dancing now?"

"Yeah."

"In that outfit? You trolling for creeps or something?"

"Something like that." She laughed.

"Be gentle with them."

"I'm always gentle with those who are gentle with me," she said. He noticed the fire in her eyes.

Chuckling, he turned back to his monitor, "You're in one of those moods, huh?"

"Something like that."

"Get gone," he said, turning back to his computer.

Purse, umbrella, and raincoat in hand, she left their apartment, locking the door behind her. She thought about taking her car, but decided that if she was going to drink, it might get in the way. Nobody knew better than a cop how stupid it was to drink and drive. She'd hail a cab at the curb or take the elevated train, one of the great advantages to living in the city. She felt a little better now. Benny would be okay. Tough bastard. Sometimes she felt like the entire world wasn't big enough to knock him down. And she'd be okay, too.

The rain had ceased. Bloated gray clouds still slid slowly and easily through the dark void of the night sky. But she could see the moon through breaks in the cloud cover and a few stars bright enough to outshine the city's light pollution. She'd prepared for the weather and now she didn't need the gear. She wondered if the clearing skies were an omen. Just as she thought that, the heavens opened again.

Shaking her head at such superstitious nonsense—omens, for God's sake!—she closed the gate behind her and walked into the rain. She hailed the first cab she saw.

As it slowed and turned toward the curb, a footstep scuffed the pavement behind her. She turned quickly, nervously. Nobody in sight. She heard somebody chirp their car alarm and climb into a car. Sandra gave a sigh of relief—nothing to worry about—and got into hers.

"LaSalle Street and Monroe, please," she told him. She wanted to be right in the heart of the city, to feel Chicago's millions of people all around her as she danced.

She paid the driver, overtipped him, and got his card in case she needed to call a cab to get home. *I need a drink,* she thought. Something, anyway. The combination of her dream last night, the murders, and the redhead in the trench coat who seemed to be following her had her jumpier than she'd been in years.

Sandra headed for the Top Hat, a blues club a friend of hers had turned her on to. She'd been there before, and had liked it well enough. The scene was a little rough around the edges and the people were interesting. Most of them, at least. The entertainment tonight was a band from New York reputed to be pretty good. Edward—the friend who'd taken her here the first time—said he'd seen them before and they weren't to be missed. Sandra couldn't remember the group's name—Dirty Dimes, Spare Change, something like that. She walked up to the door. There was a poster of the band in the doorway. Dusty Nickels. Close enough.

She recognized the bouncer. He'd been working the door on her previous visits.

"Nice to see you, lady," the tall, gaunt young man said as he took her money for the cover charge. He was dressed well—Calvin Klein urban waif from head to toe. Nodding, she slipped past him.

Though she didn't smoke herself, Sandra loved the

swirling backlit haze that marked a real blues club. It made her feel caught in the solitary embrace of a surreal world where the whining of the lead guitar was the speech of the realm and nothing was too bright or too frenetic. Exactly what the doctor ordered.

She sat down at a small round table close to the stage and ordered a screwdriver. The waitress returned quickly with the drink. Sandra grabbed the glass like a lifeline. The sting of the alcohol was pleasant on the back of her throat, and the sweetness of the orange juice provided a pleasant contrast to the sour taste of the unsuccessful day she'd spent hunting for a killer.

The band had finished their first set sometime earlier. She smiled and slouched back in her chair. The clock on the wall said ten till nine.

A roadie came out onto the stage and crouched before one of the amplifiers, fiddled with a knob. The audience was growing, people filtering in for the second show. The bar became crowded and the noise level grew. She watched the customers move and squirm past her. Good old Stevie Ray Vaughn was on the sound system, lulling the patrons with comfortable familiarity before they started their venture into a new sound.

A tall man in a light sport coat wedged himself in the chair across the table from her. He flashed her a Dentine smile and ordered a rum and Coke. She gave him no more attention than anyone else in the throng and waited for the band to begin.

She didn't have to wait long.

As soon as the man fiddling with the amp left the

stage, the PA system went silent and the band walked on.

The lead singer, a black man with thick dreadlocks, took the microphone. He was of average height, with a multicolored vest hanging open over his lean, well-muscled chest. His baggy pants looked as though they had been made from the fabric of a black parachute. He looked like someone who belonged in a reggae band, not a blues band.

"Check. Check." His lips touched the mike. His resonant voice boomed throughout the room and thrummed in the bones of Sandra's rib cage.

He gave the audience a smile, the private smile of someone who's about to share a secret. Sandra found herself immediately attracted to him.

"You folks ready for some blues . . . ?"

A spatter of applause.

The singer nodded, grinned, and raised one hand. The band kicked in with a rush of sound that was pure pleasure wrapped up in a C-seventh chord.

The club went wild.

It was going to be a good night, Sandra thought. She sipped her screwdriver as the Dusty Nickels thrummed into an old Muddy Waters song. She closed her eyes and let the music fill her. The lead singer's deep voice seemed to caress her with each word.

She knew it was time to get out there and dance.

Leaving her table, she was the first one to move underneath the lights illuminating the tiny dance floor. That was often the case. She didn't care one way or another what the rest of the crowd thought of her. She did this for herself, for her sense of self.

She was vaguely aware of others following her lead, more people joining her, moving to the music. One song led into another as she danced. Most of the time, she kept her eyes closed, opening them just often enough to keep from running into other dancers or into one of the tables surrounding the tiny, packed space. The music spoke to her even as the dancing healed the psychic abrasions of the day. She felt the freedom of movement and the gratifying coolness of her own sweat beading on her brow.

She bumped into someone, but refused to let the small collision break the spell. She apologized without looking up, and moved on.

But when she was bumped again, she opened her eyes and realized the man was intentionally trying to dance with her. He had dark skin, black eyes, and black hair, and was slightly shorter than she was. If she had to guess, she'd place him as coming from middle-eastern stock.

"Hello," the man said in a thick Arabic accent. His hot gaze undressed her. "My name is Omar. What is your—"

She frowned at him, stopped dancing, turned and walked off the floor, leaving him standing alone, his mouth open, looking foolish and hurt.

Sandra could tell he was angry, and she waited for the confrontation, feeling the muscles along her shoulders go tense. She'd decided not to look for anything, but if something came—well, that wouldn't be so bad, either. He wasn't a little redheaded street punk, but he would do.

The man locked his angry stare on her, but when she returned it steadily, he finally shrugged and turned away. He started dancing again, trying to act as if nothing had happened.

Her icy brush-off had been instinctive, and she immediately regretted it. Something about him had bothered her, but it wasn't anything she could put her finger on. Still, she'd been unnecessarily rude. She could have bowed out gracefully. No point in *looking* for trouble . . .

Because looking for trouble was stupid. Coming to a crowded bar and dancing alone always attracted attention, whether a woman wanted it or not. That wasn't fair, but it was the way the world worked. She sighed as she pushed her way in between two people at the bar and ordered another screwdriver.

She should probably apologize to the man. His fragile male ego had undoubtedly been wounded, and it wasn't as if he'd done anything wrong. Just bad timing. But apologizing to a man who hit on you was tantamount to saying you wanted him to try again. No, better to just let it drop. She gazed out into the crowd, but avoided looking at the dance floor.

She sipped her drink. Benny was right. Sometimes, she *was* crazy. Breathing slowly, she felt the alcohol begin to pull at her. One drink at home and two here so far. The lazy burn was suffusing her with a pleasant glow. She relaxed.

And she slipped into the game, the one she always played in a roomful of strangers. She'd begun to play it when she started training as a police officer, at first with conscious effort, then almost automatically. They taught classes at the academy on how to study people so that you could ID them easily afterwards, days, weeks, or even months later. She had learned how to put together spot psychological profiles on people simply by looking at them, watching them interact with others.

The process didn't always work, of course. Some people had elaborate social facades, facades that didn't reflect who they really were. But the game worked most of the time. Using such techniques, she could separate the dangerous from the harmless with some degree of certainty a few moments after entering a room. There were standard indicators of those who might use deadly force if given cause, who were just looking for an excuse to do so.

She focused on a heavy, balding man in one of the booths across the room from her. Smoky tendrils and moving people obscured his face from time to time, but Sandra kept an amused eye on him.

He seemed uncomfortable and fidgety. The lines on his doughy face indicated a low-burning worry, and her first impression was that he didn't really like the blues. He was here for another reason. Across from him sat a younger, attractive woman. Her wavy hair was teased and tied up at the crown of her head.

No, Sandra decided after a moment's study, she wasn't younger. She was just better kept. Even from across the hazy room, Sandra could see the experienced way the woman held herself, the careful motions of her hands as she talked to the fat man, and Sandra would bet that if she got much closer, the signs of repeated plastic surgery would be obvious. And they were married, she saw. Matching wedding rings. The wife liked blues, liked getting out. The husband didn't. The crowd, the noise, the situation made him uncomfortable—and he was trapped by his own appeasement of her, despising himself for it, maybe even despising her, but unable to help himself. He probably thought it was love.

Nasty . . .

A man in a black sports jacket caught her interest. He seemed like more of a blues lover than the fat man. His black clothing fit in with the ambience of this place. He wore dark sunglasses, mafiosi-style, though the room was about as bright as a coal cellar. She narrowed her eyes and wondered if he was as dangerous as he thought he was. He wore the clothes of a bad-ass . . .

No. It was a con. He was all surface, no substance. The curve at the corners of his mouth was too contrived. If a bar fight broke out, he would run in the opposite direction. Just then, he caught her gaze and gave her a come-on kind of smile.

She looked away.

There was a very serious-looking girl sitting at the booth in the corner. The girl was underage. God, people were strange. Tubby, hating himself over in the other booth, had a wife trying her damnedest to look twenty-one, while the girl in the corner tried hard to look a jaded, cynical forty.

The beat from the stage shifted as the band swung into a new number. As Sandra turned to look, something shifted in the deep shadows behind the last booth, a flicker of motion that tugged at the corner of her eye.

She caught herself, forced herself not to turn, not to spook him. It was hard to see in the smoke-filled murk, but yes. There it was. No doubt. The swirling edge of a coat, moving as he turned to stare at her. A very familiar trench coat.

She set her drink down on the bar, hitting the scarred surface too hard and sloshing the dregs of her drink onto the lacquered wood. He seemed to sense her sudden attention, because he turned suddenly away, fading back into the crowd. But not before she had seen the pimples, the freckles, and the red hair. It was him.

The redhead was here. He'd followed her, and she hadn't noticed him. How had he done that? She looked for him again, but he'd vanished. Fronds of some plant blocked part of her view.

He knows I'm a cop, she thought uneasily. *Punks don't follow cops around. Not unless they're psycho. Or they want something . . .*

Unconsciously her fingers traced the heavy shape of the pistol in her purse. She pushed away from the bar and headed toward the spot where he'd been standing.

Okay, you found me, scumbucket. Now what?

I came to dance. So, punk, let's you and me dance . . .

eleven

She picked her way slowly toward the spot where she'd seen him, but he was gone. Then, amazingly, she spotted him again, further back in the shadows, trying to blend in with a dusty thicket of fake shrubbery.

Maybe he didn't know she'd spotted him. And her first hot surge of anger was subsiding. Her fingers moved against the weight of the pistol concealed in her purse. What was she thinking? A scrawny doper kid. What was she gonna do, shoot him?

No, but talking to him seemed like a good idea. Although so far he hadn't seemed to want to talk, not after the first encounter. So go slow, get right up on him before . . .

"Hello."

As keyed up as she was, she nearly shot him.

"I'm sorry. Did I startle you?"

She turned and found herself staring up into dark, shadowed eyes. *Blue eyes,* she thought at once, though how she could tell, she didn't quite know. They were deeply set in an aristocratic face, compelling and vibrant even in the club's dim light. The man's long, straight nose gave a fox-like aspect to his face, but his strong jaw squared it off nicely. He wore a loose black silk shirt, open at the throat, and well-cut jeans. She thought she saw the glimmer of a silver chain around his neck, but she couldn't be sure.

"I didn't mean to." His voice was mild, deep, and bore a distinct English accent.

"No, no. I'm fine." She realized she was still clutching her purse like a weapon, and forced herself to relax.

She found herself smiling at him, almost against her will.

At any other point in her life, he was exactly the sort of man who would interest her, but not tonight. She was tempted to ignore him, or maybe tell him to go away, but—those eyes!

"Hi," she said, not sure exactly where she wanted to go from there.

"I'm sorry to bother you, but I believe I know you."

"Is that so?" She raised one eyebrow, trying for studied indifference—and knowing that she failed.

"Indeed." The man had not moved to take a place beside her at the bar, as someone looking to hit on her might. Instead, he stood across from her, just far enough away to avoid making her uncomfortable, but close enough that she could feel the heat from his body, catch a subtle scent of some expensive men's fragrance. He radiated calm assurance. No matter where he stood, it was a completely natural place for him to be. The polite brush-off she'd intended to give him froze in her throat.

"Really? Where from?" She was becoming interested in him almost against her better judgment.

"I realize that this sounds like the oldest pick-up line in the world, but allow me a moment to explain."

Sandra smiled, despite herself. "Okay." She relaxed a bit.

"You like games, don't you?"

She watched his eyes, and said, "*Not* really."

"Of course, you do. All detectives like games. Otherwise they wouldn't be detectives."

She felt uneasy. A chill ran up her spine and her eyes narrowed. How this man knew her, she had no idea. She'd never met him before in her life, she was sure of that. He was good-looking enough that she would have remembered him.

Yet she sensed this was not some Don Juan who liked to play games with people's heads. She felt no smug superiority in the man, no selfish lust hidden beneath a slick surface. Instead, what she sensed from his eyes was . . . a challenge. Not one which would drag her into danger, but the kind normally issued between the best of friends.

He wanted her to run. He wanted her to back out of the situation. He seemed to expect it.

She was no longer frightened. She was intrigued.

She glanced toward where the redhead had been trying out his potted plant imitation. But the kid was gone. She felt an odd flash of relief. So much for that, then.

"You must spend a great deal of time around detectives, if you know them so well," she said, looking up at him.

"Not actually. You can divine a great deal from a person in short order if you know what to look for. Don't you agree?"

She thought about the game she'd just been playing in her own mind, about the fat man and his wife, about the fake mafioso. "Maybe. In a way. So what else have you *divined* about me?" He was well-educated, Sandra decided. She didn't know many people who used the word *divined* in conversation.

"Gaining your confidence is a difficult thing, I'd guess. I wager that the faster I play my trump cards, the better chance I have of continuing this conversation."

Sandra smiled. "You could be right."

"Shall we proceed to the game, then?" he asked, raising an eyebrow. "Here is the problem: tell me how I know you."

"How many questions do I get?" she asked.

"That is a question in and of itself."

"Excuse me?"

"How many questions do you require?"

"Three questions," she decided. "What about time limits?"

"Again, restrict yourself by your own judgment." He smiled. His blue eyes twinkled.

"It shouldn't take long. Give me a moment to decide on my questions." Sandra stared at him, tried her damnedest to find a place for him in her memory. Nothing surfaced. Okay, she'd have to do it the hard way. She paused for a moment, tracking down possibilities. Finally, she said, "Are you related to, a friend of, or in any way connected to Law McKenzie?"

"No. And may I point out that you have just asked three questions?"

"Not true. It was a single sentence. You've seen me working a case. That's how you knew I was a detective."

"Yes."

She nodded and sipped her drink.

His eyebrow raised. "You seem satisfied."

"I am."

"And your deduction?"

"You live in the same building as Jack Madrone."

He shook his head, looked disappointed. "No."

"Then you were visiting. Either way, you were in the crowd clustered in the hallway."

"Indeed. I'm impressed, truly. How did you decide upon that?"

"I have an almost photographic memory for faces, so I knew I couldn't have met you. Which means you saw me, but I didn't see you. Also, you knew I was a detective. So I had only two lines of possible inquiry, really. Either you know me through someone who knows me, or you've seen me at a crime scene."

"Very well then. How is it that you knew I had seen you at only one crime scene? I'm certain you've been to quite a few more than one. You are a detective, after all."

She nodded. "Well, the fact that you recognized me at all pretty much nailed the crime scene down for me."

He shook his head. "I'm afraid I don't understand."

She smiled. "For most of my adult life, up until a few weeks ago, I was a blonde."

He laughed.

"I dyed my hair in college to try a different look. It seemed to suit me. I wore it for years. Recently I decided I wanted my natural color back, so I dyed my hair brown again."

"I see, and you've only had one major case between your visit to the beauty parlor and now?"

"No." She shook her head. "But the other crime scenes didn't attract a crowd."

"Bravo."

Sandra thought for a moment, then grinned. "You want a drink?" She tipped her head to the space beside her at the bar. "I'll buy."

"Of course, you would, wouldn't you?" he said. "A modern independent woman. Allow me this, then. I accept on the condition that I buy the next round."

"You assume there's going to be a next round."

"I can always hope."

She was flattered. He was certainly the most attractive man she'd met in months. Years. "What's your name?" she asked.

"Justin. And yours?"

"Well, I'm surprised. You don't know?"

"I may have heard something, but somehow I don't really think your name is Bruce, Detective McCormick."

"Huh. You heard Mac."

He nodded, an oddly formal gesture, but somehow endearing.

"He calls me that. But I'm Sandra." She offered him her hand and he took it, brought it to his lips. His lips were warm, and she enjoyed the sensation despite herself. "Cute," she said, "but a little old-fashioned. I'm a modern woman, remember?"

He shrugged. "Certain customs should never die." He ordered Glenfiddich on the rocks.

"What do you do, Justin?"

"I own a nightclub here in the city."

"Are you casing the competition?"

"Hardly. I enjoy the blues. One doesn't want to spend every night within one's own house."

"What's the name of the club?"

"Gwendolyne's Flight."

She whistled softly, recognizing the name.

The music ceased thrumming through the bar for a moment as the band closed their second set. The dance floor emptied out. The sound system kicked in with the siren call of a Duke Ellington riff.

"So tell me, Justin," she said, "What are you doing here? Don't you have responsibilities back at your own place?"

"At times, certainly," Justin said, "but I'm careful about who I hire, and business is good enough that I can afford to hire the best. The sort of managers who operate better when the boss is gone."

"Are you planning on leaving?" Sandra asked.

"Not permanently, but I like to travel, and I don't like to be tethered to my business. What's the point of living if you aren't free to enjoy it to the fullest?"

"Are you a rover, then?"

"I used to be. I've seen every corner of the world and lived to tell the tale."

"But going places is not your full-time avocation these days?"

"No. I have roots here in Chicago."

"A rolling stone with roots?"

He laughed and Sandra smiled. Ever since her marriage had turned into a waking nightmare, she'd lost her ease with men. But even under these circumstances—the redheaded kid and her recent inexplicable paranoia about being stalked by something—talking with Justin felt natural, like he was an old friend. She wondered what it would be like to spend time with him when she wasn't feeling half-crazed.

Still, the more they talked, the more they talked about. Perhaps it was the alcohol, or just the unique perspective Justin seemed to have on everything, but Sandra found herself enjoying his company. He talked a great deal about England. He'd only been in the U.S. three years or so. He admitted to parents with old money, but said he had been something of a rebel when he was young. He had run away from home and played in a punk band in his teens, then worked as a bouncer at a tough club in London before he'd reconciled with his parents as an adult. He also told her how glad he was that he'd made his peace with them then—his parents had died in a car accident five years ago. He still missed them. But he'd been spared the guilt of losing them without ever apologizing for the things he did as a wild kid.

At first, Sandra stayed close-lipped about her own

life, but as Justin offered more and more, never pushing for details from her, she began to loosen up. She talked a little bit about what she did as a detective. She could tell he was intensely curious about that, but she usually shied away from that topic. It surprised her that the words came so easily. She was surprised to find that she really did want to tell him what her life was like. Wanted him to understand.

"I can't talk about current cases, except in generalities. I will tell you this, though. That case where you saw me—it's the weirdest fucking thing I've ever worked on."

"That's a broad term, especially for Chicago. What constitutes 'weird' to a big city cop?" Justin asked.

"Let me put it this way. It's got everything you'd want for a *Twilight Zone* episode, up to and possibly including dragons." She smiled a bit as she pictured the strange scale in her mind. No one had been able to classify it yet. Dragons were as likely a supposition as anything anybody had managed to come up with so far.

Justin's eyebrows lifted in surprise. "Dragons? That's a new twist on big city crime. Do you like dragons?"

"Don't know many dragons." Sandra sipped her drink—maybe it was time to switch to straight orange juice. She was talking too much.

"I was enamored of them as a child." Justin said, "Perhaps it's an English thing. I knew more about dragons by the time I was twelve than a literature professor knows about Shakespeare."

"How odd. Did you seek help?"

"I got better."

They ordered another round and as Sandra began sipping her new drink, this time OJ straight up, she studied Justin. Silence hung between them. Neither felt the need to fill it immediately, but finally Sandra spoke. "So I think it's time I turned your game on you."

"Is it?"

"Indeed." She affected his English accent. "I know how you got my name. So let's try something a little more difficult. Using the data you have so far, what else can you deduce about me?"

"I feel outmatched. I don't do this for a living."

"Try anyway."

"Right. Very well, then. You are a detective. I would guess you've been one for a while, but . . ."

"But?"

"This was not your first career choice. I would wager that your decision to go into law enforcement came about through something which happened in your life. You seem to regard crime as a personal affront."

She smiled. "Not bad."

"You are a detective out of a need to impose justice, not out of a sense of vocation." He paused. "I have a question for you, if I may break the bounds of the game for a moment."

"Maybe," she replied. "I don't promise to answer it."

"If you were a criminal, what crime would you commit?"

She pursed her lips. "Not as tough a question for me to answer as you might think. Definitely—"

Something besides small talk captured Sandra's attention, and her words trailed off into silence. Through the smoke and milling crowds of people, she saw the redhead in the trench coat moving toward the door. He paused and looked right at her, inclining his head toward the exit.

"You want to do me a favor?" she said to Justin, but never taking her eyes off the kid in the trench coat.

"Certainly," Justin said. He craned his neck to see what she was looking at.

"See that guy by the door?"

He narrowed his eyes. "Yes. Red hair?"

"Yeah. He's been following me."

"Would you like me to confront him?"

"Get your head out of the fourteenth century, Justin." Justin choked on his drink and almost dropped it. He looked at her, startled.

"What did you say?"

"I said get your head out of the fourteenth century." Sandra took her attention off the punk long enough to give Justin a wry, mocking look. "I'm a modern girl, remember? And I'm a cop. If he needs confronting, I'll handle it."

"Yes. Of course." Justin turned back to look at the trench coat-clad punk, but there was a tension in him that had not been there before.

Slowly and reluctantly, because she was curious about Justin's reaction to her offhand comment, Sandra returned her attention to the redhead. The kid motioned toward the door again. Sandra nodded, still speaking to Justin. "Look, I do want to talk to him, but I will ask your help for something."

"Is he a criminal?"

"Maybe."

Justin nodded. "Very well. I'll be happy to help, Officer."

"After I've left the room with him, you go to the phone. You can see out the front window from the phone by the bar. I'll try to stay in view. If anything bad happens or if I get out of your line of sight, dial 911."

"Is it that serious?"

"I don't know." She flashed him a smile.

"As you say."

"Good."

Sandra moved away from the bar and crossed the room. The redhead saw her coming and left the bar. Sandra followed.

When she walked outside, she found him leaning against the wall of the building, looking out at the street. His stained green trench coat made him look like a refugee from a Mickey Spillane novel. His face was shrouded in shadow.

Sandra checked the bar's front window. She thought she could see Justin by the phone, but the window was dark and smudged, and it was hard to tell.

"C'mon." The redhead pointed toward the mouth of an alley some twenty feet distant.

"Right here is fine," Sandra said. She stepped closer. "What's your name, pal?"

He shrank back. "It's uh . . . Maxie. Look, I don't like talking in the middle of the street—"

"And I don't like walking into a dark alley with some asshole who jumped me once already."

The redhead snorted. "I didn't jump you! You were going to haul me in. Then you got in the way when I tried to run."

"What I need now, asshole, is a reason not to bust your ass right here."

He twitched, looked over his shoulder, looked back at her. "Get off your high horse, lady. I'm tryin' to help you."

"So stop with the bullshit and help me. You got something to say, spit it out."

This kid was right on the edge of withdrawal. Quivering and jittering, a thin trail of snot leaking from one nostril, pupils the size of nail heads.

But he'd wanted to talk to her enough to forego his high. That, for a junkie, meant it was important. And he was coming on like a C.I.—a confidential informant. A snitch. But how had he found who she was in the first place?

"Christ, Madrone was never this hard to deal with."

Madrone. Finally, it began to make a little sense.

"You sing for Madrone?" Sandra asked.

"Yeah."

"What about?"

"The demon. I heard the demon bragging."

"The *demon* ?"

Christ. Little fucker was hallucinating on her.

He caught her sudden withdrawal. "Okay, okay," he sputtered hastily, "maybe he's not a demon. He's just the demon's little dude or something. But, like, see, I told Madrone about this guy at the bar who killed the lawyer."

"Hey, whoa, hold on. What bar?" Sandra asked. "Which lawyer?"

"That lawyer guy on TV who took on that gang even though they shot up his car. So I talk to Madrone, and all of a sudden he gets his heart fucking ripped out." The redhead's wild eyes whipped around, looking over his shoulder again. He glanced over at the bar window nervously. "And I wonder if it might be me next, so I think I need a hundred bucks before I tell you any more."

"Lemme get this straight," she said. "You snitched off somebody to Madrone on the Wheeler murder?"

"Yeah, I already told you. You want more, the toll's a big buck. Like I just said."

She thought about it. "I don't have a hundred on me. You take a personal check?"

"What do I look like, Bank of America?"

She rummaged in her purse. "How about twenty?" She waved the crumpled bill under his nose.

He snorted. "You don't know a good thing when it's looking you in the face, bitch. I'm outta here." He put his hand on her shoulder to push past her. Sandra caught his wrist and pulled. She slammed him into the brick wall just beside the window. He shouted and tried to free himself, but she twisted his wrist into a joint lock and he finally stopped struggling. Just for good measure, Sandra gave another small twist. One way or another, this punk had managed to ruin her whole day, and it was time for a little payback.

The redhead started running through an unimaginative litany of street language in a low, desolate croak.

Sandra put her lips up to his ear. "Don't cop that shit with me, butt-boy. You came here to talk, so talk. If your stuff pans out, we'll talk money. But not until."

"All right! Okay! Back off, all right?"

Sandra let him go and stepped back. The kid grunted as he massaged the feeling back into his arm and shoulder. She watched dispassionately.

"That hurt, dammit!" he said.

"So you heard a guy at a bar talking about killing Carlton Wheeler," Sandra said. "And then . . . ?"

"Yeah. That's right," the redhead said in a surly tone. "That's what I heard."

"And you dropped a dime to Madrone."

The kid nodded.

"So who was this guy? What bar was he in?"

Sandra heard a door open behind her, but she kept her eyes on the redhead. The kid stared at whoever was coming out of the door. She could practically see the blood drain out of his face as the shock set in. The redhead sucked in a sharp breath. His face bleached out to the color of rancid cottage cheese.

"Jesus!"

Sandra spun around. The Arab guy who had tried to dance with her earlier stood looking at her.

The sound of footsteps on the pavement yanked her attention back to the redhead. He was already halfway to the end of the street.

"Shit!" Sandra said, sparing one questioning glance

back at the middle-eastern man before she took off after the kid. He was still watching her. Almost as if he *knew* her.

But he could wait.

As she ran, she heard the bar door crash open. She looked back. Justin was barreling out of the door, shoving the middle-eastern man roughly aside and joining the chase.

Fine. Galahad to her rescue. She just hoped he'd called the police first. *Men!*

The kid was fast, fueled by panic and withdrawal. But so was she. And this time, he didn't have a three-block head start. She raced down the sidewalk after him, gaining on him with every step. He was wearing combat boots. She knew from experience that it was tough to get into a sprint wearing kicks like that.

Red turned the first corner he came to, heading toward Grant Park and the shore of Lake Michigan, his trench coat flapping around his calves. Sandra followed, with Justin close behind her. Car headlights illuminated Red's running form. People moved hastily out of their way, staring curiously at the oddly mixed trio pounding past them. Red shot a glance over his shoulder and seemed surprised that she was so close. Bending his head, he tried to pour on the speed.

When Sandra was nearly within tackling distance, the kid veered sharply off the sidewalk and into moving traffic. Tires shrieked and horns blared. Sandra hesitated. She wanted him, but not enough to die for it. A blue Toyota swerved and slammed on its brakes, just missing the kid. He made it safely to the other side and bounded up on the walk.

"No way. I'm not letting you go now," she growled, and dived into the swirling traffic after him.

"Sandra!" Justin cried. A small truck roared by her so close she could feel its fender brush her leg. Screeches and honks filled her ears. Then she was on the other side of the street, and she could still see her quarry. He was leaning against a wall a block away, trying to gulp down enough oxygen to supply his racing heart. As soon as their gazes met, he turned and took off like a damned deer. Sandra was about to follow when she heard tires screeching and a horrible thump behind her. She spun around to see Justin pitched forward, slumped over a parked car.

Damn it!

Civilians!

Sandra glared at Red, dashing down the street, fading in the distance.

Feeling horribly responsible, she hurried back to Justin. The car that hit him had stopped and the shaken driver was getting out. The car's front right fender was crumpled. Sandra could only imagine what Justin would look like.

When she reached him, she expected to find pools of blood, compound multiple fractures, a crushed skull. Instead, Justin was levering himself to his feet, leaning against the parked convertible he'd landed on. The corners of his eyes were wrinkled in pain, but he was moving well, and when he looked up at her, she could tell he was not seriously injured.

Oddly enough, he seemed angry at her.

"Don't worry about me. I'm fine."

"You just got hit by a car!"

"So? Go on after him. I'll catch up!"

Sandra turned and ran after the kid. It would have been hopeless, except that he was a strung-out junkie, not a marathon runner. He had to pause every so often to double over and catch his breath. He was actually puking when she finally caught up with him.

He ducked into an alley and she followed him. Trash cans created an obstacle course for the two of them, but she closed the distance quickly. The end of the alley was near. She could see lights and hear the sounds of traffic from the next street over.

Again, Red surprised her. As she reached out to grab the tail of his fluttering trench coat, he turned and pulled a trash can over, sent it rolling.

The can crashed into her legs. She tumbled. She tried to turn her fall into a roll, but her body slammed hard onto the blacktop. Instead of rolling, she and the trash can ended in a painful tangle against one wall of the alley.

With a grunt, she managed to crawl to her knees in time to see Red jump on the back of a garbage truck that was just pulling out into traffic and speeding up. The kid even had the nerve to wave good-bye.

"Son of a bitch!" she snarled as she hauled herself to her feet and began to walk back to the street. A passing pedestrian gave her a startled look.

Justin came hobbling up behind her.

"What happened? Did he get away?" he asked. With

that British accent he sounded like a refugee from the Royal Shakespeare Company.

A sudden thought struck her. She started to laugh.

He looked puzzled. "Well? What?"

"Did you see that kid hop on that trash truck? Can you think of a more fitting getaway vehicle for the little asshole? Garbage for garbage?"

Her smile was infectious, even though he still seemed confused.

"I see," he replied. "Did you hit your head very hard?"

"No." She patted him on the shoulder as she leaned back against the wall. "I can't believe it. Man, I was so close. So damned close."

Justin nodded, pulled a pack of cigarettes from his pocket, and whacked it against his palm. He offered one to her.

She looked at it and shook her head. "I don't smoke anymore."

"Ah, yes. Quite understandable. Cancer and all that. You're a modern woman." He paused for the length of a heartbeat, then, "Cigarette?" He offered the pack to her again.

She looked up into his blue eyes and shrugged. "You're too much for me. Sure, why not?" She slid a cigarette out of the packet and held it to her lips. He pulled out what appeared to be a solid gold Dunhill lighter and held the flame under the tip of her cigarette. She inhaled. The smoke flowed into her lungs in that old familiar way. She leaned against the wall and relaxed. Her knees and elbows hurt where she'd skinned them hitting the ground. She grimaced as she finally got a good look at herself. Nothing she had on would be fit to wear again, between the rips and the stains. She took another drag on the cigarette.

"Nasty habit," she said.

"Undeniably." He lit up and puffed. "Strangely appropriate for moments such as this, though, don't you think?"

She smiled and leaned back against the wall. He was right. She couldn't deny it.

A moment later the nicotine buzz hit her and the world became pleasantly fuzzy. The insistent pain from her scraped skin receded to a distant hum.

"I'd forgotten what these things do to anybody who doesn't smoke them regularly."

"Ah, yes. Nicotine has quite a kick in isolated doses."

She nodded. Someone shouted at someone else down the street. A passing cab hit a puddle and sprayed a crowd of tourists on their way to the Buckingham Fountain. Sandra couldn't believe she was enjoying standing on State Street on a rainy night in the heart of downtown Chicago. But she was.

"Did you call the police?" she suddenly thought to ask him.

He shook his head. "I apologize. I saw you disappear from the window and my first reaction was to run to help you. All due to my head being stuck in the fourteenth century, I'm sure."

Sandra laughed. "Ahhh, it's for the best. The backup would never have arrived in time to do any good. He'd still have gotten away."

She let the matter drop. She wondered if Madrone's files would have anything on where the kid hung out, where he could be reached. Cops were supposed to write up their snitches, but a lot of them didn't.

She let the city noises and the company soothe her. The chill of the night air was cool on her skin, a pleasant sensation after her run.

"So," Justin said, "I had just asked you a question when you took off."

"You had? Ah, yes. I remember," she said. "Sorry about that."

"You said you knew which crime you'd commit. Which crime would that be?"

"Murder," she said.

He looked startled.

"It goes all the way back to Cain killing Abel. Murder is the oldest crime in the world. I believe everyone is capable of murder. And I've seen enough grief caused by evil men that I know some people need killing. Even people who don't need killing can make you mad enough to want to kill them. You should've seen me with that redhead back there, when he banged me around earlier today, I wanted to rip out his throat and make him eat it."

She paused, startled at her own vehemence.

Justin frowned. "It's your crime to choose, of course, but murder isn't the oldest of crimes."

"No?" she asked.

"Certainly not. Curiosity is the oldest crime. Eve ate the apple long before she had children."

Sandra considered that. "Perhaps. If it was a crime."

"You don't agree with the old tale?"

"I just don't consider curiosity a crime. Or a sin."

"Of course, you don't," he said. "But curiosity is your primary weakness. Like Dr. Faust, hungry for knowledge, you go out and stir up who knows what kind of trouble as you seek your answers. You could have been killed tonight, you know, and I could have been, too, as a result of your actions. I believe you would sell your soul to get all the killers in Chicago."

She shrugged. "Maybe. Catch them or convict them?"

"Bring them to justice. To whatever you call justice, in your own heart."

She took another drag of the cigarette. "Yeah. You got me there. But make a deal with the devil for it? Tempting, I have to admit. But I don't think so. There'd have to be another way."

"What do you mean?"

"Deals with the devil always backfire. I'd rather depend on my own resources. If you want something done right, you have to do it yourself."

"I must disagree with you there. One can always do business with the devil, provided one is willing to pay his price."

"I don't buy it. The world doesn't really work on credit."

"Certainly it does. Look around you. Our society is built upon credit—and credit, at bottom, is nothing more than trust."

"Trust. You should try my job for a while. You wouldn't trust anybody. And you'd be a fool if you did."

"Doomsayers go to their graves unrequited."

"Cute. Did you make that up?"

"I don't remember," he said. He had a brooding, shadowed look, as if he didn't much relish the direction the conversation had taken.

"I'm a cop," she told him. "I've seen too much to ever believe that you can sell your soul and get it back. Nobody ever comes out of a deal with the devil unscathed," she mused. "Ask the scumbags I deal with every day. Ask them if it was worth it—at the end of ends, they'll tell you their lives would've been better if they'd never made the deal at all."

"Not necessarily," Justin countered. "If they chose well, if they chose something truly wonderful, how could they possibly regret it? Don't you think any misery the devil visits upon them afterward could be worth it? Wouldn't you sacrifice your own life, for instance, to achieve goodness worldwide?"

"You're asking if I'd sell my soul for peace on earth? Sure I would. In a minute. But the devil is too careful, too clever for that. There's always a wicked catch in the offer. Look, there are no free lunches. The devil is the lord of lies. Perhaps he doesn't even have the power to fulfill the deals he makes, only the power to create the illusion of fulfillment. Besides, I don't think even God could wave a wand and have peace on earth. People have free will. God could lay peace wrapped in a big, red bow at the feet of humanity, but we'd screw it up before we even had the box unwrapped. It's our nature. It's *human* nature, if you know what I mean."

"Ah, so it's not the devil you fear, but yourself. You think humanity is irredeemable? That from the moment Cain raised his hand against his brother, we've never been able to stop the violence, the killing?"

"No. Not at all. I know some people can live in peace. That's what *civilized* really means. People living together and not letting the dark urges in our hearts get the better of us. I just don't think all people can live in peace. The ability to keep my blood lust in check is what separates me from the murderers I hunt. I may feel like killing ten times a day. But I control those urges. I wanted to kill that redhead, but I didn't do it."

"So you never follow your urges?"

"No, I wouldn't say that. But I believe in fairness and justice. I strive to find them and give them to those around me, and I don't let my urges push me off that path. Civilized people don't."

"So far I've heard you profess to believe in a devil, but what about the side of the angels? That's a little hazier."

She shrugged. "I try to believe in God. I would like to believe in him, but I need proof. And I've never seen real proof—the kind you can touch and feel and smell. I have questions about the nature of God that have never been answered to my satisfaction. I go to St. Joseph's Cathedral sometimes, to think. I usually feel better when I leave than when I went in. It just feels right that I should ponder important questions in a place like that. I'm not sure why. Maybe it's because God actually is there. I don't know."

Sandra took a last drag on her cigarette and tossed the butt into a nearby trash can. It gave a sharp spit as it hit the puddle at the bottom of the can. Justin offered her another, but she declined. It suddenly occurred to her that they had been talking like two people who already knew each other well and wanted to know each other better. And she hadn't batted an eyelash. She probably should be worried about it, but she wasn't.

"If my primary sin is curiosity, then I think yours is melancholy, Justin," she said. "The more I know about you, the more I see this huge dark cloud hanging over you. You do put up a good act, though."

She turned to look at him and found his gaze fixed on the pavement, his brow furrowed. Sandra winced, wondering if she had crossed some unseen line.

"You've caught me." He seemed reluctant to speak, but then continued anyway. "I've made choices in my life that I often regret. You remind me of someone who was once very dear to me."

Sandra raised an eyebrow, "Is that why you picked me out to hit on?"

He shook his head, smiling, "No. I hit on you because I like the way you dance, actually."

"Good, so do I." She paused. "Who is she, this person I remind you of?"

"My late wife."

Sandra whistled. "Hey, I didn't mean to step on a tender spot. Let's just—"

"No, it's all right," he said. "I lost her a long time

ago. The pain is an old friend by now. A habit as much as anything else. Some of the things you do remind me of her."

"Were you together long?" she asked.

"For centuries, it seems."

Despite his assurances, Sandra felt she had stepped over some line, into forbidden territory. She decided it was time to change the subject.

"So how'd you end up in Chicago?" she asked. "You'll never pass for a native here, you know."

He flashed a relieved smile. "Would you believe I liked the look of Wrigley Field?"

She looked dubious. "You look more like a polo aficionado to me."

She paused. "I'm cold," she said, rubbing her arms. The scrapes on her shoulder and her elbow were beginning to sting again. "And we should probably get you to a hospital for a few X rays. I'm pretty sure you're fine, but you'll want some baseline stuff for the insurance company in case you wake up in agony tomorrow. And who knows—maybe the police are looking for you. I could fix all that while we're at the hospital."

"I'm fine, really. Barely a scratch. And I could afford to buy the hospital, so I won't need to bother the insurance company. As for the police, well . . ." He grinned at her. "As you say, I already have a connection with the police. Or do I?"

She grinned in return. "Maybe . . ."

They headed for the street. Justin hailed a cab. It stopped by the curb. He held out a hand in invitation as he got into it.

"I've enjoyed our adventures tonight. Come with me, and let's see if we can continue them."

Sandra paused before replying, sorely tempted. Since her marriage, she'd been almost entirely celibate, only occasionally soothing her urges with the odd one-night stand. After Chuck's abuse, she'd never been able to trust a man enough to think about a relationship

And the age of AIDS had made those one-night stands even more dangerous than they used to be. She'd be a fool to take this man up on his offer, no matter how much she liked him.

On the other hand . . . those *eyes*!

She took his hand, stooped, and slid into the taxi next to him.

"Where are we going?" she asked.

"We'll figure that out on the way," he said.

twelve

Sandra slid to the edge of the bed. The air in the room felt cold on her bare skin as she slipped out from under the covers. She stood up slowly so as not to disturb the sleeping man beside her, and her feet sank into the plush carpet. The room smelled like every other hotel room she'd ever been in. Impersonal. Neutral ground.

Sandra had not wanted to take Justin back to her place. She had no desire to listen to Benny give Justin the third degree, which he'd certainly do if given the opportunity. Although he meant well, Benny considered it his right, both as her brother and her friend, to screen her male acquaintances.

Justin, for his part, had said he would rather not return to his home. He'd told her that it was above the club, and he knew if he went back, he'd undoubtedly have to check in on things downstairs and wouldn't come back for hours. It was, he said, one of the joys and hazards of owning a business.

He had suggested he splurge on a luxurious compromise, and so here they were.

The room had that sumptuous feel the best hotels strive for. True to his suggestion, Justin had arranged for a beautiful suite in the gorgeously restored Conrad Hilton on Michigan Avenue, overlooking Lake Michigan.

They'd checked in, and for a few short hours Sandra had forgotten all about her troubles—the kid, the murders, her paranoia about something following her, her nightmares. All she'd thought about was Justin: the texture of his skin, the way his expressions flitted across his face, the gleam in his blue eyes, the way his hands felt on her body, the way he made her feel when he touched her just so . . .

Her skin tingled in the cool air. She could feel the pull and twinge in seldom-used muscles as she walked across the room. It had been an evening to remember in more ways than one. Justin had made her feel cherished, adored, and—finally—wild for him. She'd forgotten everything, even her own name, in the resulting rush of pleasure.

But now she was scared.

It had been too good. The perfection of the night frightened her. She needed her mind clear to solve the murders she was investigating. She needed to be a cop first, a woman second, until she had the killer behind bars. She needed her emotions under control and her energies focused. She simply couldn't afford to fall head over heels for an English aristocrat, no matter how charismatic he was or how fabulous he was in the sack.

If this night had been a casual one-night stand, forgotten almost before it was begun, it would be different. And that had certainly been what she'd planned when she'd gotten into the cab with Justin. But it had very quickly become something else, a soul mates-finding-each-other bonding experience that had her scared to death.

Maybe she should've accepted the other man's advances—that middle-eastern guy had clearly wanted to jump her bones. She was sure she could've screwed him and dumped him without a second thought.

Since Chuck had nearly destroyed her, she had made a semiannual habit out of one-night stands. She was no longer the trusting fool who'd married a handsome monster with love in her heart and stars in her eyes. She didn't think she could trust a man enough to have a long-term relationship. Not after Chuck.

She'd learned the hard way that the law and social mores didn't adequately protect her if something went wrong between a man and a woman. All the restraining orders in the world couldn't keep a man out of her life if he was determined to destroy her. Right up until the situation between her and Chuck had escalated into assault and attempted murder, and even after that, the law couldn't—hadn't—done a thing to help her. Not until she'd had witnesses and proof. Now she was a cop. In a way, she understood. But it still sucked. And it probably had a lot to do with why she'd *become* a cop.

Still, just because she felt unable to have a successful relationship with a man didn't mean that she didn't like sex. Until it had become as abusive as the rest of their marriage, she'd always enjoyed the physical aspect of her life with her husband. And she'd discovered that she still needed the kind of release only sex with a man could give her. As dangerous as it was—and because she was a cop, she knew exactly how dangerous it could be—she would still, once or twice a year, go out looking for Mr. Goodbar. She figured she did it to prove to herself that she was still a sexual being, that Chuck hadn't taken that away from her along with everything else.

Tonight had been one of those nights when she needed a man, any man. And Justin had been handy.

But somewhere during the velvet depths of the night it had turned into something much more complicated.

She turned and looked down at Justin. His black hair was spread out over the pillow, gleaming like a raven's wing in the dim light. She liked him. Really liked him.

But she was afraid she might feel even more for him, certainly as she came to know him better. Maybe this warmth in her heart had ignited the moment he'd rushed out into traffic after her—like the name of that old Joe Cocker group, Mad Dogs and Englishmen. Maybe it was the way he'd understood her longing for a cigarette to help her get through what had happened, or the way he seemed to know her so well even though they'd barely met. Maybe it was the fact that he talked interestingly about so many subjects, and actually listened to her replies. But however it had come to happen, she knew that she really liked him.

She looked at him again, sleeping quietly on the far side of the huge, canopied bed. Part of her wanted to snuggle up beside him, to sleep through till morning and wake up in his arms in that glorious bed. But she could not allow that. She had a job to do—one he would get in the way of if she let him into her life in any real way. And, more importantly, she had no intention of giving her soul to a man again.

Never, never again.

Chuck had destroyed any hope of that forever.

She found her clothes and her possessions, scattered in passion scant hours before. She slipped the garments on, most of them, though they were sadly the worse for wear, and picked up her purse. She left her underthings behind—they'd been torn past the point of usefulness in their first breathless rush of passion. She hoped those scraps of silk were all she was leaving behind.

But she feared she'd lost something much more precious than a few shreds of clothing to Justin. She was desperately afraid that, somewhere down there in the tangle of clothing and pillows on the plush carpeting, she was leaving behind a big piece of her heart.

She tried not to think about it. Whatever she feared had happened last night, it was over now. It would end right here, right now. She would see to it.

Pausing one last moment beside Justin's sleeping form, Sandra watched his chest rise and fall with his breathing, the way his eyelashes fanned out over his cheekbones, so long and thick they almost appeared to be fake. She wanted to touch him, kiss him. She shook her head. After all she'd been through, you'd think she'd have learned. Men were predators, and women their preferred prey. Even the best of them expected the house to be clean, the meals to be on the table, and the shopping to be done while they were off doing manly things. The worst of them would kill or maim at the slightest excuse. *Use them or they will use you,* she thought. *Nothing good can come of this.*

She turned and fled the room.

Home at last, Sandra emptied her pockets onto her dresser in the first faint blush of morning. She thought about turning on a lamp but left it off. The darkness was comfortable.

She felt like the weight of the world was on her shoulders. Her stomach was queasy and her head hurt, the alcohol and nicotine chasing each other in a painful relay through her body.

She had gone out seeking clarity. Instead, she'd indulged in a wonderful distraction that was likely to cause her more pain than it was worth.

Frowning, she decided she wouldn't let it get to her. She had too much at stake to fall apart over a man.

Unbuttoning her blouse, she started digging through her closet for something new to wear. She tossed the ruined blouse on the floor.

Think of the case, she told herself. She'd been so close to catching that snitch last night . . . *damn it!*

If he wasn't bullshitting her, maybe he knew the man who had killed Carlton Wheeler, and possibly killed Madrone, too. At the very least, he could've provided new leads.

But Red was crazy skittish, even though he'd gone out of his way to talk to her. The moment that Omar guy had stepped outside the bar, Red had bolted like he'd seen a ghost.

As she finished stripping off her clothes, Sandra drew in a deep breath. Justin's scent clung to her, mingled with her own, making it hard for her to concentrate on anything else. She should take a shower, but she was exhausted, and she had to go to work in a few hours. She'd rather spend the time sleeping, if she could.

She really should go to bed, but her mind was restless, unsettled. Resting her fingertips lightly on the window, she leaned in, put her forehead against the glass, looked down. It was a trick she and her girlfriends had learned in high school, when they'd gone to the Sears Tower. Lean over the rail, put your head to the glass, and look out. It seemed like you were going to fall, all that way. It made you dizzy.

Now only the alcohol was dizzying, and the feeling was hardly the pleasant glow she'd felt in high school. The view from an eighth-floor condo was nothing compared to the sights seen from the vast height of the Sears building.

She thought of the killer, out there somewhere in Chicago's mean streets. Was that the source of her weird paranoia, that feeling of being stalked she just couldn't seem to shake? Madrone had been a cop, and she was a cop. And Madrone was connected to Baxter, and to Wheeler. And she was connected to Madrone now.

Somebody had killed one cop. Why not another?

Why not me? Am I jumping at shadows?

Jesus . . .

Hopefully something would turn up in this dead-end case. She'd find the redhead and squeeze him. She still had the dime bag she'd taken from him yesterday. In the shape he'd been in, if she could find him before he scored again, he'd probably trade anything he had for a taste.

It was an appealing thought, at least. She walked to her bed, climbed in, and pulled her heavy comforter up around her neck. She set the alarm to give herself four hours, settled into the buoyant down pillows, and closed her eyes. A moment later she was snoring softly.

Justin opened the door to his apartment. The rooms were dark, though outside the rosy pink glow of dawn was painting Chicago's skyline with gleaming highlights. But he made no move to turn on the light. He wanted no part of the light. The darkness had been his home for centuries.

It's true, he thought. *I have been shrouded in the dark, working for the light.* The Dragon said it was the curse of those who would truly change the world. That only the rare few were brave enough to wade through eternal darkness to give others light.

I am tired of it, he thought. *How can a man serve others forever, without gaining something for himself?*

Justin had done more than just observe Sandra tonight. He had joined with her, had probed her mind. He had lain with her and tasted her essence. And he knew now that she was smart enough, driven enough, to put the pieces together. His dilemma with his role as the Dragon's scalpel had increased tenfold.

He did not want to kill Sandra. He had not believed it necessary before this night. He had sought her out to prove to the Dragon that he was right. But the Dragon's fears were well-founded. Now he knew he'd have to control Sandra or kill her. If she was given half a chance, she would learn everything there was to learn about Justin and his master. He'd find her snooping around his club, just like Madrone. At the rate she was moving, he'd find her coming after him before another day had passed.

Justin moved across to the huge picture window in his living room and opened the heavy drapes to let the daylight stream in. He stared out over the city to Lake Michigan, glinting golden in the dawn.

She'd trusted him last night, had slept in his arms after they'd made love. He could have killed her then, painlessly, and she'd never have known that her time had come. Her last thoughts would have been soaked in pleasure, her passing a gentle release. But he had not done it.

Justin turned his thoughts to the past—to Hong Kong in the 1920s. He had made a different choice then. He'd been standing just like this, looking out over the dark waters of Victoria Bay, and there had been a dead woman in his bed.

The body cooling in his bed had been Angela Mary Godfrey, archaeologist and adventuress. Justin had loved her, he supposed. More than that, she had been a taste of glowing life to him, at a time when he'd been drowning in death. Perhaps it was that sensation he had coveted, rather than the woman who gave it to him.

Angela had been a vibrant woman, a woman who lusted for knowledge and experience, who lusted for Justin the moment she had laid eyes on him. And when Angela saw something she wanted, she took it. In the twenties, she had been an anomaly. She would have been branded an outcast in the tightly restrained society of the time, Justin supposed, if her father hadn't been so wealthy, or if she'd shown the slightest signs of caring what people thought of her, or if she had stayed in one place long enough to be branded anything.

Justin had only known her for a few weeks. She'd been searching for evidence that dragons had once existed, and she'd carried with her a sword she'd said had once been Saint George's. The Dragon wanted her dead because of it.

Justin's hands pressed the cold glass until his fingers turned white. He shut his eyes as if that could ward off the memory of Angela's dead face against the blood-soaked pillow, the strands of her sun-gold hair stained with her own blood, her beautiful eyes gone cloudy in death. The tragedy of it had traumatized Justin. He had lost his faith in the Dragon after that night and had only regained it when the Dragon had finally shared his plans with Justin.

Justin still retained a link with Angela—a sapphire ring. He had not thought of Angela since he had packed it away before coming to the States. But thinking of Angela always made him think of the ring.

The ring . . .

Justin left the window and went to his bedroom. He threw open the closet door and pulled out the huge trunk. All these years and he still knew exactly where it was. There was a small storage compartment in the lid. Justin reached in, withdrew the battered old box he'd placed there so long ago, and opened it.

The ring was exactly as he'd remembered it. The silver band was wide and ornate as a gothic cathedral. The stone was set in a heavy bezel, a blue cabochon stone cut square, with a small, darker blue imperfection in the center . . .

The Hong Kong marketplace seethed with sound and motion. Justin laughed at a street performer. Angela threw some coins into the juggler's hat, squeezed Justin's arm, and pulled him on to the next stall. The bazaar was a crazy jumble of vendors, performers, and artisans, all trying to sell their wares.

"Have you tried this?" She pointed at a vendor selling meat on a stick.

"No, nor will I, until I know where it came from" he said, dubious. She tugged him in that direction and bought two.

Before they'd finished their snack she saw something else that drew her attention, "There!" she said. "Monkeys! C'mon!"

"You go," he said. "I'll watch. I've seen monkeys before. I don't like them much."

"No sense of adventure, that's you," Angela said, letting go of his hand and moving toward the monkeys. Justin smiled, chewed the spicy meat, and watched the people milling about. Every now and then, another Chinese merchant would accost him, beg him to buy this bag of nuts, this piece of jewelry, that pair of sandals. Justin refused politely each time.

Then he'd noticed the little old man. There was something different about the man and his boat. Much larger junks were berthed all along the harbor, with others sailing everywhere their keel depth would let them go. Nobody paid the boats any attention. But when the old man rowed his tiny, weather-beaten rowboat up to the pier, all seafaring action seemed to cease. And when he secured his craft and jumped onto the dock, the congested mass of humanity parted for him, let him pass. In the chaos that was Hong Kong in the twenties, that required something close to a miracle.

Watching curiously, Justin became even more interested when the little old man made a beeline for him. Watching the crowd scramble to get out of the man's way was like watching the sea part before Moses.

He came to a halt right in front of Justin and for a moment, Justin felt like he should move aside.

The old man did not introduce himself, did not attempt a preamble of any kind. His wide-brimmed reed hat tilted back as he looked up at Justin. His slitted eyes and sun-browned face wrinkled into a contagious smile.

"Sir, gift to you." The old man spoke softly in broken English. "Give you heart's desire."

"Oh, it's lovely!" Angela exclaimed, who had just come

up beside Justin. "You must have it, Justin dear. How much?" she said to the old man.

He smiled even wider and nodded. "Not mine. For you." He inclined his head toward Justin.

Justin was confused. "From who?" It was something Justin would have expected to see at Sotheby's in London, not on a wharf dock in Hong Kong. The ring was incredible. The dark imperfection in the center of the sapphire looked like a flame.

"Not mine. For you," the old man said again, offering the ring. Justin hesitated, but Angela took it and put it on his finger.

"It looks as if it was made just for you!" Angela said. "Is it not simply perfect?"

"Quite . . . perfect." Justin was stunned, unsure of what to say. The old man tugged at Angela's cuff and she leaned down. He whispered something and then, with a bow and a smile, turned and shuffled back to his little rowboat.

"What did he say?" Justin asked.

"How extraordinary!" she said. "Did you know him?"

"No. Not at all. What did he say?" Justin pressed.

"He said this ring holds the blue flame of indomitable will. It will remind you of the Tao. The way of love over hate."

Justin smiled. "I thought Tao was the way of balancing good and evil."

Angela shrugged. "Everyone has their different interpretation of the facts, dear Justin. There is always more than one truth. More than one way."

Justin had taken the ring off that night, just after his master told him to kill Angela. He had not put it back on since then, though he had kept it with him. He'd always wondered if the old man had actually said the whole bit about the indomitable will, or if Angela made it up. After all, the old Chinese man could barely speak two words of English, and that was quite a complex speech. And it was exactly the sort of thing Angela would do, pull a romantic proverb out of the air to flavor the day. Probably she had hired the old man to make his appearance and give Justin a gift she knew he would refuse if she offered it to him directly.

Justin turned the ring over in his hand. He put the tip of his finger inside its silver circle.

"Justinian!" The deep, grinding voice thundered through the silence of the dawn.

Justin jumped, slammed the ring on his finger in his surprise at hearing the voice. He turned to face the mirror above his chest of drawers.

The Dragon stared back at him. Its dusky scales were obscured by smoke, but its burning eyes were clear, glowing behind the haze.

"After all this time, you still doubt me."

Justin swallowed, but he said nothing. He could not deny it.

"Have I not made you privy to my plans? Do I not strive with every ounce of energy I have to guide this world to the point where it might be safe for my return?"

"Yes, my master."

"You know my mind. You know that our activities must be kept secret from the people until they are ready. You know this. And yet you suffer this witness to live. I care not what you do with your time, Justinian. But do not choose to consort with those who endanger our cause. You know your race is not yet ready for my presence. They are still too fearful, too superstitious. We have guided them closer, closer every day, but they are not ready yet. Be patient, Justin. You can see the truth of my words. Look at their books and films about the unexpected, the unknown, the impossible. Soon they will be ready for me again. Just a few more generations."

"I know, my master."

The smoke from the glowing eyes spiraled upward as the Dragon's gaze held him captive.

"Then do my bidding. I know you fancy this woman. But I also know there have been many women in your life to fancy. I would like to be merciful to this one, as I have wanted to be merciful to each before this, but mercy is a weakness for those who care more about themselves than the difficult task at hand. You have chosen yourself over me. You have put your personal gain over the good of all. And you must be punished for that."

Justin swallowed.

"Do you accept your punishment?"

"Yes, my master." Justin bowed his head.

"Open your mind to me, Justin."

Justin obeyed, and the Dragon's powerful psychic claws dug in. Searing flames enveloped him, burning him inside and out to the point of madness. Justin did not cry out.

The price of disobedience.

The flames rose higher. The pain intensified.

The price of dissension.

Yet the pain felt better than contemplating Sandra's death. It distracted him from contemplating that awful task. From that, at least, he was free for this one moment.

He burned until his flesh bubbled and popped, purifying him in the Dragon's fire.

The price of freedom.

thirteen

Wet leaves slapped her face. Sandra ran as fast as her aching legs could carry her. She stumbled around tropical tree trunks and thrashed through wet bushes. Yellow rays of oppressive sunlight flickered through the thick foliage overhead.

The black fox had been tracking her. It remained at a distance, watching calmly, sprinting to keep up with her, loping alongside sometimes, stopping with her when she had to rest. In contrast to her own noisy progress, it never made a sound, slipping through the dense rain forest like a dark ghost. Or perhaps she simply couldn't hear it over her own ragged breath, over the blood that pounded heavily in her temples.

A golden crow cawed overhead and she ran past a white gorilla shaking the banana tree. She had to get away. He was back there, somewhere, and getting closer. Of that she was sure. If she didn't run faster, if she didn't get out of this accursed jungle, he would catch her.

An unseen root smacked her in the shin. The root was a

trash can and it clanged loudly as it tangled up in her legs. She cried out and tumbled to the forest floor. The black fox moved closer.

"No!" she screamed, warding it off with her hands, but the fox stopped a few feet away from her and sat on its haunches, watching.

Her chest rose and fell like a bellows. Her jeans and T-shirt were soaked with sweat, pulling at her as she tried to twist to her feet—

Too late.

She screamed again. The sun illuminated him. His red hair flamed. His trench coat was dry, despite the wet forest, and it rippled lightly around his ankles. Each pimple, each freckle, was a diseased spot on his face. He raised the knife over his head.

She forced herself to roll out of the way. The blade plunged into the earth. She dragged herself to her feet and tried to run.

No sooner had she lurched away from him than she stumbled again, clipped by a bush.

She fell . . .

. . . and fell . . .

. . . and landed on the hard, flagstone floor of the Cathedral of St. Joseph. The jungle noises stopped. No tropical birds cawed overhead. No chameleons took slow, careful strolls across scaled trees. The leafy ceiling had been replaced by high, ribbed vaults. The hot sun had given way to the cool, tomb-like echo of the church.

Her breathing reverberated around her. Slowly she rose to her knees, hampered by the white dress she now wore. She looked down at it. The gown was floor-length, had no belt, *and was made of a heavy fabric that was threatening to suffocate her. Already the sweat of her body was wetting it, causing it to cling to her skin.*

A slight scuffling sound caught her attention and she looked up at the altar. The black fox stood there, watching her.

Her breathing had begun to slow. Her heart had begun to calm.

"Oh, God, no . . ." she whispered.

"Did you think you could escape me?" The voice came from behind her.

She spun around, stumbled back against a marble column. The redhead in the green trench coat moved closer. He was fully seven feet tall. His shoulders were powerfully wide and the hands protruding from his coat were veined and gnarled. A knife shimmered at his side, clenched tight in his massive fist.

"Did you really think that, bitch?!"

She pushed harder against the column, wishing she could somehow push herself through it, somehow escape this horror.

She closed her eyes. Her feet scrabbled against the stone. "Please, God . . . please . . ."

A hand closed around her throat. Her eyes opened and she looked at the face so near hers.

Slowly the features of the teenager melted away and reformed.

"Chuck . . ."

"Did you really think you could escape me?"

Sandra struggled to escape his iron grip, tried desperately to remember her training, all those years of lessons that had taught her to deal with this sort of thing. But the memories wouldn't come. Her skills had abandoned her.

"God . . . no . . ."

"Your god is nothing here. You're nothing."

The knife sliced into her chest.

The pain was excruciating. Sandra gasped, choked. Hot blood burst from her mouth. Chuck's hand twisted the knife. Sandra felt her body jerk reflexively as her life ran out of her veins.

The bloody knife clattered to the floor.

"One more thing," he said. "Your heart is mine. It will always belong to me."

Chuck's hand reached into her chest . . .

"No," she screamed. Her hand pressed hard against her breastbone. Her heart was still there, securely inside her unmarred chest, still beating. Her sheets were covered with sweat.

For a moment, in the darkness of the room, she'd thought she was still in the church. Early morning light filtered through her white gauze curtains. She closed her eyes and opened them again.

No, she was not in the cathedral. She was safely in her bedroom. It had just been a dream.

She heard a door open not far away. Rubber wheels rolled down the hall. A knock on her door . . .

"Sandra?" It was Benny's voice, concerned and hesitant.

"Yeah." She tried to control her breathing. Pulling the sheet up, she spoke again: "Come in."

Benny opened the door and wheeled in. He immediately rolled to the side of her bed and looked deeply into her eyes. He didn't say anything, just took her hand in his.

"Thanks," she said.

"Are you okay?" His voice was soft and low.

"Benny . . ." she started to explain, but couldn't manage to get the rest of the words out. She pulled away from his reassuring handclasp and put both hands to her face. Dammit. The tears started to come and it was too late to do anything about it. Benny waited patiently until she cried herself out.

"I can't believe it," she mumbled.

"What were you screaming about?" he asked.

"It was Chuck. Another nightmare about Chuck."

"Shit, Sandra," Benny swore. "I'm so sorry."

"I just can't believe it." She started to cry again, "It's been ten years since I left him. Ten years! I haven't had a bad dream about him in more than two years, and now they're back."

"Same ones? He's holding you under the water until you drown?"

"No. He chased me with a knife this time. It's never been that way before."

"With a knife?"

"Well, it wasn't him to start with. It started out being a black fox, then this asshole junkie who's been following me around, and then it changed into Chuck. I don't know why. Why would I still be afraid of him?"

"They say it sticks with you, Sandra. He beat you almost every day of your married life. Even if you can wipe up the floor with him now, it doesn't matter. You're still remembering that time when you couldn't."

"But not for years. Why now? I think it's this case. This stupid case. It's got to be."

"So drop the case."

"No." She shook her head adamantly. "You know I can't do that."

He reached out and touched the sheet she had gathered to herself. "Your sheets are soaked with sweat. You were screaming loudly enough to wake the dead."

"Sorry, Benny," she said. "I don't run anymore. I don't run, and I don't back down. Forget it."

"Sandra . . ." he started, took a good look at the uncompromising lines on her face, then sighed in defeat. "Okay. I just think—"

"I know." She smiled, reached out, and lightly traced a scar on the left side of his ravaged face. She spoke more slowly, more softly. "I know. And I thank you. If it weren't for you—"

"Flip sides to everything." He cut her off with a wave of his hand. "You've been there for me at least as often as I've been there for you. I just wish you'd listen to me more often than you do."

"I listen," she whispered. "I really do."

"Yeah. But do you act on what I'm saying?" He sighed. "All right." He shook his head and began to back his chair out. "I'm going to make some breakfast."

It surprised Sandra that he'd said nothing about how late she'd come home last night. He had to be curious about what she'd done, but he said nothing. It was Benny's way. He needed his space to survive, and he respected other people's need for space, as well.

He left the room, shutting the door behind him.

I could probably learn a few lessons from Benny, she thought.

Sandra went to the shower and washed the physical evidence of her adventures from the night before—both the good and the bad—from her body. She dried off and dressed, trying to shove the dream out of her mind.

When she finally emerged from her room, Benny was just putting the finishing touches on some eggs and toast, and the smell of fresh-brewed coffee filled the kitchen. She poured herself a cup and sat down at the breakfast table with a sigh of contentment.

"You're a saint," she said as he wheeled himself up to the other side of the table.

"I know." He smiled at her.

"You're too good to me."

"I'm saving up for a time when I'm going to be really *shitty* to you."

She smiled back at him and began eating her breakfast.

"Oh," he said. "Some guy called for you last night, a Dr. Dawes, I think. I wrote the name and number down next to the phone. He said you could come talk to him today. Said he didn't find much, but that he's got someone you might call."

She sighed again, but with a different tone. "Damn. I was hoping he'd be able to figure out something for me."

"Well, he's got someone you can call."

"Yeah, but I'm not too hopeful. He was supposed to be the best."

Benny shrugged.

"It beats going into the office, I suppose," she said. "Damn. I think I've got another lead if I can just find that redheaded punk. But if I can't, and Dawes can't help, then I'm at a standstill with this case. I just—"

The ringing of the phone interrupted her sentence. Sandra looked down at her scrambled eggs, half eaten and cooling quickly.

"You want me to get it?" Benny offered.

She shook her head. "No. It's probably for me." She crossed the room and picked up the phone.

"Yeah?" she answered.

"Bruce?"

"Hey, Mac. What's up?"

"We got another one."

Her body went cold. "Another ripper? Shit!"

He paused. "You okay, Bruce?"

"Yeah, I'm fine. It's the same MO?"

"Mostly," McKenzie said. "We don't have access problems this time—it's pretty obvious how our psycho got to the victim—but there's a kid with a hole in his chest the same size as the others. The crime scene guys are still looking for the heart. The evidence seems to indicate the killer tossed it to the ground, just like always, but that some scavenger, probably a dog, made off with it."

"The victim's a kid? Jesus, Mac . . . how old?"

"Eighteen."

Sandra swallowed. "Why a kid?"

"I don't know. Who the hell ever knows? Not till we nail some bastard—and maybe even not then, huh?"

"Who was he?"

"Name's Zachary Miller. The killer got him with his pants down. Literally. Kid was humping a girl in a parking lot in Burnham Park down near Soldier Field. The killer hauled him out of the car and did him right there, right in front of his own car. It looks like the killing was slow this time, like it lasted for a while. Both Baxter and Madrone were pretty much instantaneous, but it looks like this kid got thrown around some first. There was blood on the car and all over the blacktop. Maybe our guy is starting to get a taste for—"

"Wait, in Burnham Park?" she said.

"Yeah, why?"

"What time, do they think?"

"Early. Just after sundown. About seven o'clock, why?"

"Jesus, Mac, I was right there last night!"

"You were there?"

"I mean, close. I was at a blues club a few blocks from the entire thing."

"No kidding! What were you doing there?"

"Blowing off steam."

Sandra swallowed, thinking of the redhead she and Justin had chased.

Into his thoughtful silence, she said, "Any witnesses?"

"Kind of. Well . . . it's strange, Bruce. We got someone who saw the whole thing . . . and then some. The girl our victim was trying to boff. A girl named Tina Danforth. Seventeen. A nice, normal kid—good student, caring parents, no signs of substance abuse. She and the victim were dating. But her story's just too fucking weird. I mean bad weird."

"Why?"

"She says she knows who the murderer is, but every time she starts talking about it, she starts raving about monsters and angels or something. I think you need to talk to her. You're a woman, and maybe . . ."

Sandra's blood went cold. "Monsters?"

"I don't understand it, either, Bruce. Like I said, you're going to have to talk to her."

"Who called the cops?"

"A waitress at a cafe near the park. She heard screams, but didn't see anything. So the uniforms took their sweet time getting there. They found the girl nearly naked, beat up, covered in blood, just standing there on the street waiting for them. She led them back to the car where the murder took place. The crime scene's a zoo. We got footprints everywhere, at least five different sets in the victim's blood. Strange thing is, they tally with the girl's story. Well, sort of.

"By the way, our witness says the victim was the one who trashed her, not the killer. She says the kid was trying to rape her, and the monster yanked him out of the car and killed him."

Silence stretched on the phone line.

"You still there?" McKenzie asked.

"God, Mac."

"Yeah."

"Do you think it could be her? Could she have killed the kid?"

"No, I don't think so," Mac said. "She's a flyweight. Monsters would be more plausible than that."

"Yeah? I know some girls who could put up a pretty good fight. I could."

"Maybe so. But the victim looks like he got put through a meat grinder before his heart got ripped out. Cut up, choked, beaten, tossed at the car hard enough to half mash it, then thrown all over the place. No way the girl could pull that off. You see her, you'll know. No way."

"Okay, but that leaves us with another problem. This doesn't track with the other two our psycho's killed."

"I know. So he's nuts. Freaks do freaky things."

"I mean, you've got to figure he went after Baxter for reasons of his own, then went after Madrone because Madrone stumbled onto something that might lead to Baxter's killer. Or because he hates cops. So why go after a kid?"

"Beats me, Bruce."

"Mac?" she said.

"Yeah."

"There's something I need to tell you."

"Yeah? What's that?"

"Where you at?"

"I'm at the scene. The forensics guys are just getting started."

"Okay, I'll meet you there."

•   •   •

The crime scene had been cordoned off and uniformed officers were doing their best to keep the rubberneckers back. Fucking ghouls. People bitched about crime and violence, but they couldn't resist a bucket of blood.

And there was blood everywhere. Sandra squatted, getting a better look at the scuff marks on the blacktop, the blood, the footprints both in the pooled blood and leading away from the site. Five sets, just like Mac said. The congealed blood was still thick and faintly sticky in the damp morning air.

She looked at the dents in the Camaro. That little cheerleader type might be strong for her size, but there was no way she was up for smacking around the victim hard enough to put deep impact craters in the sheet metal of the car.

She moved to the edge of the parking lot, where the blacktop gave way to rough grass scrub along a slope that descended to the water below. Lake Michigan was dark under the gray sky.

Mac wandered back from where he'd been chatting up one of the forensics techs, a young woman with a nice rack and dancing blue eyes.

Men.

"You shoulda let me know about Madrone's snitch last night, Bruce," he said seriously. "Maybe there's some kinda connection. Same general neighborhood and all, where you ran into him . . ."

She shrugged, walking along the edge of the dirt, "No way, Mac. That eaten-out junkie probably isn't even in as good shape as the girl."

Narrowing her eyes, Sandra knelt by a couple of

marks in the mud. They were tracks—like an animal's footprint. A damn large animal. Something with three splayed toes. Damn large toes. And they looked a lot like that unexplained print in Jack Madrone's carpet.

"I wonder how he left the scene with no one seeing him. After doing the Miller kid, he had to be covered in blood," she mused aloud.

"Dark out, Bruce. And the park's usually pretty empty. Wouldn't be that hard."

She looked around. About a half block down the street there was a big storm sewer pipe. Given the weather the past few days, it was—not surprisingly—gushing water in a steady stream. If he was willing to risk five or six major diseases, the killer could have washed off in that. A man soaked head to toe wouldn't seem very out of place in Chicago, what with all the rain lately. And these tracks seemed to be heading right for the pipe.

"Take a look at these," she told her partner, pointing at the imprints in the mud. "What do you think?"

He crouched down next to her. "I don't know. What do you think?"

Sandra swallowed and looked around. She suddenly felt as if she was being watched. Was this the same kind of discovery Madrone had made before he died? "Shit, I don't know. Looks like the same thing we found with Madrone. But like an animal track, you know?"

She peered around at the shadows beneath the trees, at the thickets and shrubs. Lots of places to hide. "Something maybe wandered down from the 'burbs? Or further?"

"Yeah. And climbs the sides of condos and unlocks windows."

"Well, the girl claims she saw *something*. Dragons, right?"

Mac shook his head in disgust. "Yeah. Dragons. You know what, Bruce? This whole case stinks," he said as he stood up. His knees made sharp popping sounds. His eyes never left the animal tracks. "It just keeps getting creepier."

"Yeah. Gets your blood pumping, doesn't it?" Sandra said, still feeling the chill. She couldn't believe some of the things she was thinking. "You want to be the one to tell the captain that we've maybe got a man-shaped reptile running around stalking people and ripping their hearts out?"

"Oh, man, that's not funny at all. And you know what, Bruce? It worries me. I feel like we're stumbling around, blind, in a mess that just keeps getting bigger and uglier."

"So what have we got so far, Mac? One scale, two sets of very weird footprints, and a missing redheaded snitch. All somehow connected. Maybe. If the snitch wasn't lying in the first place."

"Not much," Mac said.

No, it wasn't much. She knew that. But it didn't matter. Shit like this was why she'd become a cop in the first place, spent the long years working her way from the academy to patrol and finally into investigation and homicide.

She knew she needed to test herself, to see if she was tough enough to take down the worst the city could throw at her. If she couldn't prove herself—and keep on proving herself—she was afraid that her fears would catch up with her, that she'd hide from the world forever. She'd done it for a while after her husband nearly killed her. She knew that darkness was still with her, waiting to fill her up again.

The only way out of that arena was to take a path straight through the things she feared the most. To do it anyway. Turn her face to the fire and believe she'd live through it.

So she would rather die than turn away. It kind of limited her options. Not that they were all that wide to begin with.

Mac twisted uneasily. "One more thing," he said.

"Yeah?"

"This freako scrags Baxter. Who was a rent-a-cop. Then he guts Madrone, who was a cop. And now we're investigating Madrone. Does that . . . ?" His voice trailed off.

"Does it put us number one on his hit parade? I dunno, Mac. What do you think?"

He stared at her. "I think I'll be real careful for a while. Watch myself, you know? And maybe you should think about it, too."

"Oh, I have been, Mac."

"Well, keep it up, Bruce. You keep it up, hear me?"

She nodded. "I hear you."

fourteen

Looking at Tina Danforth was like looking into a mirror, a mirror into her own past. In more ways than one. Physically, she looked like Sandra once had looked. But the mirror was an emotional one as well. How many times after Chuck had slammed her around had she looked just like this, tattered in spirit, battered in the flesh?

Sandra shivered as she watched the girl who lay hunched in on herself in the hospital bed. Bad, bad shit.

Tina was trying her damnedest to curl up, to occupy as little space as possible. The girl's mother perched on the edge of the mattress, sobbing quietly into a wad of tissues.

Tina was wearing one of those ridiculous hospital gowns with a single tie in the back. Her legs were tucked up against her chest, her ankles crossed, her naked feet looking curiously vulnerable where they peeped beneath the end of the sheet, tiny blue veins prominent against shock-pale skin.

Sandra knew what she was thinking, because she'd had the same thoughts herself. Tina was pretending that she was all alone in this room. Mac had been right. Sandra knew she could understand Tina better than anybody else, because she'd been there, too.

Tina's expression was as familiar to Sandra as her own skin, even though it was a skin Sandra had shed long ago. She let the memories flow over her, memories of a time when she, too, had suffered at the hands of a man, and had had to tell a policeman the awful story.

And there was something else bothering Sandra. Now that she looked again, ignoring the bruises and the bandaged scrapes, Tina really *did* look a lot like her. It wasn't just the defeated, wary aura surrounding the girl—the look she thought of in her own mind as the *Chuck* look—that caused goose bumps to rise on Sandra's arms. If Sandra had been several years younger, she and Tina could have been identical twins. Damned close to it, at least.

It was a weird déjà vu feeling to see herself as she'd once been. Then she shook off her uneasiness and stepped to the bedside. Tina looked up quickly, then shrank back from her. After what she'd been through, Sandra couldn't blame her.

Tina would not look at her.

"I'd like to talk to you, Tina, if I could, about last night."

Tina shook her head violently, her lips compressed.

"It's important. Please?"

Tina closed her eyes.

Sandra tried again. "I can get you something to eat

or drink. You need something in your stomach. It'll make you feel better. Believe me, I know. And you don't have to talk to me unless you want to."

Apparently Sandra's calm, patient voice hit a chord with the girl. She nodded.

"Okay. I'll be right back."

Sandra left the room, went down the hall to a tiny lounge, and bought five bucks' worth of sodas and chocolate bars. She brought them back and watched as Tina ate in tiny, microscopic increments. Finally, when the girl was looking a little calmer, Sandra tried again.

"Tina, we need your help. You wouldn't want what happened to you to happen to someone else, would you? We want to find the man who killed Zack. We want to stop him before he does it again."

Tina looked up and Sandra got the eye contact she wanted.

"Can we talk, Tina? Just for a while?"

Slowly Tina's eyes took on a haunted look.

"I know you don't want to talk about what happened with Zack."

Tina shook her head.

"But you'll have to, and if we do it now, then it will be over with. I want to ask you some questions about before and after you were in the car with him. Did you notice anyone hanging around the parking lot when you drove in?"

Tina hesitated, then shook her head no.

"No one parking their car and pausing, seeming to do something, maybe check the trunk or the tires or something?"

Tina barely shook her head, as if the question meant nothing to her.

"Tina—"

Tina mumbled something, too low for Sandra to hear.

"What was that?" Sandra asked.

"I-it wasn't human," Tina whispered.

"What?" Sandra said. "What do you mean not human?"

"I think I'm going crazy . . ." Tina said. "I must be going crazy." Tears welled in her eyes and spilled over. She looked up, trying to keep her chin from quivering. "I want to go home. Can I just go home?"

"Tina, don't you think—"

"Please, how can I make you believe something I don't believe myself?" Tina said. "I don't know what it was. It was big and green and it had claws and wings. It spoke my name, and it said it . . . it said it . . . had 'punished' Zack." The girl began crying. Through her sobs, she continued speaking, although now completely to herself, not to Sandra at all.

"He said he was my guardian angel, but he wasn't . . . he punched the back window out. He grabbed Zack. He just tore Zack apart. He. . . had blood. . . Zack's blood on his claws . . ." The soft words became incoherent sobs; Tina retreated into herself, closing her eyes and clasping her legs tight against her chest.

Sandra sighed. The story was *not* going to play well with her boss. The MO of the murders was bad enough. Add in a story about inhuman monsters, and if the media got hold of it, the whole city would go nuts. Not that it mattered. It wasn't her story, and it was the only story she had.

She sat back in her chair and watched Tina rock back and forth on the bed. The girl had seen something, but she was so shell-shocked by the ordeal that she wouldn't make a good witness. Even if what Tina was saying was the absolute truth—and Sandra was starting to think there might be something to it—they were going to have a hard time convincing anybody based on this testimony.

She did have some corroborating evidence. The claw prints Sandra had seen in the mud—she'd had the crime scene guys take plaster casts of the tracks. She had a photo of the print in the carpet at Jack Madrone's apartment. She had the scale that nobody could identify. But it was all too thin to hang a wild story of a lizard man stalking the streets of Chicago on.

Maybe something more ordinary was going on . . . Did the killer maybe get a kick out of wearing some kind of bizarre costume when he pulled people's hearts out of their chests? That actually might make sense—Sandra had seen weirder stuff in her years with the force. But why embark on a series of murders in a costume? Still, psychos *did* do psycho things. John Wayne Gacey, the Clown-killer, had murdered young boys while wearing a clown costume.

So far all they'd gathered were a few tracks, a single scale, and the strong smell of Chinese food. And a snitch . . .

"Tina, did you smell an odor like burnt sesame oil? Sort of an Oriental food kind of smell?" Sandra asked.

Tina looked stunned, nodded, and burst into uncontrollable sobs.

Great, Sandra thought.

Sandra let out a slow breath. Where to now? She could press the girl, pump her for more information, but she doubted it would do any good. More stories of clawed, winged men? Guardian angels bent on murder? Where was she supposed to go with that kind of crap?

Sandra turned to the door, saw Mac trying to hover unobtrusively just beyond the doorway. A hard thing for a guy his size to accomplish. She nodded at him and he winked. Then she turned around and looked at the girl. Tina was still huddled in a tight, quivering ball. "We're going to get someone to come in and take care of you, okay, Tina?"

No response.

A middle-aged Asian woman came in, dressed in gray slacks and a white blouse. A plastic photo ID card with the usual bad picture on it hung from her pocket. Wide, oval glasses enlarged her dark eyes, and her straight, gray-streaked black hair was pulled back into a severe bun. Despite her crisp, professional appearance, she had the gentle eyes of a good mother. Something about her put Sandra at ease immediately.

"That was quick," Sandra said. "I was just gonna ask Mac to get somebody in here."

"Actually, it was the captain who sent me," the woman said, her accent cool, restrained, and, surprisingly, upper-class British.

With a gentle smile, the Chinese woman looked past Sandra at Tina. "Perhaps your young witness needs something a bit different than an interrogator right now."

"Whatever you say, doctor." Sandra shrugged and moved to the door. Something niggled at the back of her mind, and she turned around. "Y'know, I haven't seen you before. Where's the other psychiatrist?" Sandra thought for a moment and came up with the guy's name. "Parker. Where's Parker?"

The Chinese woman said, "Parker is out right now. I'm filling in from another precinct. Captain Mahoney asked me if I would help out here."

Sandra shrugged again, "It's the captain's show. Tell me if she starts making sense. I'm Detective—"

"McCormick. I know," the woman said. "Do not worry. I will take good care of the girl."

"Right." Sandra left the room still feeling a slight bit odd. McKenzie walked up to her just as she closed the door. He was short of breath.

"Hey, Bruce. Parker's gone. Personal business or something."

Sandra clapped a hand on McKenzie's shoulder. "Captain's a step ahead of us. He already sent someone. Never seen her before, though. Must be new or something."

McKenzie opened the door quietly and looked in. He nodded at the woman, closed the door. "She looks nice."

"I'd agree with that." Sandra sighed, thinking again of how little they had on the case. "Like she said, maybe that's the only way of getting straight answers out of the poor kid."

"Being nice?"

"Yeah."

"You don't feel like being nice, Bruce?"

"Not really. Anything about this shit make you feel nice, Mac?"

"Naw. But I'll tell you what would. One of those large pizzas with everything from that joint over behind the Marriott." He glanced at her. "You ain't all that big, Bruce. But I gotta keep my strength up."

She stared at his gut. "That your strength, that thing hanging over your belt?"

He tried to look hurt. "Come on, Bruce. I didn't get no breakfast, and it's already lunchtime. Gimme a break."

"I'll do better. I'll buy. How's that?"

"*Now* I feel nice," he told her.

fifteen

Sandra sat in an uncomfortable chair in Chicago's O'Hare International Airport, listening to a bored voice announce the status of her flight. The plane was available for boarding, first-class passengers or those requiring special assistance only. The throng of people heading from Chicago to San Diego shifted and moved toward the gate.

She made one last check of the passenger waiting area, but saw no sign of the junkie in the trench coat. Which was not a huge surprise. Maybe if she'd had a hundred dollar bill in her wallet *then,* she'd know *now* whatever the hell it was he wanted to talk about. She doubted he'd be chasing after her again. It wasn't likely he'd enjoyed their meetings much. So now she'd have to track him down.

What a pain.

Mac had checked the jackets on all of Madrone's cases, and in the Wheeler jacket he'd found a grubby, handwritten note that referenced a snitch, a kid Madrone had listed only as Maxie—had to be the same guy. The first-name-only dodge wasn't all that strange—a lot of cops were secretive about their snitches. At least there had been a phone number, but the phone turned out to be a hot-sheet welfare hotel. They found one Pakistani clerk who, based on the kid's description, thought he'd seen him around.

No, he hadn't seen him around lately, though. As for the phone, it was in the lobby of the hotel, and was obviously a one-stop communications shop for dopers and their dealers. No help there.

And Dr. Dawes had been a disappointment. He had nothing for her. Or practically nothing. His only contribution was the name, number, and address of some herpetologist who lived in southern California, a little town called Fallbrook. According to Dawes, if anybody could identify that scale for her, this would be her guy.

"I should warn you. Dr. Simmins. He's a little . . . odd," Dawes had said.

A little odd? What the hell did that mean? Another loony? She'd just about had it up to here with loonies.

As she watched the first-class passengers trudge onto the plane, she thought about what she had. One weird scale, several weird footprints, a weird method of murder, and three connections.

Baxter, Madrone, and Zack Miller had all been brutally murdered, their hearts ripped from their chests. That was one connection. The second possible connection was that Baxter and Madrone had been cops, or Baxter at least sort of. But the dead kid named Zack wasn't a cop, so maybe that pattern didn't hold. Or maybe it did, and Zack had been a murder of opportunity.

A further, even more tenuous connection involved methods of access. The killer, in the cases of both Baxter and Madrone, had gained access in apparently impossible ways—high floors, no obvious entrance. And Madrone had been investigating a high-profile case with a similar access problem. But with Madrone's case, the victim had been shot, and his heart left untouched inside his rib cage. So was that a real connection or just smoke? Mac was probably right—it was a hell of a reach. Still, a hell of a reach was better than nothing at all.

She made a mental note to take a look at the Carlton Wheeler jacket, maybe even check out for herself whether there were any mysterious scratches or gouges in the walls beneath his windows.

In the end, all of it added up to not much. She had the scale and the prints. And the junkie. If she could find him again.

Every homicide cop knew that the vast majority of killings either were solved more or less on the spot, or through somebody—the killer, a friend or relative of the killer, or some other informant—dropping a dime. And all of Sandra's instincts told her that Maxie, the junkie, might have something. But what? He claimed to know who killed Carlton Wheeler. But beyond her own gut feelings, there was nothing solid to link Wheeler to her own psycho killer. The mere fact that Madrone had been investigating Wheeler's murder, and had gotten scragged by the ripper, wasn't much to hang her hat on.

Madrone had been investigating a lot of other cases, too.

Still, similar access problems, and Madrone's murder. Maybe something. Not much, but maybe something . . .

So find the kid. Find Maxie. It shouldn't be too hard. Junkies were junkies. They had a limited worldview. The world was junk. Watch the junk, find the junkie.

Mac was working on that while she hauled her small glass vial off to California. At least the scale, whatever the hell it was, was something *real*.

She also had high-resolution digital photos, both disk and prints, of the weird tracks they'd found at both Zack's and Madrone's murder scenes. Forensics said they were of the same type, but they had no idea what type that was.

Some big animal. Maybe a lizard. Maybe something else. Maybe a setup . . . she was inclined in that direction herself. If Dawes hadn't been able to identify the scale—and also hadn't recognized the prints as belonging to any reptile species he knew about—then maybe it was just a psycho playing games. She'd read stories about Bigfoot, about how hoaxers deliberately left fake footprints around to bolster their scams. She did have a witness, though. Tina what's-her-name. And Tina said a big guy with wings and claws. And *scales*. Some kind of dragon-like monster. Not a real dragon, of course, but a dragon man. And some weight-lifting bozo wearing a Godzilla suit, complete with claws and big feet, would account for what Tina thought she'd seen. That is, *if* Tina hadn't been smoking something really *serious* before she climbed in the backseat with her former boyfriend . . .

Another mental note. The hospital had taken blood samples from the girl. That was standard. If the samples were still around, run a check for drug traces. The girl—and her mother—had claimed she wasn't a doper, but who knew? Kids didn't tell their parents everything, and parents sure as hell didn't know everything about their kids.

She hauled out her cell-phone, dialed the District, and left a message for Mac to call the hospital and take care of it.

Still, even if the girl had actually seen what she claimed she'd seen, it didn't answer why. Why off some punk kid? There was *no* connection between the crime scenes. Two were indoors, in hard-to-reach places, with absolutely no witnesses. This was outdoors, in the open, and the killer had left a witness behind. One he didn't have to leave behind.

And what about that other guy? The one Tina had said sounded like an Arab? Who'd *also* tried to kill her, or at least threatened to? And the Asian karate kid. Where the hell had *he* come from?

Jesus. Smoke, mirrors, and no idea in the world *why*. Still, did *why* matter?

No. *Why* mattered only if it would help her catch the scumbucket. Means, motive, opportunity. She had problems with all three. How did the killer, even if he was immensely strong, manage to rip out the hearts with one punch? Forensics said the kind of strength those wounds demanded was beyond even the most powerful man. So he used something, maybe some kind of home-brew weapon . . .

Motive. Who knew? With a real psycho, it might be anything from the voice of the devil to a conviction that his victims were possessed by Martians. As for opportunity, how the hell did this clown, complete with lizard suit, get into Madrone's apartment, Baxter's museum, and maybe . . . into Carlton Wheeler's apartment?

That was a thought. Wheeler had died before any of the others. Was that the first strike, before the killer put on scaly long johns and figured out how to keyhole punch a major cardiac arrest?

Still one hell of a lot of smoke. And there was only one thing to do when you had a lot of smoke. Take what you *did* have and work it as hard as you could.

She had a scale and some photos of weird footprints. And she had a name of some guy in California who might be able to identify them.

It was worth a trip, even if Captain Mahoney hadn't been real enthusiastic about signing off on her travel voucher. But he knew how thin everything was, and he was also painfully aware he couldn't keep a lid on this thing much longer.

"Push it as far as it will go," he'd muttered, his eyes bloodshot, his thick white hair rumpled. "Once it comes out, then the mayor gets involved. All the pols. And we're in a shitstorm up to our eyebrows."

Shitstorm . . .

That was a fair enough description of what the media would generate as soon as they got hold of the details. With sweeps week coming up, the local TV stations would throw armies of hysterical reporters at the case. And at her . . .

"Passengers in aisles one to fifteen, please board now."

The bored voice of the airline attendant cut through her revere. She gathered her things, stood, and walked onto the plane.

The flight was a direct one, lasting about four hours. The kid sitting next to her spilled his juice on her lap, nearly ruining her expensive woolen slacks. She'd brought a book—the latest thing in murder mysteries—but the cops in it were so unrealistic she finally put it aside. How come bad mystery writers always made their cops idiots?

The flight landed on time. She lugged her carry-on to the rental car desk, then got on the shuttle bus and went to a parking lot at the outskirts of the airport to pick up a cramped little Dodge, all the Chicago P.D. would spring for by way of transportation.

Dr. Simmins's home was an hour's drive north on I–15 to the small, inland town of Fallbrook, not too far from the Marine base at Camp Pendleton.

She spent her drive admiring the scenery and listening to the stereo. At times the terrain between San Diego and Fallbrook was stunning—rocky highlands and lush green hillocks. But much of it had been what they called *developed*. She passed more than one golf course, seen through distant trees, and thousands of tract homes, each so like the next that it was a miracle the owners managed to find the right house every night.

Finally she hit the freeway exit for Fallbrook. Her directions sent her on a winding road that took her through fruit groves. She recognized the orange trees, but some of the trees hid their fruit behind large green leaves. Limes, maybe? Avocados? Whatever they were, the surroundings were idyllic.

And almost without realizing she did so, she found herself thinking about Justin.

He had not called her asking why she'd left in such a hurry, without waking him. Despite herself, she liked that. He hadn't needed to chase after her, didn't seem to expect anything from her in particular. Had he assessed her desires so correctly that he'd figured out trying to hold onto her was exactly the wrong course of action? Or had it just been a one-night stand for him?

She wished it had been a one-night stand for her. It would be so much easier that way. But she couldn't stop thinking about the way he smelled, about how his eyes glistened as he looked down at her, the feel of his body pressed against her.

She frowned unconsciously and looked out the window.

Puffy white clouds floated across the blue sky, their shadows sliding over the land. Beautiful country. She wished she was visiting California on a vacation, rather than on business.

Dr. Simmins lived off the beaten track. She'd left the freeway, and now she turned off a twisty, gravel lane onto a dirt road. She guided her rented car up the side of one of the larger hills, climbing through groves of fruit trees whose trunks looked as if they'd been whitewashed.

After fifteen minutes of bumping and pounding along, she began to wonder if she'd taken the wrong turnoff. The further she drove, the rougher the terrain became. She almost got her car stuck twice but finally made her way to the top of the hill.

The road ended in a parking area of sorts. There were three old 4x4's in various stages of disintegration sunk into the ground and grown over with grass.

As she got out and shut her car door, Sandra stretched and admired the view. As Mac put it, any-thing—and anybody—that wasn't nailed down too tightly tended to roll to the West Coast. But standing here on this hilltop and looking out on paradise, she could understand why people flocked here. There was a windswept wildness to everything that was appealing to her city-bred heart.

She looked up at the sky. The clouds were turning gray, and darker still along their heavy, bulging bottoms.

Rain in Chicago didn't bother her much, but that dirt track she'd come up on, as bad as it was dry, was likely to be much worse in a downpour. She decided to make sure she wound things up and got the hell back to a real road before the storm broke.

The house sprawled out across the entire east side of the plateau, expansively if not elegantly. Wood-slat siding curled away from the studding in places. Where the paint had not been completely stripped by the ele-ments, paint flakes hung tenuously to the boards. Most of the structure was hidden by foliage. Dozens of lush trees formed a barricade around the house. At least one of every kind of fruit tree she'd seen on the way up seemed to be planted here. Ivy carpeted the ground, climbed across the windows, and reached up into the sagging eaves.

She walked toward the house, looking for a path to the front door. She saw flashes of a wraparound deck, also sagging, through the luxuriant greenery. Broken pavement blocks partly covered in green moss were half buried in the ground, but they seemed to lead in the general direction of the porch.

The trees closed in on her immediately. Between the increasingly dense cloud cover and the thick, leafy canopy, it felt as if she had gone from day into night. She stepped under a low hanging branch. A chirping noise off to her left caught her attention. Something scuffled next to her left ear and she turned around.

A chameleon was making its slow journey across a branch, its thin legs releasing their long-fingered hold one at a time, stretching and looping around to grasp the branch again and pull itself forward. Its tail curled slightly and uncurled, as if it were some horizontal periscope, sensing her position. It stopped for a moment. Large, scaled eyeballs swiveled, focused on her, studied her.

Sandra stared back at the little jeweled lizard, fascinated. Things were alive in here, she realized. Probably a lot of things. Now that she listened, she could hear them moving.

She continued on, and finally emerged into the roughly cleared space surrounding the old house. The deck and yard—if you could call the jungle of weeds that surround the house that—was enclosed by a rusty chain-link fence. A sign on it warned NO TRESPASSERS.

A tremendous splash sounded from somewhere out of sight. What the hell?

Following the fence line, Sandra trekked along the edge of the yard, burrs scratching at her hose. Damn. They were new, too.

Another stretch of chain-link bisected the space between the house and the original perimeter, and within that was a swimming pool.

Lounging in and around the pool were a half dozen alligators. The one who had just splashed into the pool opened its long, toothy snout and swiveled its head around, searching for prey. Sandra stared at it. What kind of nut-case kept alligators in his yard? The sign on the fence took on new meaning. She suddenly felt very naked and exposed. What other little surprises might be hidden in the riot of greenery at her back?

Something brushed her shoulder. She let out a half gasp/half scream and spun about. Reflexively she struck out, hit something, and heard a muffled grunt as whatever she'd hit fell away.

"Oh, my God, I'm so sorry!"

She ran to help him stand up. "You startled me. Are you Dr. Simmins?"

"No, no. I'm the one who should apologize," the little man said in a high, nasal voice. He shook himself, dusted off the seat of his pants, stuck out one hand. "Yes, I'm Simmins. And you are . . . ?"

He was just under five and a half feet tall, wiry and thin. He wore baggy Hawaiian shorts and a tight tank top that hugged his pot belly, making it look like he'd stuffed a bowling ball under there. His stork-like legs stuck out from the gaudy shorts and his gnarled toes were crammed into old yellow flip-flops. His thick, black-rimmed glasses were askew on his long, triangular nose. In what looked like a habitual gesture, he immediately pushed them up on his face. His eyes, made tiny by the glasses, were coal black. He regarded her with a feverish intensity.

"I'm Sandra McCormick."

She held out her hand and the thin man took it. His grip was soft, damp, somehow tentative.

"Doctor, I really am sorry. I got spooked. The alligators . . . I've never seen them outside of a zoo."

"Just some of my pets." He smiled. Sandra noticed how his nose, long and pointed, twitched when he spoke.

They stared at each other. With the introductions out of the way, he didn't seem to know what to do next. He kept smacking his lips. After an awkward moment he nodded toward the house.

"Come on in," he said, stepping past her and walking along the fence.

"Uh, sure," she said. She followed him through a corroded but still sturdy gate, keeping one eye cocked nervously in the general direction of the alligator pool. As she followed him along, she noticed a double set of indented scars in the back of his left calf. Probably a souvenir from one of his pets. She grimaced. Ugly thought . . .

He opened his front door and ushered her inside.

"You probably think my setup here is odd," he said.

She remembered Dr. Dawes using the same adjective to describe Simmins. Well, he'd been right about that.

"I had to install the fence systems a few years ago to avoid any further contamination of the local ecosystem. I'd misplaced a Burmese python. The locals weren't amused."

"No," she said faintly, "I guess they wouldn't be."

His living room held a few benches and innumerable *National Geographic*s and scientific magazines stacked on every level surface, including the floor, most of them featuring reptiles on the covers.

She pretended not to notice the three geckos clinging to the wall by the light switch. As he led her deeper into the interior, she almost stepped on a lizard. It scurried under a nearby table where it did a series of quick pushups as it stared at her with calm, lidless eyes.

The enormous house seemed to be buried in clutter. Posters of dinosaurs, snakes, lizards, alligators, and jungles plastered the walls. Bookcases burdened by all manner of scientific texts were piled high in disarray.

"Come on through here," he said, negotiating a path between teetering stacks of mud-spattered magazines on the floor. He led her though the kitchen, a part of which was cordoned off with a fine mesh wire cage. Sandra began to get the unnerving feeling that she was in a huge cage, as well.

"I put up the wire to keep the larger ones from getting into the cupboards."

"The larger ones?"

"Iguanas."

"Oh."

"They like the saltines."

They exited the kitchen and entered the den. More pictures and posters of reptiles, real and fictional, covered the walls, though the clutter was marginally less. She eyed several posters from the movie *Jurassic Park* that seemed to be mostly huge white teeth.

"So," he said, gesturing for her to sit, "Dr. Dawes said you had something that stumped you. Something weird."

"Yes," she said. She opened her bag, reached in, and withdrew the vial containing the scale. She handed it to him. He raised it to the light and squinted.

"Um," he said, "where did you get this?"

Sandra told him, explaining how Madrone had it in his sleeve when they'd found him murdered.

Simmins stood up, eyeing her sharply. "Do you know what this is? What it might be? I've been waiting for something like this for a long time."

"Do you recognize it?" Sandra asked.

"Well, it's a long story, but I used to have one. Well, a lot of them. An entire skin."

"What?" Sandra stared at him.

"Uh-huh. A skin found in London in November, 1888. A human-sized lizard. Larger than human sized. The scales were this same color, translucency . . . the same size, texture. No doubt about it."

"Did they find the animal it belonged to? What was it?" Sandra tried to keep the eagerness out of her voice.

"For a couple of days, the London papers suggested that Jack the Ripper was a giant reptile. But that didn't last for long. Anyway, a cold-blooded creature could never have lived in a climate as cold as England in autumn. Unless," he shrugged, casually gesturing to one of the dinosaur posters, "Bakker's theory about dinosaurs being warm-blooded is true."

"What about the skin?" Sandra persisted.

"Well, I learned about all of this when I was studying in the Sorbonne in Paris. They had it in one of their archive drawers. A shame. No one ever paid much attention to it, and the skin was just rotting there, forgotten. So I . . . well, I . . . they let me have it." He shifted uncomfortably on the couch.

Sandra shrugged. She didn't care how he'd acquired it. "So do you still have the skin? Can I see it?"

"Well, um." He shifted again, brought one of his skinny legs up to cross the other. His thin, gnarled fingers clasped his shin. "Not exactly. I sold it."

"You what?"

"I know, I know." His eyes were downcast. "I was young and foolish and, well, you know how the saying goes. You never know what you have until it's gone. I had the skin for years. I had only told a few of my closest colleagues about it. For, um, certain reasons I didn't want it to be public knowledge that I had it, but . . . then *he* showed up."

"He?"

Simmins stared up at the ceiling. "Now that's the strange thing. I can never remember his name. I have a hard time remembering his face, too. He was a very polite, very well-dressed Chinese gentleman. He visited my apartment in Paris and we got to talking. We must have talked for hours about my theories. In the end, he told me he wished to purchase the skin. Of course, I immediately said I didn't have it any longer. But he insisted and finally I admitted that I might be able to put a hand on it. He told me the price he was willing to offer and, well . . ."

"You sold it."

He nodded. "For a lot of money."

"How much was it?"

"Enough to buy Jurassic Park. Or at least this research laboratory. And then some." He paused. "You have to understand, Detective. I was poor. I thought about all the research I could do, all by myself, with no sponsor, with the money that he offered."

He sighed. "I've never been able to decide whether I regret parting with the skin or not. Obviously it was the type of thing a person stumbles across only once in their lifetime. But then, so was the offer the Chinese gentleman made me."

"So you don't have *any* of it? Not any *part* of it?"

"No."

"No photographs?"

"I didn't think about that until it was too late. I can tell you basically what it looked like, though, if that will help. It was almost eight feet long. It had roughly the same shape as a human, except it had six limbs. Two that looked like legs, I suppose. Two that were arms, and then two that were wings coming out of its back. That's what I assumed, at least. There were no wings along with the skin, only ragged holes in the back of the skin that suggested it. It was really the only evidence of a six-limbed reptile ever discovered. There isn't even any fossilized evidence of such a creature. Of course, such a large creature could never fly. The condor principle, you see, times four. Never fly, unless, of course, my theory about the creature's bones is right. They could have been formed of hexagonal protein crystals, and that would've made them light enough. That would explain any lack of fossilized evidence, if in fact these creatures existed in large numbers long ago."

Silence fell again, and Sandra watched his face as he watched hers. She had no idea if he was telling the truth, lying, or delusional. Her private opinion was that he was a nut-ball and had been one for years.

"Could this scale have come from some large, trained lizard?"

"But . . ." Simmins looked puzzled. "I told you where it came from."

She sighed. "Yes, an eight-foot, six-legged reptile with wings. A lizard man."

"Well, that's not completely sure. I mean, it's only supposition that it was a lizard *man*. It could have been a completely separate evolutionary strain that just happened to be shaped very much like a human."

"I see."

"There may be one other possibility mentioned in the literature," he said thoughtfully.

"Oh?"

"They're called the Drakkers." He scrunched up his face. "No . . . that's not it. Drakmers . . ." Again, his face contorted into a disappointed frown. "No. The Drokpas! That's it—the Drokpas."

"The Drokpas?"

"It's been well reported by those who have traveled there that there are dragon men who live in China. High up in the Himalayas. I've never seen photos, mind you, but there's been enough talk for me to believe the story's true. And there are many cites in respected journals. Older ones, of course, but . . ." His voice trailed off. There was a noise to his left and they both glanced in that direction. An iguana was making its way across a line of stacked books on the shelf under the window.

"Dragon men. In the Himalayas," Sandra said. Her voice was flat.

He spread his hands. "Perhaps it's a bit tenuous . . ." he said. "But I've told you everything I can think of."

She rummaged in her purse and brought out the digital prints. "We found these at two of the crimes," she said, handing them over.

He stood up, took them over to the window, and brought them close to his face. "Yes, yes. The same. See the triple claws, the way the arch is twisted slightly?"

She stood up, walked over, and joined him. He pointed out anomalies in the prints, how one claw was somewhat larger than the others, equivalent to a human heel. "This is no crawling lizard, Detective. Whatever it is, it stands on its hind legs."

She shook her head in frustration. "But you don't *know* what it is."

"Well, the Drokpas I mentioned . . ."

"Right. Them."

They stared at each other again. Finally his watery gaze dropped.

"I'm sorry I couldn't be of more help," he said softly.

She retrieved the scale and the prints, put them back into her bag. "Oh, you've been a help," she said.

He brightened. "That's good. Isn't it?"

She felt a wave of sudden pity for this misfit living with his cold-blooded reptiles in the back of nowhere. "It's a help," she said. "I just don't know what *kind* of help."

He nodded. "Will you keep me informed? If you actually find anything?"

"Of course," she said. She glanced out the window. The clouds beyond were now a vast purple bruise across the sky. "I'd better get going," she said. "Looks like rain."

He escorted her as far as the front gate. "Be careful now," he called. "It's not a good road."

The last she saw of him, he was standing and watching her, one hand slowly waving good-bye.

She waved back, then plunged into the gloomy thickets that barricaded his house from the rest of the world.

"Chinese dragons," she said. "Drokpas. Lizard men with wings."

Some sort of sticker bush scratched a long tear in her already tattered hose.

"Jesus!"

It was three o'clock when she left her mad scientist's lair. She drove down five miles of winding highway before she came to Fallbrook's main street. The highway entered the town, weaved back and forth a little and then abruptly turned to the left onto a straight drag.

She stopped at a small Chinese restaurant, surprised but pleased to find one in such a small town.
The place was practically deserted. The food was good,
though nothing to compare with the best of Chicago's
Chinatown. She ate mechanically and stared out the
window into the parking lot. It had finally begun to
rain.

As she watched the water pour from the heavens,
she allowed herself to think of Justin. She remembered
his hands on her. How good it had felt to be touched.
Maybe to be loved, if only a little, if only for one night.

Still thinking about her options—first, whether she
had any options regarding Justin, second whether she
wanted any—she glanced out the window next to her
table. A man was looking at her car. He seemed familiar.

The hairs on the back of her neck stood up. Where
had she seen him before?

And then she had it. He was the middle-eastern
man who had tried to dance with her at the blues club.
The one who had stepped out of the bar and maybe
caused the redhead to bolt.

What the hell was he doing staring at her car in a
parking lot in Fallbrook, California? She'd come here
almost on the spur of the moment. How had *he* gotten
here?

Sandra watched him. She couldn't see his face full
on, only his profile, indistinct through the rain-blurred
glass. Suddenly he seemed to sense her attention. He
turned and vanished toward the side of the window, in
the direction of the entrance.

A moment later he walked into the restaurant. Up close, it was him. He turned to face her, his gaze boring into her.

What had been a dismal failure of a day as a detective had suddenly turned into something else. What it had turned into she wasn't sure. Not anything good. The hesitant, boorish persona the man had shown before, at the blues club, had vanished. Now he radiated danger.

He walked straight toward her, his eyes burning. Hidden beneath the edge of the table, her hand worked the catch of her bag and came to rest on the butt of her pistol.

"Hold it right there, pal," she said to him. "No closer."

The man—hadn't he said his name was Omar?—wore a wide-collared shirt—a fad Sandra could've sworn had died in the seventies—and baggy bell-bottoms.

He looked down at her and snorted contemptuously.

"And if I don't? Are you going to shoot me, Detective?" His voice was as dry as the desert, heavily laden with that piping accent. He stopped just in front of her.

Sandra suddenly, desperately wished she had stood up before he blocked her in the booth. She didn't show it. "Stay right where you are and we'll get along fine," Sandra responded coldly. "I don't—"

The man lunged for her.

She jerked out the pistol and pulled the trigger. The gunshot cracked and the man stumbled back, crashed into a glass-topped table. The glass shattered, scattering across the floor.

A woman emerging from the rest room screamed.

Sandra slid from the booth, took a shooter's stance. Both hands gripped her pistol and she locked her elbows, staring straight down the barrel at the man.

He was lying on the ground, not moving.

Had she killed him? At that range she couldn't have missed.

She remained cautious, keeping her distance. The restaurant had become deathly silent.

"Call 911," Sandra commanded the terrified lady by the bathroom, coming around to where she could see the inert man's face, never taking her eyes off him.

Then his eyes snapped open and he grabbed for her leg. Sandra fired again, but the man's speed was unbelievable. She'd shot him again, she knew she had, but he kept coming after her, and she stumbled backward, careening into another table. It rocked and the glass plate slid off a bit, but did not fall over.

And then he had a grip on her arm, twisting with frightening power. She felt her bones grind together. Christ, he was fast! How had he gotten to her that fast?!

Sandra leaned into him, trying to dislodge his hand, but he let go and shoved her away from him, not with any fancy technique, just with raw power. His hand snaked out, chopping at her wrist. Sandra's gun clattered to the tiled floor. She gasped at the pain raking across her wrist.

She lashed out with a low kick at the man's kneecap, following it up with one to the balls. But what would have put any normal man on the ground, curled up, holding his groin and trying not to puke, didn't faze him at all. He grunted softly and, without pausing, launched himself into the air. His feet rammed into her chest at the crest of his jump. The air exploded from her lungs and she smashed into the side of a table like a wrecking ball. The table went over with her on top of it. Glass shattered all around her.

She struggled to breathe, tried to raise her head. There was a vast ache like a vise around her chest, choking off her breathing.

Omar straddled her, then sat down hard on her belly, pinning her to the ground. His hands wrapped around her throat and squeezed. She struggled desperately, pounding at his face, but to no avail.

Seconds later, as she felt her consciousness ebbing, the man relented, relaxed his grasp on her throat.

"Listen," she croaked, "you know I'm a cop, the police are on their way, and you've got witnesses, lots of them, watching through the front window! Get out while you still can!"

With one hand, the man kept her neck pinned against the floor. He used his other hand to spring the magazine from her gun and toss it away.

"If you have no gun, you are no longer the big cop woman, are you?" His Arabic accent was guttural and very pronounced.

"What do you want?" Sandra asked.

"I want you to stop looking for things you know nothing about," he said.

"Thanks for the tip," she said. "I didn't realize I was getting close to something." Sandra wanted to keep him talking, wanted to start a dialogue. The longer she kept him talking, the longer she stayed alive—and the more chance the local suits would come riding in to save her. She shifted her body a little, hoping to gain a bit of leverage she might use to throw him.

He pulled her head up by the hair. Sandra gritted her teeth from the pain. His mouth descended close to her ear.

"I want to kill you slowly," the man murmured, his voice insidiously intimate. "I want to treat you like the whore you are. You cannot beat me. Your gun is nothing. Compared to me, you are nothing. Stop looking, or I will find you again. I will kill you. This is my first, last, and only warning. If you—"

There was a loud shout and someone slammed into the killer from behind. Suddenly free of his weight, Sandra rolled to her feet, crunching glass. It was the busboy! He stood lightly on his feet, facing the middle-eastern man, who was glaring murderously at the young Asian kid. His dark hair was tied back. He wore a grease-stained white apron.

"Get out, kid," Sandra said. "It's not your fight."

The kid ignored her. He was staring intently at Omar. "My uncle would say you are being unwise, good sir," the boy murmured to the man. "You have chosen a poor path, he would say. What would your uncle say?"

The man looked at the boy curiously. "What the hell are you talking about?"

"I think he would disapprove of what you are doing. He would think badly of you, as any good uncle would.

Do you wish to bear the disapproval of your uncle?"

The wind seemed to go out of Omar's sails. He looked around nervously, then looked back at the boy. "Who the hell are you?"

"We all have uncles, sir. We must be wary of their disapproval, mustn't we?" the boy answered.

Sandra stood in mute bewilderment. What in the world was the boy talking about? Why was the man listening? Sandra eased slowly closer to her gun. The man had not removed the bullet from the chamber. She'd kill him this time. This time, she would make sure he did not get up.

"Fuck you!" the man raged suddenly. "Fuck this!" He turned and sprinted toward the bathroom.

With a grunt, Sandra lunged for the gun, snatched it up, and chased after him. She flung the bathroom door wide and stepped in, crouched, ready for anything.

And found nothing.

Omar was gone.

Sandra looked at the tiny window just to the left of the toilet stall. Closed. She whipped her gun around the edge of the stall and—

—empty.

"I don't believe this!" she muttered, feeling fresh waves of pain rise from her battered wrist to meet her crushed ribs. She looked over at her reflection in the mirror and nearly dropped her gun in shock. The mirror's surface seemed to be liquid, shifting like a receding ripple on a pool of water.

"Christ . . ." Sandra shook her head, closed her eyes, and rubbed them gently. Her eyes were playing tricks on her. Probably shock. He'd hurt her enough for that.

When she looked again, the mirror was stable, normal, as smooth as if the liquid ripples had never happened at all.

A siren sounded outside.

Where was the cavalry when you needed them?

And now that they were here, what the hell was she going to tell them?

sixteen

J ustin woke with a start, sweat standing on his brow, a rotten taste in his mouth.

For a moment he had no idea where he was. Then he began to recognize the gloomy outlines of his shuttered bedroom. His bed.

He raised one hand and stared at it. The impossible dream was still fresh—*burning* fresh—in his mind.

But he *never* dreamed. Not when he was truly asleep. He'd lost that ability seven hundred years ago! He'd gone two thirds of a millennium with never even the ghost of a dream to disturb his Dragon-bought rest.

He realized his hand was shaking, and with an effort lowered it and hid it beneath the bedcovers.

What did it mean?

He closed his eyes, but the details still danced behind his eyes. He had dreamed he stood on a high place. Behind him was a woman whose face he couldn't see, but he knew her hair was dark. Like Gwendolyne's had been . . .

In his hands he brandished a great silver sword, a razor of gleaming light, as he stood beneath a sky livid with fire. And from that fire, stooping like an avalanche, a vast, glowing form surged down upon him in a tsunami of terror.

As he raised himself to meet it, bearing up his own silver flame, his battle cry came rushing to his lips: *"Strike for the Sword! For the Light!"*

Now his lips moved silently as he shaped the words in the dim confines of his room.

Once again he felt the fear of the dream, the terror and, somehow, the exhalation as he waited to do battle with—

Surely a nightmare. A fantasy. For he knew that dark shape thundering down the sky, knew it as well as he knew his own form. And he would never oppose that one, never. Had he not proved himself over the endless centuries?

So why had the Dragon sent him this dream? He had no doubt the Dragon was capable of such a thing. The Dragon was capable of anything. But why, after seven hundred years, had he chosen to disturb his disciple's empty sleep now?

Perhaps as a warning . . . ?

But a warning of what?

Suddenly uneasy, Justin threw off his covers and rose from his bed. He padded about silently until he was dressed, then crossed to the far wall of the room. His hands moved against secret catches. Half a minute passed, and then he heard a sharp click, and a section of wall swung back, revealing a room beyond. The secret entrance in the wall moved slowly, ponderously, as if it was very heavy. It was.

Justin stepped on through, the last wisps of his dream falling away. Blessedly so. Nevertheless, the feeling that he was in danger still prickled at the base of his skull.

The room was long and narrow, about thirty feet by ten feet. The walls were cinder block. The only door into the room was made of steel a half-foot thick, set on hinges an explosion wouldn't damage, and now, as he watched it swing shut with a soft thud, it was closed and locked tight. The only way to open the door from the outside was by punching in the correct code and waiting out a delay of thirty seconds.

The only way to exit the room from the inside was by getting past him.

Incandescent light bulbs in the I-beam ceiling shed a harsh light—a light that was reflected in each of the twenty-five mirrors that lined the room's walls. The mirrors were of varying sizes and shapes. The largest were propped up against the far wall. Other, smaller mirrors hung on the wall. No mirror was smaller than half the size of a man. Each mirror had come from a different part of the world.

Justin knew of six other "Disciple Rooms" like this one. One was in Kalzar's mansion in Saudi Arabia. Another was in Lyon in France. There was one in Capetown, South Africa, one in Moscow, one in Rome, and the latest had been set up in Brasilia. Each of the mirrors in the Disciple Room connected to one of the Dragon's disciples who had served him for more than a hundred years. When the disciples passed that mark, they were given access to these rooms and could travel at will between their cities and the abodes of each of the seven Elder disciples.

Any disciple, or any trainee with an Elder disciple's permission, could enter any mirror with ease—traveling through the master's fiery realm to their destination.

Justin waited, staring unceasingly at Omar's mirror, like a cat waiting for a very large mouse.

The mirror began to ripple.

Omar's face slowly appeared, contorted with effort, frozen in time. Finally he moved. The watery surface of the mirror pulled away from his skin, and his flexed arms and clawing hands came through. He opened his eyes and began to prepare for the drop to the floor.

Omar's mirror was a smaller one, and perched high on the wall, the sign of a younger disciple or a trainee.

He tripped on the border between worlds and fell headfirst to the floor of Justin's room. Traveling through the Dragon's world was difficult for the younger ones. Often times they remembered nothing of it. If they remembered anything, it was only a flash of fiery red and a droning, baleful voice. Their minds, unaccustomed to such a drastic shift of reality, compensated by putting them, for all intents and purposes, to sleep.

Slowly, wincing from the impact, Omar struggled to his feet. He rubbed his head, blinked a couple of times.

Then he saw Justin, leaning patiently against the wall.

Omar was a disciple of the Dragon. He could not age. His immortal hands could crush bones and his eyes could see through the dark like day. No wound could mark him for more than a day; if Omar's neck were severed, his body would grope for the head, re-attach it, and heal. With every decade that passed, he became more powerful, serving his master and hoping for promotion.

As Omar rose from his crouch, he appraised Justin, trying to keep his own expression hidden and secretive.

But Justin was an Elder, and a trainee disciple could not hide from an experienced immortal. Omar's emotions flashed up and disappeared as fast as lake swells while reflecting the noonday sun. Surprise, bewilderment, curiosity, fear . . .

"It looks as though you had a rough flight," Justin said.

Omar shrugged. "The mirror I used to enter the Dragon's realm was smaller than the one I usually use. I . . . was in a hurry."

"Why the rush?" Justin asked.

Omar shrugged, glanced at Justin warily. "No reason."

For the first time, Justin allowed himself a smile. It wasn't a friendly one. "Omar, you fool. Don't try to lie to me."

"What do you want, Justin?" Omar asked. Justin heard the sliver of worry that was wedged in Omar's heart.

'Tis well that you should worry, Justin thought.

Omar looked longingly at the exit. Justin stepped closer. Omar would never make it unless Justin permitted it. They both knew that.

"What causes you to travel the mirror this day?" Justin asked.

"My business is my own."

Justin allowed his smile to lengthen. It exposed some of his teeth. "The master sent you to me to apprentice. To train. You belong to me. You have no business of your own. You keep no secrets from your teacher. From me."

"I am certain that Kalzar—"

"Kalzar has no jurisdiction over you. Not any more. Not in this place."

"Don't try to bully me." Omar frowned, but he did not move toward the exit.

Justin's eyes narrowed. "Where did you go, Omar?"

"To visit a friend."

"Where?"

"In Arabia."

Justin did not move. He did chuckle softly, though.

"If you lie to me one more time, Omar, I will rip your right arm off," he said, his voice pleasant.

"You can't harm me!" Omar said nervously. "We're all immortals. I know the rules that govern us as well as you do!"

"Do you? I would ask yourself that question again, if I were you."

"Are you threatening me?"

"Not any longer. I issue promises, not threats."

"I do not fear you."

Justin pursed his lips a little, as if he might laugh.

"Truly?" he murmured. "Truly you don't?"

The space between the two immortals crackled with tension.

Justin's voice was sharp in the silence. "Once more, where have you been?"

Omar hesitated, probably deciding whether or not he believed Justin's promise. He shifted his weight to one foot, then to the other. His hands remained at his sides, but Justin could see them twitching.

"I was in California."

"Detective McCormick is also in California today. Small world."

"Who?" Omar tried to look ignorant—it was one of his better poses.

"I told Kalzar to leave her alone," Justin said.

Omar struggled with the lie, finally abandoned it. "You toy with her to the point of danger, Kalzar says. She could find out things she should not know. She already knows things she should not know."

"Did she see you?"

Omar shifted again, and Justin knew the answer.

"Yes, and thanks to your unsurpassed clumsiness, she now knows more than she ever would have had you left her alone. She has a focus for her investigation. She is not an idiot, as you are. She will find out about you, and she will track you to us. To me. Who knows what she will discover along the way?"

"You should kill her!" Omar snarled.

Justin raised an eyebrow. "You presume to give me orders?"

"She should have died days ago. When she first discovered the scale."

"When she discovered the scale? Am I to kill everybody, then, you fool? How many do you think have seen
that scale? Her partner, the technicians, other police
officers. This is not the primitive Arabian backwater of
your birth. Killing her would accomplish nothing more
than to call attention to her case. To the scale. To *us!*"

He paused, then sighed in disgust. "You have no
imagination, Omar. You are stupid and dangerous to our
order. You are dangerous to me. And to *Him.* And that
I cannot permit." Justin moved languidly away from the
wall.

Omar's eyes flicked around the room. He was
openly nervous now.

"You cannot kill me."

"Your belief in your own invincibility is touching."
Justin walked toward Omar.

The trainee disciple looked longingly at the door
Justin had abandoned behind him, and Justin knew what
was going through Omar's small mind.

Under Justin's now scale-covered skin, muscles
slithered like snakes from one thickening bone to
another, lashing them tightly together with unearthly
strength. His face elongated and the cracking noise of his
teeth growing filled his head. His brow thrust out and up
until it became a solid bar over shadowed, reptilian eyes.
Wings erupted from the ripping skin on his back, spraying a token amount of his blood as they unfurled.

"J-Justin!" Omar cried, backing up. "Kalzar ordered
me—"

"I have told you before." Justin's voice was the gravelly rasp of hell. "Kalzar does not rule here."

Omar made his break. Dodging to the right, he tried to slip past Justin. But this pathetic attempt was yet another sign of his inexperience. If he had ever spent time in the dragonling form, Omar would know that Justin's senses were now heightened threefold, as were his reflexes.

Justin allowed Omar the hope that he might actually reach the door. Just as Omar passed, Justin lifted one wing.

The blow knocked Omar completely off his feet. Lying on his back, he stared, horrified, into Justin's red-slit eyes.

Justin reached down and hooked his talons into Omar's rib cage, lifted him off the ground. Blood spurted. Omar's screams turned shrill but were swallowed by the thick walls of the room.

Dragonling muscles sang to Justin, begged him to crush those brittle bones.

"I told you to leave the detective alone. I trust we need not have this conversation again?"

Omar gagged on his pain. Justin could feel Omar's heart pumping against one of his claws, which was buried deep in the writhing man's side.

"You have disobeyed my commands. I consider myself a lenient teacher, but there are times when discipline must be enforced."

Omar had regained some of his poise. Through gritted teeth, he looked down at Justin, still seeking some shred of defiance.

"Did you talk to the detective?"

Omar shook his head, but Justin saw the truth.

"I told you, Omar. Do not lie to me."

Slowly, so that Omar had time to watch, Justin brought his other claw up and grabbed Omar's right arm.

"J-Justin! She—!" Omar's response was cut off by his own scream as Justin began to pull. Justin's muscles flexed, hardened, and strained. Omar's scream ripped his throat ragged. Wet, snapping sounds thrummed through both their bodies as the muscles, tendons, and finally the skin in Omar's shoulder pulled loose. Blood gushed onto the floor. The arm curled spastically against Justin's claw and he held it up for Omar to see.

Omar's scream became a groan, but he didn't lose consciousness. It was that way with all disciples, even trainees. They could never lose consciousness due to pain. Justin knew that lesson well. It was something he learned often at the Dragon's hands.

Justin brought his long, sharp teeth close to Omar's ear. "Come with me," he whispered. "You have failed as my apprentice. You have no place in Chicago."

Turning, Justin walked through one of the full-size mirrors, leaving barely a ripple to mark his entry. He dragged the bloody, maimed disciple with him.

Omar's groan elongated as they cut the surface of the mirror. The sound stretched and coiled around them. At the best of times, a trip through the mirror was intense and uncomfortable. Wounded, it was hell.

"You don't sound so cocksure anymore, Omar," Justin cooed. The world became dark burgundy and crimson. Streaks of every red imaginable hovered in the air like water, splashing against Justin and his cargo, but never wetting him, never leaving a mark of any kind on his skin.

It was said that the Dragon had been driven from this world by Saint George. To escape the wily knight, Justin's master fled into his own reflection in a lake. Saint George drained the lake, trapping the Dragon forever, and that was why everything behind the mirror seemed like fire trapped within water. Hatred caged in shifting droplets. Venom that burned.

There was no steady point within the Dragon's world. There was no place to get one's bearings from. No horizon to keep the world upright. No land beneath the feet to walk or stand upon. Justin was not even sure if the world beyond the mirror was the Dragon's world. He'd seen the Dragon's reflection in countless mirrors, but he had never seen the Dragon while traveling the mirror world. Perhaps it was a midway station between the Dragon's world and his own. Perhaps the Dragon had to travel it just as his disciples did. Justin had never thought it polite to ask. Such small curiosities seemed utterly unimportant when facing the Dragon.

The floating globs of red splashed against them more quickly now. They whipped at Justin as if they would slash him to ribbons, but they had no substance.

Suddenly, they were gone. The whirling reds were replaced by a huge, cavernous space. Justin had always pictured it as the interior of some great stomach, like Jonah in the whale's belly. The walls glowed red, glistened moistly. He floated in its exact center. Things were more solid at this stage of mirror travel, but no more reassuring. Being surrounded by a heaving, fleshy crimson sphere still gave one no steadying point. The violent, bloody, and roiled waters through which they had already passed were only a trifle next to the oppressive weight of this prison.

"Kalzar," Justin spoke, picturing the Arabian thief. He knew he need not say Kalzar's name. This space was sensitive to thoughts, not voices, but it helped Justin to speak the object of his desire aloud.

A blinding white light pierced the stomach's wall, formed itself into a tall square. Justin floated toward the light. As he neared it, he could see through the opening into Kalzar's Mirror Room.

From this place, Justin could spy on anyone he wished. At his thought alone, a mirror passageway would open up near to the person he sought. The function of the mirror world was travel, but disciples with strong willpower could prevent themselves from being forced through the doorway. They could hover for minutes, sometimes even hours, watching their prey. Such a wait was rarely worth it. The compulsion to go further, go through, to kill, hammered at the heart and the mind constantly. But Justin had stared at many of the models for his drawings from this place.

He had no desire to linger on this trip. He had business to tend to.

He stepped through the doorway.

Unlike Justin, Kalzar spent the greater part of his time in his Mirror Room. While Justin's was a hidden vault, Kalzar's sprawled in a high-ceilinged, palatial space.

Fine divans and cushions dotted the white marble floor. Silk curtains fluttered in the tall windows with their pointed arches.

Cool air hit Justin's skin. Entering the mirror was an assault on the eyes, not the skin. It did not seem as if he were stepping into a furnace, and so it always puzzled Justin why leaving the mirror world was like stepping into an icebox. The real world hit him with mind-clearing clarity, and only then did the mirror world seem to be a place of stifling heat.

Kalzar lounged on a great, overstuffed divan, reading a book. He looked up, his expression mildly curious, as Justin came through. His features quickly tightened in outrage when he saw Omar.

Justin tossed the lesser disciple to the floor in front of Kalzar, as effortlessly as if he discarded a used rag, but he kept the arm. Omar's blood spattered on the pristine marble as he landed sprawling at Kalzar's feet. He tried awkwardly to rise. He groaned, looked up at Justin with naked hatred, and then over to Kalzar for help.

Kalzar, his face flushed, didn't spare a glance for Omar. He stood up, faced Justin.

"What is the meaning of this?" Kalzar hissed.

"I warned you," Justin said. "I warned him. Did you think I was joking?"

"The Dragon will flay you for this," Kalzar roared. He was on the verge of transformation. Justin's muscles twitched in anticipation. He wanted a bloody free-for-all with someone like Kalzar. He lusted to rend and tear. If Kalzar transformed, there would be a fight.

"The Dragon would do much worse to you for your

direct disobedience of his edicts," Justin roared back. "What I've done to Omar is a mercy by comparison."

"The detective needed death," Kalzar said. "Do I have to remind you what happens to disciples who let personal interests override loyalty to the master?"

"The detective needs to be killed if I say so, when I say so, and most important, *when the Dragon says so.* Not when *you* say so, Kalzar, no matter how insane your pride has become. Stay in your own backyard, or you will suffer far worse than this. Do I need to remind you what the master does to those who discard the rules to serve their own ambition?" Justin paused. Kalzar shivered with the effort of keeping his rage muted. The tension mounted.

"Think on it, Kalzar," Justin broke the silence. "And then follow me into the mirror, if you dare."

He paused for one final, disdainful glance at Omar's ruined form, spat once, then turned and stepped through the watery surface. He took Omar's arm with him.

seventeen

It was close to eleven o'clock the next evening when the cab dropped Sandra off in front of her condo. She felt both fatigued and strung out at the same time.

She punched her code and started up the stairs. What she really needed was a hot shower. She put the key into her door, twisted. Just as it opened, she realized there was someone else in the apartment besides Benny. Benny was talking, and not to himself. Carefully she peeked around the door and saw who was sitting across the kitchen table from her brother.

Her smile disappeared and her knees felt unsteady.

"What are you doing here, Justin?" she asked. Her voice was low, emotionless and, thank God, steady.

She wasn't ready for this. She was exhausted

from jet lag, she felt like hell, and she had so many bruises from her battle with Omar that she looked like a war casualty.

If Justin had thought to pick a favorable time to talk with her, he'd just struck out.

Unshouldering her bags and tossing them onto the floor, she closed the door behind her, trying to think of something to say. Benny coughed, started to say something. Sandra cut him off.

"I'm sorry. I know I should have called. My flight was delayed," she said. "That was the one lucky thing that happened to me; otherwise I might have missed it. I slept on a couch in the Fallbrook sheriff's office last night."

"I was worried," Benny said. Then he got a good look at her as she stepped into the light. "What happened to your face?" he asked, rolling over to her. He gently touched the stitched-up cut on her chin where a piece of table glass had caught her, the bruises on her face and throat. She was grateful he couldn't see the other, larger bruises hidden beneath her rumpled clothes.

Irritably she pulled away from his touch. "Hazard of the business."

Justin was staring at the lacerations on her face. She was pleased to find that his aristocratic English code seemed to preclude him asking her any shocked male questions. Questions she certainly didn't feel like answering.

So how in the hell had he found her condo? And why had he come here?

Giving her a slight smile, Justin stood up, attempting to break the awkward mood and almost succeeding through the sheer power of his presence. "Sandra, it looks as though—"

He's standing, she thought. *He's going to come over here. He's going to put his hands on me. Console me. Hug me. Something . . .*

Memories of his hands on her body rose in her mind and she knew she couldn't stand that. All of her resolutions to avoid him would crumble.

"I'm wondering just what the hell you're doing here," she said. He stopped, frozen between the chair and the table. *Good, stay there,* she thought, trying to convince herself that she meant it. *Just stay there.*

"I wanted to see you," he said. "I couldn't stay away any longer."

For a moment, it was almost okay. Her heart wanted to believe it, but she balked.

"Sandra, please accept my apologies." Justin's sweet, low voice was soothing. Too soothing. "It was wrong of me to come here. But I was worried. However, since my presence offends you, I'll leave." He started toward the door.

"It's all right. You don't have to go," she said tiredly, walking toward the hallway, trying not to look at him. "It seems you've made a friend. Benny invited you in. It's not my place to tell you to leave."

She heard Benny speaking quietly as she stepped into her own room and held the door a moment before shutting it softly behind her.

He was apologizing to Justin. Sandra snapped

the hair clip out of her hair and tossed it onto the
dresser, a gesture of barely controlled violence. The
clip skittered across the wooden surface and fell into
a pile of folded clothes on the other side. She leaned
against one wall, slumped, and ran her hands through
her mass of curling hair, then closed her eyes and
massaged her scalp with her fingertips.

*Why didn't I tell him to get the fuck out? What
am I doing?*

Somebody knocked at the door.

"Go away."

Benny came in.

She glared at him.

"What's wrong with you? What happened out
there in California?"

"Is this an interrogation?" She pushed away from
the wall. Crossing the room, she pulled the curtains
and blinds open and looked out the window into the
lighted city.

"I just want to know what your problem is."

"My problem?" She snorted. "He shows up and
says, 'Hi, kid, I fucked your sister and it was great
and I was hoping for a repeat, can I come in?' And
you just let him?"

"Of course, he didn't say that." Benny looked
shocked. "You know he didn't say anything like that.
He told me his name and that you'd gone on a date.
He said he really liked you and he thought you really
liked him, but you hadn't been returning his phone
calls. He had no idea what he'd done wrong. I liked
the look of him. So we got to talking. He's inter-

ested in you, Sandra, and he seems like a great guy."

"What the hell do you know about guys, great or otherwise?"

"I *am* a guy!"

"You know what I mean." She turned around. "You've never been fucked over by—" She stopped, shook her head. "I take that back—I'm sorry. It's just that I'm beat. I don't need this right now. I don't need *him* right now."

"You're not being fair to him."

"To him!" she exclaimed. "What about me?"

"You're not being fair to yourself, either," Benny said.

"I don't believe this," she muttered. "My head hurts. I want to lie down."

"I don't think it's healthy, what you do. I think it's time you stopped being Chuck's ex-wife and started being a woman again. For God's sake, Sandra, it's been ten fucking years!"

"Damn it, Benny!" she snapped. "You're in no position to talk. When was the last time you went on a date that wasn't off in cyber-land?" As soon as she said it, she wished she hadn't.

Benny flinched back as if she'd slapped him. Slowly he nodded, and his jaw set. He swallowed and his voice was husky when it came out. "Yeah, well, at least I talk to every woman I meet," he said. "The ones that actually look me in the eye, I ask out. So far, no one has accepted."

He had a terrible dignity at that moment.

"I'm sorry. I didn't mean—"

He brushed it aside. "Give him a chance." He managed a smile. "Trust someone. Trust me. I'll look out for you."

Sandra deflated like a cheap balloon and collapsed limply on the bed. She stared up at him. "You know what?"

"What?"

"I like him. I do. That's why I had to leave when . . . that night . . ."

"That night when you didn't come home until dawn?"

"Yeah. It was some first date."

"He told me." Benny grinned.

Now she was the one who looked shocked.

"No, ya dingus," Benny said. "Just the part where you chased down the guy in the trench coat. The other part I guessed. You know, you may be a good detective, but other people can add two and two. Even stupid little brothers."

"All right. All right."

"I invited him to dinner," Benny said.

"You did, huh?"

"Yeah. Will you go? I promise to watch out for you."

She grinned. "All right, I'll go. But if it ends up in the dumper, I'm going to erase your hard drive."

"Deal." He reached out and rubbed her shoulder. "It'll be fun. You can tell us all about your trip."

"Yeah, right, there's an incentive. But"— she paused—"before I go anywhere, I'm taking a shower, so you'll have to entertain him until I get myself cleaned up."

"Got it covered," he said.

She grinned at him. "My brother, Mr. Cupid."

His expression grew smug. "Got that covered, too."

She threw a pillow at him, but he was gone.

Justin said he knew a little place that was open twenty-four hours a day. Sandra figured him for something more posh, but instead he led them to a hole-in-the-wall restaurant called Venicci's, a tiny Italian joint with checked tablecloths and candles in red glass globes. The place was wedged between a dry cleaner and an appliance store in Wicker Park, a part of town she was surprised Justin even knew existed. The restaurant was dark, with wood-paneled walls, rough-hewn rafters, and wooden booths. Black, wrought-iron chandeliers hung low from the center rafter and the candle-lit tables gave the entire place a smoky, almost medieval feel. The food was marvelous. Sandra was surprised she'd never heard of it before. She thought cops knew all the good spots, but evidently she'd somehow missed this one.

The conversation started out slow, with Justin keeping a polite social distance from her and Benny, trying, she guessed, to ease the tension she felt. They began by discussing simple things, like the weather and the wine. Benny flirted good-naturedly with the waitress, but it seemed to make her uncomfortable, so he stopped after she brought their orders.

After the first bottle of wine, the meal turned into the mellow, glowing social event Sandra had half hoped for and half feared. Time slipped past quickly. Justin was a skilled conversationalist whether he was talking about the weather or about matters of the heart. He kept them both smiling.

"So why don't you tell us what happened on your trip?" Benny said finally. "Mac called twice, by the way. Sounded worried."

Sandra winced. "Oh, God. Mac. He'll go nuts when he sees—" She gestured at her face.

"So what happened?"

Slowly at first, but then with growing intensity, Sandra told them. She edited her run-in with Omar a bit, making him a random mugger, and leaving out any mention of having met him before. She wished she could leave him out entirely, but her face was chopped up badly enough to make that idea ridiculous. Not to mention that her bruised muscles had gone so stiff she stifled tiny groans almost every time she moved.

Justin sat back, his blue eyes glinting thoughtfully. "This Dr. Simmins sounds like a strange man." An amused smile played at the edges of his lips. "He has truly dedicated his life to this study? Of lizards, dinosaurs, even dragons?"

"Sure. If you believe in dragons."

"Some people believe that dragons actually existed," Justin said. "It is a much more common belief in England than here. There, a few scholars even maintain that some of the bones which are thought to be dinosaur bones are actually the bones of dragons."

"Are they saying that maybe dinosaurs were actually dragons?" Sandra asked.

"Sort of, but it's not that simple. Legends speak interchangeably of wyrms, dragons, behemoths, fell beasts, and so on. One has to read between the lines, consider the subtle difference between this word and that, as used by Benedictine monks writing in Latin hundreds of years ago. However, when I looked very hard at the forgotten stories, and sought out the oldest Welsh storytellers to ask them what their grandfathers said—" He paused, thoughtful. "When I truly come to live in the world of those moldy old books, then it all starts to become clear."

"In other words," Benny interrupted, a piece of bread still in his mouth—his words muffled as he chewed, "you're pulling this out of your ass."

Justin's mouth twitched in amusement. He looked at Sandra. "As he says."

"Well, pull away," Benny encouraged.

"Not all the great fell beasts and behemoths of lore are dragons, in very much the same way that not all primates are humans," Justin continued. "Dragons were simply a very intelligent variety of dinosaur."

"Back up, here . . ." Sandra said. "If dragons are intelligent dinosaurs, then why don't they have any wings on the skeletons in the museums?"

"Ah." Justin smiled. "Our ever alert detective asks the pertinent question."

Sandra sat back, done with her meal. She

crossed her arms and regarded Justin, feeling entertained by his fantasy. Benny twirled his pasta in marinara sauce, pleased that they were getting along so well.

"Ultimately the answer to your question lies in the tragic demise of dragons." Justin paused again, staring directly into Sandra's eyes. Sandra's smile faded as she felt a tightening in the pit of her stomach. Those *eyes* of his . . .

"The deaths of the dragons were the single worst thing that has ever happened to our world. Dragons were magical beings. They held within themselves great wisdom and beauty, as well as terrible powers of destruction. They spoke to the wind and knew the oldest thoughts of the oldest stars. When they were around, anything could happen. Nothing was impossible. They were like the gods, but gods you could see and feel. Not gods of words and ideas and faith, but gods of flesh and bone. Gods that made love, gave birth, dreamed, fought, grew old, and died." Justin sighed. "And they died mostly because we killed them. We killed them for their wings. You see, the power of a dragon is in its wings. Dragons were magical beings. Besides their intelligence, their skill in magic set them apart from their gigantic reptilian counterparts. The wings were the physical manifestation of this magic. Science tells us that nothing as massive as a human could ever fly by the force of its own muscles, let alone something the size of an elephant. And something the size of a castle? Ludicrous. Unless, of course, the rules of physics as we know them do not apply."

"So what are you saying?" Benny asked. "That dragons had wings, but didn't fly?"

"Not at all. Dragon flight was mystic. A dragon flies the way a painter captures an ironic smile with a few wisps of color. The way a great singer brings a tear to your eyes with a few words that, if merely spoken, would be bland, or even silly. Reality keeps us within a fence line, and dragons flew over that fence before it was even built.

"Dragons respected their own power and knowledge," Justin continued quietly. "So when a dragon died, its children would always return to feast upon the wings. The wings were a final bequest, an act of love and hope."

Sandra watched Justin's face, mostly his lips. She tried to keep herself from thinking what it would be like to have those lips kiss her again.

It was a disconcerting thought. She pushed it away, and tried for lightness.

"No huge dinosaur corpses with wings 'cause the kids ate them? That's an interesting theory, but it doesn't explain what happened to the skeletons of the last generation," Sandra said, and the moment she did, she winced.

It was a cop thing to say, a cold, analytical hammer shattering a beautiful story. What she wanted to say was that she liked the story, and she wanted him to continue. But she'd said something else instead. *Why did he make her so self-conscious?*

"I don't see the tragedy," Benny interjected. "What did humans do that was so wrong?"

"What did humans do that was so wrong?" Justin smiled, but his expression seemed somehow bitter. "We were jealous. It's the oldest story in the world. In the Bible, a serpent told Eve that if she ate of the forbidden fruit, she would become like God. Where do you think that story came from?

"Long before humans could write such things down, a foolish young dragon befriended a human woman. This young dragon, this *serpent,* told Eve of the power in a dragon's wings. Eve was a jealous woman and convinced her husband to slay the dragon so they could eat its wings. Once the deed was done, there was no going back. They tasted the forbidden fruit, brought the shadow of evil into paradise. Eve, her husband, and the entire human race was cast forever from the Garden of Eden where man and beast could live in peace and harmony."

"Are you saying that the reason there are no dragons now is because we killed them off?" Sandra asked.

"Why didn't the dragons stamp out humankind first, if they were so much more powerful, with their magic and all?" Benny asked.

Justin shrugged. "How can we be certain? Perhaps, at first, the dragons did not take humans very seriously. Being solitary, philosophical creatures, the dragons left the humans alone and expected to receive the same treatment. They expected better of us, and we killed them for their mistake.

"Being what we are, we humans could not help ourselves. The lure of forbidden knowledge was too great. The power gained by eating a dragon's wings was too real. Adam and Eve passed this knowledge on to their children, who in turn went off to slay their own dragons. Thus began the pharaohs, God-like beings who ruled the known world in that time.

"Once the killing of dragons started, it never stopped. There are examples in some of our more well-known legends. Tiamat in Babylon. Hercules killing the Hydra. Siegfried killing Lindworm. Beowulf and Grendel. Saint Martha and La Trasque in France.

"These people are revered as heroes, great men and women fighting great evil, but that's all a lie. It's history from the mouth of the victor. People must believe they are in the right when they commit atrocities. Otherwise their own guilt will destroy them. And so humans, out of their own necessity for self-justification, named the dragons evil. They were reputed to be linked with Satan, and thus we had to exterminate them, by the edict of God. That is how the unfortunate young dragon killed by Adam and Eve was recast as the voice of Satan in the Garden of Eden. If the same lie is told often enough, people begin to believe it. And then, of course, even lies can become self-fulfilling prophecies after many years.

"By the time of Saint George, no doubt some dragons had become enraged by the methodical extermination of their species and were determined to avenge themselves. But most dragons left Europe to escape the madness, rather than try to combat it.

Their brethren in the East had no such problems with their human cohabitants. Humans in the East were no less violent than the shaggy Westerners, but they were certainly more respectful of dragons. It is said they admired their dragons and saw them as harbingers of power, fertility, and well-being."

"So the dragons are all living in the East now?" Sandra asked.

"Alas, no, none are."

"None?" Sandra asked.

"Sounds like they just sort of curled up and died," Benny said.

"Ah, that is a very Western perspective on the situation. An Asian would see it much differently. In the Orient, one must be very careful never to ask someone for something they do not want to give you. If you ask for it, they are honor-bound to give it to you. Then, once the Asian has given it to you, he will hate you forever for asking for it."

"That's ridiculous!" Benny said.

"Perhaps, but it is also very polite. And the dragons of the East did the polite thing. When the day came that they were not wanted, they left. But I assure you, they were not happy to go. Ever since then the dragons of the East, also called by some the dragons from Beyond, have been plotting to exact their revenge."

"Sounds like a conspiracy theory to me," Sandra said.

"And what do you think of the state of the world today? Somewhat conspiratorial?"

"It's a bit shaky," Sandra said.

"And how do you account for that?"

"Human nature?"

"Human nature with a bit of outside help from the dragons from Beyond."

Benny laughed. "Good for them. I hope they wipe us all out."

"Unfortunately I think they would have," Justin said. "Except that we have someone in our corner."

"Who's that?" Sandra wanted to know.

"The last Western dragon. As I said, there were many dragons that were enraged by the idea of being driven off by these humans who had only just arrived upon the earth. By the time of Saint George, some dragons had become the evil we painted them to be. George became a hero for slaying them, but he was hardly saintly. The older accounts of his life portray him as a greedy, ambitious man. He saw himself destined to rule the world and convert it to his religion."

"No wonder he's the patron saint of England," Sandra grinned.

Justin smiled, a warm sincere smile. "*Touché*, Yankee."

Sandra's skin tingled with the wine she had drunk. The warmth cradled her. She suddenly realized she was staring at Justin, caught herself with a slight start, and turned her gaze toward Benny.

"Go ahead," Benny said to Justin. "I want to hear more."

"The king of Libya asked Saint George to slay a dragon who was demanding the king's daughter as a human sacrifice. The popular legends say Saint George subdued the beast with the sign of the cross and stabbed the evil monster through the heart. Other, older legends tell a different story.

"Saint George was a large, powerful, good-looking man. He had a voice that could fill an entire field. When he preached, people believed. When he gave orders, people followed. He traveled with a huge entourage of mystics, alchemists, Arabian magicians, and wise men from the far east. George had slain dragons before, but this dragon was not such easy prey. This dragon was the last of his kind. He was wise, and clever, and had thousands of years of anger burning in his belly. This dragon feared no man, but George was unlike any other man. And he had eaten quite a few dragon's wings himself at this point.

"The Great Dragon escaped from the traps George laid for him and led the saint on a merry chase across Northern Africa. The dragon—perhaps the most powerful of its kind ever to exist—had no wish to fight Saint George. And this dragon had learned to disappear into its own reflection. When hunted by dragon slayers of the past, it would fly over a still pool of water and disappear without a trace.

"The dragon tried this on Saint George, but Saint George was not so easily fooled. If this last dragon was the strongest of its kind, then likewise Saint George was the strongest dragon slayer ever to hunt it. And so when the chase led to a small lake, and the dragon disappeared, Saint George was able to guess what had happened.

"Then Saint George used his cross to agitate the waters so they could never form a reflective surface and the dragon could never escape its haven. While maintaining his vigil, Saint George had the king of Libya dig a huge trench to drain the pool, trapping the dragon there forever."

They all sat in silence for a long moment. Justin did not move, except to swirl the wine in his glass around and around. Then he leaned forward, set his wine down, and placed his elbows on the table. He beckoned them closer. "Do you know what they say of dragons?"

"No," Benny whispered, enjoying himself.

"They say that the last dragon did not die. They say it still lives within its own reflection on the far side of a pool that no longer exists, and for the last twelve hundred years it has lived there, influencing humankind, trying to steer it from its evil, barbaric ways in the hope that someday it will be safe for the dragon to return."

"Well, I hope it succeeds." Sandra raised her wine glass. "Let's drink to the dragon."

"To the dragon," said Justin. They clinked their glasses together.

"Where did you learn to tell stories like that?" Sandra asked Justin.

"Call it a childhood passion. I read everything I could get my hands on. When I told the best of the stories, I always had a large audience. I would make it my task to keep them riveted."

Sandra scooted out of the booth, stood, and

stretched. Her muscles responded with a chorus of dull aches, and she winced. "Whatever you did, it works. Where's the ladies' in this place?"

Justin pointed.

She turned and left the table, skirting the returning waitress.

"Is there anything else I can get for you?" the girl asked, her voice a bit taut. She looked briefly at Benny, then focused her attention on Justin, something akin to relief on her face. He shook his head. Benny stared up at the young woman's face.

"I'd like something. A large helping of smiles. I'd like some of that, if I could. Do you have any tonight?"

The girl hesitated. Then she grinned nervously and gave a forced laugh. And kept looking nervously at Justin, who ignored her.

"For Christ's sake, the least you could do is *look* at me. I'm not that ugly," Benny said abruptly.

The girl hesitated, obviously at a loss for what to do. Benny glared at her, waiting for a reply.

"Benny, don't." Justin put his hand gently on the younger man's shoulder. He nodded for the girl to go.

She fled.

Benny slumped into his chair, fuming. Justin let the silence rest for a moment.

"It's not her you're mad at," Justin finally said.

Benny nodded, but only looked more miserable. "I know. I didn't mean to explode, but it was like she would've felt more comfortable if I didn't exist. Did you notice how she couldn't stand to look at me? And even when she did . . . I just get so sick of that fucking look in their eyes. They look at me like I'm some kind of a monster. You don't know what that's like." Benny fell silent.

Justin realized that his own jaw was clenched. He forced himself to ease it.

"I dream about it all the time," Benny said softly. "At night. Even daydreams. I picture myself walking up to a pretty girl and asking her to dance. And she smiles and I take her out there and dance until I . . . we—we just float away. I almost never had the guts to do that before my accident. And now it's too late."

Justin said, without looking directly at Benny, "You know, I was very sick once. I watched my body waste away, become swollen and hideously ugly. Repulsive. I thought I was going to die. I would have given anything, paid any price to make it all go away."

"Yeah." Benny let out a long breath, shook his head. "That sounds like the beginning of a familiar story. Does the usual come next?"

Justin blinked. "The usual?"

"Yeah," Benny replied. "The part where you tell me you sold your soul to the devil for looks, class, money, a killer accent, and a date with my sister . . ."

Justin grinned. He shook his head. "Fortunately, it wasn't the devil who showed up that day."

"Well, if he does ever show up, send him my way. I've got a hell of a deal for him." Benny laughed suddenly, then reached for his glass and downed the rest of his wine.

Sandra returned from the rest room in time to catch Benny's last words.

"Send who your way?" Sandra asked Benny.

Benny smiled. "The devil," he said. "But he ain't here right now."

"One can never tell," Justin said.

"*I* didn't invite him," Sandra pointed out.

"He's invited into our world all too often," Justin said somberly. Then he looked up at her and smiled. "But I think you scare him away when you're around. Your soul shines too brightly to let him in."

When they got back to the condo, Justin insisted on walking them to their door. He and Benny exchanged mumbled pleasantries and goodnights. Benny then beat a strategic retreat, leaving the two of them standing alone just outside the door.

"Thanks for the dinner," Sandra said. "And the story. Best I've heard in a long time."

"Did you like it?" he said.

"Very much."

They both paused. The silence grew nervous, exciting.

"Well, I'd better get some sleep," she said.

He nodded. "Of course," he said, but did not move. The last of Sandra's restraint vanished. She moved against him, lifted her face, and kissed him, long and hard.

"Go to bed—alone, this time," Justin said softly, as he finally stepped back from her.

Sandra nodded.

"I'll call you," he said.

"I'll look forward to it."

He turned and headed down the hallway. She backed into the doorway, but watched him until he got into the elevator and the doors closed behind him. He walked steadily and didn't look back.

She heard a click and turned around to find Benny frowning at her.

"What?" she said. "What's that look supposed to mean?"

"Well," he said, "at this point in the fairy tale, you're supposed to get on your white horse and carry him away."

"Given my luck with men, he's more likely to turn into a frog." Sandra ran an affectionate hand through his hair as she walked past him and headed for bed.

eighteen

Justin Sterling's eyes closed slowly. He nodded, caught himself, then looked out the picture window in his living room again. The city's lights twinkled like jewels on black velvet, reflecting in the glass sides of the buildings downtown and far away on the waters of Lake Michigan.

It looked like a peaceful scene. Yet he knew that peace was an illusion—it was likely that somewhere in that glittering night, someone was murdering—or planning to murder—someone else. Maybe it was a junkie knifing his pusher. Maybe a terrorist mixing a bomb. Most likely it was two men in a bar parking lot, fighting over some imagined slight or a woman they both coveted.

Peace was what mortals thought they desired, but they lied to themselves. What they really wanted was wealth, power, and control over others. They would destroy peace in a heartbeat to get it.

Even those who lived solitary lives—who cloistered themselves from the world—fought, even if it was only within their own minds. In fact, Justin was fighting now. He lacked someone to attack, so he waged war upon himself.

Justin looked out at the city, thinking of the millions of people living there. Their lives were so different than his.

He rose from his chair in silence, the raucous sounds of Chicago deadened by the expensive glass window. He lived forever—and his life was now safely insulated in a perfect, technologically engineered cocoon. A wonder of the modern age. He had the money it took to purchase the illusion of peace. He reached out and put a hand on the glass. It was cool and smooth—an illusion hiding the gritty reality of the city beyond the glass.

He turned away from the window. He must go into the city again tonight. The Dragon's voice was quiet for the moment, but Justin could feel the master's presence behind every reflective surface, watching. Did the Dragon approve of Omar's punishment? Was the master furious at Omar? At him, for punishing Omar? Or did the master simply not care one way or the other?

And that was a puzzle, wasn't it? Why hadn't the Dragon intervened to resolve the conflicts between himself and Omar, himself and Kalzar? What did it mean that Kalzar was free to approach him through the mirror, when he hadn't been before? And now he too could enter Kalzar's private domain, from whence he'd also been barred before.

It was difficult for Justin to tell where he ended and the Dragon began. Was his rage the master's way of speaking to him without using the mirror? He had often wondered how much control he really had over his own life, even when he walked the earth in human guise. He knew full well that he had very little control, if any, in the Wyrm state. He'd built a life as a man here in Chicago. He had the club, his home, his art. But were they really his? Were each of the drawings he had created somehow manifestations of the master's will? Was everything he felt somehow influenced by that quiet, powerful voice? Were his feelings for Sandra McCormick the product of his own heart or an obsession implanted by the Dragon?

He was drawn to her. He could not argue with that. She felt real to him. She glowed with the force of her personality, lit up every room she entered—something he had not experienced in centuries, at least, and perhaps only once before in his life. He knew the original attraction was based on Sandra's physical similarity to Gwendolyne. Like Tina, she had that classic bone structure, dark, glossy hair, a subtle smile, and fair skin. There had been many women in Justin's long life. But very few of them touched him in any real way. Most never even knew he was watching them—as Tina had not, before he showed himself to her. And even Tina had no idea that beneath the monstrous form of the Wyrm lay a man.

Sometimes he had interacted with them. Most of the time he had not. But he had rarely been tempted to share all he was with them—and he had never acted on those urges. Sandra, after such a very short time, tempted him almost irresistibly.

Sandra had her own demons. And somehow Justin felt that she alone might understand his.

"So what will you do now?" he asked the glass. He wasn't sure whether he was talking to the Dragon or to himself. Certainly the master lacked a soft spot for the desires of one of his immortals. Justin knew what the Dragon thought. She was getting too close to the truth. And he was helping her. Telling her the old stories. What on earth had possessed him? Why was it so important that she know the weight of his burden? The source of his power?

Justin studied himself in the glass. He was human now. He wondered whether she would recoil in horror if she saw him in his Wyrm state.

He remembered his wife, Gwendolyne, as she'd been before the plague took her.

Despite their similar appearances, she and Sandra were nothing alike.

Oh, on the surface they could have been twins—their long, tumbling hair, their dark eyes, their elegant faces and pointed chins, the slight upward tilt of their noses. But inside, they were as different as chalk and cheese. He wondered about his memories—was he seeing Gwendolyne's face on Sandra now? Or Sandra's face on Gwendolyne? He didn't know anymore.

One thing he did know—the Dragon had good cause to fear her. Sandra had almost all the pieces of the puzzle now. She was fighting her conclusions—and who could blame her? In the modern world, stories of marauding, murderous, man-shaped killers were the sort of things sold to tabloid journalists, not Chicago detectives. But she knew in her heart what was going on. She might have figured everything out, even by now, even in the intervening hour since he'd left her, and decided to move her wild theories to the forefront of her murder investigation. It would take only one tiny lateral leap in her thinking. After all, he thought, he had more or less given her the last clues she needed to buy into the story at dinner.

The phone rang.

The club phone. Someone downstairs needed him.

He crossed the room, past the dais with the mirror. There were only two reasons his manager was supposed to call him. One was in the event of some cataclysmic emergency. The other . . .

"Mr. Sterling?"

"Yes, Edward."

"There is a young woman here to see you."

"I see. Is she as I described her to you?"

"Yes, sir."

"Do not keep her waiting."

"Yes, sir."

Justin hung up the phone.

Minutes later, he heard a knock on his door. Justin was sitting in his chair in the dark, waiting. He stood.

"Come in," he said.

Sandra opened the door. He watched her every movement. Every subtle shift of her body under the white Angora sweater she wore, every firm muscle encased in her snug jeans. She carried a small backpack in one hand and the wide neckline of her sweater had drooped over one bare shoulder. The hallway outside bathed her in soft white light. She glowed in it like an angel.

"What, no gentlemanly greeting at the door?" Sandra chided him. Her voice sounded calm, but he could feel her nervousness. She lingered in the doorway, delayed entering the room.

Her eyes adjusted rapidly to the darkness, and she looked quizzically at him.

"I wanted to watch you enter my dwelling," he said. "Watch you coming to me."

"You make it sound like such a big deal. Like crossing the threshold. Well, do you want me to come in?" she asked. "Or don't you?"

"I can't decide." Yes, he wanted her. No, he feared her. Feared *for* her. Feared for himself.

"I fought with myself before coming over here," she said.

"We have both been warring then. Has the war been won between us?" He got up and moved to greet her.

He was very close to her now. He could feel her breath. He thought he could hear her heart beating.

"Is this a war?" she asked. "Is that what we've got going here? Are we adversaries in some sort of battle?"

"Of course," he murmured, so close to her, but still so far apart. "The oldest war in man's history—

the union between man and woman. It is always a struggle. A contest of wills."

"Then let the battle begin." She stepped over the threshold. "It's dark in here," she said. "I can barely see you. But I can see your eyes. I can always see your eyes."

He reached a hand out toward her, then let it fall.

"I would touch you," he said. "But where? Your lips . . . your throat . . . your hands . . . ? They are all so tempting. I can't decide."

"Here . . ." Her voice was barely audible. She took hold of his hand, placed his finger on her lips. "Start here."

He kissed her. Her eyes closed and shock flashed through them both like lightning, paralyzing them for an instant. The feeling that held them in its grip was overpowering. It was as if all the energy in the universe flowed through that single kiss. They abandoned themselves to it.

At last they parted. His heartbeat sounded loud in Justin's ears.

Sandra, too, seemed overwhelmed. She swallowed, whispered, "My, my." Her pack thumped to the floor. He took her in his arms again and kissed her thoroughly.

"I think, Justin . . .," she whispered into his ear, " . . . we just won that war . . ."

Omar paused for a moment after he hopped the fence surrounding the safe house where the Drokpa agent masquerading as a psychologist in the Chicago police force had taken Tina Danforth. He was as careful as it was possible for one of his impulsive nature to be. No one heard the rattling of the chain links. Omar scratched at the stump of his arm and seethed. It would heal, but the newly forming nerves itched like crazy. It would be at least another couple of weeks before it was completely regenerated, Kalzar said. The infernal itching as it grew back was driving him mad.

Omar turned his attention away from his lost arm. A large black man in a white uniform walked around the corner of the brick building, wheeling a trash barrel out to the Dumpster. Omar stared at the man, then walked toward him.

The orderly turned when Omar was a scant few feet away. He jumped in surprise, then frowned. "Hey, man. You shouldn't be here. Get out of here!"

Omar continued walking forward. The orderly retreated, got back against the Dumpster, and balled his fists, ready for a fight. He was a large man, very strong, and clearly sure he'd win any sort of confrontation.

"What the hell you doing here, anyway?" the orderly said.

Omar paused a couple of feet from the man. He narrowed his eyes and looked at the orderly. After a moment's silence, he spoke.

"Trying to decide how to kill you without getting blood on your uniform."

• • •

Tina awoke in the darkness of the strange room and sat up. Everything seemed odd to her—she'd been disjointed and confused ever since that terrible night. She had been dreaming about the dragons, some dreams terrible nightmares that dragged her screaming from sleep, others reassuring her that she would heal and times would change. She couldn't remember exactly how the last dream—one of the lovely ones—had ended. She hadn't wanted to wake up, but the dragons said she couldn't stay right now, that she had to go back.

It was important, they said.

Now she just had to figure out where they wanted her to go.

As the reality of the dark room took hold, Tina heard something outside of her door. Fear tore through her. Now she remembered what the dragons had said and why she had to leave, leave now. The dragons said that danger would come for her tonight.

Do not be afraid, they had said, but be swift and prepare.

The door handle turned and a shaft of light fell across the floor. Tina slid her feet off the bed and stood up to face the intruder.

The man came in and closed the door behind him. He wore a white orderly's uniform, but Dr. Shiang said the orderlies would not come into her room at night unless Tina called them.

The man paused. Tina could barely make out his features, but she saw enough to recognize him. He was the man who had attacked the Chinese kid just after

Zack's murder, who would've killed her if she hadn't run for her life. Tina had talked about it with Dr. Shiang. The doctor told Tina the man's name was Omar.

"I know who you are," Tina said, feeling a strange calm. Her dreams, while a warning, had somehow settled her nerves.

"Do you?" Omar narrowed his eyes. He lunged across the room, slamming Tina up against the wall. She gasped, completely unprepared for his speed and brutal power.

"Good," Omar said. "Then you know I'm the one who's going to rip that pretty face off your skull."

Tina struggled against the iron hand holding her captive. She kicked at him, scratched at his eyes. Nothing worked. He was toying with her like a cat toys with a mouse, enjoying her futile struggles while he contemplated the best location for his killing blow. Tina felt herself unraveling. Her calm dissolved as if it had never been, and she felt herself returning to that dark place deep within herself, the place where Dr. Shiang had found her.

Then she remembered the dragons' voices from the dream and she ceased her struggles. The dragons seemed to speak to her again and soothe her fright. If Omar really wanted to kill her, she would now be dead. Perhaps he would hesitate long enough for her to escape.

Tina swallowed against Omar's relaxed grip and spoke hoarsely. "I've heard the voices of the dragons from Beyond," she said. "I have heard their singing. I will never be the same again."

"Then you've joined the wrong side," Omar said, a snarl curling his lip. He threw her across the room. She crashed into the bed, overturning it. The lamp, the digital clock, and a box of tissues clattered down around her. She cried out, sprawling onto the floor. She pushed herself up and turned to look at him, crying, sobbing through the pain.

Omar's eyes were glowing red. He stood over her, waiting for something. Tina noticed that he had an empty sleeve where his left arm should be. At that moment he looked even more threatening than if he'd been whole, his body and his expression twisted and malevolent.

Tina swallowed, steeling herself, and said the first words that came to her. "You are just a minor disciple. You can't take the dragonling form."

That seemed to affect him. His triumphant smile turned into a snarl. "Soon enough, pretty one, I'll cross that threshold. I don't know who's been telling you so much, but they obviously haven't told you enough." He moved toward her and Tina scuttled backward.

A shaft of light tore across the room again, and a cool voice came from the doorway. "It will be difficult to rip apart your victims with only one arm."

Tina melted with relief. Omar turned to face Dr. Shiang. The small Chinese woman stood quietly in the doorway, outlined by the glow of light from the hallway. Her long, black hair was unbound. She looked as if she had hurried here. Tina had never seen Dr. Shiang look hurried before.

"That will be a problem for you," Dr. Shiang continued, stepping into the room between Tina and Omar.

"Who the hell are you?"

Dr. Shiang answered his question with a question. Her voice was a warm breeze in the cold room. "If they have already taken your arm, the rest will not be far behind, don't you think?"

Omar responded by backhanding her sharply across the face. Dr. Shiang stumbled across the room, but did not fall. She righted herself and stood calmly once more, waiting for the next attack. She did not once look at Tina, but Tina could almost hear Dr. Shiang's voice inside her head.

Run fast! Now!

Scrambling to her feet, Tina went for the door.

She reached the hallway at a dead run and heard Omar yell. Over the pounding of her own heart, she heard his footsteps crashing after her.

At the end of the hallway was the physical therapy room. Tina fumbled with the handle and threw the door wide open, rushed inside even as she slammed it in Omar's face. Weight-lifting equipment in all shapes and sizes filled the room. Six-foot-tall mirrors covered every wall.

The mirror! Dr. Shiang's voice whispered in her head. *Into the mirror!*

Tina's rational mind couldn't quite see the point of that, but her rational mind seemed distant and small in these circumstances. She had seen things in the past few days that defied explanation. Tina had only one certainty right now. She trusted Dr. Shiang with her life.

That was the only certainty she needed.

She leapt at the mirror. It rippled as she passed through it.

Omar's fingernails scraped Tina's nightgown as she plunged into the mirror. Her actions caught him off guard, and he missed her. He leapt after her, reaching for her disappearing leg. He caught hold of it just as his senses were overwhelmed by the mirror world. Keeping his grip firm, he thought of Kalzar's mansion as his mind was forced into sleep.

When Omar's consciousness returned to him, he knew something was wrong. The surface of the mirror at Kalzar's house parted for him like water, and he stumbled onto the marble floor. The bright sun blinded him for a moment.

Omar looked at his hand. In it was a girl's slipper. Tina Danforth was nowhere to be found.

With his mouth agape, Omar stared up at Kalzar, who had noticed his arrival. Kalzar rose from where he had been lounging on some cushions. His eyes narrowed.

"Where is she, Omar?" Kalzar asked in a quiet voice.

Omar shook his head. "I don't know. I had her . . . I know I had her . . . I will return at once and—"

"So you have failed me again," Kalzar said. "I don't think returning to fetch her will be necessary."

"But, Kalzar, it wasn't my fault. The dragons from Beyond—"

"Yes, yes . . ." Kalzar nodded. "I know."

Omar watched in terror as Kalzar's face elongated. Teeth cracked and grew large in his jaws. Wings burst from his back, ripping through his shirt and spraying blood.

Omar screamed and leapt for the mirror.

His hand broke the surface just as Kalzar's claw closed on his ankle . . .

But Kalzar captured more than a shoe.

Kalzar threw the bloody rug at the base of the steps. It fell open, revealing what was left of Omar. Already, the lesser disciple's parts were trying to fit back together. Eventually he would reform, but there was a trick Kalzar had learned long ago when one of his protégés had disappointed him, and he had used it many times since.

I'd better hurry, he thought, *before he assembles himself enough to start moaning again.*

Kalzar crouched before one of the stone walls of the cellar and hit a hidden lever. A section of the wall moved and he reached within and pulled out a large, iron-bound trunk. Setting it aside, he pulled out a second, identical container.

A thump broke his quiet contemplation, and Kalzar turned. No shadow marred the light spilling from the stairway. The thump sounded again, and Kalzar looked down at the trunks. A slow smile curved his lips and he laughed.

Softly at first, then with growing strength, a voice came from inside the other trunk. Kalzar produced an ornate key and opened it.

Half of a man struggled within. His body ended roughly at the base of the rib cage. His wild eyes rolled and squinted at the light. "Please!" he cried, "I'll do anything! Please!"

"Hassan," Kalzar said pleasantly. "Do you know that I had completely forgotten where you were? You're looking much better than when I put you there. Would you like some company? I'm sure you and Omar will become the best of friends."

Kalzar scooped up roughly half of Omar from the rug and tossed it on top of Hassan's upper body. It didn't really matter what went in, as long as the spine was roughly in two pieces, and those two pieces weren't allowed to touch. A lesser disciple would grow back any extremity in time, but if the spine was halved, the disciple would remain in two pieces. Kalzar wasn't sure if that was the case with the Elders—he'd never had a chance to experiment—but he'd always been curious about it. Perhaps he'd have a chance to find out soon.

"Oh, dear God, no!" Hassan screamed.

Kalzar opened the second trunk and threw the rest of Omar on top of Hassan's legs, which were kicking. He closed and locked the container, then turned back to the original trunk. Hassan had managed to push himself on top of Omar's remains, and he was clawing at the sides, trying to drag himself out. He grappled with the edges of the trunk, but Kalzar patiently removed his hands and pushed him back.

"Hassan," Kalzar began, "Do you think, after all this time, you have learned your lesson?"

"Yes, master. Oh, yes, master."

"I don't."

Kalzar slammed the lid shut and locked it. The horrified scream from within afforded him a great deal of pleasure. He couldn't even remember what Hassan had done to invoke his displeasure.

Perhaps Justin was right about one thing, Kalzar thought as he shoved the trunks—one moaning, one reverberating from desperate kicks—back into the alcove and closed the wall. Omar had turned out to be a bitter failure. Kalzar decided that he must be much more careful about the allies he chose in the future. Or perhaps he should do away with allies altogether, start tying up the loose ends himself?

Yes, that would suit him. The general would take the field again. Why should the lackeys have all the fun?

nineteen

The clacking of keyboards and the buzz of voices in the precinct made a comfortable, familiar sound as Sandra breezed into the Eighteenth District the next morning.

The station felt like home, and it was good to be home, even as difficult as it had been to leave Justin. The memory of the night she'd spent with him brought a smile to her face. But then, just about everything was bringing a smile to her face today. The rain had let up and the sky was robin's egg blue with a few white puffy clouds—a very nice change from the unending storms of recent days. She'd even heard a bird singing just outside the garage as she turned off West Chicago.

She had wanted to linger beside Justin all morning, or do something stupid like make pancakes and fresh-squeezed orange juice and have breakfast with him in bed. After hours of lovemaking, each time sweeter and slower than the last, they had finally collapsed in exhaustion. The miracle wasn't that she was late. It was that she'd come in at all.

If she'd been juggling her usual caseload, if it had been any other day, she would have been tempted to stay in Justin's arms. But things were coming to a boil. And the monster was still out there.

She walked into the detective squad room to the familiar sight of Mac talking to his wife on the phone. Linda always called at the beginning of the day, about an hour after he got to work. Mac was nodding without really listening and saying, "Mmm hmm," at random intervals, and nodding some more, until he saw Sandra.

"Honey? Yeah. She just walked in. I gotta go." He paused. "Who? Sandra! Who do you think?" He shook his head. "Right. Okay. I've got to go. Bye." He put the receiver down and regarded Sandra silently for a moment.

She gave Mac a sweet smile.

"Glad to see you could finally make it in," he said.

"It's good to be back."

He looked at his watch, "Really? You wouldn't know it by the time."

"Relax, Mac. Nothing ever happens before ten o'clock."

He narrowed his eyes. "What's up with you?" he asked.

"I'm not sure what you mean, Mac." She shrugged and looked around. "Did they wash the windows or something in here? Seems brighter."

"Little Miss Sweetness and Light . . ." Mac sat back in his chair and smiled a little. "I don't believe it."

"What?"

"You've got that barnyard egg look."

She raised an eyebrow at him.

"Just laid," he said, chuckling. Mac was his own biggest fan. "Ever heard that one before?"

She felt her face heat with embarrassment.

"And well laid, from the looks of it," Mac continued.

"Not funny, Mac."

He held up his hands in surrender. "Don't get your hackles up, Bruce. But questions like 'Gee, did they wash the windows?' and that goofy smile you're wearing are a dead giveaway."

"Focus, Mac. Think *focus*, okay?"

Across the room Lewis was cussing at his computer again. O'Mara was trailing the captain to his office door, trying to convince him that she deserved this weekend off.

Mac chuckled. "Focus on what, Bruce?" He blinked with spurious innocence.

"Dragons, maybe. Dragon men."

"Aw, jeez, Bruce. Not that weird shit. Please."

"So what else have we got?"

"We picked up a redhead in a green trench coat."

"Yeah? When was this?"

"This morning, before ten o'clock. Breaking and entering. I snagged him out of the general tank. He's in the cage in interview one, just waiting for you."

He handed across a sheaf of photocopies. "He's got what you call your basic history, the usual hairbag crap. All of it pretty minor, junkie stuff. A real winner, our Maxie."

Sandra skimmed through the pages—several drug-related arrests, some hot check charges, a couple of shoplifting arrests, but no convictions. The kid had been defended by some high-powered lawyers.

She raised her eyebrows. "He's got a lot of clout for a punk. How come?"

Mac shrugged. "Not him, but his daddy. Rich guy, and up until recently, he was paying the tolls."

"Oh." Sandra nodded. "Nothing violent."

"Hell, Bruce, he weighs about ninety pounds dripping wet. And he's a junkie. He gets violent, your granny would crush him."

"Well, let's go talk to him."

"Hold on, tiger. What happened in California? You look like you stuck your face in a meat grinder."

Sandra described all the events that had happened since she'd last seen her partner. Mac listened thoughtfully, nodding here and there. When she finished, he said, "Omar. That Omar fuck. That's the weird shit. First you run into him at the club, and then he tries to whack you out in sunny California. That ain't no coincidence, babe."

"No, I don't think so, either," she told him. "And there's more. The description we got from that girl, Tina. An Arab, she said. An Arab who tried to scrag her, but got stopped by some Chinese kid. Just like what happened with me."

"Christ, Arabs? Now we got, what? Terrorists or some shit like that, to go along with monsters? Tibetan dragon men?"

"I don't know. I'm thinking maybe it's some guy in

costume, or maybe an animal trainer using some sort of predator that's been trained to kill on command. Some kind of huge lizard or something that could claw through a man's chest." Sandra shook her head. "Maybe this Omar asshole's working with a partner in a dragon suit."

"Oh, God, Bruce, that's screwed up."

"I know. Everything about this is screwed up. And getting screwier, right?"

He stared at her. "You don't buy this lizard monster shit, do you?"

She shrugged. "I don't know what I buy right now. But we do have one thing that's real." She flapped the papers. "We got Maxie."

Mac grinned. "Yeah, we do, don't we?"

She slid her rear off the edge of the desk. "So let's go see just what it is we got."

Sandra stood in front of the one-way glass. It was him, all right. The redheaded, pimply youth on the other side sat uneasily in his chair. He moved restlessly, fidgeting and shifting, never completely at rest. He picked at a zit every now and then. Sometimes he reached up reflexively to adjust his trench coat, but the officers had taken it from him when they arrested him. His hands would hang in the air over where the collar should've been, and then he'd notice what he was doing and put them back in his lap for all of two seconds before he began to tap the table, or twitch, or ruffle his short-cropped carroty hair.

"Nervous, isn't he?" Sandra said.

"He's pulling out of junkie heaven. He'll be even uglier in a few hours or so."

Sandra nodded, then opened the door into interrogation room one. The moment Sandra stepped into the room, the kid recognized her. He seemed caught between relief, fear, and the pain of his withdrawal.

"Hey, the cop lady," he mumbled, his dark-ringed eyes a startling contrast to his pasty, freckled complexion. He hunched down into himself, never taking his haunted gaze off of her.

"Maxwell Bergot. Your parents must be worried sick about you." Sandra said.

He snorted and looked away. "Fuck them," he said.

She nodded. "You're a real sweetie, aren't you?"

She pulled up a chair opposite him, spun it around, and sat down. She leaned her chin against the back and stared at him.

"I got a question for you, Maxie."

He shrugged, looked at the table, then back up into her eyes.

"Why've you been following me?" she asked.

"I told you."

"Yeah. You said you wanted to give me some information, and then you ran. People who want to give me information usually stick around long enough to deliver. They're a lot more likely to get paid that way."

"Shit, you weren't gonna pay. You tried to stiff me. I should've just left you alone. Should've learned from what happened to Madrone. Stupid. Now I'm dead."

She raised her eyebrows. "Yeah? Why are you dead? Little drug deal gone bad?"

"Cut the druggie shit, okay?" he snarled, "I was doin' you a favor, and now I'm probably gonna die for it! Just like Madrone."

"What do you mean, Maxie? What do you know about Madrone? Who killed him?"

He gave her a cynical smile. "You cops are so stupid. I swear I drew Madrone a white line straight to the guy, and even then, he fucked it up, got himself killed."

"Madrone?"

"No. The Easter Bunny. Fuck it. Look, I told him where he could find the guy that done the lawyer guy."

"Wheeler," Sandra said.

Maxie nodded.

"Where?"

"I was in a bar for . . . ," he paused, looked up at the one-way mirror and frowned, ". . . for something, and I overheard these guys talkin'. They were talkin' about that lawyer guy, and I heard one of 'em say he did it and how much he loved it and everything. Then he tries to say he didn't do it, like it was a joke, but you can tell, you know? I mean, if you seen somebody who really killed somebody, you can tell them from someone who's just talkin' shit. This guy done it, even though he said afterward that he was only joking."

"What was his name?"

"I don't know. Something strange. Ozar or Okar or something. Omar, maybe. I think that was it. I can't remember. It started with an O."

"Omar?" She caught it right away, but a moment later, she caught something else. "So that was why you ran that night. The guy was standing right behind me!"

Maxie snorted. "Hooray for you. Pat yourself on the back and dig my grave."

"Who was he talking to at the bar?"

"The bartender," Maxie shifted again, and this time he broke eye contact and looked at the wall. "He'll come after me, you know. If he could get to Madrone, he can sure as hell get to me."

"We'll protect you." Sandra said.

"Like I got a helluva lot of choice now, right?" Maxie said.

"What's the bartender's name?"

"Nick," Maxie said. "His name is Nick Seder."

"Where does he work?"

"Gwendolyne's Flight."

Gwendolyne's Flight? Justin's bar—Sandra had just left there, just left his apartment above the bar.

". . . told Madrone he should talk to Nick, he wanted to find this Omar asshole. Next day Madrone turns up dead."

"Why'd you keep running away from me all the time?"

"'Cause you kept bein' a bitch!" he exclaimed, "I risk my ass to help you, and you take my stuff, rip me off, then you wanna bust my ass!"

Sandra eyed him without emotion. "Yeah, life's tough like that. Especially if you're an asshole."

Maxie squirmed and looked at the wall.

She nodded. "All right, Maxie. We're going to keep you here for a while. You'll be safe. You think good and hard about any details you might've missed. I'll get back to you again."

"You're gonna lock me up, book me?" Maxie asked.

"You scratch our backs, we scratch yours. That's how it works. For right now, protective custody. Your own private cell. I'll tell 'em room service." She reached into her bag, pulled out a twenty, handed it over. "Order a pizza if you want."

He took the money. "You got something else of mine, too. Maybe you wanna give that back?"

"Sorry, Maxie. The only turkey you get here is cold turkey. Or I could just boot your ass back onto the street, see if Omar looks you up."

It was obvious he was tempted. But then he subsided. "Naw. I think I'll hang here for a while. Till you grab the guy. You are gonna grab him, right?"

"Oh, yeah," Sandra said. "We're gonna grab him." She rose to leave.

"You sure you can't help with a taste?" Maxie said, the sick whine of need in his voice.

"Fresh coffee in the hall," Sandra said, and went out to find Mac.

"Omar," he said. "Again with this Omar guy."

"What do you think?" she asked.

"It's a lead. I say we drop by this Gwendolyne's Flight joint, say hi to Nick Seder."

She swallowed, hesitated. Fortunately Mac didn't notice.

"Yeah," she said.

"You know where it is? You're the big bar hopper, after all."

"Yeah," she said, "I've been there before." For some reason she couldn't bring herself to tell him she'd *left* there only a couple of hours before.

Most likely the murderer was just a guy who came into the bar, got too drunk, and said too much. Most likely. The old stupidity factor. And maybe Justin just happened to know a hell of a lot about dragons. Or dragon men.

Maybe . . .

Cops, she thought, don't much believe in coincidences, though.

As they left the building, they walked past the little cell where Maxie sat, fidgeting and staring uneasily at his reflection in a small shaving mirror affixed to the wall over the sink. Staring as if he saw something besides his own ugly, sweating mug there.

Something scary. Bad scary . . .

twenty

Nick Seder walked up to the back door of Gwendolyne's Flight and fumbled in his pocket for the keys. He was beat. The party at his house last night had wiped him out, and he wasn't looking forward to a busy Friday evening. Fridays were always busy at the Flight. Nick was, however, looking forward to a Bloody Mary to calm the thumping in his head. He'd bitched about the rain yesterday, but he would have preferred an overcast sky to this blindingly bright fall day.

Lost in his own pain, he did not see the two figures approach him until it was too late. A meaty hand fell on his shoulder and spun him around.

"Hi, Nick," McKenzie said, flipping open his badge case. "How ya doing?"

"What the hell do you want?" Nick looked from McKenzie to Sandra and back again.

"Hey, Nick, my man. Script says we ask the questions, right?" McKenzie spun him around and pushed him up against the wall. "And I'll bet you know the position, don't you? Ah, you do. What a surprise."

Grudgingly, Nick spread his feet, put his hands out, and leaned against the wall as Mac body-searched him.

"Aw, man! I haven't done anything! You can't just—"

"Sure I can, Nick," McKenzie said. "You know I can."

"I don't believe this," Nick whined. "You can't just take a guy and—"

"Hey, Nick? Shut the fuck up, okay?"

Nick frowned, but said nothing else until McKenzie was finished.

"Okay, turn around."

Nick turned. His eyes widened as he saw what McKenzie was holding in his thick fingers.

"What have we here?" Mac held the two small glassine bags and a small black film canister up against the sun. "The baggies look like smack. Would that be about right, Nick?"

Seder's mouth opened, closed, then opened again. "Hey, you don't just walk up to me and go through my pockets, asshole. Ain't you never heard of a fucking search warrant?"

Ignoring him, McKenzie opened the canister. "And coke, and some little pills here." McKenzie shook the plastic case. "What would those be, Nick? Speed? Downers? What else you got on you?"

"Hey, those aren't even mine."

"Right. They don't have your name on them, do they?" McKenzie said. "Guess you put on the wrong

Margaret Weis and David Baldwin

jeans this morning, huh? They're your roommate's, right?"

"That's right," Nick said. Then, sullenly, "So show me a warrant."

McKenzie sighed with mock patience. "Don't need no warrant, Speedy Gonzales. Not when Detective McCormack—that's her, right there—and me, Detective McKenzie—saw you behaving in a suspicious manner. And in the process of us investigating your suspicious mannerisms, we happen to notice evidence indicating that you might be holding in your very own possession this dope here. Which we found in the process of checking you for weapons. For our own safety, of course."

"That's all bullshit and you know it."

"You aren't that stupid, are you, Nicky? Judge'll buy it in a New York minute, right?" Mac grinned at him. "Am I right?"

All the air seemed to go out of Nick. "What the fuck you want, then?"

"You got the right to remain silent, Nick. And you got the right to a lawyer. If you can't afford a lawyer—"

"I know the fucking drill, man. What the fuck you *want* with me?"

Sandra stepped forward. Mac handed her one of the baggies. She lifted it, dangled it in front of Nick's nose. "You got a sheet, Nick?"

He shrugged.

"Bet you do," she said. "Bet this won't help any. Enough here for a felony possession for sale, I'd guess. And we got three strikes in Illinois now. How many strikes you got already, Nick? One? Two?"

"Aw, come on. What do you want from me? This ain't no fucking dope bust. Is it?"

She stared at him, considering. "Maybe not."

His shoulders slumped in relief. "So we can deal, is that what you're saying? Okay, fine. Deal. You want names or something? That's cool. I got names."

Mac eyed him with distaste. "Man, loyalty's always a fine thing. My dad used to say that. 'Course, he'd never met a slime-sack like you, Nicky. You're a piece of work."

Seder avoided his gaze, stayed focused on Sandra's face.

"Lady, tell me what you want, okay?"

Sandra considered a moment longer, drawing it out. Then she nodded. "I want to know about Carlton Wheeler. Who killed him."

Nick's resentful posture faded, and he looked scared. "I d-don't know what you're talking about," he stammered. His brow furrowed.

"Nick," Sandra said kindly, "how we going to deal with you standing there lying your ugly face off?"

"Look, I didn't have anything to do with no god-damn lawyer, and that's the truth!"

"Just like these drugs aren't yours?" McKenzie pressed.

"Okay, fine! Pin the drugs on me. You bastards wanna roust people who're just going about their business, fine! There's nothing I can do about that. But I didn't kill nobody!" He paused. "And I want a lawyer. I got nothing more to say."

"We didn't say you killed anybody, Nick." McKenzie leaned over, close to the bartender's face. "We just want to know what you know about it."

"And you know something, Nicky. You know Carlton Wheeler's a lawyer. And I don't remember telling you that. Did you tell him, Mac?"

"Nope. Maybe he's a mind reader. How about it, Nicky? You read minds?"

"I . . . uh . . . man, I dunno nothing about none of that shit. Honest to God."

McKenzie shrugged. "Hey, look here, cool. Play it that way. See if I give a shit." He pushed the remaining bag and the canister into his own jacket pocket. And pulled a pair of cuffs off his belt. "Turn it around, Ace. Hands behind your back."

Nick's gaze leaped from Sandra to Mac and back again. Suddenly he licked his lips. "Wait a minute . . ."

"Naw, no more waiting, Nicky. We thought maybe you knew something, maybe you'd wanna help us like any fine, upstanding citizen would." He shrugged. "But if you don't feel that way, well . . . just stick 'em out." He grinned. "You can be one of the thousand tales of the big city."

Nick's face crumpled suddenly.

"Okay, okay, wait just a minute . . ." Nick held up his hands in front of him. "Maybe we can cut some kind of a deal?"

"Now you're talking," McKenzie said, moving so close to Nick's face that the bartender had to take a step backwards. "Let's just go back to the station house, and you can tell us everything you know. You know enough—maybe we can talk deals."

"No, that's not what I mean! I just mean, well, maybe I might know something."

"Then you'd better tell us." McKenzie smiled, but it wasn't a happy face.

"No way. I'm not telling you something and then having you take me in for drugs anyway. Forget that."

Sandra moved forward again. "You talk to us, we forget this ever happened. We don't even know you." She glanced at Mac. "Is that right, Mac?"

"Nicky who?" Mac said, grinning.

Nick blew a blast of breath out of his mouth and looked at his shoes. "I can't believe I'm trusting a couple of cops," he muttered.

"Listen, you cockroach," Sandra said, "I don't give a shit whether you trust us or not. You're not in a good bargaining position here. Or are you too stupid to figure even that much out?"

"All right, all right!" Nick looked at each of them in turn, and then began.

"You said Wheeler, that lawyer, right? That's what you want?"

"Yeah," Sandra told him. "That's what we want."

Nick chewed on his lower lip a moment. "Okay. It was a couple of weeks ago, I think. In the bar. This guy came in and was drinking. It was pretty late. Close to closing time."

"This guy? What guy?" Sandra asked.

"Omar something."

Sandra nodded.

"What did he look like?" McKenzie asked.

"Short. Black hair. He looked Libyan or something.

Really dark black eyes. He had a wide mouth and he seemed kind of paranoid, you know, freaky?" Nick paused, thinking. "But kinda like he could take care of himself, like he didn't give a shit. Like, I dunno, like nothing could scare him, he could handle it all. He *knew* he could handle it." He paused again, then shook his head. "Hard to describe, I guess."

Actually Sandra thought Nick had described him pretty well. Omar just kept cropping up all over the place. She wondered what he would look like in a lizard suit. But even as she thought that, she knew she was missing something.

"Is he a regular?" she asked.

"He comes in often enough."

"So what did he say about Wheeler?"

Nick shrugged. "He didn't say much but he laughed really loud. Since it was pretty quiet, I looked over to see what he was laughing at, and it was the TV. There was something on about the Wheeler guy. Some big case he'd won just before he was killed. How he was supposed to be some kinda champion of justice or something. Anyway, I mostly remember this Omar dude laughing— he sounded sort of weird, y'know?—and so I asked him what was so funny."

"'Big guy, big man,' he said. 'Champion of the downtrodden.' Or some shit like that, and he laughed some more. 'He pissed in his underwear and all over that stupid kimono when he was looking down the barrel of a gun. Some fucking hero.'"

Nick paused, looked down at his shoes. He shrugged. "I wouldn't have thought anything of it. Just some guy talkin' shit, except I knew a girl who was Wheeler's girlfriend for a while before he got famous. She came into the Flight a lot. When he first started hittin' the news, she used to brag about it, a little, how she shouldn't have let him go, and all that. I asked her what he was like. She said he was a really nice guy, not like some of the celebrities you hear about. She said he was pretty normal except he had a few eccentricities." Nick paused. "Like wearing silk kimonos around the house. It was just another story. I'm a bartender. I hear stories all the time. But it stuck in my head because I thought the kimono was weird. I mean, isn't it a Japanese woman's dress?"

McKenzie shrugged. "Beats me."

"Well, anyway, that's why it stuck in my head, and when this guy said that, my blood kinda froze, and I looked at him, and I knew he'd done it. I knew he was the murderer and he was sitting right there at my bar, bragging about it. I must've looked weird, or he must've realized he was talking stupid, 'cause he shut up all of a sudden. I didn't say anything or let on that I believed him. I think I just said something like, 'Yeah, sure buddy. You want another one?' So he looked at me really hard for a second, and I played like stone dumb, 'cause I didn't want him thinkin' that *I thought* I'd just heard a confession. The guy was creepy, you know? I mean, I didn't want to have him following me home and putting a bullet in *my* brain. No way. He was so twitchy you'd think he'd do something like that. Like maybe he wanted to do that, and was look-ing for any excuse." Nick shrugged. "Well, that's all I know. But if you want my opinion, he wasn't lying. He did it."

"You see him around a lot?" Sandra asked. "Does he come into the bar on any kind of schedule?"

"Naw. Not recently, anyway. He used to come in almost every night, but he and the owner got into a fight or something. Mr. Sterling doesn't like him. I haven't seen him in the last week or so."

Sandra gave a small sigh of relief. Reassurance splashed over her. Justin had recognized an asshole when he saw one, and had kicked him out of his club. Good. She was glad of that . . .

"Anything else?" McKenzie asked.

"No, that's it. I didn't follow the guy or anything. I didn't ask him over to play poker. He was creepy. I just wanted him out of the bar. I was glad when Mr. Sterling told Rocky not to let him back in. There's another one of 'em, though. I think it's his boss or his brother or something. He still comes in."

"Another what?"

"Another one of them fucking Arabs. We get a lot of them, but these two, Omar and the other guy, they were together a lot. And the other guy treated Omar like a flunky or something, always made him come to the bar to get the drinks, like that."

"So, you know the other guy's name?" Sandra said.

Nick chewed on his lip some more. "It's uh . . . I dunno for sure, some weird name—begins with a K, I think. I didn't go up and introduce myself to them."

"Why didn't you go to the police?" Mac said.

Nick stared at him. "You kidding? Me, go to the cops?"

"Okay," Sandra said. "That's it? That's all you got?"

"That's all I got," Nick said.

Mac and Sandra glanced at each other. Mac shrugged.

"See you around sometime, Nicky," Sandra said.

"Hey, wait a fucking minute!"

Mac paused, then turned. "What? You just remember something else?"

"My shit. You got my shit. You took it off me, and it's mine."

He was almost crying.

And Mac grinned at him. "Shit? You know anything about any shit, Sandra?"

"Only the asshole I'm looking at right now," she replied.

"Oh, you fuckers," Nick breathed softly. "You thieving fuckers."

Mac stared at him. "Don't you need to be getting to work, Nicky? Instead of standing out here in the hot sun, giving me shit?"

Nick's eyes went slightly wild, and Mac shifted his weight on his feet. "Don't even think about it, asshole," he said softly. "You can't even begin to imagine what a pleasure it would be."

After a moment, Nick's gaze dropped and his shoulders slumped. Without another word he turned, opened the door, and stepped on through.

"Nice guy," Sandra said.

"Asshole," Mac replied.

Sandra stared at the back doors of the bar. Two doors. One door was large and one was just ordinary sized. She'd worked in a few restaurants when she'd been married to Chuck. None of them had had more than one back door. Despite the difference in size, the doors both looked like utility doors, except one was caked with grime, like any well-used back door to a club or restaurant should be. The other door was polished metal. Why would anyone polish a stainless steel utility door?

For no reason, she stood before the door, staring at her reflection until McKenzie touched her shoulder. "Hey, Bruce? You okay?"

She gave a slight twitch, caught herself, forced a grin. "I'm good, Mac. I'm just fine."

Sandra sat quietly in a corner booth near the front door of Gwendolyne's Flight. The place was hopping. Colored lights splashed across the crowd. A smoke machine sent billowy white clouds snaking around the dancing bodies. The smoke's slow, sinuous movement accentuated the frenetic pace of the dancers. The club was packed and she was keeping a low profile. She did not want to alert Justin to her presence. If tonight was the night they nabbed Omar, and Omar turned out to be the killer, then she could relax into Justin's arms after it was all over.

She had been tempted to let Justin in on the deal. He could have made things easier for her and McKenzie. But as much as she hated to admit it, there was still a nasty, lingering doubt about his involvement in her mind. Omar had been a regular in his bar. The redhead had bought drugs from Nick in his bar. Maybe it was coincidence—this was a big, popular place. But she couldn't guarantee it. One of the first cop rules was that coincidences usually weren't. So she wouldn't risk the entire case by telling him anything. Because if Justin *were* involved . . .

Don't think about it, she told herself. *He's not involved. Just focus on this Omar sonofabitch. Let the rest take care of itself . . .*

Moments later she watched a guy cross to the bar and order a drink from Nick. The guy reminded her of Omar, but he wasn't Omar. Nick made the drink and handed it over. As the guy turned away, Nick caught Sandra's eye and nodded.

This one did look very much like the man who had mopped up the floor with her in California and then vanished into thin air, the man who'd tried to dance with her at the blues club. But it wasn't Omar. This character was very well dressed. He acted like a wealthy snob, watching the dancers with a detached air of amusement, like someone thinking about ordering one of them from a menu. When the cocktail waitress arrived at his table to see if he needed another drink, he barely acknowledged her existence.

McKenzie showed up soon after. His bald spot was slick and his coat was splattered. The rain must've started up again. He did not come to join her, but glanced at her. She nodded toward where the Arab was enjoying his drink. McKenzie nodded back, shook off some of the rain, and headed straight for the guy's table.

Deep down inside, despite his formidable appearance, McKenzie was a teddy bear. Nonetheless, McKenzie could be very intimidating when he put his mind to it. When he didn't smile, his face looked stony. With his steely gaze and his immense bulk, he was a much more effective intimidator than Sandra was. They had used this routine before. McKenzie was the front man. Sandra was the backup nobody expected, just in case things got out of hand.

McKenzie approached the man and Sandra watched them exchange words. The Arab shook his head. McKenzie leaned over the table and said something else. The Arab stood to leave, obviously not with McKenzie.

Putting his big hand on the Arab's shoulder, McKenzie started to shove him back into his seat. The man didn't move. Instead, he reached up, grabbed McKenzie's wrist, and did something to it. Sandra saw the pain lance through McKenzie's face as he stumbled backward.

She was instantly on her feet. McKenzie staggered to his knees against an adjacent table, scattering the people seated there. He shoved his good hand into his coat and pulled out his gun. The people at the table jumped up and scurried away, as did several others nearby. The commotion caught the attention of the bouncers, who started pushing through the crowded bar in Mac's direction.

The Arab walked calmly but quickly toward the kitchen doors.

McKenzie's eyes caught hers. She could see the pain in them. The Arab must be devilishly strong! Mac was cradling his arm close to his body and looked hurt, but not in any real danger.

He nodded at her and she saw him say "Go!" though

she could not hear a thing over the music and club commotion. She hesitated only long enough to see the Arab push open the kitchen door, and then she bolted for the front door.

There was only one place the Arab could hope to escape to, and that was the alley. She burst past the startled doorman and sprinted out into the pouring rain. She skidded a little as she rounded the corner of the building, then she poured on the speed.

She stopped at the mouth of the alley. There was no one there. Her heartbeat thudded in her ears.

The falling rain muted the streetlights, so the alley was darker than she'd have liked. She crept closer to the Flight's back door. Their guy might've already emerged and hidden. She drew her gun and looked carefully in every direction. With each step, she looked over at the two back doors, the big grimy one, the small shiny one. Soon she was soaked to the skin.

She checked the two Dumpsters as she passed, but no one was hiding there. Her eyes adjusted to the dim light, and she started to wonder if McKenzie had grabbed the guy in the kitchen.

She abandoned that thought when the large, dirty utility door rattled sharply, then burst open. The expensively dressed Arab stepped out. His white silk shirt was instantly plastered to his dark skin. He did not have a chance to look around before Sandra yelled.

"Freeze, asshole!"

He looked at her, mildly startled, then smiled. It was that same supercilious, amused smile he gave the dancers inside.

"Hands in the air," she commanded, walking slowly closer, keeping her weight centered and her arms rock steady, the pistol leveled at his chest.

His grin widened . . . and he disappeared.

"What the hell?"

Shocked, she dropped her arms, then snapped them back up, pointing all around, scanning the alley. She heard a strange noise, a kind of cracking sound.

Then there was nothing. Only the sounds of rain and traffic slogging through the Chicago night.

"Where the hell did you go, you bastard?" she said, moving to the doors, her gaze still jumping from shadow to shadow. Nobody there. She opened the dirty door and looked inside. The light from the kitchen flooded over her and she squinted.

"McKenzie!" she called. "McKenzie! Talk to me! Where are you?"

No answer. She was about to step inside when a hand clamped on her shoulder.

She gasped at the strength of it. Pain shot through her, but her training came to the fore and she spun. She could not see her opponent, but she centered her balance and sent the force of the attack beyond her. The grip on her shoulder faltered and she slid out from under it. But whatever had grabbed her had claws, and it ripped her shoulder as it tore loose.

Sandra gasped and gritted her teeth, raised her gun. What was this thing? Invisible? With claws? Her heart started pounding faster. Sandra felt as if she'd stepped into some weird nightmare. No one could just become invisible!

A whisper of air warned her that she was under attack again. Claws raked her hand, knocking away the gun. Blood flew and she cried out, pulling her wounded hand against her stomach and cradling it.

The silence fell again, but she could feel the thing there, somewhere very close. Her mind reeled. This wasn't happening. This couldn't be happening!

She backed away, looking desperately for her gun, not knowing where her attacker was, frantic to find someplace to take shelter, someplace she could defend herself. But her mind wouldn't function right. Should she run? Where? How could she escape something she couldn't see?

A claw scraped blacktop to her right and she spun to face it, almost falling. It scraped again, and then it had her.

"No!" she screamed, trying to roll with its weight, but it had picked her up off her feet, giving her no leverage whatsoever. Its arms squeezed her until she thought her ribs would break. Something like a tentacle wrapped around her legs, muffling the kicks she launched.

She gasped for breath, hoping to force air into her lungs. At this rate, she would pass out in seconds. She tried to scream and couldn't. Terror gripped her.

Helpless again. Just like with Chuck. All her cop training, all the martial arts, and she was helpless once again. Her furious tears mixed with the rain.

A fetid smell surrounded her, and she felt something smooth, hard, and wet against her ear. Was it a tooth? Teeth? A quiet, gravelly voice began speaking.

"You look just like all the other women in Justin's

drawings. I'm surprised how many of you he finds, women who look so much like his dead wife. But you. You're different, aren't you? He must really fancy you. He defies the master to keep you alive. That's sacrilege. It will cost him everything he has. He knows it will, and he does it anyway. He need not worry anymore, though. I'll do him a favor tonight."

A rough hand closed over her left breast. She could feel the points of his claws digging mercilessly into her chest.

"I'll kill you now—his way," the voice continued. "That will make him feel much better about the whole matter, I'm sure." Throaty laughter from the shadowed, invisible creature holding her vibrated through her entire body.

Suddenly the monster's body rocked and she heard the sound of flesh ripping. Its grip went slack and she fell to the blacktop. A great cry burst from the beast and she realized that the ripping flesh was not her own. There was another low growl and a new voice that seemed vaguely familiar.

"I told you not to touch her."

"You will suffer dearly for this, Justin. The master will twist you into a bloody rope," the first voice said.

Sandra sucked in a pain-wracked breath and tried to see what was happening, but there was nothing to see. She could only hear the noise of a terrible fight between the two invisible creatures—their slashing, their biting, the rip of flesh and crunch of breaking bones. The ground shook with their battle. Something slammed into one of the Dumpsters, knocking it three feet back into the building on the far side of the alley. A huge dent appeared in its side.

As she watched, mesmerized, dazed, she thought she could make out two barely perceptible shadows in the rain, charging each other, grappling, limbs pulling back and descending in fierce blows with blurring speed. The growls and ripping sounds came from that direction.

"I don't believe this . . ." she whispered, trying to collect her senses, trying to think what to do next. "This isn't real. I've lost my mind. This can't be real."

She pushed herself to her feet and lunged for the back door. Snatching up her gun in her good hand, she turned and concentrated again, was able to pinpoint the almost-invisible combatants. Bringing the gun to bear, she locked her elbow and began firing into the huge shadows. Two pain-filled roars split the night and blood spattered on the far wall.

The shadows broke apart and one of the shadows ran toward her. She followed it, continuing to fire until the chamber clicked empty. A harsh wind slammed past her and she threw herself to the side. The footsteps suddenly stopped. They didn't slow or scrape to a halt. They just ended. Sandra looked to her right, but she couldn't make out anything. Just the wall and the two doors. She thought she saw the smaller, polished door rippling, but she concentrated on it and realized she must've been mistaken.

A tremendous flapping of wings began down the alley. Sandra spun, even as she hit the catch on her pistol, letting the empty magazine fall to the ground. The flapping faded slowly upward. Then she heard nothing but the sounds of the city.

She thrust her hand into her coat pocket and withdrew another clip, jammed it in the gun. With her back against the wall, she pointed her weapon outward as she slid toward the door. This was crazy! It was all crazy! She couldn't think anymore. She let her body move instinctively while her mind reeled.

"McKenzie!" she yelled, pulling on the cold metal handle, opening the grimy back door with her foot and slipping through. She butted shut the heavy door behind her, then turned the dead bolt. From what she had just experienced, it would hardly keep them out, but maybe it would give her a warning if they burst through. Like that would help. The strength of those things was unbelievable!

They had been invisible!

Lizard men . . .

Dr. Simmins's words floated through her overworked brain.

No, she thought. *Impossible. That's not possible!*

Don't think about it, she told herself. One step at a time. Find McKenzie. Find—

Sandra looked down as she turned the corner into the kitchen.

"No!" she cried out, falling to her knees. McKenzie lay chest down on the red tiles. His head was twisted all the way around, his dead eyes fixed on the ceiling.

"No no no no no . . ."

She grabbed a fistful of his jacket and laid her face against his back. He was cooling already. Already inhumanly cold. Rage and remorse slammed into her, and she gritted her teeth so hard she could hear them grind. A waitress came around the corner from the interior.

She froze and screamed.

Sandra could hardly blame her.

"I'm a cop. Shut up!" Sandra snarled, fumbling for and then flashing her badge with her wounded hand, still clutching her pistol in her good one.

"Just shut up . . . call the police and an ambulance. Tell them an officer is down. Got that? An officer down!"

The girl scrambled away, her eyes wide.

She leaned over McKenzie's back again. The butt of her pistol smacked angrily into the tile, cracking it. She held her dead partner in her arms, cradling him, even though it was too late to save him.

Tears ran down her face, spattered across Mac's dead, staring eyes, a river of unbearable, unending pain.

twenty-one

Justin dropped in through the sky-light and landed heavily on the floor of his apartment. He bled from a dozen slashes Kalzar had put into him, but he was sure that Kalzar was in far worse shape. His injuries were healing even as he watched.

Justin's Wyrm body wanted to find Kalzar and rend him into such small pieces they could never be reassembled. He trembled as he tried to control the rage that surged through him.

Slouching over to the dais, Justin sat down and took a rapid inventory of his injuries. In addition to the gashes, he had taken three of Sandra's bullets. They'd burned like fire—one through his wing, one through his forearm, and one into his upper side. The first two had passed through him harmlessly. But the third bullet was lodged between two ribs next to his breastbone, and he must remove it, or he would walk around with lead in his chest forever.

As happy as his dragonling body was to do harm to

others, it was not nearly so excited about ripping holes in itself. Slowly he used his claws to widen the wound. The shiny green scales of his hide resisted him. He growled. He could not easily reach the bullet. It was too far inside him and too awkwardly placed to get a grip on.

He paused a moment, then growled again and punctured a new hole in his back, trying a different direction. There it was. His claws closed on the lead slug, and he plucked it out.

Levering himself to his feet, Justin stumbled into the bathroom and brought out an armload of clean towels. He threw them over his chair to protect its upholstery, then slumped into it.

He considered returning to human form, but the dragonling body would heal faster, and he must go out again soon. He had to find Sandra.

The huge mirror behind the dais rippled. Kalzar's scales were the color of Arabian sand, and he had a slighter build than Justin, longer and thinner. His elongated face resembled that of an alligator. Justin was pleased to see how badly he'd wounded Kalzar. Great lines of red crisscrossed his chest. A huge chunk was missing from his neck and the back of one arm. One of his slender wings hung at a strange angle as he picked at a gaping hole in his thigh.

The bullet came free and he tossed it onto the dais. It clacked down the steps and came to rest on the carpet.

"I haven't been shot by anything that painful in a hundred years," Kalzar said. "I'd forgotten how much it hurts. The last time I was hit this nasty it was a musket ball in Palestine. I had the taste of lead in my mouth for weeks."

Justin rose. Kalzar's narrow eyes followed Justin's progress as he walked toward the dais.

"I am going to make something perfectly clear to you, Kalzar," Justin rasped. "Sandra is mine. Don't touch her again. I will fight the master himself if that is what it takes to keep her from harm."

Kalzar was unmoved by the threat. "Kill? Me?" His many rows of teeth shone in the light as his too-flexible lips peeled back in a smile. "You can't kill me, Justin. And we both know it."

"We are both Elders, Kalzar," Justin said. "But you do not know all things. If you were a studious man, you would never make such a statement. Try frequenting libraries for a century or two, rather than staking out stray kittens and peeling the skin from their bodies."

"Your bluffs are transparent, Justin," Kalzar said.

"And your ignorance is immeasurable," Justin replied.

"There is no way to kill us."

"Read your *Beowulf*, Kalzar. There is a way. Cross me again, and I will show it to you. I promise you that."

As he spoke, Justin again saw the thing in its hiding place. So commonplace a cache for something so deadly to one of his kind. He'd found it in the most unlikely of places, doing his master's work; had found it, realized what it was, and bundled it up to take along with the artifact his master had sent him to fetch.

The museum guard had interrupted him as he was doing this. The guard's name had been Baxter, though he hadn't learned that till later. But Baxter's death had been a necessity, not only to protect the Dragon, but to conceal any possible knowledge of what he'd found in the room Baxter had tried to guard. To conceal that knowledge *even from the master* . . .

Kalzar's eyes narrowed, as he tried to determine whether or not Justin was lying. "The master will hear of this," he said as he backed through the mirror and disappeared.

Good, Kalzar, Justin thought. *Tell the master. I have suffered your incompetence long enough, and now it is time for you to fear, for I have come to the end of my patience with you.*

As he stood there, staring at the disappearing Kalzar, Justin felt the mirror catch hold of him. He tried to turn away, but he was caught. Letting out a breath, he waited for the long-fanged face to appear. He waited to see the enormous dragon's head, a head as large as his own body.

Instead, it was Justin's reflection that began to talk to him, except that the eyes were smoldering red. The voice was deep, low, and tinged with enormous age.

"My servant, tell me," the master said to him, "do you not think the time is ripe to put aside your small amusements?"

Justin closed his eyes and fought the impulse to immediately cry, *Yes! I will kill her now, for you, my master!*

His defiance took every bit of strength he could muster.

"I would ask you, master, to give me time—"

"Time? I have given you enough time, Lord Sterling. Such a response is unacceptable. How much time do you require when all of eternity is before you?"

"I wish to turn her, my master. She is worthy, resourceful, intelligent. I want her to become a disciple, to serve you as I do, forever."

The master narrowed his smoking eyes. The Dragon made no quick response to the request, but studied its disciple. It was the first time Justin had ever known the master to hesitate.

"What kind of offer is this, Lord Sterling?" the Dragon asked at last. "I have a purpose of my own—a noble cause. That purpose requires all my attention— and all of the attention of my servants. It is not in me to offer boons to you for your idle enjoyment. The trappings already bestowed upon you are sufficient for the work which needs you as its champion."

"She would be a great asset to you, I assure you. I have watched her. Have you not watched her, as well?"

Again, the master paused. When the Dragon spoke, its voice was barely a whisper, "As I do watch you, Lord Sterling."

Justin said nothing.

"You have served me well, Lord Sterling," the Dragon continued. "Under this consideration, I do give you a single day to accomplish this. If she looks in the mirror with welcome in her heart, I shall make my own decision upon the span of your lady's life."

Justin gulped and nodded.

"One day, no more," the master said.

And then Justin's reflection was his own again. His own blue eyes looked out at him, blinked once, and looked at his clawed feet.

One day, no more. Justin rubbed his finger, looked down in curiosity at the sapphire ring the old Chinese man had given him so many years ago. It was an enigma to him—the only item of his apparel that had ever survived the transformation from his human form to his Wyrm form and back again unscathed. He'd left it on ever since he retrieved it from the trunk—it seemed to speak to him sometimes, to calm his rage, to flare with internal fire at each change of his emotions. It burned his flesh now as though someone had put it in an inferno . . .

twenty-two

The cathedral was practically empty, but it was always open for those who needed to come in and pray. Because it was in a big city, the hours of this church bent to the strange schedules of its inhabitants. The priests kept the sanctuary open twenty-four hours a day, even though they risked the worldly evils of looting and other urban dangers.

Sandra's priest said that God was present at all hours—therefore, his house should be open to those who needed him at all times. There was no organized ceremony tonight. A few people wandered the side aisles, admiring the rows of sculpted apostles, prophets, saints, and patrons in the Gothic structure and lighting candles in the lady chapel. The building was filled with that wonderful smell—a hundred years' worth of incense and holy candles—common to all old Catholic churches.

The nave—richly ornamented with gold leaf and mosaics—was a hand-built cavern, all perfect curves and right angles. Intricate stained glass windows glowed with jewel-like colors. Carefully positioned lighting outside the church made the windows nearly as beautiful in the evening as they were in daylight. Fluted stone columns speared into the vaulted ceilings. Sandra stared at their tops. The columns, reaching to become a part of the sky, always calmed her. The medieval artisans who had built the soaring stone churches of Europe had managed to paint the emotions of religion in stone. This New World imitation of their art captured that spirit. The very stones of the church cried out the convictions of those who shaped them—that the impossible was attainable. God is near. Reach for him, and perfect yourself for his coming. Work hard. Dedicate your life to the light.

She took comfort from her surroundings. She needed that comfort. It wasn't the first time she'd sought relief from a crisis here. The church had been pivotal in her escape from Chuck. Those fluted columns had spoken to her then as well. From them, she gained the idea that she could be more than she was, that she could strive for a better fate than life as Chuck's punching bag.

And now where was she? She was back in the same place. Her lover was a monster, just as Chuck had been. A monster with claws and teeth and wings. A mythical being. A dragon. Her lover was a dragon.

She'd finally placed that strangely familiar voice in the alley. Even distorted by a transformation into who knew what kind of monster, she'd recognized the cadences of her lover's voice. The stories Justin had told her and Benny at the restaurant were not the products of his mind or his arcane reading. They were true. In his apartment was a mirror surrounded by dragons. Between the cycles of their lovemaking in that long, wonderful night, Sandra had stood in front of that mirror, bathed in her own sweat and Justin's, and studied the medieval carvings on the border, entranced. An heirloom, he had said. The oldest, most prized possession of his family. He had brought it from overseas because he had always loved it, he had said.

Did his master speak to him through this mirror? She was sure it did. What was Justin? Was he truly some sort of demon?

She rested her head in her arms against the back of the next pew. What was she going to do now? She had fled the crime scene as soon as she could, after she'd surrendered her weapon for testing, had her hands swabbed to prove she had indeed fired shots, answered the questions for her captain and Internal Affairs. She'd had the paramedics patch her up but refused to go to the hospital to have the claw marks on her shoulder stitched. She was held together by butterfly bandages, medical gauze, and some painkiller the paramedics had given her. Good stuff, whatever it was. She'd have to look at the name when she had the prescription filled. Nice to know for the next time her life fell apart.

She was on medical leave, according to her boss. Don't come into the office, he'd said. Don't call us, we'll call you.

None of it had penetrated the soft, fuzzy cocoon of her shock. She left as soon as she could to come here, stopping only to retrieve the small Chief's Special revolver that was her off-duty weapon. Now it pressed reassuringly against her bruised ribs, fully loaded. She was going to get the first priest she saw to bless it. Maybe dragons were like vampires or werewolves, vulnerable to bullets dipped in holy water or something.

It was too much. And who could she tell? Who would believe her? Mac might have, at least some of it . . . but Mac was dead.

She almost didn't believe it herself. She had no proof. Not a shred of evidence. Certainly not an eyewitness. Not that an eyewitness would have helped. If nobody would believe her, a cop, why would they believe anybody else?

That made her want to laugh, but she clamped down on the impulse. At this point of emotional exhaustion, laughter opened the gates to hysteria. She could not afford that. Her lover was out there, somewhere, with his claws and his invisible body and his irresistible strength. And his *friend* was out there as well, waiting for her. Waiting to do Justin the *favor* of killing her.

She was going to have to file a report. What would she say? There would be an office full of questions for her, and she had no answers. She had discharged her firearm nine times. She had slow-bleeding punctures around her left breast, a three-clawed gash on her shoulder and on her hand. Her partner was dead.

And Linda . . . and McKenzie's kids . . . What could she tell them? What could anyone possibly tell them? She would never again hear Mac arguing with Linda. Linda would never again call him at work. Never.

"Oh, Mac . . .," she whispered, fighting her tears. Soft footsteps intruded on her private pain, and she lifted her head, though she did not look behind her. She heard the steps move into the pew just behind her and stop. Somebody settled into the seat with the swish of fabric brushing across wood.

Fear rustled across her skin. She knew who it was, who it had to be. She didn't even need to turn around. Somehow, she'd known he would come.

"Tell me the truth, Justin . . .," she said quietly. "Tell me I'm going insane. Tell me everything I saw was a hallucination brought on by stress, brought on by something. Tell me that."

"That is not the truth," he answered, his voice soothing.

Still she did not look at him. She stared straight ahead, her eyes fixed on a statue of the Virgin Mary.

"Your friend said I look like your wife. Is that the truth?"

"Yes." Justin paused, then said, "He is not my friend."

"Where is she?"

"She died a long time ago."

"A long time ago? What exactly are we talking here—decades, centuries? Are you going to tell me next that you live forever?"

Justin said nothing.

Sandra choked on the truth. "I don't believe this!" she cried. "This isn't happening. What are you, a vampire or something?"

"No."

"Worse? A demon? One of the devil's creatures?"

"No."

"What, then?"

"You remember the story I told you and Benny at dinner the other night?"

"Of course, I remember. I've been thinking about it since . . . tonight. What does that make you, then?"

"One of the Dragon's disciples."

"You're a dragon man?"

"Something like that."

"Then that was you tonight, fighting with . . . that other . . . dragon man."

"Yes. His name is Kalzar."

"I shot my pistol at both of you. Did I hit you?"

"Yes."

Sandra swallowed. "But you're okay, of course," she said sardonically.

"Weapons can only kill me if they are appropriately blessed. I am not mortal," Justin replied. "They hurt, but aren't fatal. I was impressed, however, by your calm in being able to shoot me at all."

"You're not mortal. Of course not. What self-respecting demon would be?" She started to laugh, heard the harsh hysteria in it, and stopped herself. "Did the gunshots hurt badly?"

"Yes."

Again, she swallowed, but said nothing.

"Sandra—" Justin began.

"How do I look like her?" she interrupted him. "In what ways?"

He paused, then, "If you took your hair down, and looked into a mirror, you might see Gwendolyne looking back."

"Gwendolyne . . . Gwendolyne's Flight. You named your club after her? That was her name?"

"Yes."

"What did she flee?"

"This life. Too soon."

"And I look exactly like her?"

"Yes. She was beautiful, inside and out, as you are. Her beauty took my breath away every time I looked at her. But in other ways, the two of you are nothing alike. She was quiet, soft-spoken. She moved through life gently, like a murmuring brook over smooth stones. You're a fighter who challenges the world to come and meet you. Everything you touch, you ignite with your passion."

"How did she die?"

"We were taken by the plague, both of us. We were at death's door. The Dragon came to me in a silver mirror. I was swollen with pustules, lying on the cold stone floor in a puddle of my own urine. The Dragon offered me immortality, and the strength to change the world for the better, to fight for his cause. I accepted. Someday the world will be safe for the Dragon to return, and that day will usher humanity into a new and brighter age of evolution. The Dragon cannot come back as long as there are people who would hunt it, people like Saint George."

"Why didn't the Dragon make the same offer to Gwendolyne that he did to you?" Sandra asked, still staring at the Virgin Mary, still unwilling to turn around and let the plea in Justin's eyes threaten her resolve, steal her strength.

"The Dragon did make that offer to her."

"I see," Sandra said softly. "She refused."

"You must understand," Justin said, "she was a child of the Dark Ages, raised on stories of witches and devils. Like all superstitious people she thought anything she could not understand must be evil in nature. When she saw the Dragon's face, she saw only its intimidating appearance. She did not hear the wisdom of its words, could not know the wisdom of its years, its benevolence. Her fear of the Dragon was greater than her love for me."

Sandra paused. It was all so strange, but she had seen enough evidence to convince herself that he spoke the truth. She nodded slowly.

"There's something I don't understand. Who killed that girl's boyfriend? What great purpose could that possibly serve?"

"Does it matter? He hurt her. He deserved to be punished."

"That girl looked like me. Like your wife."

"Yes."

"So you slept with her, too?"

"No!" Justin's reply was vehement. "She was just a child."

"Then what? You watched her? Spied on her?"

"Protected her," he insisted.

"Those sketches on your wall—you didn't tell me the truth, did you? You said they were of me, but they're not. Only some of them are me. Some of them are that girl, aren't they? And some of them are other women. Centuries of women who live in your memories . . . yet all the same . . ."

"Sandra, please understand. You cannot know what it is like to live so many years and never have the chance to live a normal life. Through the years I choose people to watch and I live my life through them vicariously. My normal life. From them, I can taste what it would be like to grow up, to have mortal concerns, to love, to die . . ."

"By chance, are all of these people you watch young, pretty women with wavy hair and brown eyes?"

Justin paused. "I am afraid so. We all have our eccentricities."

"Do your eccentricities include ripping people's hearts out of their chests, by any chance? Trying to kill me? Killing my partner?"

"That was Kalzar's doing." Justin's voice was firm.

"Why?"

"You cannot understand a mind like Kalzar's without first understanding the conditions under which he was raised. He was born on the Arabian peninsula in a time of holy war and vast ruin. Everything is a *jihad* to him, a divine battle. He believes my need for a personal life jeopardizes our mission. He has taken it upon himself to rid me of what he sees as my weakness. He is a shortsighted soul who cannot appreciate the beauty at the end of the road we travel. He can only appreciate the necessarily bloody work we must do to get there."

"And you tolerate that?" she asked.

"Believe me, I would kill him if I could. But we do not die easily. And our master forbids us to fight among ourselves. That is one of the Dragon's few laws."

"And you broke that law tonight?"

"I did."

"For me."

"For you. I would break it again. Kalzar knows this. It may make him wary of coming near you. On the other hand, it may make it more tantalizing to him to try. I do not know."

"And your guardian Dragon, doesn't it care that Kalzar is a bloody murderer?"

"You cannot judge the Dragon by human standards. The Dragon is over four thousand years old. It carries the memories of every other Dragon before it. To the Dragon, a single human life is nothing. The Dragon cares for the whole of the human race, not the sum of the parts. It cannot afford to lose sight of the long view for momentary compassion. It is not a generous master, but its purpose is the highest possible."

"And the end justifies the means?"

"Of course. You know this as well as I do. You're that kind of detective. Your own police force has people trained as snipers for SWAT teams as well as those officers who travel to grade schools and teach bicycle safety. The city needs all kinds of law enforcement officers. So does the Dragon."

"Kalzar just killed my partner. Somebody killed Jack Madrone, Baxter, and Zack. And Omar, Kalzar's buddy. Is he one of you, too?

"In a way."

"Would he have killed me if you hadn't intervened that night in front of the jazz club?"

"You know a great deal about us now," Justin said softly. "That makes you a liability . . . or an asset."

Sandra finally turned around, looked into Justin's vibrant blue eyes. If he was hurting from the fight, he didn't show it. It was impossible to believe she'd pumped nine bullets into him and the other dragon man. But then, this was all impossible to believe.

"What do you mean?" she asked.

"I want you to join me," he answered. His eyes entranced her. "I beg of you."

"Become what you are?" She heard her voice as if from a great distance away.

"Yes. It is the safest option for you."

"Join you or die? Is that it?" she asked bitterly.

"Sandra, I can't always be around to protect you from Kalzar. If he is determined, he will kill you.

And he is a zealot. Few thoughts enter his small mind, but once they do, they never leave."

"You're serious . . . ," she said. Suddenly she laughed. Laughed even as she realized she was crying. This morning she'd been a cop. She lived in Chicago, a city in the United States in the twentieth century. Now she didn't know who or where or even when she was. She felt a horrifying lack of stability, as if the cathedral was made of the smoke rising from the altar candles.

"I am serious, Sandra," Justin pleaded. "I want you with me forever. I love you."

Her emotions threatened to overwhelm her. She loved him, too, but she couldn't say it. There was . . . too much between them. She couldn't just . . . an ocean of blood roiled between them. McKenzie's death. Madrone. Zack. Baxter. Wheeler. Who was Justin, really? Who was this Dragon who was prepared to grant her immortal life? And for what price?

"I want that Arab's head on a plate," she said. "You may be able to tolerate him, but I can't. I don't care how he goes down, but I want him down."

"The end justifies the means?"

"Damn straight!"

Justin smiled. "You see? I knew we were the same, you and I."

She said nothing.

He reached out and took her hand. "I have answered your questions. I have but one for you."

Sandra nodded.

"You left, that first night we spent together.

Why? It was lovely. Why did you leave?"

Sandra licked her dry lips and averted her gaze from his. "I was afraid," she said. "Benny got that right. I had a husband once . . ." She told him everything. The beatings, the verbal abuse, how she kept coming back for more of the same . . .

"I've been afraid to trust my emotions since then. After I escaped that whole fucked-up situation, I always felt that I had damned myself with my own lying heart. I . . . didn't want to do that again. I couldn't bear to lose myself that way again. When I spent the night with you, I let down my guard, and you crept in." She paused, looked up at him. "I didn't want you to be there. I didn't want to admit that I . . ."

"What?" he asked softly.

"That I'd fallen in love with you."

He reached out a hand and touched her cheek. "How could anyone strike such a wonder as you?" he whispered. "Of all the sins I have seen, that must be the greatest."

She bowed her head, then looked at him. "Your friends Omar and Kalzar have been taking turns sinning, then, since the day I met you."

"Sandra . . ." He leaned forward and kissed her on the cheek. "I would never do that."

She nodded. "I don't think you would."

He rose, still holding her hand. She looked up at him.

"You need some time alone," he said. "I think it's best if I leave for a while."

"Yes."

He let go of her hand and began walking quietly down the aisle.

"Justin?" Her voice was barely above a whisper.

He turned. "Yes?"

"Thank you."

"For?"

"For saving my life back at the club."

"You're welcome."

twenty-three

Sandra pulled into the District Eighteen lot and parked close to the door. After the events of the last few days, she saw danger in every shadow. Any little noise sent a spike of adrenaline racing through her body. She was exhausted, but she didn't want to go home. She knew the moment she touched her bed, she would fall asleep, and she couldn't afford to sleep now. Not while Kalzar still walked the earth free, in whatever form he chose. She wanted to trust Justin, but she had wanted to trust him before, and now Mac was dead.

Sweet, loud-mouthed, dependable Mac. Sandra dreaded talking to Linda more than anything else. And she hadn't, not yet, at least. She had her own pain to deal with first.

Sandra spent another hour at the cathedral after Justin left, trying to pull herself together. Somehow, she felt he was watching her the entire time. The sensation left her with conflicting emotions. Was the dragon at the door to protect her from other dragons? Or to devour her the moment she stepped outside?

She went up the stairs to the precinct and to her desk. She didn't see who was working graveyard, and she didn't care. She had only two purposes here now.

Her fingers felt numb as she scribbled out a note and signed it. She had no idea what time it was. Looking at the windows, she realized it must be near sunrise. The night was giving way to day along the eastern horizon in the faintest of pastel glows.

After folding the note, she searched through her desk for an envelope. Not finding one immediately, she started toward the captain's office. She was too tired to be bothered with details.

"Sandra," the captain's voice stopped her. She looked up to see him standing in his doorway. He was a stocky man in his forties, a little taller than she was. His dark red hair had a few streaks of white in it. She had always been impressed by how muscular his forearms were, all covered with that curly, crimson hair. His face had always seemed old to her, which was odd because he had almost no wrinkles. Only a few at the corners of his eyes. Perhaps it was just the way he looked at her. It seemed like he knew more than anyone alive. He appraised her, checking for injuries.

"Captain . . ." She blinked, swallowed, and tried to think of something to say. She hadn't expected him to be in the precinct at this hour. "You're here early."

He nodded. "I told you not to come in, unless IA called. You're on med. leave, Sandra. Why the hell are you here?"

She held up the note. "I'm sorry this isn't couched in official language on the proper form, but I just can't handle going through all the channels right now."

"What is it?" He raised a bushy red eyebrow in inquiry.

"Request for a formal leave of absence. Of indefinite length."

"Sandra . . . I'm sorry about Mac. He was one of my friends, too."

She nodded. "Yeah. I know." She passed him the piece of paper.

"You sure you want to take this kind of leave right now? A medical is understandable, but people will talk about this. It might not be so easy to come back." He paused. "There'll be questions about you . . . about your mental health."

"I know. I don't care."

"Will you at least bring Johnson and DeWitt up to speed on where you and Mac were with your cases?"

"It's all in my files—every bit of it. Though I think I can guarantee they're not going to like my conclusions." She thought for a minute. "If you want, I'll write it up now."

"Later is fine."

"Good." She turned and started walking away. The captain didn't say anything. As she passed Mac's desk, she looked down at all his paperwork, scattered about. She could hear his phone ringing in her mind. She could see him picking it up, talking to Linda with that patient expression on his face. Grunting and nodding and shrugging at Sandra as she waited.

The tears threatened to overwhelm her again, and she turned away. The captain had followed her. He was talking to her, but she hadn't heard a word of what he was saying.

"—they can call you if they need help or background on your conclusions, right?"

She shook her head.

"Don't you want us to catch this guy, McCormick?"

She shook her head. "Yes, sir. I want him caught. Just, maybe, not the way you think . . ." She cut herself off and began walking away again.

"Sandra." The captain's voice carried across the room. It had that tone she had heard so many times when he was warning an officer away from a course of action. "Don't try anything on your own. We're cops, not vigilantes."

She kept going. Following the hall she'd walked so often with her partner at her side, talking about nothing, him teasing her, getting on her nerves. She couldn't get his voice out of her head, so she just listened to it and remembered. Mac smiling. Mac laughing. Mac talking to Linda.

Yeah. Yeah, okay. Yeah, I gotta go. Look, Sandra's here, I gotta go . . .

Sandra got in her car and drove to the coroner's office.

She pushed through the door and went inside, followed the darkened hallway to find an attendant.

He was a tall young man with a big nose, bony and a little bent to the side. She'd seen him around. He'd been working here for more than a year. He was handsome in a lost-little-kid way.

He glanced up from a microscope and smiled hesitantly. "Hi," he said, "how can I help you?"

"You worked on the Zack Miller case with Dr. Benson, didn't you?"

He nodded. "A little."

"Can you help me? I need to know some things about the Miller kid."

He nodded back. "Sure . . . uh, what, exactly?"

"I want you to see something. Pull the file and meet me in the examination room."

"Okay." He seemed confused, but he went to get the file and Sandra continued into the examination room. One wall was all stainless steel, covered with twelve square doors, each about the size of a dorm refrigerator's. The meat lockers. Bodies were kept here, chilled and waiting, until the police were finished with them, and then they were sent to the city morgue. Miller's body would be long gone, but that was all right. The coroner kept extensive records, videotapes, and photos.

The young doctor returned a moment later with a file. Sandra had looked it over before. Among the contents were photographs of Zack Miller's grisly wound, and a few suppositions as to what could have caused it. Nothing concrete. But now Sandra knew what could rip a hole in a man's chest like that. She had felt those claws rip into her own body.

The young man was shuffling through the photographs. Looking up at her, he said. "What exactly did you want me to review?"

"The wound."

"Oh. Okay. Yeah, I remember. Unknown puncture wound, punched through the rib cage. Probably a steel mechanism. Powerful launching device."

"Right." She paused. "What's your name?" she asked.

"Joe," he said.

"Okay, Joe. I want you to look at something for me." Sandra began unbuttoning her blouse. Joe actually took a step back, gulping and turning red to his hairline. He blinked several times, and seemed to be searching for something to say, and something to look at far above her head. Finally he just closed his mouth and tried to look elsewhere as Sandra removed her blouse and then her bra.

She ripped the bandages off her breast and shoulder to reveal the wounds. "I want you to identify these for me."

Joe coughed nervously, turned his head to look at her while keeping his body facing the other direction. "Um, well, that is . . . where did you get those marks?" He looked into her eyes, unwilling to look lower.

Sandra's gaze turned flinty and she closed in on him, took his hand, and put it on her shoulder just where Kalzar's claws had rested.

"Can we get on with this?" she asked.

"Y-yeah, sure," he nodded. He craned his neck to look. "Um, maybe you should, uh . . . maybe you should lie down. I'm sorry. All the people I'm used to working on tend to be, um, lying down."

Sandra hopped on one of the tables. Joe grabbed some latex gloves out of a cardboard box and pulled them on. He did seem more relaxed once she was on her back, although he got a little flustered every time she moved. The fact that her chest rose and fell as he examined the wound seemed to unnerve him a little. But she waited patiently, and finally he was finished looking over her injuries.

"Okay . . . ," he began. "I . . . well, what did you want to know?"

"This was obviously done by some sort of claw, correct?" she asked.

He nodded.

"Imagine that what killed Miller was also a claw."

"Okay," Joe said.

"Is it the same claw that made this mark on me?"

Interest lit in the coroner's eyes and he shuffled through the photographs of Miller's chest, pulled a few out, and then focused on one in particular. Sandra remained still while he probed at her again, looking at each of her small wounds in turn, and then backing up and looking at them as a whole.

He held the photograph he'd chosen up against her chest as he looked. Slowly he shook his head. "No. Not the same."

Taking the photograph from her belly, she handed it to Joe as she sat up. Immediately he was nervous again. She put her bra on.

"Why?" she asked, pulling her blouse on.

"Well, um, do you mind if I ask you where you got that wound?" He indicated her chest.

"Yes. I mind. Why are they different?"

"Oh, well, Miller's killer's claw—if it was a

claw—was larger. The incision points were wider than the claw wound around your . . . on your chest."

"And that's all? It's larger? Are you sure it wasn't the same claw simply opened up wider?"

"Well, no, because it's not just the size that's different. Miller's claw had four incision points. Three and one—like an eagle's talon. Three claws on one side and one directly opposite on the other side. Yours is like a human hand would be if it had claws. Well, more so than an eagle's talon, anyway. You've got four wound points on your chest. Three and one, except the opposing claw isn't directly opposite, but off to the side like a human thumb."

Sandra slid from the table as she finished buttoning her blouse. Looking him straight in the eye, she asked, "You mean there is absolutely no way these two wounds could have come from the same claw?"

"No. If they were animals, I'd say they were similar, but a different species. Close, but definitely not the same creature."

Sandra made a fumbling, dazed attempt at tucking in her shirt.

"That's not the answer you wanted, was it?" Joe asked hesitantly.

"No," she said as she headed for the door, leaving the rest of her blouse untucked. "No, it wasn't."

twenty-four

On a normal day, Sandra would race up the stairs to her apartment at a steady pace, giving her legs their daily workout. This time, she plodded. Using the elevator would have been faster, but she had no intention of being trapped in a closed space right now.

Mac was dead, Kalzar wanted to kill her, and nobody around here was safe—including Benny. Even Justin had said he couldn't protect her from Kalzar forever. And why had Justin dragged Benny into it? Had Justin made that connection with Benny just to have something to hold over her? Or did he like her brother for himself—Justin would certainly be able to see beneath the scarred surface to the real man inside. Sandra couldn't help wondering why Justin had taken such an interest in Benny. She worried that it wasn't a good sign for Benny's continued health.

Could she just grab Benny and drive to another city? She doubted it. But she had to try. He was the only person they could use against her now. She wouldn't lose him like she'd lost Mac. Once she had Benny safely hidden, she would come back.

It was past time for a reckoning. Kalzar would pay for killing Mac. But Benny had to be safe first.

And Justin? What about Justin?

It was too confusing. Her thoughts whirled. She could find no clear resolution for the situation. There was a part of her that would gladly spend the rest of her life with Justin, but the rest of her immortal life? Serving a master who could, and did, force his servants to murder the innocent? Could she reconcile the part of herself that loved Justin the man with the part of herself that loathed him for what he became at the master's hands? He was a killer. She'd spent her adult life bringing killers to justice. How could she possibly still love him? Did she?

Sandra's fatigue pulled at her. She wanted to sleep, but she didn't dare. She didn't have a moment to spare. Kalzar was still out there, walking free, and Mac was dead. She knew she wouldn't find rest until that situation ended, either with Kalzar in jail—or dead. For Mac's sake. For Benny's sake. And for her own sake, and her unshakable belief in the power of justice.

She entered the condo and found Benny looking out the window. Awake again, despite the early hour. It was unlike him. The lights were off, but the sun was just up, pink dawn light streaming into the room throwing long shadows.

She wondered if he'd awakened because he was worried about her. She didn't know if she could face him telling her how happy he was that she had loosened up and spent another night at Justin's— tell her that she needed to trust men again. If only he knew . . .

"Benny," she said wearily, closing the door behind her. He didn't move. "We've got to leave. We've got to leave Chicago. Today. Now. In half an hour or so. I want you to—" Her brother still hadn't moved. His back was to her, and she couldn't see his face.

"Benny?" she cried, her voice going tight in terror. "Benny!"

She crossed the room, shoving aside a table that blocked her path. Grabbing his wheelchair, she spun it around.

Benny jumped up out of his chair. His arms encircled her in a big hug and he lifted her off the ground, laughing.

Inside her, something went over the edge. She heard herself screaming. Terror filled her heart. Ducking low, she broke the grip of Benny's arms and shoved him, hard. He landed in a tangled sprawl of arms and legs. She stepped back from him, shocked at what she'd done, fighting to get herself under control. Benny was lying on the floor, looking bewildered. He shook his head a little.

"Whoa, ace, remind me never to surprise you." He stood up. He was *standing!*

"B-Benny?" she said, her breath coming fast.

"Isn't it great?" He laughed and leaped into the air, pointing at his nose. His perfectly straight nose. It was completely normal, healed. All the scars on his face were gone. All the deformities wiped away as if Benny had stepped from the distant past into this present day, whole and well.

"What . . . what have you done?" she asked, backing away from him. She bumped into his wheelchair, stumbled past it, and leaned up against the wall.

"Me? I've become whole again. I'm walking! I'm jumping! I'm sparring with you, I guess! I don't know! Look at me, Sandy! I can *walk!*" He started toward her, as if to prove it.

"Stay away from me," she yelled. Her wide eyes flicked from him to his wheelchair and back to Benny's face.

Benny stopped dead as if she'd shot him. His smile vanished. "Sandra . . .," he said, concerned. "It's all right. I know it seems strange, but . . ."

"I'm going crazy," she whispered. She shook her head, closed her eyes to see if the strange new world she'd walked into would vanish when she opened them again.

"Benny . . . tell me how this happened."

"You won't believe how wonderful it is, Sandra. You can't imagine what it's like to go from being able to walk to not being able to walk and then back again. I feel like I could kick the walls down. No more pity and disgust in people's eyes. Fuck that.

Fuck them!" His eyes radiated a strange combination of joy and contempt.

"Benny . . ." Sandra heard her voice go flat, as the truth began to dawn on her, the only truth it could be. "How did this happen to you?"

"Justin showed me a mirror. I looked into it and—"

"A mirror! No, Benny! When?" Sandra gasped.

"A little while ago. He came by and—"

"He did this to you?" Sandra's throat tightened. She couldn't move. Despair settled around her like a black cloak, followed by a searing, white-hot rage.

"Did this to me? You make it sound like a sin, not a blessing." He paused, staring at her, then shook his head. "No, it was the Dragon."

"Where is he? Where's Justin?" she snarled.

"He's not here now. He left, but Sandra, don't be angry. He told me what happened at the club, about Mac. I'm sorry about him, but look . . . just look at me! Sandra, he showed me the mirror. Inside it . . . you wouldn't believe. The Dragon was the most beautiful creature I'd ever seen. That story Justin told us at the restaurant, it's all true! It was the Dragon in that mirror, and he's everything Justin claimed he was. The Dragon looked inside me, said it could see the strength trapped there, and it asked me if I wanted to be released."

"Save me from this . . .," she whispered. Sandra's mind filled with images of Benny slaughtering Zack Miller, of Benny punching a hole through Jack Madrone's chest.

"I said yes," Benny's voice lowered, awed, "and he gave me my life back."

"Oh, no, Benny!" Sandra pressed back against the wall. "God, no, Benny . . . !" When the Dragon decided to kill her, would it send Benny after her?

She felt herself falling, and Benny was there, holding her up, just as he'd done when she'd fled from Chuck. Just as she'd done for him after the accident.

"Don't touch me," she said. She felt herself sliding down the wall. Benny grabbed her, held her upright. His arms were incredibly strong. "Please, no. . . ."

"Don't be silly," he said unhappily. "It's still me, Sandra. Your crazy brother Benny. Everything is going to be all right. I promise."

"Don't make promises you can't keep," she said, breaking his hold and shoving him away. He stumbled backward a couple of paces and she tried to run past him. She bumped into his wheelchair. She picked it up and hurled it to one side.

He watched, stricken, as she ran from him. She clutched and fumbled at the front door, flung it open, and lurched out, slamming it closed behind her.

Benny walked the few steps to the door and stopped before it, tragedy written in the lines of his face. An elegant figure emerged from the hallway. The man laid a hand on Benny's shoulder.

"What happened, Justin? Why did it go wrong?"

390 Margaret Weis and David Baldwin

Benny asked, his voice trembling. "I did what you said."

"She is only frightened, my friend," Justin replied. He, too, was disappointed.

"I wasn't frightened."

"Everyone reacts differently. Give her time. She'll come around."

"I guess so." Benny sounded dubious. "I just don't understand why she wouldn't be excited for me, at least. This is so amazing."

"She has not had an easy time of it lately. Keep in mind—you didn't see Mac's dead body, or feel Kalzar's claws rip your flesh. She's had reason to fear us in the past. Give her time to deal with the changes." He paused, and then spoke again. "She is still in very real danger. She is not yet one of us. We must protect her. Take a cab and follow her."

He withdrew a small, folded piece of paper. "Here is my cell phone number. I will keep the phone with me at all times. The moment you see Kalzar or any other suspicious person near her, call me immediately. Do not hesitate, because they will not allow her to live unless she accepts the change. The Dragon's disciples are many. She's in the greatest danger of her life right now. We must give her our help, whether she asks for it or not."

"Don't worry about that, Justin. Sandra means more to me than any of this. They won't get to her without going through me."

Justin gripped Benny's shoulders and looked him in the eye. "Yes, Benny, they will. I know how you feel. Strong enough to beat down mountains, but it's not enough. Don't try to be a hero. You'll fail. You cannot withstand Kalzar. He will tear you open and then let you watch as he guts her. Call me."

"Okay, Justin," Benny promised. "You have my word."

twenty-five

As soon as Benny shut the door, Justin set Benny's wheelchair upright, walked to the windows, and stared out at the city. He was tired, far too tired. Perhaps it was the wounds he had received. He had never fought with another of the Elder disciples. Never. Perhaps the weariness he now experienced came from that. Or perhaps it was the Dragon's punishment for his continued disobedience.

Justin did not know. He had not come close to a mirror since the fight. He could feel his master's desire to speak to him, but he refused to respond. He felt rage surge within him. Rage at Sandra. But it was the Dragon's rage, not Justin's own. As a consequence, he did not dare change into his dragonling form for any reason. Hiding while Benny and Sandra argued had been torment for Justin. He'd had to clench both hands to keep from bursting through the door. He'd been terrified he'd end the conversation with Sandra's heart in his hand. Why couldn't she just look in the mirror and accept her fate?

Justin looked down at the sapphire ring on his finger. For some reason, it gave him comfort. It brought Angela to mind, and how he had not wanted to kill her, either. It reminded him of how terrible he'd felt afterward. He did not want to stare at Sandra's bloody corpse—the feelings he had for her were so much more intense that he knew the aftermath would be unbearable. Somehow, the thought of Angela eased his struggle with the Dragon's wishes.

He would have to face Sandra soon. The Dragon had promised Justin a day to convert her, but it seemed that the Dragon was not willing to be patient. The incessant longings for Sandra's death were proof enough of that. Why was she resisting the choice? She loved him, he knew that, sensed it in her every move. Gwendolyne, too, had loved him . . .

Justin sank down on the couch. He closed his eyes. In the darkness he saw a flash of a dream. The same dream as before. Of him, doing battle with a great, fiery shape, wielding a sword of light. Was that what it meant? His subconscious throwing up a graphic scene representing his own situation now, in essence battling the master he had obeyed for so long?

And he thought he knew what the sword of light was, too. The knowledge frightened him. Because that sword was real. Did it mean the dream might become real as well? But that would be . . .

No, it would be impossible.

He opened his eyes and sighed. How long could he wait? He would have to face her soon, convince her or . . .

Justin shook his head. Each moment he delayed was one more moment Kalzar would have to exact his revenge. Kalzar had finally found Justin's weakness—Sandra—and he would use it. He wouldn't be able to help himself. Kalzar would never forgive Justin for besting him.

Justin let out a breath, relaxed, felt his eyes closing. It felt so good simply to rest a moment. Just one moment . . .

The vision began the same way as every vision he'd had since his pact with the Dragon. Justin cried out against it, cursed himself for relaxing his guard, but there was no escape now. The red eyes of his master opened and Justin saw through them.

He floated in the high vaulted ceiling of the cathedral. Below, Sandra sat in a pew, head bowed, silent. One of the doors at the front of the church opened, and he saw himself enter, saw his dark hair and long black coat silhouetted in the sunlight of the doorway. Then he moved forward and the door shut behind him. He walked toward Sandra. She rose, afraid of him. She tried to run, but he grabbed her, spun her around. Her fists struck out at him.

She managed to escape his grip. She sprinted away, but he knew it was hopeless. He had done this too many times before. He changed into the dragonling. His powerful wings flapped twice and he overtook her. The dragonling picked Sandra up like a rag doll. Her neck snapped. Her screams died away. His clawed hand plunged into her chest . . .

•   •   •

The vision changed, replaced by another. This time Justin was in London. He could see no landmarks, but he knew his homeland simply by the feel of it on his skin.

He stood on the roof of a great cathedral. Low clouds hung over the city, and the rain fell constantly. In his hand, Justin gripped the Blade of Beowulf, the sword the legendary hero used to slay Grendel's mother, the dragon named Gyzalanitha. The blade had survived through the centuries, imbued with Beowulf's power through a piece of his thighbone, which was kept in the haft. This was the sword Saint George had carried in his hunt for dragons. When he finally died, a sliver of his finger bone had been inserted into the haft as well. Both dragon slayers had eaten dragon wings, and both had become something more than mortal. Their magic had become a part of the sword. It was the only weapon Justin knew of that could kill a Dragon . . . or a Dragon's disciple.

Kalzar, in dragonling form, stalked toward him across the great stone sculptures adorning the cathedral's eaves. He walked toward Justin with a terrible smile on his face. His smile slipped when he saw the sword in Justin's hand. The smile's last remnants froze forever on Kalzar's face the instant the blade swept through his neck . . .

The vision wrenched away, and once again Justin saw himself walking into the cathedral. Once again, he killed

Sandra. He wrestled with the dream. Again he was in London on the cathedral. Again Kalzar's head rolled to the stone facings of the great church. Then Sandra's death played out once more. And again . . . and again . . . and again . . .

Justin willed himself awake, finally escaping the clutches of the visions that haunted him. He'd never escaped such visions before until released by the Dragon, had never been able to do so. Perhaps he hadn't done it this time. Perhaps the Dragon had let him go. After all, Justin's mandate was obvious. The Dragon wanted Sandra dead. But he seemed to want Kalzar dead as well.

Perhaps not all the visions had come from the Dragon . . .

"I will not kill her . . ." Justin vowed through gritted teeth. "She will convert. I swear it."

But even as he said it, pain shot through him, burning him alive as he cried out. He staggered and slammed into the coffee table. Wood cracked and a huge, jagged splinter of it pushed through his forearm. His blood gushed onto the carpet, but that pain was peripheral to the other agonies the Dragon was unleashing on him. Now there was pressure on both sides of his head, and it felt as if his eyeballs were going to pop from their sockets.

"No." He was defiant. "I will not!" His forearm came free of its impalement, and he struggled to stand. Huddling into himself, Justin forced the pain from his body. He willed the Dragon away. Electric shocks coursed through his limbs and he screamed in agony, but his resolve did not falter. He remained hunched over, eyes shut, fighting.

With each jolt of burning anguish, a memory of the last time he had fought this battle came to him.

The other . . .

Images of her flashed across his mind and he focused on her, not the fire burning his flesh.

He was in Russia. It was the turn of the century. A young woman entered the barn. Her breath was a white cloud in the frosty air. She had recently given birth for the first time. Justin could hear the baby crying from where he hid in the barn. He perched in the loft, one with the early morning shadows.

The woman's blonde hair was a cascade of sunshine framing her soft, round face. Her movements were graceful and her happiness radiated from her. The vision of her would always stay with him, the way her lips were curved in a smile, the way her cheeks were flushed, the way she whistled softly as she worked, never knowing of the demon who hovered by her door.

His dreams had sent him here, the only kind of dreams he had anymore. She was his victim. He had seen how he would kill her. Here, in the barn. Now, as she was gathering eggs. Now, as she lifted her skirts and tucked them in her waistband, to keep them free from the straw and dirt in the barn as she collected the eggs.

He watched her exposed legs, smooth and youthful, and he remembered when he had first seen Gwendolyne. He had been in his nineteenth year, fully a man by the standards of the time. She had been fourteen, a slim and agile sylph of a girl, all hair and eyes and that beautiful smile. His first glimpse of her by the riverside had been enough for him. He'd known then that he would marry her.

He had seen too much of Gwendolyne in that young Russian girl. He had dared to love her and the Dragon had disapproved, just as Justin's father had disapproved of Gwendolyne. That first night Justin could not bring himself to kill her. He waited until she left, and that was when the pain hit. All of that day and all of the next he stayed hidden from the young woman, locked in his personal struggle with the Dragon, drinking hell by the mouthful. In the night, sometimes, he would allow himself to cry out quietly, caught in the throes of torment.

By the third day, he could not remember what it was like to be without pain. All he knew was that he could not continue the struggle for another minute without going mad. That morning, when the young Russian girl entered the barn, he was ready to take her. Her death was instantaneous. A knife from behind. A slit throat. She never had time to realize what exactly was wrong before she passed from the land of the living.

He had bought her three days with his pain. Three days. How valuable were three days of happiness? He'd had little more than that with Sandra. What price could be put upon such a thing?

Slowly Justin's memory faded away . . . and with it, the pain . . .

The phone. His cell phone was ringing.

Justin plunged his hand into the inside pocket of his coat, fumbled after the phone.

"Yes?" His voice was tight, controlled.

"Justin? It's Benny. I'm at the cathedral. Sandra's here. I had to go to a pay phone outside to call you. You told me to call as soon as I saw someone suspicious. Well, he's here, I think. That guy you mentioned. Kalzar."

"Kalzar," Justin managed to say.

"Yeah, him. He came in and sat by the door. I think he knows who I am. The way he looked at me . . ."

"It's possible. Elders can often tell when a younger disciple is near. Very well. I'll be there as soon as I can. Stay as close to him as you can without revealing yourself. Don't fight him, but do what you can to keep him away from Sandra."

"How do I do that?"

"I don't *know* . . . but you have to *try*."

"Okay." Benny hung up.

Justin folded the phone and slipped it back in his pocket. Was the Dragon sending Kalzar to kill Sandra? Or was Kalzar operating independently? If it was the latter, then Justin might buy himself time by killing Kalzar. If it was the former, Justin could never protect Sandra. There would always be another disciple assigned to kill her. One of them would eventually succeed.

There was only one way to protect Sandra forever . . .

Justin stepped out the door and sensed them immediately, though they weren't readily apparent to human eyes. He wasn't surprised when two men stepped from the shadows near the corner of the building.

They were Chinese, an older man and a teenage kid. They seemed familiar, though Justin couldn't place either one of them in his memory. Justin looked down at the ring on his finger, looked at them, then narrowed his eyes.

The two flanked the edges of the staircase that descended from the door of the building to the sidewalk. Never pausing, Justin started down toward them. What would have been creepy to anyone else was merely annoying to Justin. He didn't know who these people were, but he had a fair idea who might have sent them. They could stand in his way at their peril.

"Who are you?" he asked. They didn't seem inclined to stop him, but they weren't afraid of him, either.

The man was middle-aged. His short, black hair was streaked with gray. His eyes appraised Justin, and Justin didn't like the feeling at all.

"You know who we are," the man said.

Justin nodded. "Yes, of course. You're Drokpas. Human slaves of the dragons from Beyond."

The man nodded. "Yes. We serve them, but we are not slaves. We seek—"

"I know what you seek," Justin said. "You think you can stop my master from returning to this world."

"You do not realize—"

"I realize that if you try to stop me, I will rip you limb from limb. You know I can do it."

"We know," the man said. He and the kid bowed and stood aside.

Justin brushed past them. "At any other time I would not suffer your kind to live," he growled, walking quickly down the street.

When Justin was almost out of earshot, the man yelled to him, "Remember the blue flame! It will serve you well!"

The words were so surprising he froze for a moment. He spun around to ask them what they meant, but when he faced the steps again, they were gone.

As if they'd never been.

Hidden in shadow, the two Chinese men could still see Justin as he hailed the cab. Neither spoke for a long moment.

"I fear for her," the younger finally said.

"I know. Matters are coming to a cusp," the older returned.

"I don't trust him."

"It is not our mission to trust him. It is our mission to help him understand his true nature and that of his master."

"What if he hurts her?" the younger asked.

"Then that is as it must be."

"I cannot stand by while this happens," the younger said.

"Then I will send you back to Drokpasyl," the older man said. "She is not our purpose. The earl of Sterling is. We have watched him for hundreds of years. He is the one who can end everything."

"So we may save the girl Tina, but we may not save

Sandra?" The younger man's voice was thick with rage.

"Tina was meant to be taken into the fold. So the Dragons said."

"And yet they will not take Sandra. How are we different from Justin, then? We justify these deaths as necessary things. How are we different?"

The older man turned a stern gaze on the younger. "Your passion is admirable, but your logic is lost in a sea of anger."

"I just don't think—"

"That is correct. You are not thinking clearly. You assume that you could stop the earl of Sterling as you stopped his henchman, Omar, from killing Tina. Need I remind you that if Omar had spent a little more time on you, you would be dead? There is nothing you can do to stop Justin. If you stand in his path, he will cut you down and think nothing of it. And your resistance might be the one thing he needs to work himself into a rage. And then how would you have served his future victim?"

"The Dragons could take Sandra into the fold," the younger man pointed out.

"Would you have them take her as Justin wishes to take her? Would you tell her, 'Join us if you wish to live. You have no choice'? I turn your question back upon you. How would that differ from what Justin is doing?"

"At least she would be alive."

"So Justin thinks, also. You are both correct. But neither of you are right. They both must make very important decisions. They cannot make those decisions if we do it for them. What must be will be."

The younger man paused for a long time. He struggled with himself, but finally his face became calmer, more placid. He let out a long, slow breath.

"Yes, Grandfather."

"We must trust," the older man said.

"We must trust," the younger echoed.

twenty-six

The cathedral had three entrances, the great double doors in the center, and two smaller, steel-bound wooden doors on either side. Statues of the apostles flanked the center doors. The pointed arch was a recess three feet thick, carved into delicate filigree which sloped down to the entranceway. Above the arch was a scene of Jesus weighing souls, with Mary to his right and Peter to his left. It was an impressive edifice, even to a man who had watched Gothic cathedrals being built, as Justin had witnessed the construction of parts of Westminster Abbey and other great churches.

Below those scenes was a representation of Christ at the time of Armageddon. Souls floated free, rising from their tombs. Radiant angels with beautiful wings carried the devout up toward Jesus.

But farther down, a more insidious scene took place. At the bottom of the frieze, the souls of the wicked reached imploringly for heaven, crying out in pitiful, silent shrieks of terror as long-horned demons with maniacal grins gripped their legs and dragged them down to where the flames leapt high. Within those flames, every atrocity imaginable was occurring. A huge devil, by far the largest figure of the scene, held a man in seven tentacles. The devil was ripping the man's head off. A naked woman ran through the flames, tears sliding down her face. Three snakes sank their fangs into her flesh, one at each breast and one at her genitals. Another man was being stuffed headfirst into a tub of flames by three small demons. His legs kicked fiercely.

Justin turned his gaze from the scene. If he should die—actually die—worse awaited him. Eternal torment. Yet wasn't that how he might describe his current existence?

Justin reached the right-hand door and opened it. The pain had stopped, for now. He was approaching his victim. In the eyes of the Dragon, Justin was no longer resisting his edict.

The cathedral was all but empty. Only two people—Sandra and Kalzar—sat in the pews. Benny was there somewhere, hidden in the shadows.

At the sound of the door opening, Kalzar, close to the entrance, turned around. As always, he was impeccably dressed in a gray, pin-striped three-piece suit. Kalzar saw him and grinned. For a moment Justin's rage almost slipped out of control. His hands longed to strangle the smile from that smug face, to push those glinting eyes back into his skull until they burst. But now was not the time. Soon enough there would be a more appropriate moment. Justin would wait.

Kalzar stood up, smoothed his lapels. Justin did not

even spare him a glance as Kalzar walked by, nodding in approval. He opened the door and left the cathedral.

Justin saw Benny out of the corner of his vision, standing in the shadows of the nave. Justin beckoned the newly made disciple to his side with a slight motion of his head.

Benny walked to him without a sound. Already he had slipped into a disciple's powers as if he had been born to wield them. Justin placed a silent hand on Benny's shoulder. He nodded toward the door. Benny shot him a questioning glance.

"Follow Kalzar. Keep your eyes on him if you can. I wish to know where he goes."

Benny smiled. "It will be a pleasure. What about Sandra?"

"Give me this moment alone with her," Justin whispered. "I must dissipate her fears. She will be one of us soon. It will be all right."

Benny nodded and followed Kalzar.

Justin began the long walk down the center aisle. Sandra was sitting in the same pew as when they had first talked here. Perhaps she always sat there. He allowed himself to wonder how often she came, how often she sat in that pew. The questions took his mind off the Dragon's singing desire for her death. Every cell of his body ached with the Dragon's need to destroy her.

He carefully chose a pew three back from hers and sat down. The pain returned with a vengeance as he halted. He gripped the back of the pew. The wood creaked under his tightening hands.

Sandra had not moved since she'd heard the door

open. Her back was straight, and she gripped the seat in front of her just as Justin did.

"Is it you, Justin, really?" she asked, her voice drifting up into the ceiling. "And will it? Really?"

"What?" Justin asked, quietly, trying to conceal the struggle within himself.

"Will it really be all right? Or did you just tell Benny that to get him to leave?"

A pain like hundreds of small burning blades opened the flesh on Justin's back. He gasped. "That depends upon you."

She turned around. Her tear-stained gaze was hurt, angry, betrayed. "Join you or die, is that it?"

A spear of fire slammed into Justin's guts, twisting. He let out a tight breath and tried to keep his arms from shaking. The wood of the seat in front of him cracked.

He nodded. He could not speak now. The pain was too intense.

A tear ran down a well-traveled track on Sandra's cheeks. "Why did you have to drag Benny into this? Couldn't you have just let it be between the two of us?"

Fire encircled Justin's heart. The burn spread throughout his chest, choking him. He paused until he could speak. "Benjamin . . . he wanted this," Justin managed. "It is all he has wanted for a long time now. You know it's true."

"No," she said. "The Benny I saw back at the apartment was some mutated version of *my* Benny! What did you do to him?"

"He chose his path, Sandra. You should choose it, too. You are just afraid."

Sandra laughed, a hollow sound. "Of course, I'm terrified. Look at what it's done to you. Look at what you've become. The same thing will happen to Benny, and you brought him to it!"

Justin felt the pain of his fingernails being plucked out, one at a time. The hairs on his head, as well, one by one. His jaw was shaking when he opened his mouth to speak. He closed it with a snap, marshaled his strength, and spoke slowly. He could hear the pain in his voice, though. If Sandra were listening, he was sure she could hear it now, too.

"What I do is painful, and not necessarily just. I do not deny it. It is a heavy burden to bear, but a necessary one for all of mankind."

Sandra gripped her seat with white knuckles. "So killing that kid? Killing McKenzie? Those murders served the good of mankind? I don't buy it. It's not necessary! It could never be necessary!"

"I did not kill McKenzie."

"What difference does it make?" She turned to face him. The cathedral thrummed, echoing with her ire. "It's all the same! People die at your hands—Madrone, Baxter, Zack. What justifies that? Nothing could!"

"Wait. . . ." The pain intensified. "Let me. . . ." He let out a small breath. " . . . Let me tell you something, a story, before you make your decision."

"Forget it." She started to leave, but Justin cut her off.

"Please," he begged, and for the first time, she noticed his pain. She finally realized the price he was paying to let her live. She was silent, watching, wary. She sat back down, prepared to listen.

"Long ago, near the turn of this century, I was ordered to the Russian countryside to kill a young girl."

Sandra seemed about to say something, but Justin motioned her to be silent.

"I did not want to do it," he continued. "She was the wife of a poor revolutionary named Iosif Dzhugashvili. Iosif supported his small family by doing odd jobs and by keeping the farm. In his spare time, he wrote for a tiny underground Bolshevik newspaper under the name of Joseph Stalin. I did not want to kill Yekaterina. She was a wonderful woman. I do not believe I have ever seen such devotion between a couple. They were in love, despite the danger that was always a part of their lives. She had recently given birth to a son, Yakov. She was wild, spirited, and she bolstered her husband's convictions when he despaired. He lived in constant fear of the day when men would appear at his door and arrest him for treason.

"If he was the mind that helped lead to revolution, she was the backbone that kept him straight. And she was also his weakness. If she had asked him to give up his writing for her, he would have done it in an instant. But she would never ask him to give up his dreams and convictions. She was brave, and she believed that since they were right, they would be invincible.

"I struggled for days, hidden in their barn, trying to resist my call to be the reaper of this beautiful life. You . . . ," he gasped as new agonies roared through him, " . . . cannot imagine the pain of resisting my master. I could only resist for three days, and then I murdered her. I made it look as if her dismemberment was carried out by czarist aristocrats. I lingered long enough to see her husband find the body. Young Iosif's heart broke before my eyes.

"From that moment forward, nothing else mattered to Iosif but his work. He threw himself into it. Before long he was discovered, arrested, and sent to Siberia. Later he escaped and returned to the struggle where he caught Lenin's eye. By then Lenin did not see an intellectual, in love with words and ideas, dedicated to a higher purpose. Lenin saw a man of action who wanted to fight and to kill.

"I watched these events from a distance, watched as Stalin climbed to power. The millions of deaths he inflicted on his enemies, his own people, even those he called his friends, were torture to me. For I knew that I had begun it all with a single act of violence. I was appalled at the way Stalin turned his old friends against one another, the way he exiled Trotsky and later had him killed, the way he seized complete power when Lenin died. He was the worst tyrant I had ever seen. He drove peasants off their land, starved his people to death, killed anyone who opposed him. I could not believe that I had made such a man. I could not believe it . . .

"Until I saw a man who was worse.

"I detached myself from my master after Yekaterina's death. I avoided him, I hid from him. I could not believe in him any longer, not after what he'd made me do.

"But when I walked through the frozen streets of Stalingrad after the Russians captured the 'indestructible' German Sixth Army, turning the tide on Nazi Germany forever, I knew that the Dragon's long view had out-reached me again. Whatever Stalin was, he was not Hitler.

"Stalin was a cruel and bloody leader, completely ruthless. It took a man like Stalin to defeat Hitler.

"That day I reconciled with my master. He saw the understanding within me, and he bestowed a new gift upon me. In those frozen streets, I first assumed my dragonling form, with all the strength and power that accompanies it. That day I became an Elder disci-ple. I flew across the countryside, viewing the carnage. Millions died in the six-month battle for Stalingrad, but it was not the Dragon's fault. He was trying to guide them away from war. As he puts it, monsters that destroy need monsters to combat them. That is his philosophy. You cannot stop a sword's blow with-out steel of equal quality. As harsh as the Dragon's methods may seem sometimes, he is our only hope of reaching past this bloody nature of ours. He is our only hope of reaching true civilization. . . ."

When Justin finished his story and looked up, he realized that Sandra was sitting next to him. Her eyes were red rimmed, full of sorrow, wet with tears. The back of the pew in front of him had disintegrated under his clenched hands.

Her light touch trailed across his tensed jaw. He jumped at her touch, delicate as it was.

"Join me . . .," he said in a hoarse voice.

"I was you," she whispered. "I was just like you. Look at what you endure for him." She never wavered in her gaze. "My dragon's name was Chuck, and every time he struck me, I told myself that he didn't mean it. Every time I stared in the mirror for hours at a time, watching the bruises darken on my face, I told myself that he really loved me. He was just frustrated, and needed me to help him get past this tough time in his life. I needed to help him achieve his dreams. I told myself he hit me because I had to learn. I believed it for so long. But Justin . . ." She paused long enough to draw a deep breath. Both her hands reached up to touch his face. "He lied."

"What?" He peered through the agony, focusing on her face, concentrating on her words. "No. . . ." He shook his head.

"Yes. Don't you see?" she urged. "We believe their lies because we want to. We make them our own and call them truths. Because we let our fear have us. Because we won't face the devil we don't know, as opposed to the devil we do. And we hate ourselves for it."

"No. . . ." Justin's memories pulled at him, and the Dragon's pain threatened to rip him apart. Gwendolyne's face hovered in his memory, pleading for her life. "No, it's not like that . . . she was just afraid. She was . . . she couldn't face . . . it was what she wanted. I didn't . . . I didn't force her. She was just afraid. It wasn't me. It was the plague, not me . . . the plague that killed her. She didn't choose in time, and. . . ."

Sandra's hands came away from Justin's face. He opened his eyes, which he'd closed in a desperate bid to block the pain. He looked up into Sandra's eyes.

She had risen and was backing away from him. Her face was a mask of terrible surprise, as if she were seeing him for the first time.

"I've been a fool," she said.

"Sandra." His voice was the dragonling's voice. Dear God, he was changing . . . he resisted the change with everything in him. He concentrated on making his voice sound human. "Don't back away. Please don't leave me. She left me alone. All alone. . . ."

"You killed her," Sandra said, staring at him with terrified eyes. "You said she died of the plague, but you lied. You lied to yourself. You lied to me. All of it . . . lies. You killed her, didn't you?"

"Sandra! I . . . no . . . I couldn't have . . ."

"You did. You're lying. You lie about everything. The ends justify the means. That applies to everything for you, doesn't it? You've lived it so long, you've lost touch with everything else, haven't you?"

There was a wet crackling deep in Justin's bones. Skin crinkled and hardened, becoming scales. The scales flowed down his arm like a disease.

"Sandra, please!" Justin's voice was an animal howl buried in a man's words. He clutched his scaled arm to his side. "Join me. Quickly!" He held out a hand to her. His fingers were slowly disappearing, curling and hardening into thick, scaled talons. His thumb twisted around his hand, opposite the hooked claws.

"You're just like Chuck. What is it with me . . . every man I ever love is always just like him. . . ." Sandra bumped back against a fluted column, trapped between two pews that ended there.

"Quickly!" he roared. "We need a mirror." He grabbed her wrist and dragged her toward the altar, where he could see a gleaming silver urn.

Sandra screamed as a bone in her wrist snapped. "Please . . . let me go . . . I can't do this," she begged.

"No! Quickly!" He grabbed the urn and shoved its reflective surface at her face. "Give yourself to him!"

She turned her face away from it, looked at the wreck of the man she loved with sorrow in her eyes, pain in her heart.

"I will be . . . myself." She reached into her coat and drew out her gun.

Justin's claw lashed out, ripping her open from armpit to wrist. Sandra screamed. The gun clattered to the floor. Blood sprayed across the altar, across the steps, soaked the dark red carpet.

Sandra slumped against him, staring at her ruined arm, staring at the blood that pumped out of her in steady spurts. "Please, Sandra," Justin pleaded, holding her gently in arms desperate to crush her, "all the pain will go away. You'll live forever. We'll be together forever! You will *live!* Choose to live!" His muscles sang to him. He had to restrain them from crushing her into a pulp, from bashing her head into the flagstone steps. "For the love of God, look into the mirror!"

"The love . . . of God . . ." Sandra's body shook. "Yes . . . that *is* the answer . . . " She looked up at him. "Justin . . . you will . . . have to live with yourself again. You cannot have me. You go . . . with your God. I will go with mine. May he have mercy upon you . . . upon your soul."

Her words blasted into his brain like shrapnel. He staggered back from her as if she'd hit him. Her words were Gwendolyne's words. Gwendolyne had spoken those exact words to him before her death. She had prayed for his soul, damned him for his decision to join the Dragon.

Justin lost control.

With a powerful surge, he leapt forward and snatched Sandra by the neck. Her scream was cut off in a gurgle and a wet snap. His taloned fist drew back and he plunged it into her heart . . .

. . . into his heart.

twenty-seven

Sandra's body slid down the length of his arm, her red blood staining his skin. She fell on the altar, then tumbled to the stone floor in a crumpled heap.

Sandra's eyes, always so full of passion and pain, were glassy now. They stared past his left shoulder at nothing. Her last breath gurgled through the blood pouring from her nose and mouth. Her arms were broken, as was her neck, and her body lay on the blood red carpet of the church aisle, all unnatural angles and bruised and torn flesh.

Justin stared at what he'd done, horrified. Sandra's last agonized look was engraved on his memory, merging there with Gwendolyne's dying agony. Both . . . he had killed them both . . . both of the women he had truly loved . . .

"Well done, my servant."

Justin looked at the silver urn. The Dragon was there, all smoldering eyes and long teeth.

"You have served me well this day, Lord Sterling."

Justin roared. Grabbing the urn, he threw it the length of the cathedral. The urn flew across the building to the front of the church, where it clanged against the double doors and fell to the floor.

Justin launched himself into the air. His powerful wings carried him toward the stained glass rose window over the altar.

Glass exploded into the air. Sparkling shards fell. Pedestrians in the street screamed. Brakes squealed and cars slammed into each other.

His wings pumped furiously, carrying Justin instantly away from the scene. People had seen him, watched him fly away. He didn't care. Let them scream. He could harness the light rays, bend them around his body to make himself invisible, but what did he care if they saw him? What did he care if they screamed? They *should* scream.

Justin roared. The concrete canyons of the city echoed with his rage.

His wing clipped a building. Its brick facing ripped into his shoulder and sent him spinning downward. Chunks of brick came with him. He smashed into an awning.

Again he roared. He launched himself back into the sky. His muscles roared with pleasure, wanting more, wanting to fly into the crowds of the city and unleash carnage. But he curbed the desire. He flew straight to Gwendolyne's Flight.

It was nine in the morning. Chairs were neatly upended on the tops of the tables, waiting for the new day.

He smashed through the plate glass window, landed on the wide dance floor, cracking its paneled wood surface. As soon as he looked up, he saw the Dragon's reflection gazing at him from the huge mirror behind the bar.

"Listen to me, Lord Sterling . . ."

"No!" Justin snarled, grabbing a bar stool and pitching it at the glass. The Dragon's image shattered and fell to the floor in a rain of silvered glass fragments. Two pillars at either side of the bar were also mirrors, and the Dragon's face began to appear there. Before the master could speak, Justin smashed them. Methodically he found every mirror in the room and smashed them all before the Dragon could speak another word.

At the end of his rounds, Justin collapsed to the floor, exhausted.

"Sandra . . .," he wept. His fists crushed the floor into dust. "Gwendolyne . . . both of you . . . how could I have killed you both?"

Clenching his long, spiked teeth, he willed himself back to human form. Slowly the dragonling body collapsed. His wings rumpled in upon themselves and his muscles slithered back, away, underneath the scaled skin that pulled away from him.

Ripping his way out of the skin, he stood, naked and wet in his deserted club.

A chair scuffing the floor caught his attention and he turned. He had not heard the door open, but Kalzar sat calmly at the end of the bar, swirling bourbon in a cut crystal glass.

"Terrible service in this place," he said. "Must be bad management."

Justin said nothing. His hands curled around a tall, thin statue at his end of the bar. It was an Art Deco piece—two elongated lovers intertwined in a kiss.

"You know, I've often tried to imagine the quickest way to put you in the master's disfavor, but you outdid anything I could imagine today." Kalzar chuckled, "You really lost it this time, Justin. I suspect I'll be dreaming about you tonight."

"You won't be dreaming about anything tonight," Justin vowed.

Grabbing the statue in two hands, he lifted it and smashed it on the bar, revealing the thing he had hidden there. Hidden from everybody, from the Dragon, even in a way from himself. The other artifact he'd taken from the museum.

Justin brushed the chalky debris off the steel edge and lifted the broadsword from the statue's wreckage. It gleamed with rivulets of fire in the light from the shattered window.

Kalzar's grin faded. His thin lips tightened.

"What is that?" he asked, taking a step back.

"Why don't you tell me?" Justin said, moving toward him. Kalzar backed up another pace. "You can feel the power just the same as I can. Beowulf used this sword to kill Gyzalanitha. Saint George killed countless others of our kind with it. Using this blade, he chased our master into a lake in Libya. That was where the priests trapped the Dragon. The king drained the water away and thus ended the Dragon's ability to return to this world." Justin smiled a terrible smile. "What's the matter, Kalzar? Haven't you read up on this? I am surprised at you. Such a powerful artifact, and you didn't think to look for it? Well, I did. Until I found it by accident. Or perhaps it wasn't an accident."

"The master will have your head if you—"

"Fuck the master," Justin yelled, stepping forward and swinging. The blade caught Kalzar in the ribs, ripping into his expensive suit, his muscular chest, trailing blood in its path.

Justin pulled the blade back for a second blow. "Can you feel it? It howls for our blood. Even as I hold it, I can feel it wanting to turn on me, as well. It was made to kill our kind. Much as it wants me, it wants you more, Kalzar. I am honored to aid it in its quest."

Bleeding from his terrible wound, Kalzar bolted for the men's room. Justin cut him off with a swipe of the sword.

"So that was how you came in? The mirrors in the bathroom. I thought I'd gotten all the mirrors in the place," Justin said. "Now they're your only escape. The doors are all locked. You'd never get through one before I cleaved you in half. All of the other mirrors are shattered. Now, which way will you run, Kalzar?" Justin stalked his old enemy, sword point first, making sure to stay between him and the bathroom door.

Kalzar's eyes flicked from Justin to the blade, then back to Justin. "Calm yourself, Justin. This is not what you want. The master will forgive you if you repent. You know he will. His Elders are valuable to him."

"Begging now, Kalzar? How very unlike you."

They crossed the floor slowly, Justin waiting for Kalzar to make a move, Kalzar biding his time. Then he heard it. The telltale bone-cracking sound that preceded the transformation.

Justin leapt forward, but Kalzar was a split-second faster. He launched himself into the air. The sword caught his foot, slicing through two of his clawed toes. Kalzar howled, but while he was in the air, his transformation completed itself. Wings broke through his back and unfurled, spraying blood. His snout grew long and fanged. His suit ripped along the seams and tan scales bubbled all over his body. His howl of pain became a roar of fury. His wings flapped. His burning eyes turned to look back at Justin.

"I will rip the flesh from your bones," he growled.

Justin's urge to metamorphose into his own dragonling form was almost overwhelming. A mortal's chances against a dragonling were low. Even a lesser disciple could not fight an Elder, as he had shown Omar. But Justin refused to transform. To do so would be to enter the Dragon's realm again. That body was a gift from the Dragon, susceptible to the Dragon's manipulations.

Kalzar dove. Justin swung the sword. The blade slashed Kalzar's chest. He howled again and backed off. That wound would not heal, the toes would not grow back, and his side still bled from where Justin had slashed him while he was still in human form.

For most of his immortal life, Justin had felt nothing but contempt for Saint George, the man who had driven his master from the world. But Justin had only faced the Dragon's reflection in the mirror. Saint George had fought the Dragon flesh-to-flesh. He had sent Justin's master fleeing, using only this slender span of metal.

For the first time in many years Justin felt fear. The Dragon's powers had kept him safe from harm. But he had spurned the Dragon, and now he fought one of the Elder disciples with nothing but a sliver of sharp metal and the power of a faith he'd forsaken for centuries. If Justin failed, Kalzar would carve him up with Justin's own weapon, and that would be the end of it.

"Give it up, Justin!" Kalzar cried. He scooped up handfuls of shattered mirror and began throwing the glass at Justin.

The tiny shards ripped into Justin and he gasped. Glass rained down on him with hurricane force, and he fell back, bleeding from a dozen wounds.

Justin jumped inside the DJ's booth and slammed the door. Kalzar attacked the booth, shattering the glass.

Holding Kalzar at bay with the sword, Justin flicked on every switch in the booth. Thundering music blared out of the speakers, smoke poured out of the machines. Strobe lights cut through the white, billowing clouds. Colored lights danced.

While Kalzar tried to make sense of the chaos, Justin ran up a staircase that led to the metal balcony encircling the dance floor. He didn't go far, but positioned himself directly above the DJ's booth, hidden in a gout of smoke that chugged out of a spout just below.

It took Kalzar only a moment to realize that Justin had escaped him. By the time he looked back, Justin had disappeared into the smoke that already hung thick over the booth. Justin knew the limited visibility would turn Kalzar's advantage of flight into a disadvantage. Kalzar would be forced to fight blind against an opponent he could not kill, while a wild slice from out of the smoke could mean death for him.

Kalzar flew toward the DJ's booth, intent on turning off the machine before the entire club filled with a white cloud of smoke.

And Justin was waiting for him.

Fearing a trap, Kalzar hovered cautiously near the balcony. Justin leaped outward—Kalzar flapped his wings in a sudden lunge for safety, but it was too late. Justin's sword bit deep into the dragonling's side, severing the left wing and deeply cutting into the right one.

Dragonling and man crashed to the ground. Justin landed on the bottom, his sword clattering onto the floor, sliding out of his reach.

Justin gasped for a breath and lurched to his feet. Kalzar was stronger, quicker. Despite the vicious wound in his side, despite the fact that his wing was torn from his body and was not mending, he lunged for the sword. Justin lunged for him.

Dragonling claws grasped the hilt of the sword just as human fingers gripped the edge of the wounded wing. Justin pulled. The wing tore free. Kalzar dropped the sword, screaming and falling to his knees.

Justin kicked the sword away just as Kalzar reached for it. The dragonling lashed out at Justin. Kalzar bunched his legs to jump, but his injured foot betrayed him, and he slipped in his own blood. He took a step forward and leapt again.

Justin dove for the sword, snatched it up, and flipped over on his back just in time to meet the hurtling form of Kalzar. Justin swung. Kalzar slashed at him with his claws. Both slammed into the floor under the force of the dragonling's charge.

The blow knocked the breath from Justin's body. His left arm snapped under Kalzar's weight. But Justin managed to drive the sword deep into Kalzar's thigh. Kalzar roared again and rolled away from Justin.

Justin dragged himself to his feet and, breathing heavily, looked at his opponent.

Kalzar was writhing on the floor. His two clawed hands grappled at his leg, which was nearly severed at the thigh, gushing blood.

Justin mercilessly chopped the remaining stubs of wing from Kalzar's body. No screams this time. Only a pitiful grunt. The giant dragonling shrank, its magic snipped away. Kalzar's human form lay in a sack of scaled flesh. With a flick of the sword, Justin slit the sack so that he could see Kalzar's face.

"You've . . . killed me!" Kalzar croaked in a barely audible voice.

"I told you that I would," Justin said.

Justin stood over Kalzar, the sword gripped in his good hand. His left arm crackled and snapped under his skin as his broken bones knit together.

"You . . . hesitate . . ." Kalzar gasped. "Why don't you finish it?"

Justin said nothing.

"I see . . . now. He chose you . . . so well . . ." Kalzar whispered. "Everything . . . you do is what he . . . wants you to do. He wanted he . . . dead. And she . . . is dead. He wants you to let me live now . . . and you . . . cannot kill me." Kalzar's choke became a coughing laughter. "You cannot . . . defy him . . . not really. None of us . . . can. He chose us . . . too well."

Justin's expression was flat and emotionless. Stepping forward, he brought the blade of the holy sword down on Kalzar's neck. Steel chopped cleanly through flesh, bone. Kalzar's head fell to the bloody floor. The face—even in death—wore a shocked expression.

"You're wrong," Justin told the dead man.

twenty-eight

Benny watched from an inconspicuous entryway at the front of the club as the coroner's van pulled up. Police cars flashed their red beacons, turning the facade of Gwendolyne's Flight into a nightmare of crimson. He had followed Justin all the way from the cathedral. And now he waited.

Two gurneys rolled out of the front doors. One gurney held a body which, though draped with a white sheet, was headless. The other gurney also had a sheet draped over it, but it was impossible to tell from the outline of fabric what it concealed. A crowd had gathered in the street. People flocked to watch, but Benny didn't care. He had seen all he needed to see. Nothing further that happened here could alter his sworn course, one way or the other. He knew what he had to do.

The body wagon pulled away from the Flight and started down the street. Benny stepped from his shaded alcove. The van slowed to a stop at the first red light, and Benny ran to open the passenger door.

"Hey!" the man inside protested.

Benny grabbed the passenger's head and slammed it into the dashboard twice. Blood sprayed from his broken nose onto the windshield. The driver yelled, opened the other door, and scrambled out. Benny threw the unconscious body of the paramedic onto the pavement, jumped into the driver's seat, and pulled the van into the intersection.

He could not hope to escape the city in the stolen van, especially when he'd taken it by violence not half a block from a crime scene filled with cops. But he didn't want the van.

He drove for a couple of minutes, then turned into an alley. Tires squealed and rubber smoked as he slammed on the brakes and skidded to a halt.

Leaving the engine running, Benny opened the back and looked at the two gurneys. The one with the dead body did not interest him. He knew who it was, and Kalzar could rot there for all he cared. But the other gurney . . .

Benny whipped the sheet off and looked at the blood-smeared plastic bag. In it was a head and two gory masses of bone and flesh that most people would not be able to identify. But Benny knew what they were. They were what he wanted.

Ripping the plastic open, he dragged the two wings out of the van. A fence bisected the alley. He threw his bundle over and climbed to join it. Once on the other side, he knelt and looked at the wings. They were badly damaged, ripped or cut off at the joint, but that shouldn't matter.

He could not stay here long, and he had much to do. He brought the first wing to his mouth and bit into the bloody flesh of the shoulder joint, scales and all. Slowly he chewed, forcing down his urge to gag.

No sooner had he swallowed than he began to feel the power course through him. A wide grin spread over his crimson-spattered lips. He ripped away another bite with great zest.

Yes . . .

"Now you are mine, Justin," Benjamin McCormick vowed. "There is no place you can hide where my master and I cannot find you."

Tina huddled close to Li on a Chicago rooftop. She trusted all the Drokpas, but she felt the most comfortable with Li. Maybe it was because they were so close in age, but Tina figured it was mostly because Li had saved her from Omar in the very beginning. Li was the bravest person she had ever met.

They watched Benny quietly as he devoured Kalzar's wings. When Benny finished, he loped off into the dark. Li sighed and moved away from the edge. He rolled onto his back and stared upward.

"This was not foreseen," he said.

Tina nodded. "We'll have to ask the others to keep an eye on him." Tina didn't like to see Li so downcast. "But the rest is going as they hoped it would, isn't it?"

Li closed his eyes and Tina could see his pain in the lines around his mouth.

"Sandra's death saddens you," Tina said.

He nodded. "I wanted to save her. I was overruled."

"Dr. Shiang says—"

"I know what she says. I know what Grandfather says. I've heard it all before, okay?" Li pushed himself to his feet and walked toward the fire escape. She saw the tears streak down his face.

"I'm sorry," Tina said, following.

"Don't be sorry," Li said, shrugging. "Everyone is so sorry. Sorry doesn't do anybody any good."

epilogue

Vincent Carthy didn't know why he had been chosen to make this meeting or these arrangements. It all smacked of something highly illegal, and if he hadn't been given the impression that his job hung in the balance, he would've turned down the assignment. Certainly no one else had wanted to do it.

Stanford & Bentley Financial Consultants did not usually send their employees on errands for clients, and especially not a junior partner like Vincent. But here he was, with a checklist of the most bizarre instructions he'd ever been given, a checklist he had filled with the precision for which his firm was famous.

Again Vincent checked his watch. His client was thirteen minutes late, going on fourteen. Vincent wondered nervously what he would do if the guy didn't show. How long should he wait? Vincent wanted to leave now, but . . .

Vincent looked up and jumped. One minute he'd been staring at a deserted country road. The next he was looking at a man in a black trench coat, with long hair, Ray-Ban sunglasses concealing his eyes, walking toward him. Where had he come from? Vincent wanted this over with.

Vincent smoothed his lapels and waited by the BMW with the matte black paint. The man walked straight up to him and stopped. He did not remove his glasses.

"Good afternoon, sir," Vincent greeted him.

The man nodded. "A good afternoon to you," he said, in a crisp English accent.

"Here is your car, sir." Vincent made an eloquent motion with his hand. "Exactly as you requested. All of the modifications have been made. The chrome trim and surface paint have been covered in matte black."

"The windows have been smoked on the inside, as well as the outside?" the man asked.

"Yes, sir. It reduces visibility."

"I shall have no trouble seeing, rest assured."

Vincent nodded. "You realize that it is not legal, not without any mirrors whatsoever?"

"I am aware of that."

"Very well, sir."

"And the other matter?"

Vincent cleared his throat. "Yes. The funds have been wired, sir. The purchase has been made." He extended his hands with a ring of six keys. "These are for the ignition and the doors. This one is for the trunk. These two are for the yacht ignition, one for the doors on board. I took the liberty of labeling them for you, sir."

"Thank you." The man took the keys. "And the name?"

"I have contracted the work. It should be complete by the time you arrive. 'Sandra's Truth' in black, across the stern. Correct?"

"That's correct. Thank you."

The man stared at Vincent a moment longer, then nodded. "I have instructed a limousine to pick you up here in ten minutes. I hope you do not mind the wait."

"Not at all, sir."

"Good." He went to the door of the BMW and opened it.

"Sir?" Vincent asked, his curiosity finally getting the better of him.

The man turned. "Yes?"

"I realize that it is none of my business, but might I ask where you're bound?"

For the first time, the man smiled. "There are some people in China I have to meet."

Vincent furrowed his brow. "I see, sir."

"I doubt it."

"Excuse me, sir?" Vincent asked, confused.

"Do you believe in dragons?" the man returned.

"Sir?"

"Dragons. Do you believe they exist?"

"I can't say that I do," Vincent stammered.

"I had a dream," the man said softly. "A dream that perhaps someday they won't."

Vincent's mouth dropped slowly open.

The man closed the car door behind him. The engine roared to life, and he pulled out onto the highway.

MARGARET WEIS is the *New York Times* bestselling author of over thirty books, including the Star of the Guardian series, the Death Gate Cycle, the Darksword Trilogy, and the Dragonlance series. She lives with her husband, Don Perrin, in a converted barn in Wisconsin.

DAVID BALDWIN has held a variety of jobs in his twenty-eight years, including security guard, tattoo artist, and carpenter. In addition to his writing career, he is a Harley Davidson mechanic.